Candy Corn Curse

Aria Daze

Contents

Dedication   VII

Content Warnings   VIII

1. Genesis   1

2. House Party   9

3. Parting Gifts   61

4. Yours   79

Fullpage image   112

5. Mine   113

6. Ours   163

Fullpage image   197

7. Destiny   198

8. Reality   224

9. Home   250

Fullpage image   286

10. Heaven   287

11. Hell   325

12. Highwater   341

Epilogue   356

Appendex   360

Thank You!   363

Human Resources   364

About the author   367

Also by   368

Dedicated to my beautiful Natasha.

You came into my life like warm spring rain on a sunny day. You were refreshing, gentle, and so very kind. You taught me more about forgiveness than anyone and I am forever grateful that I got to experience loving someone as kind and beautiful as you, even if it was only for a little while. Thank you, darling. Your memory will be forever enshrined in a legacy of love and grace. We miss you everyday.

To those who eat candy corn. May you find solidarity with your fellow wax eaters here.

Content Warnings

Hello, and thanks for checking out Candy Corn Curse. This romantasy is a work of fiction, but it does contain references to real-life situations and scenarios that may be distressing to some readers. **Your mental health is important, and if this story negatively impacts at it anytime, please discontinue reading.**

Below is a list of possibly distressing material. If you find that I have missed a topic, please email me at ariadazewrites@gmail.com so I can resolve it. Thank you.

- Potentially triggering topics include, but are not limited to:

- Rape (Mentioned. Not between MCs)

- Kidnapping (Acted upon)

- Passive Suicidal Ideation

- War

- Violence

- Crime

- Murder (explicit)

- Character Death

- Depression

- Anxiety

- Specieism (Magical racism)

- Amoral Government Acts

- Parental Neglect

- Verbal abuse (Not between MCs.)

- Physical abuse (Not between MCs.)

- Explicit Sex (Definitely between MCs.)

- Non-Con (Non consensual sexual acts. Related to primal play.)

- Stalking

- Primal Play

- Unprotected Sex

- Pregnancy

- Child Birth

If you find yourself weighing the option of suicide, please call 1-800-273-8255 for US assistance and 0800-58-58-58 for the UK or 111 for the NHS. Life can be hard, but it's still worth living, and there is absolutely no shame in asking for help.

Genesis

Candy

Recurring nightmares. The doctors call it parasomnia because I always have this dream. It's so vivid it's maddening, and I've had it every single night for the last twenty-two years. Hell, maybe even longer. Fortunately, my memory of this dream doesn't stretch that far back. I usually have premonitions masquerading as nightmares, but tonight is normal. Tonight I'm in the grocery store and they have a good sale on yams. $1.99 a pound. The aisles are clean and organized tonight, and no one is staring at me as if I clawed my way from the deepest cavern of Hell because of my skin. So I relax. I peruse. I fill up my entire cart and head for checkout before the edges of my tattered vision suddenly darken. Then I'm thrown headfirst into a new reality.

Not again. My temples throb while my vision comes back into focus. The pain blanketing my head and neck is terrifyingly corporeal but I know not to panic despite how evocative it feels. Because it will vanish when I wake up. It always does. So I inhale and calm my hammering heart. I slowly open my eyes to pure white snow surrounding my cream and black form. The damp flakes fall in a frenzy, collecting moonlight as they cascade to the ground. A few of them even gleam with blue before they assimilate into the mass collecting on the frozen Earth. What a sight to behold.

I'm content watching the snowfall, but I can't will that experience for myself although I know this is a dream. I move. Or rather, something moves me. Either way, I'm not allowed to remain sedentary. I'm walking the moment I blink away some of the precipitate accumulating on my long lashes. I walk towards nothing for what seems like forever. Snow crunching underneath my feet. Head and body aching, begging me for reprieve. I blink again to stop just as suddenly as I started. Then I saw a little cabin on the horizon, windows filled with light, and smoke billowing from the black-brick chimney.

"Help!" I cry.

I don't know why I'm crying for help, but it's a constant. Just like the involuntary walking. I can feel the cabin stir although no one comes to the door. So I press on and let the frigid air fill my lungs to yell again.

"Help! Someone please!" I scream.

My screaming transitions into a choking sob, and I collapse to my knees. My muscles are sore, my throat burns, and my eyes sting from salty tears. My vision has been fixed on the cabin door just like always, but no one comes. I briefly forget this is all a dream and I start to wonder if I'll meet my end by assimilating with the snow. Honestly, it's not the worst way to go out, but then a loud snap draws my attention.

Him. My vision is still clouded with tears, but I can see the intimidating form in my peripheral. He's tall. Too tall. I can tell from his shape that he's not quite a man, but not quite a monster. He's something else altogether. Something otherworldly and wicked. His gaze switches from the dehydrated branch that snapped under his weight to my trembling person, and then he starts to run for me.

Run.

I want to run. I want to run towards the cabin. Run back from wherever I came. Run back to reality. But I can't. I'm frozen in place by a force greater than my own will. So I blot my eyes instead, knowing that it'll end soon.

This is how the dream always ends. I always scream before collapsing in the snow. *He* always notices me, always comes for me, and I'm always awake before I can even make out his features. At least I'm given that kindness. I never have to see what happens next. The dream never changes. He never changes.

He charges for me with determination. The soft blur surrounding him sharpens into the hard edges of the trapezing muscles that are working to pursue me. My heart hammers as he surges forward, pushing warm perspiration through my chilled skin.

Run.

Unfortunately I'm still frozen by the divine, but it's fine. Soon I'll be awake and this will just be another sleep journal entry for my psychiatrist. Like always.

He's only four yards away so I began to countdown from seven. It only ever takes him seven seconds to reach me. Six. Those gigantic feet of his pound against the frozen Earth as if he were a bison. Four. His horns come into focus. Grand, gleaming, and slightly curved inward like the tines of a salad fork. Two. His rich skin contrasts with the fallen snow. He's a shade of brown that looks unnatural for a human, but it's captivating nonetheless. I could stare at it for a lifetime. Zero. He plucks me from the ground.

Wait. He plucks me from the ground? This wasn't supposed to happen. I should be awake. The dream never changes. I never see what happens next. I never... I'm left breathless, realizing routine is another illusion of security. But at least the madness of the unknown is gone. The creature peering at me is hauntingly beautiful. His rapt, rust-colored eyes are lined with thick, lengthy lashes that curl away from his eyelids when he blinks and rest on cheekbones hung as high as the full moon shining above us. His skin is matte and nearly identical to his eyes, and his horns peek through a rounded mass of curls similar to my own. His bottom-heavy lips draw all my attention to the singular question that rumbles from his belly.

"How?"

My response is interrupted as I jolt awake, temples still throbbing. Unlike always.

Corn

Ah, Flowers. People say you should stop and smell them occasionally, but I've made smelling the flowers my life's mission. I purchased a small plot of land at the age of 90 and I've spent the last one hundred or so years working as a florist. I don't need to work for human money, but if I had to devote my life to something, botanicals was it. The way flowers can express joy, longing, remorse, devotion, and even grief is admirable. So I grow flowers because it's the closest I can get to devoting myself to love.

Ironically, my siblings have devoted their lives to sex, medicine, order, and riches. That's not to say those things aren't noble devotions, but we're different that way. Born of a Black American succubus mother and an Egbere father, the one thing we had in common was the expectation that we'd all be fond of sex. Except that never happened, not for me at least. I find all genders attractive and beautiful, so I think I would be pansexual if I ever got around to it. But it just won't happen. My dick never hardens. My mouth never waters, and my chest is yet to heave. Naked bodies produce a reaction similar to that of a nice ceramic vase for me. They're pretty to gaze upon, but I do not wish to insert myself in them.

My Mama says it's because I've already been claimed. She believes I have an eternal bond with someone that transcends the valleys of time and the rigor of reincarnation, and my body knows that I already belong to someone even if my mind doesn't. My father believes I need to have a drink and pop a little blue pill as the humans do. It's safe to say they agree to disagree, and I'm glad to ignore them both and do what fulfills me. Gardening. Floristing. Keeping my genitals in my pants. Minding my own busi... *Knock knock* Mostly, minding my own business.

The only thing I inherited from my father is my underbite and love of gold. My mother's genes dominated my father's so I function exactly as a full-blooded succubus would. Meaning, I have to engage in sexual activity to not die or go crazy. Although I'm beginning to think going crazy wouldn't be so bad.

"Hi, Sara- Oh, thank the ether. It's you."

My sister Nafisa is at my door with a stack of papers which means her visit was not a social one. She was here to badger me about my required annual embassy visit which we both knew I would put off indefinitely. Still, being harassed about keeping appointments was better than dealing with a lovesick elf. Pushing her way in, she drops her hefty stack of paper waste onto my poor overcrowded coffee table and wastes no time getting to the point.

"Corn, why haven't you been to the EUM yet?"

"Because I don't want to. I thought that was obvious," I shrug.

Succubi are rather interesting creatures from a genetic perspective. Even if we mix with another species, the offspring we produce is still nearly always a full-blooded succubus. Demons of lust are obviously prolific breeders, and because we can easily overpopulate, The Embassy Of United Magic has a very specific set of rules in place that we must abide by to remain in the human realm. For example, all succubi must submit an annual record of all of their partners to the Embassy, all non-monogamous succubi must limit their partnerings to five beings or less, and in my case specifically, all unmarried male succubi must pay fees for the upkeep of programs such as Heat Help and Tracer, so our lot can be provided with an assigned sexual partner to prevent another *Flocking* in the human world.

"Listen, Corn. I know the questions are a little invasive," Nafisa says with an unconvincing head tilt.

"I have to get my balls weighed. And they usually always assign me the same woman, and she *always* makes a comment about how they shouldn't even try with me because it's inevitable," I reply.

I understand the EUM's concerns, but it doesn't make submitting to the examination any less demeaning. They don't even care if your sexual preference is truthfully cold ice cream and hot brownies.

Everyone gets the same invasive unnecessary interview. Even my mom, who's been partnered to the same Egbere for a millennium.

"Well, do you go when your balls are full?" Nafisa counters. "Because that's an easy enough fix."

I mumble a quick prayer to the goddess, asking her to please strike me down where I stand lest I have to talk about my junk with my oldest sister.

"I'm not discussing my balls with you. I'll go when I get the time."

"Before the end of the week, Corn," she says firmly.

"Yes, yes. Before the end of the week. Can I get you some tea? I've made a lovely orange blossom scone."

"I'll take a scone, but I will have to pass on the tea. I'm watching my caffeine," she smiles.

My sister completed grad school in two realms with caffeine patches covering every available surface of her body while still getting her daily iced strawberry latte. So her watching her caffeine intake could only mean one thing.

"Congratulations! When are you due?" I exclaim, wings unfurrowing from excitement.

The house doesn't quite shift in time so my right dact knocks into a wall clock and makes even more of a mess on my mum-covered living room floor. Sometimes I hate that I literally wear my emotions on my sleeves, but I've learned to accept them in the near 200 years I've been alive.

"February 14th," she smiles. "It's a boy."

That's less than five months away and if I know my sister, I know she's freaking out. She has to find a daycare that will take the new edition, baby-proof the house, and sort out her oldest, my niece Charlie.

"Well, if Charlie needs to come hang out with me for a few days when it's time, I'm more than happy to help. Are you and Sven having a baby shower?"

Sven, my sister's husband, is a lizardman. They met in college and married prior to the EUM's banned partnership list and now they were working on their second child. My mother was originally weary of the cold-blooded brute, but he's a good egg. He's always been taken with her, so much so that he said good riddance to his own stickler for the rules-ass family. I like him. I'm happy they're together.

"Nah, Sven says no one gives a fuck about the second kid, and from what I've seen telling Nilla and Cyrus, he's right. You're the only one besides Mom who even congratulated me."

"Typical," I click, thinking of my DINK sister and brother. "Well let's get you two scones so you'll leave Charlie's be. And I promise I'll go to the EUM next week so they'll leave you alone."

I originally planned to wait the full year until December 31st, but everyone at the Embassy knows I'm Nafisa Hark's brother so they'll just harass her until I come in. I won't add to her stress no matter how much I hate that place. Ugh. Fuck me and my sensitive inclinations. They're going to end me up in Hell.

House Party

C andy

"Hey Fren, what are you doing for Halloween?" Betty asks over the top of our shared cubicle. Beatrice is my best friend and we've been inseparable since highschool. We went to the same college, pledged the same sorority, and even managed to end up at the same job.

I love Betty, but I hate that she always asks like the answer is somehow magically going to change. I'm 34, I'm single, I live with my parents and my most frequent outing is Bingo Thursday with my 85-year-old grandmother. So unless she's about to suggest something, my plans are exactly that plus plastic dollar tree vampire teeth and a Target cape.

"Would you believe I'm completely free?" I answer sarcastically. Betty, sensing my facetiousness, pinches my armpit with a scowl. Clearly my open schedule remains unappreciated.

"Well, now you're not. We're going to a house party in Joliet. Dress sexy. Ask Grandma Kita if she can loan you something."

Ok, first off, rude. I know my wardrobe has a thrift-goth milkmaid vibe going on, but milkmaids can be sexy! What isn't sexy about a lace-up bustier?

"Don't even pull up with that red poof-sleeve bustier situation," she chides.

That's it, I'm doomed.

"Ok, I'm changing my mind. I don't wanna go to Joliet and I'm definitely not letting my granny dress me for a party."

Granny has great taste, but her days as a sex kitten heavily influence her dress. She was a bombshell in her day. Big hair, big tits, little waist. Unlike myself who was a healthy size 20 with my two scoops of boob which are in stiff competition with my shelf booty.

"Why not?" Betty cries. "So what if you show a little tit?"

Little was a crazy understatement. I'd have my whole areola out waving to people knowing Kitara Castille, so that was reason enough to refuse. Still, the issue of location remained.

"But it's in Joliet," I whine. "Everything down there closes early as fuck and we're gonna be drinking. I'm not trying to party on an empty stomach, I'm too old for hangovers."

"There's food there, there's Pedialyte punch, there's even rooms available for rent at a discounted price at a couple of hotels. There's also fine-ass men who will be willing to crack your back like a jumbo glow stick. All you gotta do is say yes."

I won't lie, the prospect of getting my back cracked after an eight month dry spell sounded appetizing, and Granny's little Bingo friend was always harping on me to get out more and enjoy my youth and good knees.

"Fine," I say, avoiding her cheerful squeak. "But I am not having Granny dress me."

"Hey, people," I greet, kicking off my shoes.

I'm finally home after a long day, and my loving family ignores me. I only get synchronized hums of acknowledgement from my TV-hypnotized parents before Granny pops around the corner with a smile.

"Hey, Sugar. I heard you need a dress," she replies.

Damn you Betty! I curse inwardly. I knew it was a bad idea to let them exchange numbers. All they did was gossip and conspire. It was like they were in some kind of club. Extroverts Against Introverted Peace or something.

"Hi, Granny. I do not need a dress. I'm just going to wear something out of my summer stuff and put a long sleeve under it."

"She definitely needs a dress," my mama mumbles.

I look up, attempting to shoot daggers in her direction, but I'm just a hair too slow and she's back watching her program before I can even reply.

"I've been working on just the thing," Granny winks before pulling me along. "Let's try it on."

I follow her down the hallway to her craft room with a sigh. Fighting is useless.

Sometimes it feels like Granny has lived a hundred lives. She's been a schoolteacher, a show girl, a nurse, and even a costume designer.

Working on things like Gone With The Wind, The Sound Of Music, and even The Addams Family. She's insisted that she loved every single one of those jobs equally, but I don't think that's true. I think she enjoyed everything else, but she **loved** being a costume designer. The black velvet gown hanging from the dress form in the middle of her room is all the proof I need.

"Granny, this is gorgeous."

Humility is not one of her more enduring qualities and she wastes no time reminding me of that.

"I know," she replies rather arrogantly. "It's exactly what you need."

Somehow I find the courage to try it on and I hate to admit she's right. It's exactly what I need. The dress has a Queen Anne neckline that does everything for my boobs. The sleeves are elegant and lend to the overall drama of the piece, and that leg slit? Yeah, I was definitely getting my back cracked like a glow stick.

"I kinda look like Elvira," I whisper, as she pins a few bust alterations in place.

Somehow my breasts are pushed up even further and at this point, I began to draw similarities between me and the pinups lining the walls.

"Indeed. I think it's a fitting homage," she chuckles. "Hopefully it helps you lure someone young and strong. Heaven knows you're over-due."

"Granny!" I scold.

Ok. So I'm thirty-four and I've never been in a serious relationship. That's not a crime. True, I've also balked at the petitions of lots of men in recent years. But they were facially challenged, broke, or rude, and fat does not mean desperate. I won't settle for some dustball who gets his limited understanding of women from a podcast bro. I'm going to break it in hives just thinking about that.

"I don't need a man, Granny," I sigh.

"I know that, Candrima. You've always been plenty capable on your own and I'm proud of you," she smiles, taking my hand in hers. "But goodness, are they fun to have around! Especially in the winter. Don't you youngins call this cuffing season or something? Ain't nothing wrong with keeping your bed warm."

My expression sags. The Internet was the worst thing to happen to Kita Castille. What started as using Urban Dictionary to decipher simple shorthand had become a full-blown integration with today's slang.

"Granny, I thought we were having a moment. Why does everyone want me to be a damsel in distress? I'm fine. I have a good job, I have a great family, and a cool cat."

The cat in question rubs against my calf as if he both appreciates and understands the compliment. I scoop him into my arms and scratch his little fuzzy chin and he rewards me with a deep pur.

"See? Aster agrees."

My grandmother shoots my cat a frustrated side-eye, one I swear he briefly returns.

"Aster is part of the problem," she sighs. "But no one's saying that you're a damsel in distress, sugar. We just want you to have some companionship. You got a long life to live and eventually, you're going to want someone to share it with."

We have this conversation at least once a month. I'm sure it's due in part to Granny's age and some fear that after she's gone there'll be no one to take care of me, but I don't need a man. My life is complete. I'm ok with just having them and Betty.

"Granny, I'm fine," I insist.

Granny looks like she might fight me on it but the lightbulb above us flickers off briefly. It's weird, the lights in our building have been doing that a lot lately. I wonder if it has something to do with my penny-pinching daddy and his love of refurbished lightbulbs.

"Alright, sugar. I won't beat a dead horse," she waves. "Just do me a favor and dance for me, yeah? So I can live a little through my beautiful baby."

She reaches for me and I bend so that she can cup my cheek. I can't remember a time when my grandma holding my face didn't relax me and I hope I never will. Despite our disagreement on the man thing, Kitara Castille is my girl.

"Of course, Granny," I nod.

Corn

I hate visiting the EUM, and that's saying something because I'm not bothered by much. As if the embassy wasn't pretentious enough on its own, it's also located in Heaven. Heaven is beautiful with its airy pink clouds and ivory courtyards, sure, but entering Heaven strips away all simple appearance charms so I have to enter as a demon. It's also the week of Hallow's Eve, so the realm is overrun with magical tourists and Wayward Gods who are preparing for the festivals. If that wasn't bad enough it also started raining the second I left home, so now I'm forced to air out my wings in public. I don't know who controlled the Halloween weather, but I needed a word with them.

"Goodness, look at that beast," a snooty cherub comments as I flap to rid my wings of the excess moisture. "I see why they have annual check-ins."

I consider telling them I can hear their ignorant comments loud and clear, but I decide it's no good. My protest won't change their mind, so it's best to save my mental capacity for the interview portion of my day.

"Bankole!" A voice calls.

I sit down at the tiny, dust-veiled desk in silence. I've learned that it's best to avoid being personable in the last 170 years I've been doing this. No amount of joking was going to stop them from measuring my bits and pieces.

"Cornelius Esqin Bankole. 188 years of age, of African descent, residing on Earth in Morris, Illinois. A city in the United States. Is that correct?"

"Yes," I nod.

The goblin interviewing me has flawless cerulean skin and an unfortunately dry speaking voice, but I don't care. I'm just happy I finally got a new intake specialist. It is a true miracle because I've been reporting the previous lady about her inappropriate comments for a decade and no change came about, so I wasn't going to complain about a disinterested tone.

"Says here you work on earth as a florist. No sex work, correct?"

I nod again.

"That's a real shame," she mumbles.

The relief I felt just thirty seconds earlier incinerates and I wrap my tail around my leg for comfort. Lots of succubi participate in sex work, but a lot of us don't. Yet we're continuously reduced to stereotypes of hypersexual machines who don't find joy or meaning in anything else. It's hurtful.

"Moving on," the goblin says, refocusing me. "How many sexual partners do you currently have?"

I reluctantly answer one.

"No hookups, flings, or digital sex?" she asks.

"No," I answer.

I don't even want the one partner, but a demon's gotta eat. Human food will keep my physical energy up, but if I don't feed off of lust I'll eventually go feral, which can easily get me killed. The EUM has a zero-tolerance policy for feral succubi, and no, they don't care that I'm sex repulsed. It's eat or be eaten.

"How often do you all engage in unprotected intercourse?" the goblin, Helvetica asks.

"Never."

"How often do you all engage in protected intercourse?"

"Also never."

"What? Then what do you do that classifies as sexual activity?" she balks. This is my favorite part. The part where I get to tell an underpaid stranger that I lick coochie to stay alive.

"Cunnilingus," I sigh.

"What about during your rut?"

"Yeah, I don't do that," I shrug.

"What do you mean you don't do that? All magical creatures have heats and ruts. You're an S tier succubus. One percentile in both height, weight, and wingspan."

"Listen, I understand what the paper says. But I personally don't rut."

"That's impossible," Helvetica argues.

"It's not," I say, shaking my head. "I don't experience sexual arousal. Ever. Not even during hormone highs."

"Do the physicians know about this?"

"Yes, but they don't care because I'm very unlikely to cause a flocking. They just take my measurements, adjust my tag, and send me on my merry way. Do you think we can get to that part?"

"I can't believe this. You don't even have sex. Why are you here?" she asks, gripping her clipboard.

Truthfully? Because the magic system is irrevocably broken, discriminatory, and biased. Magical beings claim to be wiser and more accepting than humans but they're not. Still, I know my opinion is unpopular.

"Beats me," I answer.

Helvetica gnaws on her bottom lip before pulling out the infamous Who Not To Fuck chart. She circles a few things and then slides the printout my way with an exasperated sigh.

"Look, kid. Between me and you, rules are changing at the EUM. The average succubus lives a millennium and a half. That's 1,500 years of exams and interviews, and that gets expensive."

I nod, not quite understanding where she's headed with this.

"Starting next year the embassy is going to be changing these check-ins to once a decade for **partnered** succubi. They figure if you're stable, you're no trouble and they don't have to spend as much time on you. Which saves money."

So if I partnered, I'd be free? At least for ten years anyway. Still, ten was heaps better than one.

"Just mind the list," Helvetica says. "Pick the wrong creature to partner with and it'll be more trouble than it's worth."

I slowly review the inky paper in front of me. Fortunately, Succubi are compatible with most beings. Witches, humans, fae, elves, and even animangi. Yet with all those approved options, one no-no still stood out to me.

"I thought witches and sorcerers were the same?" I ask.

"No, absolutely not," she says. "Think of it like this, you're a succubus, and Succubi are demons, but you're not a Hell Spawn. Hell Spawn and Succubi are marginally related. Witches and Sorcerers are marginally related," she continues, noticing my sprawling look of confusion.

"So why are sorcerers on the banned list?" I ask, unable to quell my curiosity. Helvetica looks at me with doubt simmering in her golden eyes before dropping her voice to a whisper.

"The offspring you two would produce would be cataclysmically unstable. The EUM likes order. The unsupervised creation of all-powerful beings does not facilitate order. The consequences would be grave for everyone involved."

With that, I swallow the rest of my questions and give her a grateful nod. I'm on the EUM'S shit list by default, and I have no desire to make it harder on myself by choice.

Ever.

Candy

"Ou, Granny! You did that!" Betty claps.

We got dressed together at my place since she needed Granny's help with a minor alteration, and while Betty has seen me in plenty of my grandmother's creations, this dress was a showstopper. The curve of the neckline against my breasts and the unsubtle decadence of the plush black velvet was one thing, but that split? That was something else. It was tastefully high, stopping just before the swell of my hip, making me grateful I invested money in good jewelry. In place of my usual lace garters were two thigh chains, one of the waning moon and the other a silver link of hearts. It tied together the masterpiece Kitara Castille so painstakingly crafted.

"She really did," I nod. "I'm kind of sad this is being wasted on a Joliet party."

"There's no such thing as a wasted outfit, Candy," Granny interjects. "Besides, who says the party has to stop in Joliet?"

I quickly glance between my grandmother and best friend. Betty is in her own little world, dancing to a song only she can hear, but Granny's cola brown eyes are full of mischief.

"What are you two plotting?" I ask cautiously.

Granny waves me off with a disarming smile.

"I'm too old to plot, sugar. Besides, it's bingo night. I have my own plans. All I ask is that you be open to whatever comes your way."

"Especially if it's a man," Betty nods.

I throw my head back and groan. Honestly, some midnight snukie sounds good but I'm not going to tell them that. If I'll do that, they'll break out the prayer candles and summon me a man.

"Please stop saying that before the universe hears you and gives me something I ain't ask for," I chide.

"All I'm saying is, you look good," Betty offers. "They're going to be eating you up."

I grin in the mirror as an equally beautiful Little Red Riding Hood joins my side. Betty's loose locs are pulled high off her face, she's glowing with an ethereal plum shimmer that was made for her umber complexion, and her dress, a combination of corsets, ribbon, and tulle, is to die for.

"Well then I guess this is a buffet," I say, twirling her. "Let's roll."

The party wasn't in Joliet, it was in fucking Minooka. An hour away from home. Gone were my hopes of popping in and out and leaving Betty with the car while I took the L home. Now I was going to have to participate.

"Look at this shit. You got us out here with all these damn white folks!" I fuss at Betty. "Why do I let you take me on these Get Out ass adventures?"

We rolled past a closed Casey's and I noted that the night was still technically young, only 9:30pm. This wasn't our first time being in places with Casey's gas stations, but it was certainly the most inconvenient. Nothing was open, just like I feared, and I wasn't seeing a whole lot of skinfolk either.

"Calm down, Candy. It's just a little out the ways, but check this out. Check this out."

She pulls up the party's Instagram and starts listing off amenities like we were visiting a day spa or something.

"There's a maze, a cider dunk, a bonfire-"

"I'm not hearing you mention anything about there being other black people here," I interject.

"Shh, I was getting there. It's being hosted by Callum Perry and his sister."

"Callum Perry? The CFO of our company, Callum Perry? Oh, Betty..." I groan.

This sounded like trouble, something Beatrice Calvin was known for. Fraternizing with an executive was dangerous. She put blood, ramen-induced sweat, and tears into building her career and this man could take it all away in an instant if things went bad. Granny always did tell us getting head where you made your bread was a recipe for disaster.

"I know, I know," she sighs. "It's complicated. I'll tell you everything later tonight."

"You better," I grumble.

Ten minutes later, we arrive at our destination. A barnesque mansion settled in the middle of an Autumn-stricken cornfield. I notice that all the vehicles we parked among were high-end new booties, and that made me feel further out of place. My little 15' Honda Accord screamed Blue-collar povo compared to all the custom-colored Benzs, BMWs, and Cadillacs in attendance.

"Beatrice Renee Calvin, I swear to Big Robes if we get sacrificed to the elite because of you, I'm going to figure out a way to haunt your apparition," I hiss.

"Shush! You're scaring the hoes," she chides.

"What hoes?" I reply, swinging my head to confirm we're alone.

"The skeleton hoes," she snickers. "Plus the hoes from the other side.

They can see you, you know."

"Oh, great. Thanks for reminding me that you can see spirits. Cause what I need right now is Betty The Big Titty Witch."

I wasn't a believer of magic persay, but when Betty confided in me that she could see and talk to spirits, I didn't not believe her. The universe is vast, and much about our world is unknown. Who am I to deny the possibility of something existing other than your standard bipeds?

"Then I hope they see that I prefer my men big and tall. Thick, but not pre-Ozempic Rick Ross. I need something like the OG Kevin Gates, back from when his music was nasty," I say, referring to the spirit hoes.

"Girl, shut up!" she cackles. "But I'll let them know. Now go forth and shake that ass!"

Despite my earlier hesitations, I was happy to see the party jumping like a mid 2000's club. The living room was decorated in floating candles, cauldrons, cats, and everything crawly, an impressive snack station was visible from the left, and classics such as Get It Shawty, and No Hands poured over the multitude of bass-rich speakers. So shake that ass I did, for about an hour until my left knee started squeaking.

"Oh, auntie can't do this like she used to," I say out loud.

I need to find a lounge, so I start looking at the party's map provided on their Instagram, only to be distracted.

"I'd pay good money to see how you used to do it," a voice replies.

I look up from my phone and meet a pair of indulgent brown eyes. Tall? Check. Handsome? Check. Certified Big Boy with thick thighs? Double check.

"Hi," I say, locking my phone and abandoning my side quest.

"Hi," he chuckles. "I'm Steph."

"Hello, Steph." I purr internally.

Steph and I retire to one of the many couches not currently hosting a show to talk. I learn that he's 37, a Howard Grad, a game show enthusiast, and an avid gardener. I practically salivate learning that. Picturing a man that fine swinging a big hose will do that to you.

"So what do you like to do for fun?" he asks.

My eyes widen as I try to think of one hobby that won't make me sound like I'm secretly 50 and renting out a 30 year old's skin, but the longer I think the harder it becomes to lie.

"Honestly? I like bingo nights, soap operas, and reading. I'm a week away from saying fuck it and buying knitting materials," I laugh. "Does that make me old?"

Steph grips my knee in a way that makes a pulse start to reside in the lower part of my body and gives me a gentle smile. God, he has such a nice smile. White, perfect, lickable.

"Honestly? Yes. But that's ok! I've always wanted to make a cougar purr."

Yeah, he was going to make a kitty purr alright. Tonight was that night.

Steph must've been a professional panty wetter though, because he immediately caught the vibe. The leather seat stretched and dipped as he shuffled closer to hook his arm around my waist.

"So, what do you like to read?" he asked, grazing my ear with what had to be the world's softest lips.

"What the fuck do I be reading?" I thought as my brain lost functioning capacity.

Truthfully, I liked reading about all the things I was hoping he'd do to me. So bending, hunching, kissing...

"Romance and fantasy," I answered breathily.

"You know I never could get into fantasy," he whispers against my lips. "But maybe I could be a fantasy guy with you. Maybe you could show me all your favorite fantasies."

YES PLEASE! Smoother than Mr. Clean with a fresh wax? Check, check, motherfucking check!

Tonight had been an amazing success and we were only two hours in. The hard part was over. All I had to say was yes.

"I'd lik-" I start.

"Stephhhhhh," someone groans, interrupting me.

An equally beautiful, but catastrophically drunk man ambles over to where we sit on the couch and hangs on the side of Steph.

"I think we should go. Trell passed out in the hay," he sighs.

Concern shows on my face causing Steph to shoot his friend the world's dirtiest look.

"What?" he mutters before noticing me. "Ohhhh, you were getting your mack on? My bad bro, we can just Muver."

He then leans way too close to his friend's face and whispers unbearably loud,

"She kinda fine. She look a pretty ass dalmatian with all those spots."

And 10 points to the formidable, Ms. Vitiligo.

"Okkkk," Steph says, rising from his seat beside me. "I'm sorry, but I have to get going. I'm the designated driver for my people tonight, and I do not trust them to get home safely like this."

He looks sad like he's ruined his chance, but little does he know, I love a caring man. He's turning down guaranteed pussy to make sure his friends are good. I eat that shit up.

"That's ok," I say with a gentle nod. "Do you wanna exchange numbers?"

Steph nods back, only to be interrupted by his friend.

"His number is 773-65-"

"I can put it in your phone," Steph says, covering his friend's mouth. "Just shoot me a text when you get the chance."

He saves his contact as Junior Cougar Tamer Steph with a little heart and I have to remind myself that backing into this man like a cat in heat is uncivilized. Modern humans use words.

"Will do," I smile dizzily.

Steph leaves after plucking the rest of his crew from various outhouses and fields so I set off on a mission to find Betty and tell her about Mr. Cougar Tamer. Except, she was nowhere to be found. Not at the bonfire, the outhouse, or the chilly pumpkin fields. We made a plan to check in every half hour, but I should've known better when I saw her pouring shots down Callum Perry's throat. She was probably somewhere out of reach in this big ass house, wrapped around that poor man. Still, I gave my search a good twenty minutes before my bladder started screaming at me. Damn that pineapple passion punch.

After relieving myself in an outhouse that was more luxurious than any indoor bathroom I've had the pleasure of squatting in, I fling open the heavy wood door to spot Betty.

"Beatrice! Where have you been?" I chide, seeing her sway carelessly. While waiting for her answer, I notice her glorious cape is rumpled and her fishnets now have holes at the top of her thighs. Not to mention her obvious lack of a bra.

"I've been getting ate up," she hiccups.

That sounds about right. I can practically smell the man lingering on her skin from where I stand five feet away. I would scold her in any other situation, but I'm jealous, truthfully.

"I honestly thought you'd be in the same boat. No luck?"

"I had one hopeful, but he was the designated driver so he had to leave," I explain.

"Was he fine?"

"Mhm."

"Bummer. You get his number?"

"You already know," I smile, feathering her fingers with mine in excitement.

"AYEEEE! We gone get some dick to-"

"Betty! Inside voice!" I chide.

Betty nods and then whispers in lowercase.

"We getting some dick, friend!"

We do a joint happy dance in the fallen foliage before Callum interrupts us with his authoritative boom.

"Betty? Are you ready to get going?" he asks.

Callum Perry is a man who's spent his whole life in charge, and boy does he sound like it. Still, I can't help but notice how his voice softens the tiniest bit as he says Betty's name. If he wasn't the deciding factor in whether or not I had a job, I would definitely be swooning. I liked him for her.

"Ditching me?" I tease.

"Yes, I'm sorry," she sighs. "But I got your gas and dinner."

"Don't worry about it, babes," I say, hugging her. "I had a great time and I'll see you on Sunday for Granny's brunch."

"Ok," she nods. "But don't tell Kita about tonight. I wanna tell her myself!"

I smile as she skips away, right into the muscled arms of her boss-turned lover. Callum lifts her with ease and positions her into a fireman carry, only grunting when she nuzzles his neck with a soft kiss.

Yeah, she's going to have to tell me everything on Sunday. I just know that shit is fire sauce.

I realize I'm alone as the music changes from dancehall to 90's slow jams. I could go fishing again, but I really like Steph, and I've never been one to double dip when I found a good thing. Plus it's creeping up on midnight. So I decide to grab a few snacks and hit the road. I hoped it would be a quick trip back, but unfortunately, after suffering an unbearably hot summer, mother nature decides that we should have an equally treacherous fall and makes snowflakes litter down from the sky. The earlier rain was fine. Cold, but fine. But this snow? The roads are slick and slushy not even five minutes after it starts.

I grip the wheel tighter, trying to keep my car as straight as possible in what I hope is a lane. My headlights are bright, but they're barely cutting through the thick flurry of fluffy white snow, and I can see no more than 20 feet ahead of me. Then to make matters worse, my phone decides that the perfect time to die is right as I look up to try to figure out what exit I was taking. Whoever was in charge really had it out for me.

I drive for another mile, but I still haven't come across a familiar exit, so with one hand on the steering wheel, I began to search through my junky purse for anything that feels like a charging cord. Only to have the post of an earring pierce the sensitive skin under my fingertip. I snatch away violently, and the car jerks, skidding along an icy shoulder. My tires screech as my brakes temporarily stiffen, but I gain control of the car in a nick of time, right before I go careening over the metal barrier and over a steep hill. My heart hammers in my chest. Maybe I should've just stayed put for the night. Maybe I should camp out here until morning. Wherever here is.

Only the more I think about it, the lighter the storm becomes. The road in front of me becomes clearer, and the snow falls in a light, easygoing pattern.

"I'm just overreacting," I tell myself. "I've driven home in worse snow than this."

That much is true, but I also knew where I was going. There's not much that makes me leave my insular city, so I had my way home memorized, but here I was in fucking Minooka. Luckily, this is the age of technology, so all I had to do was pullover, plug my phone in, and then GPS my way home. Nothing major.

I find my charger in the front pocket of my purse, plug my phone in, and attach it back to the mount. It powers up a minute later and I load the directions a minute after that. Good news? According to the weather app, this storm was local, so I only needed to head about fifteen miles north before I was in the clear. Bad news? I had been traveling in the wrong direction for the last half-hour, so I was now ten miles outside of Morris, south of Minooka. Damn it! Why'd I let Betty talk me into this?

I calm myself. This wasn't Betty's fault. I wanted to party with my friend and find someone to crack my back, and I let my phone die, looking at eyeliner tutorials instead of charging it when we were getting ready. This was on me and I needed to be a grown-up about it. I was the one who was directionally challenged. Once I get over my fit, I start back down the road. I need to take an exit in two miles to turn back around, and then it should be a straight shot up I-80. That was simple enough.

I turn on my slow jam playlist, crank up the heat, and let the sweet ballads of Alex Isley take me home. I actually start to enjoy the snow once I tame my anxiety. The falling crystals catch the moonlight like silver chunks of glitter, reminding me of the once-inescapable magic of Halloween. I wish I had more time to enjoy these parts of life. Simple things like witnessing the seasons change, enjoying the moonlight, and watching a deer cross the road.

"Wait, what the fuck!?" I scream. "Is that a deer?"

I don't know why I asked like there wasn't a buck standing 500 feet in front of my car. Of fucking course it was a deer.

I take my foot off the gas, but the roads are so slick that the tires didn't need my help to propel forward. So I settle for honking my horn as loud and frequently as I possibly can. Only the damn thing doesn't move. The buck stays frozen in the road, eyes glued on my headlights. Hitting the deer is not an option. If I survived, my car definitely wouldn't, plus I'd be killing an animal in the process. But my brakes have once again stiffened, the ice is still sending my car forward, and the deer is still standing there. That leaves me with one other option. I veer out of my lane on the two-way highway, just barely missing the buck, and managing to keep my car intact.

"Whew, that was a close one," I say out loud.

I then try to reign my vehicle back into the correct lane, but where one danger is avoided, another appears. My wheel is stuck, and judging by the harsh scraping sound coming from my undercarriage, something I ran over has immobilized my axel. Quick thinking had saved me all night, but not this time. I pulled and yanked at my wheel, hoping that by some divine miracle, whatever was caught under my car would be freed. Eventually, I realized that divinity was far and few in between. So like the buck, I was paralyzed by fear as my car went barreling off the road and smashing into a tree, finally stopping me for good.

I must've passed out when my brain realized the impact was un-avoidable, but I'm alive. Noticing the smoke coming out the back, I kill the engine and try to shuffle out of the door. Only for sharp pain to grip my left leg and arm as I try to move. I'm injured, but alive. I know I'll need to find help and that can't happen if I stay here, but the door isn't moving, and once I calm down enough to ask myself why, I notice that the rear driver's door has been folded into the front by the tree. My car was just a foot or two short from being completely wrapped around the ancient oak, and I know I'm lucky to be alive, yet alone coherent. Still, I can't help but push my luck. So I climb over the seats and push open the front passenger door before rolling into the freshly fallen snow.

I look up and see the hill I rolled off of some three-hundred feet away, which means I'm in a valley. I consider walking back to where I came and seeking help along the highway, but the ripping sensation in my lower leg tells me that's a dead man's mission. So I spin back towards my car. It's weird, because I feel like I've driven through Morris at least a dozen times before, but I've never noticed this. The oak was surrounded by a thicket of other trees, some appearing to be fruiting, while an entire field of fall botanicals sat behind them. Neat little rows of mums, boxwoods, calla lilies, and phlox were visible underneath the blanket of snow and when I limped closer to the apple tree on my right, I noticed there was some sort of sprinkler system running through the entire area. I was in an elaborately planned orchard or garden, and I hoped the owner's house would be nearby.

I walk until the pain in my leg makes me pass out, and when I wake I realize this is the *dream*. My head and neck throbs just like always as snow flutters down from the dark, stormy sky. Now I know why I'm always walking. If I don't, I'll surely freeze out here. Especially since I suspect that I'm suffering from internal bleeding. Who knows how long I have before that takes me under?

So I walk for a mile until I come across the same cabin. Warm light flickers against the frosted windows while thick smoke billows out of the brick chimney. It's exactly like my dream, and fear of the known almost convinces me to stay silent and fall victim to the storm instead of calling for help, but alas, I still have shit to live for. Shit like Granny, Betty, Aster, Mom, Dad, and Bingo Thursdays. So I open my mouth and scream.

"Help!"

The stinging cold strips my vocal cords, but I feel the cabin stir. So I keep walking, hoping to be easier to spot. Hoping that I reach the door before I find out what happens after he reaches me.

"Help! Someone please!" I call again, feeling my body weaken under the weight of the trauma.

I start to cry from the pain, the adrenaline finally wearing off, and then I collapse into the snow. Once again, the cabin is quiet and I'm afraid that this is how my short life will end.

But then I hear it.

The winter-stricken branch snaps then his eyes meet mine before the countdown begins. I should be terrified seeing this creature stomp through the snow, but it's so familiar it's almost comforting.

Seven.

His warm breath fills the chilly winter air like a plume of smoke as he moves towards me.

Six.

Those gigantic feet of his pound against the frozen Earth as if he were a bison.

Five.

His muscles glisten with melted snow as he sprints masterfully through the ice.

Four.

His horns come into focus. Grand, gleaming, and slightly curved inward like the tines of a salad fork.

Three.

His tail snakes forward, clearing small debris from his path with impressive agility.

Two.

His rich skin contrasts with the fallen snow. He's a shade of brown that looks unnatural for a human, but it's captivating nonetheless. I could stare at it for a lifetime. Mabe even two.

One.

His sinewy arms extend outward, ready to collect the pitiful shell of a woman before him.

Zero.

He plucks me from the ground.

I smile because although he's terrifying, he's so beautiful. Something about his curious eyes searching mine makes me want to collapse against him and never leave. We stare at each other in complete silence for a moment longer before he asks me a simple question,

"How?"

The pain overtakes me before I can answer. After everything that has happened, my body finally gives up, and my eyes slam close as I wilt into his arms.

Corn

This is not good.

Don't get me wrong, nothing about today has been great, but this takes the cake. See, after another round of intrusive examinations and questionnaires, I was finally free of the hell of Heaven, so I flew home only to get caught in a snowstorm. The rain I could handle, but I was wholly unprepared for the snow, especially since it wasn't in the forecast. I hadn't winterized my fields or cut much wood, and although I have some task magic, it was hardly enough to power everything I needed to do before midnight. So after wasting a day at the EUM and five grueling hours of preparation, I was finally able to sit down with my knitting project and a cup of tea. Only for my property alarm charm to go off.

The first time I thought it was a fluke. It went off an hour ago, but when I went to check the panel, no movement was visible for a hundred yards. So I figured it must've been a quick hare or a nosey deer, and went back to working on my blanket. Only for a woman to call out for help shortly after.

At first, I wondered if I was hallucinating because the EUM took too much blood since the intruder appeared human.

That was impossible.

Humans could not seek me out because my property was cloaked under a powerful government-issued deception spell. This area appeared as a grassy field from the highway, and even if someone did veer from it, the tree was as far as they could come without being automatically teleported back to the road. Yet somehow, this little human was wandering around in my front yard. And she was hurt.

"Fuck, fuck, jamanichei!" I curse, watching her from the panel.

The last thing I needed was for the EUM to accuse me of luring a human woman into my home, but she looked worse for wear and although I'm selfish, I'm not selfish enough to let an innocent woman die. So I crept out of my chimney, into the trees, and watched her from a distance. She was covered in dirt and blood, and the way she dragged her left leg through the snow led me to believe it might've been broken. Which was confirmed when she wailed for help again before collapsing on the ice. If I didn't help her, she would certainly die.

I creep from my spot in the trees, trying to remain as quiet as possible, only to step on a fucking branch. A horrendous snapping sound travels through the woods, causing us to lock eyes when the human looks my way. I'm nervous at first, but after noticing blood pooling around her mouth, I know I have limited time to get to her before she finally succumbed to her injuries. So I ran.

I run for a woman who was clearly terrified but oddly motionless. I figured she'd be in shock, still, I thought she'd faint from seeing a demon run after her. Instead, her eyes stayed trained on mine the entire time. Then, when I finally plucked her trembling body from the Earth, she smiled at me as if we were old friends. Which is odd, because her energy felt so familiar that I couldn't say we weren't. She did feel like an old friend, if not something much more.

"How?" I ask, wondering if I did somehow lure her onto my grounds.

I hoped she could tell me that this was all a dream and that I had actually passed out in my chair two hours ago, but it didn't happen. Her smile faltered briefly before a content sigh escaped her, and then with one final, shaky breath, she passed out in my arms. So now, here I was, a S tier, unpartnered Succubus, with an unconscious human woman in my possession.

"Fuck!" I scream again, clutching the cold woman to my chest. "This is not good."

It wasn't good, but seeing this strange woman die would be worse. Knowing that, I hurry into the house, feed the fireplace, and get her settled onto my bed. It hurt to see my new olive sheets stained with oxidized blood, but a life was more important than bedding. Even if it was good bedding.

"Where are you bleeding from?" I ask as I examine her.

Her dress, while beautiful, was an impediment, so after much deliberation, I extended my claw and cut it from her body. The slinky velvet piles around her sides and exposes her perfect marbled skin. Then she groans, likely expressing her dissatisfaction with my decision, but a well-dressed woman did no good dead, so I continued on.

She had several injuries: Lacerations, bruises, scrapes, and two broken limbs. One being the leg I saw her dragging through the snow.

"What happened to you?" I ask.

"Accident," she replies weakly and *inaudibly.*

My tail straightens, expressing my shock as I stumble away from the strange woman. I don't know a lot, but I know this is no human.

She can pass through barrier spells and communicate telepathically. Whatever this strange creature is, she's powerful.

"Hello?" I ask, wondering if she'll answer me.

I wait in silence for a few minutes before giving up and approaching her again. I could've sworn she answered my first question, but I could just be delirious from the stress. This is the most being interaction I've had in a decade, all packed into one day. That would drive any self-described hermit mad.

The woman in my bed twitches, likely still feeling the pain of her injuries, so I snap out of my pity party and went to work. I needed to heal her enough for her to take a bath in some Calasole, and once she was all healed up in the morning, I could send her on her way and have my quiet Iife back. Now if only my tail would get the memo.

"*Soft.*" My mind purrs as my tail wraps around the thick thighs of the mystery woman.

My body begins to vibrate with possession as my tail continues to indulge in her sinful softness. Gliding over tender skin and artful curves, it tucks into itself, creating a loop over the top of her thighs. When I finally notice that she's squirming under my grip, I snap out of my trance and chastise my wayward tail.

"No! We do not touch without permission!" I admonish, freeing her from the love loop. "That is not ok!"

My tail is not pleased to be uprooted from its newfound happy place, so it sharpens itself and stabs at my hand until I slap it a few times for good measure.

"We are not unmannered beasts. We do not touch women without their explicit consent."

I hear her giggle, but she's still unconscious, which either means she can communicate telepathically, or I'm truly going crazy.

Damnit.

I knew delaying my feedings would bite me in the ass. Now I'll have to play Saraphine's game to eat again. But that's a worry for a later time. Right now I'm focused on healing the woman before me. I sanitize my hands and tail in liquid fire before carefully measuring the depth of her lacerations. Unfortunately, they're too deep, so I won't be able to stitch them. I'll have to lick her instead. What do I mean by that? Succubi spit is a regenerative agent. Why give Succubi healing saliva? I don't know, but I feel like it's a sex thing. You get a little too rough with your partner in the heat of the moment so you lick them a little and they're good as new. At least that's my theory. Someone out there probably knows the actual answer, but I've never cared to investigate.

I take a pot of grass into my right hand, and the bruised arm of the woman in my left, then I transfer the energy between the two, licking down the length of her arm until the cuts start to heal. She's seriously hurt, so that completely kills the first pot, and three more until I heal all of her outward injuries. But when I finish, something feels wrong. She's still swelling, and the flesh on her left side is starting to bruise again.

"Crap, what did I do wrong?" I groan in frustration.

"I think I have internal bleeding," she replies. *"My car hit a tree."*

I knew I never liked those metal death tubes. Flying remains superior.

Unfortunately, internal bleeding is often fatal for creatures with slow healing rates, and while I still don't believe she's human, it looks like she may fall into that category. I've never tried to heal someone internally before, but given how gnarly her initial state was, I figure it can't hurt to try. There's just one problem.

"I think I could heal you, but I'd have to insert my tongue inside you," I say sheepishly.

Of course, this is the one time she doesn't reply. I throw my hands into the air, debating if this is something that overrides moral code, or if I should just leave her be. But the longer I consider option B, the more my stomach turns with unease.

So I try again,

"Hey, did you hear me? I said I'd have to, um, be inside you."

I sit next to her and wait for her reply, but this is the closest I've been to her since grabbing her out of the yard, and I can't help but be absorbed into her beauty. Her hair is as thick as mine, but her spirals are a little looser, so her afro flows around her like a delicate dandelion pappus. Her skin is a conflicting storm of rich earth and soft cream, with the white affecting both her brows and hairline. Then while she doesn't have much of a top lip, her bottom lip is heavy and plump, beckoning even. She's stunning.

"She's mine." I growl internally.

I jump again, worried by my own thoughts. I must truly be going mad because there's no way I want to claim a woman who was a complete stranger an hour ago. However, my nervous spiral finally prompts her reply.

"I trust you." she says gently.

Unable to resist, I gingerly push her hair away from her eyes and gaze upon her fully. It would be a travesty for such a breathtaking creature to pass on this soon, so I sigh and ready my mind.

"Ok, we're going to try," I say. "Hopefully this works."

I don't trust another pot of grass to get the job done, so I move the bed into the living room and send my tail off into the yard to find an overgrown weed. Luckily, he finds that pesky tree of heaven I meant to cut down, and I wrap around it to start the transfer. I've decided that her mouth is the most chaste point of entry, and I climb onto the bed, hovering over her, admiring her one final time before I'm forced to violate her. Once I've had my fill, I slowly separate her lips with my tongue, sweep inside her mouth, then snake down her warm throat.

I won't lie and say I had the most gentlemanly reaction to the sensation, but I will say that nature was the driving force there. I hadn't willingly been inside of anyone in a long time, and their flesh never tasted this sweet. But this was for survival, I needed to heal this woman and get her back on her way. So I focused all the energy I could into her body and let my spit drip down her throat.

Platonically, of course.

It's not like I can see what's happening in there, but I don't sense much change after a few minutes, and I start to panic. What if I made it worse? What if she can't breathe? What if my chosen sacrifice doesn't have enough power to-

All my what ifs ground to a halt as the woman underneath starts to cough, lungs racking with fresh strength before, with one final spasm, she ejects me from her mouth. I scramble off the bed and check her side. The bruising is fading, and her breathing is evening out. I've done it. I've healed her.

Like the loser I am, I do a little happy dance to celebrate our triumph. I did not kill this woman! I healed her! However, with that comes a separate realization. She will need food, clothes, and entertainment until she's strong enough to leave, and we're trapped in a truly ornery storm. I don't have anything for a woman. I eat twice a week and walk around naked most of the time. So now I have to get creative.

I don't have much protein available, but I do have beans, rice, yams, and tomatoes. All of which I use for a stew. I hope she doesn't mind spicy food because that's the only way I know how to cook, but something about the content sigh that escapes her when the veggies becomes fragrant tells me that won't be a problem. Part of me wants to test my luck and ask her what her favorite food is, but I know she needs rest. So I immerse myself in my tasks. With the stew going, all we need now is something sweet, and luckily, I know just what to make.

Once the tart is done, I work on fashioning her some proper clothing. I have a bag full of granny squares left over from various projects, so I pick a few that coordinate and stitch them together to make her a dress. The hardest thing about it was disturbing her to get her basic measurements, but my tail doesn't seem to mind the extra physical contact. Even if it is making me lose my already fragile mind.

Soon I'm back to working on my project; A blanket for my nephew. I only have a few more rows left before I can work on embroidery, and despite how my evening started, it's peaceful now. I'm sitting beside the mystery woman while I work, watching her chest rise and fall underneath the mountain of blankets. I have so many questions about her. Who is she? What happened with her car accident? Why is she able to walk through my barrier? Why is she so beautiful? I consider asking the questions for the sake of getting them off my mind, but she'll need as much rest as possible to tolerate the Calasole bath. So I table my concerns and focus on the delicate countenance of her breath for now.

Just as I finish my last row, hunger begins to set in. Thankfully though, it's just physical hunger from utilizing so much of myself, and not the sex magic kind that makes me want to sniff the creamy, pink-painted toes of the woman in my bed.
I bet they'd smell good though. They look like they smell good.
But rather than inciting my tail by thinking about the strange woman's toes, I rise from my position on the couch, fetch two bowls, and cut into a pan of cornbread. Then just as I ladle some vegetables into my bowl I hear the softest,
"Uh, Hi."

I quickly spin around, sending the broth in my hand sloshing out of the bowl and onto the floor as two cinnamon-colored almond eyes bear into me. My heart catches in my throat as my brain works furiously to catalog every single perfect atom of the woman in front of me, and as her lower lip settles into an effortless pout, my wings unfold and knock a perfectly good canister of pineapple jasmine tea onto the floor with the soup.

Candy

"Oh, hello," he rumbles.

If the gigantic wings, sloping horns, and flickering tail didn't make it obvious, his voice certainly would've. He sounds like somebody took a clip of Dennis Haysbert's voice and added 150% more bass to it. He sounds strong and hypnotic, certainly not human. Still, my circumstances tell me I'm safe. I'm warm, clean, and somehow alive, which I'm positive is thanks to the big orange dude.

"I assume you're the one responsible for my current location, so thank you for saving me," I say.

"It was no problem," he nods. "Would you like some stew?"

A breeze nips through the front window and caresses my bare shoulder, and in the second it took me to look down and realize I was naked, the man/devil compressed his monstrous form down into that of a seemingly normal human body. Said skinwalker then prepares two bowls of soup and a plate of neat little cornbread squares, before tucking a massive canteen of water under his arm and walking toward me.

"Sorry about the lack of meat," he says, pouring water into my glass. "I'm pescaterian and I didn't know if you had a seafood allergy. So I figured I should play it safe instead of being sorry later."

"Oh, ok," I say, taking a cautious nibble of what I assume is sweet potato.

As soon as the food settles onto my tongue, the comforting flavor seeps into every nerve in my body. It soothes and calms every single one of my anxieties. This man has brought me magic in a bowl.

"What are you?" I blurt out.

The skinwalker fidgets with his hands, pinching off crumbs that aren't there.

"What? What do you mean?" he says nervously. "I'm black."

My brows marry as I process his answer. He's tiptoeing around my question, but I can't be mad. That was definitely a real nigga answer.

"No, not your ethnicity. Your species."

"I'm human," he insists. "Did you hit your head during impact?"

Whoa. I mean, I know I passed out in his yard, but that was low. He basically called me delusional via head injury.

"Are you trying to gaslight me?" I scoff.

"Yes," he nods vigorously.

"You're doing a bad job, then. I saw those wings. They knocked over a container of tea. It's still on the floor."

His head drops between his shoulders, allowing him to produce a pitiful sigh from deep in his belly.

"Can we just pretend that you didn't?"

"Fine," I shrug, sipping a little water.

I briefly make a face when I realize he's one of those weirdos who prefers room temperature water, which causes him to shuffle awkwardly.

"What's wrong?" he asks, voice heavy with concern.

I go quiet when a strange chill rushes down my spine. It almost feels like I'm back in middle school dealing with my first-ever crush, but I soon realize I'm just thrown off by how perceptive he is and how eager he seems to repair my discomfort.

"Nothing," I say, shaking my head. "I just prefer cold water."

"Oh, that's an easy fix."

Taking my glass into his hand, he mutters something quick and then condensation begins to form on the cup. Showing that the liquid inside is now cooler than the balmy 80° of the rest of the house.

I take another sip and it's ice cold.

"I thought you said you were human?" I murmur.

The stranger's eyes flash to that captivating rust color briefly before fading back to chocolate brown. Something tells me that isn't just some neat party trick or advanced light manipulation, and he confirms it.

"I did say that, didn't I?"

"So, are you going to eat me or something?" I ask.

His eyes slip down to my cleavage, where the blankets are just barely covering my erect nipples and they remain there as he replies.

"Eat you where?" he chuckles.

My face grows hot while I question my own sanity. Is he flirting with me? More importantly, should I flirt back? I mean he is my type in either body. Big boy, thick thighs, confident, and caring. He's even got me considering adding horns to my checklist.

Wait the horns!

"You're a demon?" I ask, feeling confident in my diagnosis.

"A succubus," he nods.

"I thought guys were called incubus?"

"Our names depend on the beings' preferences. I prefer to lie under. Per the Latin transcription, that makes me a succubus. Plus a lot of us don't bother with gendered names anymore. It's archaic."

"Interesting," I say, watching him free his tail.

He's slowly shifting back to his original form, having given up the facade, and I notice the house is moving with him. At first it's just the walls moving further back, but eventually, the table, dinnerware, and furniture adjusts too.

"Is your house magic?" I ask.

He looks around, realizing I noticed the shift, and nods.

"It is. It's an accomodation spell. I hired a witch to do it for me a few decades ago because I hadn't stopped growing," he explains. "Speaking of magic, what exactly are you?"

I quickly snatch my head back. I mean, I have vitiligo, but it's clear I'm black and there are no hidden wings going on here.

"What kind of question is that?" I huff.

"A valid one," he retorts with a scoff. "See, I've had a barrier spell around this property for the last hundred years. Yet, somehow, you were able to walk right into my front yard. Right into my arms."

I remember some details, but other things are fuzzy. I don't recall coming across any kind of barrier. I definitely don't recall walking into his arms.

"What? What is a barrier spell?" I ask, head spinning.

"A barrier spell is a EUM-issued deception charm often placed on the homes of creatures deemed dangerous to humans so that they are allowed to live on this plane. Meaning, I can go out, but humans can't come in. So either you aren't human, or my 100 year old spell is faulty. Which one is it?"

"I am too human!" I shout.

But my confidence in that statement is waning.

Maybe he's right. Maybe I did hit my head during the crash, and maybe I'm in a coma. Or maybe I'm dying and my brain is protecting my consciousness from the trauma with this elaborate production. Or maybe I'm already dead. Suddenly the room is too hot, because I'm certain I've died, ended up in hell, and got assigned a demon whose only job is making me question my existence. I claw at my chest, hoping I can feel something that will ground me, and in that frenzy, I scratch myself and draw blood.

"Hey, hey, hey," demon guy says, pinning my arms to my sides. "Let's not hurt ourselves. It's fine if you don't want to tell me."

"Have I died?" I whimper, feeling helpless.

"No you're not dead, sweetheart. You're very much warm blooded and alive."

"But you're a demon. And you think I'm what? Magical?"

"Yeah, kinda. You can communicate telepathically."

"No I cannot," I snort.

"See! You just did it!" he says, referencing my internal conversation.

I touch my lips, realizing he was able to hear me even though they didn't part to make a sound. Still, I remain in denial.

"How do I know this isn't just you reading my mind?" I question.

"Pfft, I cannot read minds. Nor do I want to."

"Prove it," I demand.

"Prove it how?"

"I'm going to think of a number between 1 and 20. Tell me what it is."

"This is ridiculous," he scoffs.

"What number?" I reply.

"10."

"17."

"Oh look, I got it wrong cause I can't read minds. Are you satisfied now?"

I let my gaze fall onto his handsome face. He looks irritated, but honest. Nothing about him indicates that he's telling a lie, and yet I don't believe it.

"No," I say, shaking my head. "What if you just picked a different number to throw me off?"

"Hm, I still don't see how that would benefit me, but sure, I'll entertain that theory. So say I can read your mind, think of your most embarrassing moment to date. If I get it right, I can read minds. If I'm wrong, I need you to accept that you might be a little magical and drop this."

"Alright," I agree.

"Ok," he says. "Ready? Go!"

The memory populates instantly. I was a junior in high school, it was prom, and I was a virgin. For some reason, I thought my first toe in the waters of sexual activity should be deepthroating. So I tried to swallow Arman Henry's dick only to gag and throw up hot wings and McDonald's strength sprite everywhere. Everywhere, including my champagne-colored dress.

"Ok, I got it," I say, cringing.

"Ok," he nods. "So I'm sensing a bathroom. I'm also sensing feathers."

"Feathers?" I chuckle.

"Stay with me," he says, taking my hand. "Ok. So I can see you tried to, uh... adopt a bird!"

I picture myself with a parrot perched on my shoulder and erupt into laughter. As if Aster would ever share my love with another pet, let alone one he considers a snack.

"Ok, I'm adopting a bird."

"Yes, you're adopting a bird. But it's hot outside when you adopt Donte."

"The bird's name is Donte?"

"Yes of course. That's a great name for a bird," he laughs.

"Why didn't I name him Birb? That's a better name."

"That's his last name. Donte Hephzibah Birb."

"Lots or biblical references for a demon," I shrug.

"Hey, who's telling this story?"

"You're right, I'm sorry."

I try to contain my laughter as he continues.

"Right. So you bring Donte home, give him some fruit, then go take a shower because it's hot. But you forgot to close his cage and he flies out."

"Oh no."

"It's ok though, because Donte joins you in the shower. Only he mistakes your hair as his landing, and you freak out, knock over your soap, and end up covered in feathers," he explains.

The picture is vivid in my mind. A sticky summer day, a clingy bird, soft gray feathers everywhere.

"This is ridiculous," I snort.

"Yes, it's so ridiculous," he nods. "Cause I can't read minds. Luckily I'm great at improv though."

"Ok," I sigh, finally accepting the truth. "So I can communicate tele-pathically. What if I'm like a seer or something? My best friend says she's a seer."

The demon brings a hand to his chin, considering my answer.

"Mhm, I think seers still fall on the human side of the spectrum. You might be a witch though. Lots of witches don't get powers until later in life. Then some only have simple task magic and true sight."

A witch, huh? I guess that would explain my goth milkmaid vibe, the cat, and my recent string of mixed luck. Bad luck aside, at least I didn't die.

Wait.

What happened to my injuries?

I pull back the layers of blankets and run my fingertips over my skin. There is no bruising, no cuts, no blood. I'm fully healed. It's like the accident never happened.

"How is this possible?" I ask.

I notice that the demon is staring at the ceiling instead of my now exposed naked body.

"Uh, how is what possible?" he asks, face twisted in agony.

"I'm healed!" I shout, sticking out my once-fractured leg.

"Yeah, my spit can heal. No mind reading, but that's pretty cool, right?"

Suddenly the memory comes rushing back. I remember his warm tongue gliding over my skin, licking my arms, and sliding down my throat. I blush, because that part in particular made my girlhood tingle. His tongue was long, soft and thick.

"I wonder what else is thick on him?"

Suddenly, the demon looks strained.

"Hey," he croaks. "Can I interest you in a bath?"

I realize I might've said that last part out loud, or directly to him.

"Yes, um, sorry. But thank you for healing me."

"It's no problem," he nods. "Still, you need to soak in some Calasole to help your cells get back normal. Demon spit can rewrite your DNA."

"Oh," I exclaim, once again realizing that he is a demon. "Wait, what's Calasole?"

"It's a recovery herb," he explains. "It restores your body to prime condition if used correctly. Once you've already done the brunt of healing."

I finally look at the walls. While the big guy has a maximalist decorating style based on the odd statues and paintings in every nook and cranny, his house is also made cozy with a library of books. There are books against the windows, books stacked nearly on the table, books hiding in the kitchen, and even books behind glass on the ceiling. He has a library that rivals national archives. A collection that would take two lifetimes.

"Can I read about it?" I ask.

"Yeah, sure," he nods. "Let me start running your bath and I'll grab a book or two."

A short while later I'm carried to the bathroom. I initially tried to walk, but my legs were so weak that I collapsed on the floor and gave the big guy scare. I guess I did need the Calasole.

When we enter, I'm surprised to see that it's a literal bathroom. A large soaking pool is in the center of the room, level with the floor, while an immaculate 360 shower sits to its left. There are large candles on the ground, lighting the room in warm yellow light, while plants hang freely from the ceiling and spill out of pots near the floor.

"So I take it you're a plant guy?" I ask, as he lowers me into the steaming, green water.

"I'm a florist," he answers. "So yes."

My body relaxes into the pool, becoming heavy and warm as the herb does its job. I only know this is normal because the book he gave me was quite informative. It even detailed how the plant is able to use osmosis to regenerate damaged cells.

"Do you grow Calasole?" I inquire.

He shakes his head no.

"I have to get it from Heaven. It's illegal to grow on Earth. The EUM has long learned that humans do not need access to tools of immortality."

I'm relaxed, but not relaxed enough to disregard my obvious shock.

"Wait, you're allowed in Heaven?" I balk.

I don't claim Christianity, but it's hard not to treat it as a universal default while living in America. We have it shoved down our throat constantly. God is good, Satan is bad. Demons are the antithesis of angels. Based off that, I would assume demons chilling in Heaven is a big no no.

"Of course," he nods. "Actual Heaven is much different from what humans believe it to be. It's another plane of existence, just like Hell and Earth."

"Oh," I say.

I fall quiet as I try to reconcile my version of Heaven with reality. It must be full of magical creatures and quite large. Especially if it's hosting several full sized Succubi like him. It also sounds kinda pretentious. Why are they the keepers of the recovery herb when Hell is right there? Traveling to Heaven to get a magic herb sounds like a dream. Traveling to Hell though? Sounds painful and oddly itchy.

While I get lost in my thoughts, I twirl a strand of hair around my fingers. The Calasole has worked wonders on my dry curls and I consider asking him for a little to mix in a spray bottle if that's allowed.

"I should twist my hair down so it can stay moisturized. Especially since I don't have a bonnet." I think. Except I didn't think it. I said it telepathically. So the big guy meanders to a nearby shelf, grabs two combs, then squats beside me.

"What are you doing?" I ask, as his feet slide in the water.

He dips the wider of the two combs in a jar of liquid first before starting at the ends of my frazzled, winter-eaten hair.

"What? You said you wanted your hair twisted."

"Yeah, but this is a little intimate for strangers, don't you think?"

"We're hardly strangers," he chuckles. "We share custody of Donte Birb, plus my tongue has been down your throat."

I snort, catching a whiff of his scent in the process. He smells like fresh squeezed citrus, rosemary, and good leather. But not the leather you'd find in a modern day department store, no. He smells like the kind of leather that was produced by a tanner who had perfected their craft over a lifetime. He smells timeless.

It's intoxicating.

"I don't even know your name," I sigh, as he detangles my roots with his large, yet nimble fingers.

Call me traditional, but I was taught to learn someone's name before taking a bath in their home. Or sleeping in their bed. Or having them twist your hair. Or moan while they twist said hair.

"Well that's an easy fix," he cooes. "My name is Corn. Or Cornelius if you're a stick in the mud. And who might you be, lovely young witch who walked through my barrier spell?"

"Candy," I giggle. "Or Candrima if you're extra."

"Candy and Corn. What a combination."

"Indeed," I agree, finally realizing the play on words. "It's nice to meet you, Corn.""The pleasure is all mine," he says, scratching my scalp.

I seriously doubt that's true, but I let him tell me his sweet little lies. Now's not the time to be self-righteous.

I finish my bath, and Corn offers me a dress and dessert. It's weird because I hadn't given my nudity much thought past the initial shock. It felt completely normal to be walking around him in my birthday suit, even though he was quite literally a sex demon. Still I accept the dress, it's pretty and it fits me strangely exact. He says it's a rush job, but I just think he suffers from perfectionism. I'd pay at least $300 for something like this back home.

"What's for dessert?" I ask after getting dressed.

"Flourless chocolate tart," Corn answers while preparing two plates. "I hope you don't mind. I have ice cream, but it's made of ehikuzimu milk."

"What's a Ekumiso?" I ask, completely butchering the pronunciation.

"Oh right. I forget you're new to this. Ehikuzimu literally means hell cow. They're indigenous to the mountains of Diasi."

"What's Diasi?" I ask.

"A kingdom in Hell parallel to what we would consider modern day Africa."

I realize he referenced a single kingdom in relation to an entire continent.

"Oh my God. Hell must be huge," I mumble.

"It is. Some people spend a thousand years traveling Hell and they still don't see everything."

"There's tourism in Hell?"

"Of course. Hell is a popular destination for magical tourist. Especially the hedonistic ones."

"Sorry, I know I have a lot of questions," I sigh.

Corn offers me a gentle smile before sitting next to me with our tart and ice cream from hell.

"You can ask me anything. I don't mind," he offers.

I don't know why that does it for me, but goddamn it does. He's already saved my life, made me dinner, and made me a dress, but him offering his knowledge at my disposal is the icing on the very delicious cake/pie thing we're eating. It should be a sin for a pastry to be so buttery. It probably is.

"This ice cream is good," I say, nudging him.

"It's my favorite," he laughs. "It's the only reason besides my sister that I visit Hell."

"Too hot for you?"

"Nah, my family is just a bit overbearing. They keep reminding me that I'm well past marrying age. All my siblings are partnered off so now I'm the odd one out."

"Wow, so that's a universal experience?" I laugh. "Figures. I have that conversation twice a week."

Corn shakes his head at the sentiment, but I'm amused to know some things never change across species.

"I don't even know what to say to that. You're still very young. What are you? Like 40?"

"Hey!" I shout, slightly offended. "I'm 34!"

"Oh, goddess. That's worse. Here I am a hair under 200 and a thirty something is being pestered about partnering. I'm doomed."

My eyes quickly leave my plate and land on Corn's face. He's got a little bit of a five o'clock shadow, but his skin is still smooth, tight, and elastic. His cheekbones are high, his eyes are clear, and his smile is white. Corn is very handsome, and he definitely does not have the skin of someone two centuries old.

"You're two-hundred!?" I gasp.

"Almost. I'm 188. I just had a birthday last Tuesday."

Figures he's a Scorpio. If that type of thing even matters when it comes to demons.

"Wow. Sorry, for my outburst. I just wasn't expecting that. I thought you were my age."

His cool laugh fills the room and calls my body to attention. I don't know what it is about that low rumble, but it does devious things to my body without even trying.

"Don't be sorry. I like the compliments," he chuckles while scooching closer. "Especially coming from you."

My breathes catches my response in my throat because there it is again. That little nudge into flirting territory. Though I can't say I'm displeased. Sure, Corn is five times my age, but he's hilarious, smart, interesting, and kind. He's also fine as fuck. Tail, horns, wings, and all.

I allow myself to fall a little.

"Especially me?" I question.

Corn subtly rakes over me with his eyes, quietly cataloging every inch, finger, dimple, and toe before nodding slowly.

"Yes, especially the inquisitive little witch who told me I was fine as fuck two minutes ago via telepathic communication."

"Oh, right," I say, slightly embarrassed. "Sorry."

Corn collects my plate and returns it to the sink wordlessly. I'm 100% sure I've blown my chance, but then he returns, looking hungrier than he did five minutes ago.

"Don't be sorry, Candrima," he purrs, while scooting closer. "It's ok to know what you want. I know for certain that I want you. Do you want me?"

An eight foot tall demon just asked me if I want him. I should he terrified, I should be denying it, I should be running away. But instead, I'm leaning into his oh-so-tempting, round lips for a kiss. A kiss that could end up costing me my soul, but it's so perfect. Corn lets me take the lead, however, his lips still mold around mine with enthusiasm. After my initial intrusion, his tongue flickers out and tangles with my own, stealing my breath away, and I nibble his generous bottom lip like my life depends on it. We fall in rhythm so easily that I feel like I was made to kiss this being. Isn't that crazy?

One kiss and I was hooked.

I try to dissuade myself from falling further. There must be something that will take the magic out of this moment.

"Do you do this often?" I ask Corn.

I assume he must. He's a sex demon. That has to count for something.

"No," he replies. "I can count on one hand the amount of times I've initiated sex. But everything about you has been driving me to the brink of insanity since I saw you."

"All bloody and bruised? You must have high standards" I joke.

"I do," he nods. "Because not even the threat of death can dim your radiance. Not every being can claim such reverential beauty. Certainly not anyone I've met."

Who needs a soul anyway? Hell doesn't sound so bad. They apparently have fantastic ice cream.

I once again press my lips onto Corn's, this time slipping my tongue inside his mouth to taste him. He's sweet from the chocolate, but also slightly earthy like unsweetened tea. It's a perfect combination in my mind, one I don't see myself tiring of. Especially with how frenzied our kissing has become. Eventually I move to straddle him, hoping to increase our skin-to-skin contact, and once I settle into his lap, I find his tail curled around my thigh. The sensation is welcome, but oddly familiar.

"Sorry, my tail likes your legs," he whispers while stroking my shoulder.

He seems embarrassed, like his tail's actions are not his own, and something tells me they're not.

"Your tail can think independently?" I ask, amazed.

"Yes, it has its own central nervous and olfactory systems. It's still a part of me, but it doesn't need my direction to seek out things it enjoys. We both enjoy."

"You enjoy my thighs?" I chuckle.

His eyes began to invert, with the rust seeping out of his iris and taking over his sclera, and the black of his pupil taking over his iris. It reminds me of what happens when a shark smells blood. That pupil dilation that occurs before its instincts take over and it consumes everything in sight.

"I enjoy everything about you, Candrima," Corn rumbles.

He takes my face into his hand, tilting it upward so he can place a soft kiss on my exposed throat.

"I enjoy your questions," he whispers.

Another kiss.

"I enjoy your company."

He kisses me again.

"And I especially enjoy how wonderful you smell," he says, slipping the tip of his tail between my legs.

I fall apart while he teases me with small slow circles. So much so that I have to cling to his horns to stay upright. Corn's tail is a wonder. It's covered in soft minky hair, reminding me of suede. It's flexible, and it's precise. His strokes are perfectly timed with the placement of his hungry kisses, encouraging me to sync the rhythm of my hips with his.

"Cornelius," I moan out.

Hearing his name does something to him, and his horns erupt further. I slide down the burgeoning ivory pillars atop his head with another soft moan, then I find us on the bed with him underneath me.

"Would you like to ride my face, Candrima?" he offers sweetly. "I'll be your chair. I'll be whatever you need."

I've known this man for a handful of hours, but somehow I know he's everything I want. Confident, charming, sweet. Able to detangle 4b hair. Oozing sex appeal.

I don't hesitate to nod yes, and Corn pats his shoulders, motioning for me to climb up. Part of me wants to, but I suddenly grow nervous.

"What if I squish you?" I whisper.

I've seen that episode of The Boys and I have no desire to recreate it. Corn seems sturdy, but apparently I'm magic. Who knows what could go wrong?

Corn gently takes my cheek in his hand and rubs behind my ear to relax me.

"Candy, I'm a four hundred pound lust demon. You will not squish me," he says firmly.

I look at my current position, noting that he's nearly twice my size. I'm straddling his abdomen and he's not even breaking a sweat.

"Ok?" he says, refocusing me.

"Ok," I sigh.

"That's my good little witch, now come treat my face like a bike seat." I try not to giggle as I climb the length of his body. I know he didn't mean it to be funny, but the image that populates of his face being ridden through a park in the springtime is hilarious regardless. Right up until I finally settle in place and his tongue parts my folds.

"Ahhhhhhh," we moan simultaneously.

The head alone makes the departure of my soul and subsequently, my sense, completely worth it. Corn is not only vocal and sensuous, he's also thorough. I roll my hips to catch his rhythm, and he gives me what I want by sucking on my throbbing clit. I reach for my breast and his hands find mine to provide that much needed simulation. I shatter my own ear drums when all that pleasure finally overtakes me, and he slips his fingers into my mouth to silence me. I thought I was having decent orgasms, but having Corn lick my clit and hole at the same time while his tail plays with my ass has determined that was a lie.

After my second orgasm, I collapse against his horns a twitchy, shaking, mess. Corn politely re-positions me into his arms and runs his big hand down my back, soothing my racing heart.

"We don't have to do anything else, Candy," he says after a while. "I'm good if you're good."

I finally gather the strength to look up and I notice his eyes are slowly returning to normal, despite the massive, ominous tent in the crotch of his pants. He's so sweet to offer, but I want my back cracked, and he's going to be the one to do it.

"Shutup," I growl, hastily freeing him from his corduroy prison.

His dick springs forward, crashing against my open palm and I gasp at the weight of it. It's heavy like a grocery bag filled with canned goods and just as thick as I hoped. He's also covered in wavy vertical ridges that emit a strangely soothing glow and that same soft suede-like hair as his tail. His dick is menacing, but pretty to look at.

Until he starts to return to human form.

"Corn, what are you doing!?" I shriek.

He's still handsome as a human, but the act has offended me for reasons I can't readily explain.

"Candy, I..." he sighs sadly.

I can feel his distress so I do as he's done to me, and gently rub behind his ear. The big guy's love language must be physical touch, because his eyes flicker in between brown and rust as I rub all over him. Until his original color returns.

"I've never had sex in my succubus body," he admits.

I didn't expect that. I mean, he's nearly two hundred years old so I definitely didn't expect a virgin, but to hear he's never had sex in his own body?

"Why not?" I ask.

Corn eyes fill with something that reminds me of shame and it breaks my heart. I wonder what's happened to him to make him feel that way?

"Succubi are heavily stigmatized. So either the person wouldn't be interested in my true form due to stereotyping or they'd fetishize me," he almost whispers.

I get a vision of a younger Corn, anxious and hurt because parts of him were rejected, then a conflicting vision of the disgust he felt when he realized that someone wanted him only because of those parts. To live out some weird demon lover fantasy.

"Corn, I'm sorry you went through that," I say. "But there's nothing wrong with your body, and that's also not the only reason I like you. Really it was the tart and the conversation. Also the scalp scratches. Maybe even the whole, *Not letting me die in the snow,* thing," I say.

A shy smile returns to his handsome face.

"Are you sure it's not the over-enthusiastic tail?" he asks.

"Well," I say, feeling him wrap around my thighs. "Maybe a little. But I admit I'd like to learn more about your improv skills. I also have plans to steal your ice cream if that's ok."

"I'm completely fine with that," he chuckles, returning to his normal form.

The bed stretches back to its normal length as soon as Corn does, and I'm happy to see every demonic inch of him. Especially his mischievous tail.

"Are you sure about this, Candrima?" he asks while cradling my face. He's trying to give me one last chance to say never mind, but I don't want it. I want the big skittish succubus who's been plaguing my dreams for a decade. I want to be lost in the storm of his haunting gaze while we drown together. I want to touch him and hold him, and cause him to lose his mind a little. So placing my hand over his, I don't hesitate to answer,

"Yes."

We sit in silence for a moment, searching each other's eyes. I think he finally understands that I want this, so he allows his tail to travel between my legs and rest against my swollen bud. Corn hisses when he feels how wet I am, his eyes once again invert, and his horns extend past his thick curls.

"Repeat after me, little witch," he rumbles. "Nulla vita nova hac nocte."

"Nulla vita nova hac nocte," I say, and a bright green flash of light emits from my pelvis.

Not at all creepy.

"Hm. What was that?"

"Birth control incantation," Corn explains. "I'm immune to STDs, but I can still impregnate you. I've accepted that you might like me a tiny bit, however, I know that doesn't mean you want to be introducing your demon baby daddy to your family sometime within the next year."

"Touché," I giggle. "So how are we doing this?" I ask.

Corn doesn't reply. He just stares at me until I look away, finally noticing that his tail is curled around my waist. Then with one swift movement, my ass is placed against his steel erection.

I guess that answers my question.

I'll be riding this demon like a rodeo bull.

I slowly tilt my hips upward until I can feel his velvety tip press against my entrance, and as soon as he draws his bottom lip into his mouth, I push downward onto his length, damning my eternal soul.

I knew sex with Corn would be different, but I didn't expect him to ruin me instantly. He feels so right that words that are not my own leap from my mouth while I try to adjust to his size,

"Cornelius, meus es tu."

"Meus es tu. Meus es tu. Meus es tu," I chant while rolling my hips. His stretch stings in the best way possible and I quickly approach my first orgasm. But I'm thrown off because suddenly, the demon underneath me vibrates and the bed shakes with him. His whole body is humming and his eyes are low. A sensation that's familiar in the oddest of ways.

"Are you purring?" I ask.

"Yes," he moans before pressing his lips to mine. "You feel so good, Candrima. Please don't stop."

Fortunately for him, I can't. The purring and the ridges are taking me well past what I can handle without going crazy. I want to ask him more about the purring but my brain walked out five minutes ago. At that point, my body was in complete control. So I give up trying to think and I instead submit to the pleasure that we're sharing. I can feel everything as we thrust against each other. The heat of his flesh when he enters me, the strength in his arms as he supports me, the curves of his ridges while they push against my slick walls, and even his racing pulse as we dance. His heart calls to me the same way his body does and I want nothing more but to answer it.

"Oh, Corn. You're doing so so good for me, handsome," I say, praising him.

"Candrima," he groans. "My sweet little witch. Your beauty will plague me for a lifetime."

His wings unfold against the mattress with a woosh, expressing what I'm certain is enthusiasm and I smile, happy to know what pleases him. I continue praising him and softly scratch his scalp in between thrusts while he melts further into the bed and I melt into him. Eventually, I lose my composure and joining him becomes my main goal.

"Candy, please," he cries. "Slow down."

I know why Corn is begging me to slow down, my motions are no longer measured, gentle, and slow. I've lost control and the full weight of my body is now crashing against his hips in fast, aggressive bursts. I should probably heed his warning, but it's too late. I can't stop it. I've been teetering on the edge of a steep cliff ever since he moaned my name, and now we're both going to fall. Likely knowing that I was unstoppable, Corn gives up trying to slow me and instead embraces our destruction. He plants his hands on my hips before allowing his tail to burrow in my ass, and then he meets my pace, measure for measure.

Despite our frantic speed, our peak is a gradual overtaking. The heat slowly spreads from my chest down to the tips of my toes, compiling where Corn and I are joined, then something strange happens. One orgasm rolls into three, and during the assault of unrelenting pleasure, electricity builds in my fingertips. It's a trickle at first and I assume it's my overwhelmed brain playing a trick on me, but the lights in Corn's house start to flicker, reminding me of the cheap bulbs back home. Despite the ominous energy now oozing through the air, I can't stop fucking Corn, and that cliff I thought we'd teeter off has now become a mountain. I flex my palms, digging my nails into his arms in an effort to ground myself to reality, but it's no use. The sensation ripping through my flesh is too strong.

"Corn," I cry, feeling the heat everywhere. "Something's happening to me."

"It's ok, Candy. Just let it go," he cooed sweetly. "I won't let anything happen to you, baby. I've got you, little witch. I promise."

That's all the reassurance I need. So I peer into his eyes and let go. I let go of control, I let go of fear, and I let go of my burdens. Energy floods my body with the heat of liquor in the cold and the feeling is euphoric. White hot sparks fly from my palms and scatter across the room as I press my mouth onto Corn's. His lips crash into mine hungrily, then my final orgasm punctuates the night with a loud roar as Corn finally succumbs to the pressure of our union. I can feel him swell against my flesh, releasing his need, and as I cry out his name, his sharp teeth pierce my throat, laying claim to my voice. Right before a second set of hands join mine.

Parting Gifts

Corn

I've been asleep for too long. How long, I don't exactly know, but the smell of burning stew wakes me from my sleep. I scramble from my bed and turn off the Instant pot. So I've been asleep long enough for my stew to burn. What exactly happened? I sit at the table for a moment and attempt to fully wake. Then I notice two chocolate-stained plates in the sink, one scraped clean by my famished guest.

The witch.

"Candrima!" I shout.

What the hell has happened to my voice?

Spooked, I slap my hand over my mouth, thinking that will help. Except I noticed that my hand is now covered in strange markings. I pull my hand away to examine the images. It looks like a language I've yet to learn, and a soft white glow is emitting from the inside of the scarring. It's on two of my arms and both of my legs.

Wait.

Why are there four arms hanging from my sides?

I run through the house to the bathroom in search of a mirror, and when I finally reach it, I'm mortified. The additional appendages are front and center, but four eyes stare back at me, and when I turn to the side to get a better look at the marking on my ribcage, *both* my tails unravel from each other and began exploring the marks.

"What the fuck is happening to me!?" I shout.

My voice once again startles me. It's always been deep, but the sounds coming from my mouth are downright sinister. It sounds like I should be speaking a different language altogether, because my voice is too far into the sopranos to annunciate half the syllables correctly. I have four eyes, four arms, two tails, and a lot of anxiety. Then to make matters worse, I'm starving, and *not* for physical food.

Candrima has disappeared, my body has metamorphosed, and I'm losing what is left of my mind. This is the absolute worst time for a pop by, but I've long learned that the universe doesn't care about inconveniencing anyone. So of course there's a knock at my door while I'm in the middle of freaking out. I would ignore it, but a large part of me hopes it's the little witch, and I practically sprint to the door only to find Saraphine waiting at the threshold.

"It's been two months, C- Oh, what the fuck!?" she shrieks.

She takes her time examining me. Her eyes rove over my features like I'm a prized stallion on the auction block, then she licks her lips. The action unsettles me.

At least some things haven't changed.

"Listen, Saraphine. I appreciate you for stopping by, but your help is not needed today. I ate less than twenty four hours ago," I say gently.

At least I think I did, I still have no idea what day it is, and the hour also eludes me.

"Corn, what happened to you?" she whispers cautiously, motioning to my new body.

Ha. If only I knew. I had mine numbing sex with a beautiful creature I can only assume was a powerful witch, and I woke up disfigured and in a severe lust deficit.

This is exactly why I don't stick my dick in things and or beings. *But Candy feels so fucking good,* I remind myself. I think about her for too long and suddenly I can smell her on my skin. Her sweet scent of summer hibiscus and honey. Her heady sex. Her chocolate-heavy breath. My body responds to her memory, and my hunger pains worsen.

"Dude, your eyes are doing that thing again. Are sure you're not hungry?" Saraphine asks.

The elf reaches to place a hand on my chest, but I hardly have the chance to protest before my glowing markings spark and electrocute her, turning her skin from olive to coal black.

"Oh my Goddess! Corn, what the fuck!?" she screams.

She's distraught and rightfully so. I just fried her hand like she was a piece of buttermilk chicken. Her anger is warranted, but I have to stop her when she opens her hand to shove me.

"DON'T!" I roar, feeling my stomach flip from the surge of foreign magic. "Don't touch me. I think there's some sort of protection charm on me."

"What?" she exclaims. "What could you possibly need protection from in this scenario? A gel manicure?"

"I don't know!" I respond. "I just know the magic doesn't like your touch."

"Corn, you big idiot, think! You're a succubus, you survive off of touching other beings. That's not protection magic, that's a curse!"

A curse? That's impossible. Demons can't be cursed and Candy wouldn't have cursed me. What good would that do her anyway? This is probably just a side effect of me finally wetting my dick. I probably just need to sleep it off.

"Saraphine, I think you should leave," I say to the angry elf.

"Oh, you don't have to tell me twice," she scoffs. "I want no parts of a curse. I'll let the EUM know we're no longer involved. Good luck, Corn."

Her words hit me like a boulder. I've been trying to rid myself of the imposing little elf for the last twenty years, and all it took was one wild night with a strange woman and the uncertain threat of a curse. I should be ecstatic that I was no longer forced to deal with her, but the sentimental part of me felt bad, knowing I caused her pain and embarrassment.

"Saraphine, for what it's worth, I'm sorry," I offer.

Saraphine looks at me, eyes shrouded in grief, before scoffing.

"Don't be sorry, Corn. Be careful. You're not the only thing that goes bump in the night."

And with that, she was gone.

I'm alone again, but this time there's a Candy sized hole interrupting my solitude. I know I didn't imagine her because her presence is lingering on my sheets. Her shed curls are gathered in my combs. Her fingerprints are visible against the polished leather of my books, and her strange magic is coursing through my veins. Whatever happened between us was more than just casual sex, and I have a feeling that the direction of my life is dependent on finding her.

Suddenly there's another knock on my door, less urgent than the last. "Saraphine, I told y- Oh, Nafisa."

My sister is also bristled by my new voice, but when her eyes meet mine, I notice the dread etched into her soft features.

"Oh, no," she whispers, motioning to the extra limbs. "Corn, how did this happen?"

I don't answer her question because I don't know. I just step aside and allow her to enter my messy house. If I was in a better position, I would have tidied with a quick spell, but I understand my power is limited with my deficit.

Nafisa has been talking for two minutes straight, but I don't have the mental bandwidth to converse with her. It's taking everything I have just to remain upright. If I don't eat soon...

"Corn!" she shrieks. "I know your bean-head ass hears me talking to you. What happened?"

"I DON'T KNOW, NAFISA!" I roar. "I don't know!"

"Something had to happen, Cornelius," she says, spotting the blood on my sheets.

"The entire metropolis of Chicago goes into grid failure last night due to supernatural events, and I get dispatched to investigate a rogue energy surge in this area only to find you like this. From an Embassy standpoint, this looks so fucking bad. You have to know how bad this looks."

"It wasn't me!" I finally shout. "There was a woman."

Nafisa softens her voice and her lecture ceases.

"A woman?" she asks.

"She was a witch," I nod. "She came through my barrier spell, and she was hurt. So I healed her. But somehow we ended up having sex, and it was so weird because I actually wanted to have sex with her."

Nafisa sits beside me, extending her small hand to stroke my big back. I make a mental note that her touch doesn't trigger the magic, which is only supporting Saraphine's curse theory.

"Then what happened?" she asks.

I take a deep breath, using it to recall the events of the night previous. Candy's touch, her soft kisses, the surge.

"That's just it, I can't remember. I know we, uh, came together, but the last thing I saw was a white flash. Then I woke up to all of this," I said motioning downward.

Nafisa's examines me sorrowfully, until her eyes reach the mark on my ribcage. All of the markings look like gibberish to me, but my sister recoils at the sight of the abdominal one.

"You said it was a witch?" she murmurs, tracing the marks.

She doesn't give the chance to answer before she starts invading my space. Unlike the other two, Nafisa has always respected my preference for minimal touching, but not today. Her hands trace every accessible mark over my body quickly, then once again to make sure she's cataloged everything. After that, she mutters what I assume is a translation spell, and I'm proved right when she provides her diagnosis.

"Corn, you naive, sweet, idiot! That wasn't a witch!" she screeches.

Sure, Nafisa has a few hundred years on me, but I think I know a witch when I see one. At least I hope I did.

Fuck, I don't know if I did.

"How can you be so sure?" I ask cautiously.

Nafisa pinches the bridge of her nose, drawing her tail into her mess of curls to scratch her scalp. I realize then that whatever has happened is five-alarm bad.

"Because no witch on this plane is powerful enough to successfully engrave a claiming curse on one of The Nine Sons Of Hell. Corn, you've been bound to that woman, and you will die if you don't find her."

Candy

I'm running through a maze of rooms at full speed with the heavy fabric of a luxurious dress bunched in my hands. The smell of hot wax hangs in the air, indicative of the candles lighting my way. I've never been here before but I know where I'm going. Two more lefts and then a sharp right.

I'm sure of it.

I can't tell you what I'm running from, but I can tell you that exhilaration rushes through my veins. I run faster, outpacing the darkness that seems hellbent on extinguishing every candle left in my wake, and then I finally make it. I turn into a room with a balcony, commanding the doors to shut firmly behind me, and then I step into the light.

My skin glows platinum in response to the foreign purple moon, and I stretch my hand outward, greeting the celestial body.

Triumph surges through me and a small smile sneaks upon my lips.

I've done it.

What exactly? I'm not sure, but it feels magnificent.

Until my body begins to move backwards...

I dig my heels in, hoping to slow the invisible force pulling me, but it's useless. I'm sent reeling back through the room I came, my body bursting into nothingness as I collide with the cool ebony doors. I manifest on the other side, my newly corporeal body flailing in an attempt to grasp anything I pass in the hall. Of course it doesn't work, and I begin to wonder why until I hear a chuckle bereft of any and all humanity bounce off the walls. The darkness envelopes me like an old friend, molding to my curves like skin. A pair of hands become distinguishable as they glide over the swell of my chest and the soft apex of my tummy, then another pair joins those at my hip.

"Little witch, it appears you were incorrect," a sinister voice says. I should be terrified by all accounts. I should absolutely be pissing my pants. But for some reason, this entity feels safe. His voice is just as familiar as his lingering touch and so is the darkness I'm shrouded in. I attempt an answer, but sharp teeth prick my shoulder blade before my voice can even form.

"Your performance was unsatisfactory," he says haughtily. "Perhaps you wanted me to catch you?"

Yes, that feels right. My face heats under the accusation and desire builds in my belly. I know I wanted him to catch me. But I deny it still,

"No, I-"

My heels begin spinning against the polished floor immediately and I'm spun to meet my antagonist. A being no smaller than eight feet towers in front of me. His body is surrounded by inky shadows and carved with intricate tattoos. Some appear to be written in ancient languages. Histories are scrawled across his tight knuckles, warnings appear on his arms. His body is carved from the same ebony as the doors. He's hard everywhere except his lower belly, which kinda reminds me of the primordial pouch that cats have. But when I peer into his face, it's his eyes that leave me breathless. Rust, and rapt, and lined with thick black lashes. His gaze ignites my entire body and sends my senses into overdrive.

"Corn," I gasp.

This is not how I left him. I have so many questions but I just barely see his smile before I'm pulled from his side and thrust back into my reality.

My reality where I'm burning a hole in my quilts.

I leap from bed, too dizzy to think straight, and dump my nightstand water onto the mattress to quell the embers. Then my alarm sounds, resigning me to routine. I thought the demon in the woods was just a vivid hallucination, but this is the second time I've had that dream since I left.

And I know it won't be the last.

"Girl listen, I know you don't wanna tell me what happened, but is there any chance you might be pregnant? Because you've been sick every day this week."

I take the wet wipe from Betty's hand to clean up the third hurl of my day. How I made it to work on time is a complete mystery. Honestly, Betty poses a valid question, but I'm not sure how to explain to my best friend that I fucked a literal demon on the night of Halloween, and while no, we didn't use protection, I did say some funny words that made my coochie glow green, so I think I'm good. Oh that's right, I can't explain that shit to her or anyone else, because I sound like a nutter butter.

Truthfully, I'd probably be checking myself into the grippy sock factory if I didn't have marks on my neck proving Corn was real. Corn was very real and I missed him so much that I could feel it in my bones. Still, I knew there were limits to what I could say out loud, and the whole story of my car crash and the man of my dreams was a big fat no.

"I'm fine," I say, waving Betty off. "I just got off my period. I think it's just the stomach flu."

She gives me a skeptical glance. One that silently says, *"I don't believe you for one minute, and I hope you don't believe that shit either."*

"You know my niece swore up and down that she had the stomach flu. Now the stomach flu is turning four and her favorite color is orange."

I chuckle, visualizing the framed photo of Kenzie on Betty's desk, looking like the personification of a tangerine.

"It's nothing, I promise," I say, taking Betty's hand. "It's just stress."

That much isn't a lie. I thought sleeping with Corn would be a fun night with little consequence, but when I passed out in his arms...

I woke up in the springtime, to a warm southern wind tickling my curls. The redbrick cabin was behind me and I was surrounded by a vivid field of lavender and bee balm, something I can only assume was Corn's handiwork. My mouth was dry and my body was so heavy I could hardly walk, but a sharp pain rolled up my side and I took off. Eventually finding Corn in the field, bloody and beaten. My heart raged in my chest as I clawed aimlessly at his binds. I was working fast trying to free him, but when he detected movement that wasn't our own, he used his tail to push me back towards the house.

"Candrima, my sweet witch. It's ok, baby. Just let them take me and call Betty. You'll be safe with her."

My heart shattered for reasons I could not comprehend. How was I supposed to leave him and return to my life as if nothing ever happened? How was I supposed to breathe without my lungs? How was I supposed to run without my legs? How was I supposed to live without my soul?

"*No!*" I screamed. "*I'm not leaving you. Corn, damnit! I'm not leaving you!*"

"*Candy, they will enslave you!*" he hollered. "*Go! I will not allow your life to be traded for mine.*"

I opened my mouth to argue, but as soon as my tongue touched my palette, an arrow pierced my jaw, and when I collapsed to the ground, I saw the Earth open up to swallow my spilled blood.

Then I woke up for real. Back in the cabin, back in the fall, back in Corn's arms. Which for some reason, he now had four of. That was concerning, but the warmth of his embrace and the robust scent of citrus and leather was starting to overtake me, and I knew I couldn't stick around to ask questions. If I did, we'd both die. And while I didn't have the opportunity to learn more about him then, my dream assured me that his was a life I'd cherish more than my own. So using all the strength that I could muster, I slipped out of bed, out the door, and out of his life. Hoping that I never saw the ending of that particular nightmare.

That was only the beginning of my troubles. Because when I walked back to the orchard at the bottom of the hill, all I could think about was how cool it would be if my car wasn't smashed into the side of a giant tree. Well imagine my surprise when my car was no longer in bits and pieces. It was instead parked on the road with the keys in the cup holder, and the sensuous black dress that the demon ripped me out of in the passenger seat. There were no scars on my body, no damage to the road, and not a single scratch on my car. The only proof I had that the night actually happened was the granny square dress I rode home in, and the raised infinity mark against my throat.

I go home after work, text Betty, and take a long warm shower to mask my tears. It starts off with a light sob, and eventually I'm crying so hard that I'm choking on my own liquidated snot. But no matter how hard I cry, I never feel any better. It's been 9 days since I ran from Corn and something inside of me feels irreparably broken.

I regret it.

I regret leaving him even though I know it was for the best. That right there should be concerning because I'm grieving a practical stranger but connecting the dots has never been my strong suit.

Granny however...

"Candy," she calls.

I've been avoiding her because once I asked her about the surge, she asked me what triggered it. I didn't want to tell her that I came so hard that I short-circuited a house, so I figured it was best to pretend no part of that conversation ever happened and accept I was going crazy.

"Candrima," she says sterner.

I pause in the hall, body draped in a big fluffy robe, hair matted, and skin stripped from the unusually long shower.

"Yes, Ma'am?" I say.

I don't hear her move, but suddenly her hand is pressed against the back of my neck. I know I'm burning up before she tells me.

"Oh, Candrima. You can't stay here, baby. You have to go back."

When Granny asked me about the party after my walk of shame, I simply said it was fun, I danced, and I met someone. It was nice and vague, but her warning wasn't.

"Granny, what are you talking about?" I reply, trying to downplay the fear in my voice.

"Candy, he will find you. Go willingly, please. Don't make it harder on yourself."

I know she's right. I can feel him constantly. Searching for me, calling for me, pulling me back to him. Still I play dumb,

"Granny, I don't know who you're talking about."

"Candrima, this is not the time for delusion. He w-"

"Granny, stop!" I shriek.

The house rattles and creaks while several of the street lights flicker as a warning. The surge is back and this time I don't have enough strength to contain it. The energy surges through me, forces me to the ground, and pours from my hands, accidentally overloading the circuits on our block and causing a power outage. A series of groans and curses confirm this isn't my imagination while my grandmother silently admonishes my stubbornness.

"Ok, Candrima. I'll drop it. But just remember a hard head makes a soft ass. You can't run forever," she says.

Then she walks away.

I dream about him that night. I dream about his embrace, his kisses, and his eyes. I dream about him taking me into his arms with reckless abandon, pulling my body close to his. So close that I can feel his heartbeat dominating mine, leading my pulse to quicken. His large hand gently traces the side of my jaw, then he issues a warning.

"You can't run forever, little witch. I will find you."

My eyes dilate with a strange mix of lust and fear until I realize something important.

"This is just a dream," I chuckle nervously.

Corn gives me a dark smile in return,

"Is it just a dream, Candy?"

I nod and that prompts him to adjust us, giving him space to expose his member to me. It's just as enticing as I remember, except this time it looks painfully hard. Angry even.

I make the mistake of looking too long and when I look back up, I'm facing the wall with Corn positioned behind me. My heart hammers with anticipation while he rubs the bulbous head against my slick sex. I shouldn't want this but I do. And Corn gives me less than a second to consider the implications of that before he presses into me, skewering me on his length. My short nails scrape against the drywall while my body adjusts to his challenging girth.

"Does this feel like a dream, Candrima?" he growls, his breath heating my skin. "Do you truly think this is your mind playing make believe?"

"I-I don't know," I stutter.

"You know," he challenges with a mirthless chuckle.

As if the twine of his hips wasn't enough to drive a woman mad, I also feel the gentle laving of a warm tongue against my swollen clit. Panic rises with my mounting pleasure, because Corn hasn't changed positions once. He's still firmly behind me, stroking me into oblivion. My release comes quickly with a whimper and Corn withdraws as soon as I'm done. Looking every bit as benign as he pretended to be before.

"What are you?" I gasp, sagging into his arms.

"Yours," he replies with a kiss.

Then his head dips to nip my shoulder.

And when I wake up an hour later, the mark is still there.

It's been twelve days since I left him and I feel like I'm dying. No, I don't mean that figuratively. My energy is low, my appetite is gone, I'm pale, and I'm losing weight. I've told everyone else that it was a bad case of seasonal depression, but the Extroverts Club never once subscribed to my delusion. Luckily though, Betty, Granny, and Mama have stopped asking me about what happened, and have instead shifted their focus to keeping me alive.

"Hey, friend. How are you feeling?" Betty cooes.

She offers me a smoothie which I press my feverish forehead against. It helps, but only slightly. The cafeteria downstairs never uses enough ice.

"Fine," I lie. "Just sleepy."

That last part is true. I've been downright exhausted lately. Although that could also be the dreams.

"Food might help," she says, gesturing to the smoothie. "Granny told me you've been sans appetite."

I nod because there's no sense in lying. I look like I'm starving.

"How about we go get some gelato after this? My treat."

Despite my illest intentions of going home and rotting in my bed, I couldn't resist the temptation of a cup of Chicago's finest gelato. Topped with maraschino cherries, toasted peanuts, and chocolate drizzle. Gelato sounded like it could very well fix my life.

"Fine," I grumble. "But my presence is not guaranteed for anything else."

Betty gives me a soft smile, promising nothing. So I give up and resign myself to my daily task of making sure I don't get fired.

My liquid diet of pineapple mango smoothies gets me through the day and I have enough power left over to keep my plans with Betty. So at 5:15 P.M we're hopping on the Red Line and headed off to Vito's And Friends Gelateria. Fresh air is admittedly nice, and so is people watching with my best friend.

"Girl, what the fuck does she have on?" Betty whispers.

A woman passes us, wearing Doc Martens, dark wash ripped jeans, a pink midi skirt, a neon green sweater, and a gray bucket hat. She looks country, but she's skinny so the "pros" will call it fashion.

"Beatrice, Beatrice, Beatrice," I tsk. "You wouldn't know style if it slapped you in the face."

"She must've been styled by a Paris bed bug. Good on them for finding employment. Who says the American Dream is dead?"

I laugh so hard that it startles the man next to us and earns us a weird look. Oh well. I needed that laugh. Because the ominous, yet anxious aura belonging to Corn begins to hang over me, closer than ever before. Don't get me wrong, it's not new. He's been looking for me ever since I left. Sometimes I'd feel him miles away, and sometimes I'd *feel* him in my dreams. Granny was absolutely right. He was going to find me.

And this time I knew there'd be no running.

"Hey, are you good? This is our stop," Betty says, breaking me from my worries.

"Uh, yeah," I nod. "Just thinking."

"Well cut that out. You look creepy as hell. Come on, let's go eat," she says.

Much to my relief, Corn is nowhere to be found when we step off the L. So we walk two blocks, exchanging our jokes and discussing Betty's recent bedroom habits before we reach my personal heaven. Vito's beckons us forward with its cornea-frying neon signage, and we're transported back to a version of the 50s where black people are allowed to eat ice cream in public. Creamy mint leather booths, malt soda machines, digitized juke boxes, and 29 different pans of the best gelato in the Midwest greet us, and I leave my worries at the door.

We quickly pick our flavors and settle into a booth, my ass squeaking against the polished leather as we do. I got a salted egg yolk and caramel double scoop, while Betty got a white chocolate raspberry. As per tradition, we took the first spoonful of each other's before tucking into our own.

"Oooh ok. I see the vision," Betty exclaims.

My mouth waters from the tart raspberry and rich white chocolate before I can reply. It's a classic comfort. Especially during warmer months.

"I won't lie, yours is excellent," I say.

"Aren't you glad I talked you into this?"

"Yeah, whatever," I smile.

I eat a few bites and my shoulders lower from my ears. It's smooth sailing for as long as there's gelato in my cup. Corn who? "So hey, you know that guy you met at the party?" Betty asks.

It takes me far too long to think about someone other than the demon who sucked my soul out my pussy.

"Who?" I ask.

"Steph."

"Oh, yeah. Steph!"

It's sad really. He started off as the number one contender only for his memory to be fucked right out of my mind.

"Apparently, he's Callum's cousin," Betty giggles. "And they're stopping by to have a quick dinner with us."

Damn it! I knew Betty's promises of one and done were too good to be true.

"Beatrice!" I shriek. "Why would you set me up like this?"

Regardless of the fact that I look half dead and I can feel a giant demon searching for me, I'm also dressed in faded slacks and a peplum shirt that I've had for an embarrassingly long time. This is not date wear, and I don't want a date.

"What? I thought you liked Steph?"

"I do, but I am not in the place to date right now."

"You won't be depressed forever, Candy," she says. "Besides, it's just dinner."

Again, it's not the depression as much as it is the giant demon looming over my heart. Maybe I should come clean. She's going to tell Granny and I'm gonna sound fucking nuts, but at least she'd understand why I'm no longer interested.

"Betty, that night-"

I'm interrupted by Betty's excited squeal,

"Oh, here they come!"

Steph walks in looking like a model. A moisturized, confident, well-dressed model with an infectious smile. A model that unfortunately doesn't do shit for me. Corn really has ruined me.

"Hello, ladies," he greets cheerfully.

He bends down to kiss my hand and my stomach lurches, threatening to decorate his nice slacks with two scoops of novelty gelato.

"Hello again, beautiful."

Despite his kindness, my discomfort spreads. It feels like I shouldn't even be looking at him, let alone interacting with him. It doesn't make sense, I know. But my body is literally screaming at me to take my hand back.

"Hi, Steph," I chuckle awkwardly, placing my hand back on my cup. "Long time no see."

We had reservations at one of my favorite steakhouses, making it difficult for me to politely escape dinner. Betty knew I didn't have any other plans, and if she knew, Callum probably knew. I also couldn't say I didn't enjoy the genre of food being offered because a medium-well porterhouse with garlic mashed potatoes might as well have been a pillar of my personality. You know those muscle-bound, smoke daddy, steak bros you see online? *I* was one of the steak bros. I mean I was the fluffier, broker kind, but part of the club regardless.

So accepting my fate, I joined Steph on the walk to his Beemer while Callum escorted Betty to his Benz. Illinois' weather was amenable today so it felt like an actual autumn night instead of pre-winter, our conversation was interesting, and the crowd was minimal. The night had all the makings of a good one. Still, there was something telling me this wasn't a good idea, and that something didn't take long to make itself known. Standing taller than anything benign and draped in shadowy black, he appears from the dark alleyway and calls for me.

"Candrima."

Yours

Corn

Finding out you've been cursed sucks. Finding out you've been cursed by someone you trusted and shared yourself with though? Devastating. I cried for an hour straight after my brother confirmed that it was indeed a curse embedded in my side. One he couldn't remove at that. I was stuck. I couldn't travel planes. I couldn't eat. I couldn't sleep. All I could do was search for the creature who'd cursed me, and where do I find her, but on the arm of another man. It was insulting. He was a small human with hardly anything to show for his life but an uneasy smile.

What a waste of everyone's time.

"Candrima," I say gruffly.

It took me twelve days. Twelve days to find this little witch. I've been exhausted for twelve days. I could feel her all the time. Her joy, desire, amusement, anger, and frustration. Her pity. Her hopelessness, and right now, her fear.

"Corn," she swallows. "Hi."

One thing I've learned about being bound to a powerful witch is that telepathy works both ways. She's been apologizing the whole time I've been searching for her, while I've been begging her to return.

"Is that your boyfriend?" I ask.

She takes a step away from the man quietly, only blinking in response. Still, she's not far enough away for my liking.

"Come here before I show you what kind of monster I am."

She shakes her head, silently refusing. But I'm irritated and I haven't eaten in almost two weeks so I'm beginning to wonder if fear is a good enough replacement for lust.

"If you don't come here, I will eat him and mount his skeleton in my library." I threaten.

That lights a fire under her ass, and she separates from the man, giving him a full six feet of space.

"Hey, is everything good, Candy? Who is this dude?" the man asks.

The question wasn't meant for me, I know. Still I answer almost immediately,

"Her demo-"

"My demonstrator!" Candrima interjects, finally walking toward me. "He's teaching me how to knit, but I've been under the weather and I've missed a few classes. He's probably just worried. Let me catch up for a moment and I'll meet you guys up there," she says.

That's a lot of confidence for someone so small. A lot of misplaced confidence at that.

"Are you sure?" her friend asks.

Honestly, she shouldn't be.

"Yes, it's fine. I'm safe with Corn," she assures. "I trust him."

My heart splits in two. She trusts me but she cursed me? She ran from me. She maimed me. Witches must be proficient liars by default.

Her friends nod and reluctantly stalk off, checking over their shoulders every few seconds as she makes her way towards me. Her warm breath conflicts with the chilled wind around her, creating a visible trail as she tries to calm herself with controlled breathing. She's nervous, as she should be, but she's still beautiful. Although she does look worse for wear these days. Her brown skin has lost its warmth because she's paling, and some of the plumpness in her cheeks has disappeared. I wonder if she ever recovered from the accident.

Who cares? She cursed you.

As soon as my brain reminds me of the transgressions committed, she meets me where I stand, leaving no more than two feet of space between us. I raise my hand to her face, cupping her chin as I did that faithful night, and finally, all of the pain starts to dull. My body is no longer screaming out of hunger and loneliness. My thoughts feel clearer, no longer racing and anxious, and the ache in my stomach eases. I've been reunited with my bind and it is a blissful feeling.

Still, I'm not happy.

"You left," I say plainly, stroking her chin with my extended claw.

She takes a shaky breath in before meeting my gaze with sincerity swimming in her pretty brown eyes.

"I had to," she replies quietly.

I had a speech prepared, but seeing the sadness in her eyes makes me abandon all of that and ask the same thing I've been asking the entire twelve days.

"Why?"

Her lips part and I know she's going to fix this by telling me what happened. By telling me that it was something outside of our control. By telling me she didn't mean to break my heart, but she hesitates before closing her mouth and shaking her head again.

"I can't tell you," she says.

My stomach lurches from the sting of rejection once more.

There is no reason. She simply didn't like what she signed up for and she left. She left me to pick up the pieces. She left me to die.

"Fine," I grunt. "Say goodbye."

She pulls away, brows knit with confusion and something akin to hurt before meeting my gaze.

"Are you leaving?" she asks cautiously.

I smile, letting my eyes glow in the autumn moonlight before bending to hug her. It's a gentle embrace that hides my true intentions and I relish knowing she never saw it coming.

"No, but you are."

"Would you like some more wine?" I ask.

Dinner was great. I finally had an appetite after finding the source of my deficit, so what better way to celebrate than with a nice juicy steak? I traveled all the way to Diasi to select the finest filets Hell had to offer, but apparently Candrima wasn't a fan.

"Take me home," she grits for the fourth time this evening.

I laugh as I pluck a mushroom out of the roasted vegetables.

"You know, I remember our conversations being a lot more enriching than this. What happened?" I ask.

"Take me home!" she shouts.

I pour myself another glass of wine and finish it on the spot. I hope it will lure me to sleep since the witch is back in my possession, even though she doesn't seem too happy about it.

I wish I cared.

"Corn, I have a life! I have a family! Why would you do this?" she sputters.

Why did I take her? Wow, what a question. Feeling the effects of the wine, I finally shed my humanoid form to show off all the gifts she left me with. Everything from the tails to the eyes.

She watches in awe or maybe even horror as I transform into a beast of a demon, horns too large for even the best accomodation spell, arms threatening to rip an elephant in half, voice of something sinister. Finally I adjust fully and the chair creaks under my new weight.

"Corn," she swallows. "What happened?"

She asks as if she doesn't already know the answer.

"You happened, Candrima."

"What? I didn't do this?" she gasps.

I stretch, showing off the ominous glowing curse on my side. It's not burning for the first time in almost two weeks because property has been returned to the owner, even if the owner doesn't want it. It hurts, but what hurts worse is her playing in my face.

I just want an apology.

"You did, Candrima. We slept together, you drained my energy, then you left me with a death bond and ran away. I haven't had sex with anyone else in eighty years, so I didn't get it elsewhere. I trusted you, and you cursed me!" I sob, finally feeling the gravity of the situation.

I cry until my vision blurs and the woman in front of me splits into four. I hate that I'm so emotional. Now more than ever.

"Corn," she says, rising to wipe my tears on a napkin. "I didn't know."

She comes close, her hibiscus scent flooding my senses and sending my head spinning, but I stop her before she can make contact.

"Don't," I say firmly. "We both know what happened the last time I let you touch me."

Her body stills, her pulse increases, and tears form in her eyes. She's afraid of me now. But I don't care if it'll protect my heart.

"Until I can figure out how to remove this bind, this will be your home. I don't care about your life, I don't care about your family, and I don't care if you want differently. Enjoy owning a demon, little witch. I hope it was worth it."

Candy

Corn left to sleep on the roof last night. I tried to protest because it was raining, but he said he didn't want to be anywhere near me. I cried myself to sleep because not only was I displaced, the man I've been thinking about constantly no longer wanted me. He no longer trusted me. Granny was right, I should've just gone back on my own. He would've probably been skeptical, but not this hurt. We could've worked through it and I could've figured out how to remove the curse. Now he hates me.

I'm no fool, so I know Corn has done more than provide a strong lecture to keep me from leaving, and I'm proved right when I open the front door and it's a portal to an abyss. I can't have a phone because of the tracking capabilities, and the house is also constantly moving. We get about five hours of daylight and darkness at a time so I know we're skipping all over. Basically he's telling me to stay put or die.

I'd leave him alone and let him cool off, but on the seventh hour of darkness my stomach grumbles. It's been a full twelve hours since I've had anything to eat and I hope he's not mad enough to let me starve.

"Corn?" I call into the extinguished fireplace.

The roof creaks before his deep voice responds,

"What, Candrima?"

He sounds irritated and I almost reconsider, but then my stomach growls again. Closed mouths don't get fed.

"I'm hungry," I say. "There isn't anything in the fridge but eggs and I guess wheat?"

He sighs, then a short while later I hear his giant feet slap against the roof. However, the roof never falters or creaks. Whatever demon houses are made of must be stronger than Batman.

"Move," he responds.

I do as I'm told, choosing to sit politely on the sofa, and with a gust of wind, Corn comes barreling down the chimney in a plume of black shadow and red smoke. Leaving soot against my freshly polished floors. I frown at the mess and he sneers in return. What an asshole. I almost consider leaving it and letting it muddy, but I know that's just going to cause me more stress later. So while he stalks to the kitchen, I gather a broom and mop.

"How do you like your eggs?" he asks after a while.

"Medium," I say.

He gives me a small nod of approval before continuing his tasks. I watch quietly as takes out a small metal machine and feeds the grains in, transforming the roughage into a fine powder. He then adds a little water, a little butter, and a stick of cinnamon before setting it on the stove to boil. It becomes fragrant almost instantly. Reminding me of horchata or rice pudding.

"What are you making?" I ask.

"Food," he replies irritably.

I scoff. I know he's upset, but it's a simple question. He's being a two-hundred-year old brat. I didn't mean to curse him! He'd know that if he just asked. Men are frustrating and evidently the species doesn't make a difference in the kind of games they play. Here Corn is a literal demon, giving me a stank eye and the silent treatment.

"How long are you going to act like this?" I shriek.

Corn doesn't reply but he does begin to purr. The strong vibrations travel from where he's standing until they make their way up my back. That throws me off guard because the last time I heard him purr was when we were intimate. What is going on with him? Does he want sex?

"Stop thinking about fucking me and come eat," he demands.

He sets the modest table with two plates. His is a platter in comparison to my own but he was still generous with my serving, offering me two eggs, a bowl of cream of wheat, and leftover steak covered in a minty sauce.

"Thank you," I say before taking a bite of the eggs.

"You'll need your energy for the exams," he says, tucking in.

His words don't register because as soon as the egg lands in my mouth my brain shuts off. It's soft, buttery, and slightly chewy on the edges where it was allowed to fry, and although it's seasoned simply, it's seasoned well. The rosemary and black pepper ties everything together, and I moan with satisfaction. Something that makes Corn squirm in his chair.

Finally it dawns on me.

"Wait, what exams?" I ask.

Corn swallows his mouthful of steak before raising his water pitcher. Then he answers my question with another sigh.

"It is terribly difficult to curse a demon and it takes a great deal of skill and or power. Seeing that you clean manually, I'm doubtful that skill got you this far. Which means you can't be a witch. You're something else. Something stronger," he explains.

"What else could I be?" I ask. "Up until two weeks ago, I thought I was human."

"I don't know," he shrugs. "That's why we're going to find out. You'll need to have your anatomy examined, do a divinity test, and submit a blood panel. Then hopefully we'll find out what you are and we can move forward from there and dissolve this bond."

I look down at the inscription glowing against his brown skin. It's an ancient language, but I understand it. It reads,

"A soul belonging to one."

From what I've been allowed to read since last night, there's no doubt that it's a claim bond. I feel particularly horrible now since learning the side effects. Insomnia, anxiety, nightmares, migraines. He's been in agony for weeks now because I left him. He's mad but he's not wrong. This is my fault.

"Corn. I'm sorry," I say. "I didn't mean to do this to you."

I feel a nauseating wave of betrayal in that instant since our emotional states are linked. Another side effect of the curse.

"Eat and go bathe, Candrima," he replies. "There's a dress, a slip, and bloomers prepared for you on the bed. We leave for the 4th realm in two hours."

He then rises from his seat across from me, places his dishes in the sink, and mutters an incantation which causes the dishes to wash themselves.

"Put your cup and plate here when you're done," he says.

After I make sure my dishes are clean, I locate the washroom. It's bathed in candlelight just like last time, with lanterns and candles arranged in neat rows on the floor. I strip quickly, happy to be out of my 24 hour undies. But when my clothes hit the floor I notice that they automatically teleport to the wicker hamper tucked against the entrance. Now Corn's comment about my manual cleaning makes sense. Almost everything in this house is automated by magic.

Easing into the bath, I wonder if it was automated as well. Corn has minimized sharing space with me all day, so I'm initially doubtful that it's his doing. Until the smell of the steam settles in my nose. There aren't bubbles in the bath but the water is soft from the addition of oils. I hate to admit I enjoy it because I'm sure my mama is somewhere praying for my PH balance, however, it is nice. Especially since the oil smells like my favorite hibiscus brown sugar body lotion. He may automate everything else, but the bath was his personal touch.

Maybe I can still fix this.

Fix us.

Corn

It only takes an hour for Candy to bathe and dress. I expected it to take much longer given her previous record of ignoring my requests, but she surprises me when she walks out of the bedroom clean, moisturized, and fresh-faced.

"Thank you for the dress," she says softly.

My eyes rake over her flannel-clad form the moment she says that. Red suits her well. I've recently learned she's on the taller side for a human woman and I appreciate that her long legs are just barely bested by the garment. The dress was designed to hang loose and modest, but it's doing very little to hide her soft curves and tear-shaped breasts.

Goddess, I hate that dressmaker.

How dare she make this wretched woman look even more irresistible?

"Let's go," I reply, ripping my eyes away from her.

Despite my illogical desire to stare at her all day while she does an unreasonable amount of cleaning, I know I can't afford to. The longer this curse stays, the harder it will be to remove. If it's removable at all. Plus the fourth realm is an hour there and back, and I'm already at my rope's end because I'm in my first ever rut.

I have to hand it to my brother, he's a strong one. Because if I had to go through this for five days out of every month for the last three hundred years, I would've killed myself a hundred years ago. I'm hyper aware of Candy's every movement, every hormone shift, and every mood. When her chest heaves from a frustrated sigh, all I want to do is pounce on her and lick those delicious heavy tits of hers until she cries my name once more. I want to fill her, stroke her, and kiss her until I physically can't anymore. And it's all because of this heinous curse. I'm miserable.

"You ok?" Candy asks softly, touching my arm.

Goddess, please take mercy on my damned soul. I am not strong enough for this temptation. Her skin feels like satin and the smell rising off of her is so intoxicating I'm tempted to reschedule and indulge in my newly acquired vice instead. But if I do that, I'll be stuck like this, and that cannot happen.

"I'm fine," I hiss back, taking her waist. "Do not touch anything as we pass through the realms. Do not let go of me, and do not try to escape. If you don't want to listen, you will probably die."

She swallows anxiously as she absentmindedly takes one of my tails in her hand, causing me further distress. I immediately imagine her stroking it or taking it into her mouth, and it takes a great deal of self control not to unzip my pants on the spot.

"Oh, ok. I'll stay still."

"Good," I reply, allowing my other tail to wrap around her thigh.

I tell myself it's because we need two points of contact to travel safely through the ether, but I know I'm lying seeing as she's already holding my hand and my dart tail. The truth is, I just want to touch her however I can.

She's going to kill me.

"I'm going to hurl," Candy announces as we land in the waiting room.

I have something for the motion sickness, but unfortunately she was right. She did in fact hurl. Right in the giant Zz Nafisa got Cyrus for Christmas a few decades ago at that. Traveling through the ether is rough, especially the first few times. It's a formless and fast, so any being accustomed to a linear existence usually experiences a mind fuck, then a severe panic attack followed by a slight ego death. Candrima wasn't exempt.

"Why do I feel like I just got high off of a super shroom or something!?" she asks.

"Because psychedelics actually transport you to the ether," I reply. "Although with that it's just mental and the process is very slow. Your whole physical body just got pushed through it in a matter of minutes."

She's hunched over with her chest resting against her thighs with tears streaming down her face, and while I thought seeing her like this would make me feel better, it doesn't. It pains me deeply to see her struggle. All I want to do is fix it for her and tell her it's only temporary. It's been that way since I laid eyes on Candrima.

"Sorry," she says, meeting my gaze. "I just... I just need to catch my breath."

She thinks I'm irritated with her for being sick. My stomach sours with that realization. Have I really treated her that poorly? I was so angry that she left, but now that she's back and I'm thinking with a clear head, I realize I was cruel. I owe her an apology.

"Candy," I start. "It's n-"

"Hey, hey! What's up cursed one?" Cyrus greets.

I swivel to swing at him and he just barely ducks before noticing Candrima.

"Oh, damn. You actually found her," he says with a pointed finger. "I don't know why, but I expected her to be cragglier. How old are you?"

"34," Candy gasps. "I'm fucking 34."

Yikes, the ether took it out of her. In the last sixteen or so hours since she's been kidnapped, she hasn't cussed once. But one trip through a rip in the space time continuum has made her into an honorary sailor.

"I see you guys took the ether, so how about we get some tiyheki juice in ya before we start the exams?"

"Whatever, as long as I don't do that shit again," she replies.

I grimace, knowing full well that's how we were getting back. But at least she has a few hours.

"Alright. We got quite a bit to cover today. So Corn, what do you want to start with first?" Cyrus asks.

Candy's head snaps back fiercely, whisking a few stray curls out of her eyes so she can locate the source of my brother's audacity.

"Why are you asking him what he wants? He's not getting examined."

Cyrus sends me a wayward glance while observing my growing horns and flickering tail. Having a doctor for a brother has its perks, but this wasn't one of them.

"How much do you know about S tier succubi?" he asks.

"Nothing," Candy replies. "What's that got to do with anything?" Cyrus looks back to me and I shake my head, silently letting him know to keep his big mouth shut. My rut is my business, accidental partner or not.

"Uh, let's just start with the magic test and we'll leave the exams for last."

Good idea.

Once Candy changes into a gown, Cyrus sets up for the crystal ball test while we wait out the last of her nausea. I was adamant about not touching her all yesterday, but that's a wrap as soon as she reaches for one of my hands to steady herself. I envelope her palm with mine and began to stroke her back, silently hoping to ease her pain.

I'm such a sucker.

"This is nice." she says telepathically.

"Don't get used to it," I say out loud.

My tone is gruff and final so I'm not expecting a reply, but I also don't expect Candrima to squeeze my hand tighter. Her tender palms hold mine with innocent affection that clashes with the not-so-innocent thoughts racking in my dark mind. Goddess, this little witch. She doesn't know when to leave well enough alone.

"Ready!" Cyrus calls, freeing me from my internal conflict.

"Finally," I mutter.

She releases my hand and I tell myself that's what I want, but my body knows the truth and I jump from the loss of her contact.

I'm so screwed.

"Ok, so place both hands on here," Cyrus says, explaining the crystal ball. "Then follow the prompts. Don't worry about how well you execute the spells. Just focus on channeling as much energy as you can into the ball."

Candrima nods and Cyrus and I exit the simulation room, retreating behind the safety glass. She's shaking a little and her anxiety is so strong that it's making me sick through our bond.

"Is she going to be ok?" I ask my brother.

"Yeah, there are safeguards. Don't worry, Corn. I won't harm your mate."

I almost want to scold him for calling her my mate, but the test begins and my concern for her well-being skyrockets. For all intents and purposes, he's correct. I have a mate and she's it.

The test moves fast and Candrima performs the first few task spells with ease. Her anxiety has calmed and her speech is clear. Her energy is strong. She's executing well. So far so good.

"We're moving onto the next set!" Cyrus yells over the speaker. "These will be a little harder."

The next set of spells are location and summons magic. These will determine her ability to use divinity without a clear physical reference. This helps determine how potent her magic is.

She's shown a flashcard then asked to summon the corresponding object. The expectation is for the objects to be without defects, and Candrima quickly masters her objective by summoning a hoard of fluffy rabbits followed by an anvil, a banana, and an ehikuzimu.

"Wait, is she summoning from Hell?" I ask, pointing to the beast. Cyrus bristles when he spots the foreign heifer. The cow bares the Diasi crest on her branded ear and her mouth is full of kudkud, a grass exclusive to the 7th realm of Hell.

"I think she is."

"Should she be able to do that?"

"No."

Unease creeps up my spine. Candrima's pupils are so dilated that her eyes look black and there's a strange heat rising from her skin.

"Stop the test," I say.

"Corn, she's fine. Her vitals are good," Cyrus says. "We only have one more portion."

I shake my head in disagreement. Something is wrong and I can feel it. But if we stop now, she'll have to take it all over again. So I swallow my concerns and stay quiet.

"Great work, Candy. We have one last part," Cyrus says. "In front of you are four elements and four corresponding states of matter. For this part, you will need to use each element to power a vision."

"What vision?" Candrima asks.

"We'll keep it simple," Cyrus replies. "Show me what you'll have for breakfast tomorrow."

"Ok," she says with a nod. "I'm ready."

Cyrus gives her a thumbs up and the final test begins. The viewing room is airtight but a breeze is pulled through the glass as Candrima tries to first utilize air. She's successful in her attempt, and a projection of me rolling out biscuit dough pours from the crystal ball. But then she moves on to water. Suddenly the vision changes, and we're thrust into a future where she's the breakfast. My skin heats with embarrassment because that means my rut eventually overpowered me, but then the vision changes again. This time we're in bed, the moonlight is illuminating the room around us, and Candrima is singing to me. Her voice lulls me into a state of Nirvana both in the vision and in current life before the vision begins to change again.

Then the building loses power and the ominous feeling I tried to ignore ignites.

"What's happening, Cyrus?" I ask.

My brother is panicking as he reviews his panel. None of the controls are responding and neither is the building staff.

"I don't know," he admits. "Something's shorted out."

Suddenly the room is engulfed in a blinding white light. A light I've seen once before, Candrima's light. Dangerous amounts of unorganized energy sources swarm her, and she takes it into her palms and projects her new vision through her eyes. It's us across several timelines and universes, happy and in love.

"Corn, this is bad. She fried the systems and her kinetic energy is building, she's going to blow the whole facility!" Cyrus yells.

That snaps me out of the spell she's put me in and I jump into action. "Open the door!" I shout.

The room rattles violently as the being in front of us continues powering her grand prophecy, and my brother rightly refuses.

"Are you crazy? No, I'm not opening that door! She'll kill you!"

I peer through the glass and find Candrima's gaze.

"No she won't. You have to trust me!"

I look at the vent and wonder if I can squeeze through there to get to her, and Cyrus sighs in defeat.

"Fine, I'm trusting you," he says, while opening the exit and the exam room. "Good luck, Cornelius."

I nod and silently say a prayer to the Goddess. Should I misstep, Candrima will kill me. But if I can reach her on time, I can have my Candy back. The hatch creeks open and I push forward against a gust of hot wind. I have to dig my toes into the floor to keep from falling over. It's like being in the center of hurricane. Devastating and raw.

"Candrima!" I yell.

Her head snaps towards me and those black eyes of hers give me her location. I just need to make it two hundred more feet.

"Candrima! I'm coming!"

"Stay away from me!" she shrieks. "We will only end in death and ruin, Cornelius. Nothing will ever change."

I consider how much my life has changed recently. My body, my temperament, my home, my partner. Change is inevitable, and nothing is guaranteed, but I can promise one thing. I can promise the universe that I'll look after this little witch. I can promise to work through my issues. I can promise to try.

"Candrima, please just trust me! I'm sorry for what I did and what I said, but I need you to trust me, and I'm taking a leap of faith by trusting you not to kill me," I say.

"I can't," she mumbles as I step closer.

"You can, Candy. I got you."

"No, Corn. Stop!" she replies.

"I won't. I'm trusting you."

"I'll just fuck up and hurt you again. Stop!" she demands.

"No, Candy."

She searches for an escape with panic overflowing in her eyes, but I'm too close. So she instead raises her hand, threatening to strike me.

"It's ok, Candy. I trust you," I say, taking her hand in mine.

She cries in frustration, but she allows me to capture her body against mine, and I hold her close and tight.

"We're ok," I say, stroking her wild curls. "I won't let anything happen to you, little witch."

"Ok," she sniffles. "I'm trusting you."

Suddenly, the air in the room stills, and as the chaos collapses around me, so does my little witch.

"That was incredible!" Cyrus exclaims as we leave the destroyed divinity chamber. "I wonder if she'll wanna do that again. Now that I know what she's capable of, I can-"

"No," I growl, clutching her close.

I know my brother means well, but that was too much. She's burning up and breathing hard. Plus she's barely conscious. Besides, we narrowly avoided getting blown to smithereens. Scientists have a death fetish.

Cyrus bristles against my no, but his posture softens when I'm noticing how I'm holding Candrima.

"Corn," he starts.

"Shut up," I finish.

"Ok. I'll leave it for now. Come sit down."

I follow Cyrus into his office and curl into a beanbag with Candrima. They're for pregnant patients with stiff joints, but I feel like a drained witch is also an applicable situation. Right until he tells me otherwise,

"Corn, she's not a witch."

"Ok, what is she then?"

Cyrus checks his surroundings before casting a quick anonymity charm. Then he closes the shades and locks the entrance to the facility.

"Cyrus, what's going on?"

"She's a sorceress," he replies. "That's why she was able to curse you. Their magic is old and strong like whiskey."

My mind immediately goes back to the EUM'S acceptable mate list. Not only were Succubi banned from partnering with sorcerers, but having sex with them was also illegal. Whether casual or otherwise.

"Oh fuck! This is a nightmare!" I shriek. "We're going to get arrested. Then they're going to kill me, and exile her."

"Calm down!" Cyrus says, spraying me with water. "No one has to know. If they haven't sensed her magic on this plane by now, they're not going to."

"But Nafisa will know! I ditched my tag, my location spell, and I kidnapped Candrima!"

"She's your sister, Corn. She's not gonna snitch on you about this.

This isn't missing a checkup."

"You're right. It's so much fucking worse!" I yell.

"Calm down," Candrima interjects, touching my face. "Take a deep breath."

Her voice lulls me into a docile, tranquil state, and I do as I'm told. Once I've calmed down from my moment, she gently strokes my face, scratching underneath my goatee with precision.

"Let's not stress over what we can't control. Cyrus, what do we need to do next?" she asks.

Cyrus jumps, realizing his own name.

"Well first, we need to draw blood and figure out what kind of sorceress you are. Then we need to perform a super quick anatomy exam."

"Can we do the exam first?" Candrima asks. "Seeing as I already burned off my clothes?"

I look down and finally notice she is naked as the day she was born. Not a piece of fabric in sight. My skin heats while I lose my battle to my hormones, and my hungry eyes focus on her speckled breast and soft belly. I lick my lips thinking of the most efficient way to touch all of her at once, and then Cyrus sprays me with a water bottle again.

I hiss angrily, my body hair standing straight up.

"Good call!" he says, ignoring me. "Let's get you in another gown and get this over with."

Cyrus takes her height, and when we get to her weight, he assures her that the number is arbitrary because demons prefer a *certain* body type for long term partnering so she has nothing to worry about. It's true. Most demonic creatures like our partners bigger because we're bigger. Plus as the universe's most prolific breeders, bigger women means healthy babies in the event that something goes terribly awry. Something like a food shortage.

Not that I was thinking about making babies with her. Definitely not chunky brown babies with her same untamed curls...

"Alright this is the last thing," Cyrus says, tearing me from my disturbing thoughts. "Up in the stirrups."
We've been through an MRI, a cardiac examination, and a vision test, and now the pelvic exam is last. There's good reason for that too. Jealousy flairs in my chest as Candrima climbs on the exam table and spreads her legs. I know my brother doesn't have nefarious intentions, but seeing my mate open and vulnerable at someone else's request is a special brand of infuriating.
"Make it fast," I demand.
"Will do. I've learned my lesson," Cyrus replies.

Cyrus has angered me on purpose only once. When I was a youngling, he teased me for preferring the company of plants and hid one of my monsteras, so I clipped him across his cheek with my tail. Mama was furious, but I thought it was a lesson well learned because he still bears the scar to this day and he respects my symptoms of possession.
"Just putting a little lube on this speculum. We just need a quick swab and we'll be on our way," Cyrus explains.
Candy nods and reaches over her head to hold my hand. She still doesn't know that I'm in a rut, but somehow she's doing everything necessary to calm me. The affection quells my jealous rage and I settle down to let Cyrus do his job. However uncertain he may look...

"What's wrong?" I query as Cyrus quickly withdraws the speculum.
He holds the device up to show me what's wrong. The plastic sizzles and liquefies, signifying that something has melted it.
"Candrima, what the fuck is going on with your vagina?" I exclaim.
"Um, one second," Cyrus announces.

He then releases the anonymity charm and pages a nurse.

"Hey I need a flex cam and an ultrasound machine. Yeah, coated. Extra strength if we have it."

The nurse wastes no time portaling in with the requested items, and Cyrus immediately begins prepping a small device that will apparently be inserted inside her.

"Have you had any weird symptoms lately? Nausea, vomiting, loss of appetite, unexplained feelings of disgust towards people of the opposite sex?" Cyrus asks Candy.

"All of the above actually," she nods.

"Cool, cool. Let me just check something."

He powers the machine on and it whirrs to life, ready to view the inside of my partner. Everything about this is wildly uncomfortable to witness and very intrusive. My poor little witch.

"Uh, wait," I protest as he begins to insert the device.

"No can do, bruh," Cyrus replies. "We're already halfway there and we got about sixty seconds to get this done."

I don't understand what he means until Candy groans and an image of a glowing seal is projected onto the screen. Her seal is similar to the one on my side, except it's written in Satanic Script and oozing what I can only assume is acid.

"What the fuck is that?" Candrima shrieks, pulling herself upward.

"It appears we have a two part problem," Cyrus grimaces, withdrawing the acidic probe. "Corn has also cursed you."

He sits us down and explains everything. Candrima is affected by an intravaginal demonic monogamy bind, a rare form of a claim bond meant to prevent the recipient from mating with someone else. Cyrus is right, it is essentially a curse. Because it works by releasing hormones to curb her attraction to others, as well as destroying anything that's inserted into her that's not one of her appendages or *mine.*

"But the unfortunate part is, this is not reversible. So even if we remove Corn's bind, you will still have yours. He will be your mate for life," Cyrus explains. "It will only dissolve in the event of death."

Candrima slowly turns to me with a disturbing smile.

"You talked all that shit and you sat up here and CURSED MY COOCHIE!? What the fuck, Corn?"

The logical part of my brain knows it's not funny, but for some reason I still laugh knowing full well it's going to piss her off.

"Nigga, what's funny?" she screams.

Cyrus averts his eyes in a way that tells me I'm on my own. He won't risk getting electrocuted for me, even if I am his only brother.

"Nothing," I chuckle. "It's just a little ironic.""Ironic? Ironic how?"

"Well we actually cursed each other. It's like a big magical jinx."

That was the wrong thing to say. I knew it as soon as the words left my mouth. But it was true. I Uno reversed her curse.

"A jinx?" she tuts. "A jinx is harmless. This is not harmless! You've turned my pussy into an acid pool! What kind of Scary Movie Five shit is this!?"

"Are those movies good? I've never seen them," I say, trying to lighten the mood.

"Stop talking to me!" she hisses before turning back to Cyrus. "So now what?"

Informed by my mistake, Cyrus immediately leaps into next steps to avoid agitating her further.

"Now, we draw some blood, narrow down your species, and hopefully relax. It looks like your heat is about to come on so I wouldn't encourage either of you to mess with the bonds. It probably won't end well and Corn might go feral."

"Feral? Feral like a stray cat?" Candrima asks.

"Heh, no. Feral like a lust deficient succubus. He won't be able to maintain any task magic or any appearance charms. He'll be a big horny, angry menace."

That finally gets a laugh out of her, and I can't say I'm surprised.

"Any other questions before we draw this blood?" Cyrus asks.

Candy goes quiet with consideration and I feel a quick tinge of anxiety when her voice finally returns, sounding grave.

"Why do succubi have ridges on their dicks?" she asks.

"Candrima!" I chide.

I love my brother but that's personal. I don't want to talk to him about my dick. I don't wanna talk to anyone about my dick.

"Wait, who has ridges on their dick? Corn, is your dick grooved?"

"I'm not answering that."

"Let me see your dick then," he insists.

"You can actually go straight to Hell," I reply.

"I am overdue for a vacation, but alas, I have too much work to do. What's up with your bumpy dick? Does it itch?"

"Who gave you a medical license? Were they of sound mind?" I ask.

"It's not bumpy," Candrima interjects, raising a finger. "It's a raised pattern. They swell during arousal."

I balk at her clarification. She knows way too much about my dick from a one time encounter. How often does she recall that night?

"Often enough." she says between us.

So she can read my mind now? That's not at all invasive.

"Hm, ok," Cyrus says, looking at me. "That's not a succubus thing, Candy. That's a Corn thing. Corn, I need a blood sample from you also."

I pale in the face of my greatest mortal enemy: A needle.

"For what!?" I shriek.

"I would call it curiosity, but I'm working on being transparent, so here's the deal. Succubi don't have weird dicks and we can't put claim bonds on beings above our power level even if they consent. It will fail every single time unless it's attempted and reinforced for decades. So you claiming a whole sorceress during a one night stand seems a little suspicious."

"Unless it's not my claim bond?" I half-ask.

I know that's likely not true, but I'm trying hard to escape the possibility of getting poked. Who decided that a tiny knife through your skin was the best way to get blood? We're magic! Why can't the blood just be extracted via sweat or something?

"Bahaha, no, it's definitely yours," Cyrus chuckles. "Touching her would've poisoned you by now if it wasn't. I'll even need an antidote after today."

"Corn, stop being a wimp. Just give him a little blood, I'm hungry and I need a bath," Candy says.

I plead with her silently, but her beauty is begrudging. One quick eye roll tells me that her sympathy for my phobia is almost non-existent.

"Candy, I'm scared of needles," I say, curling my tails into my lap.

"Corn," she says firmly. "You have two needles on the top of your head."

"Yes, but I'm not impaling anybody."

"Well we wouldn't be in this situation if you weren't impaling anybody," she replies.

The finger I had raised to drive my argument quickly bends down. She's got a point. I was definitely the one doing the impaling.

"I like her. I think you guys should stay together," Cyrus says.

"Hush," me and Candy reply in unison.

"Look, Corn. We need to get this done. Do you want me to hold your hand?"

I snap my head back to stare at her fully. I am a two hundred year old demon, I don't need to be pacified.

"Are you being funny?" I ask.

"No, I'm serious. I'll hold your hand if it helps. I understand if we're being honest. I'm scared of the dentist. Especially when I have to get fillings."

A little vulnerability is all it takes for me to abandon my pride.

"Yes, please hold my hand," I nod.

Ok, maybe I did need to be pacified, because she squeezes my hand and my anxiety starts to unravel. I don't even notice Cyrus prepping the needle or his nurse cleaning my skin.

"Do you wanna eat dessert later? I could probably summon some more ice cream," Candrima says.

"Wait, what happened to the ice cream I had?"

"Yeah, I ate that last night. It's not everyday you get kidnapped."

You know what? Fair. I probably would've done the same thing.

"Maybe you could do a nice tart to make it up to me," she adds.

She's guilt tripping me hard with that adorable pout and soft voice, and unfortunately it's working. I already know I'll be making her a tart once a week for the foreseeable future.

"Candrima, you didn't have to curse me to get me to cook for you. You could've just asked," I laugh.

"Yeah, but if I did that, I wouldn't have had a good reason to call out of work today would I?"

It's comfortable joking with Candy like this, and I quickly realize I could do it all day. Unfortunately though, today's not that day, and I'm reminded of that when she shifts out of my brother's way.

"And done!" Cyrus says placing a gauze pad over my puncture wound. "Nice job, Candy."

"See? That was quick and easy," she smiles.

For the first time in a century, I've gotten my blood drawn without incident. I didn't flinch when the needle touched my skin, I didn't scream, and I didn't accidentally assault anyone. I just let my stress dissolve into nothing while staring right into Candrima's cinnamon-colored eyes. Eyes that make this cold, sterile room feel a hundred times warmer.

"Yeah. Easy," I reply.

Candy

I get my blood drawn and then Cyrus sits us down to explain how claim bonds work. Apparently us cursing each other has reinforced the bonds, so we're now in a "honeymoon" phase. Which is basically us spending 12-18 months in a state of perpetual physical yearning. I was concerned to find out that it lasted so long, but Corn was quick to inform me that magical beings live nearly ten times as long so a year is nothing in the grand scheme of it all. Magic beings also make concessions for these kinds of things since they don't fight natural cycles, so Corn isn't bothered when he was to call a few non-human clients and let them know that he won't be able to work this next year. Meanwhile I'm freaking out about losing my pitiful human job. I can't work like this. I'll definitely get fired for fucking my demon husband on the clock.

"You're anxious," Corn says simply as I pour over the honeymoon brochure.

Shit. The bind is doing its job and it's pissing me off! I just want to freak out in peace. But no, he just has to have access to my emotional state.

"Yeah, because there's no cure for my curse and I just found out I'll be tethered to you for a year or better."

"Actually, the rest of your life unless you choose abstinence."

"Gee thanks, Corn. That makes me feel so much better."

Corn winces like I've sliced him with a knife and then I feel another emotion tangle with mine. Rejection.

"Corn? What's wrong?" I ask.

Tears well in the corners of his pretty eyes. His wings flutter slightly, ruffled by his upset, and his tails curl around his legs similar to a dog that knows he's in trouble. The big guy doesn't hesitate to lay it all out.

"You don't like me," he sniffles. "Is that why you're so upset?"

I've been dreaming about this man for decades, yet I never could've imagined this. He's unexpectedly sensitive and emotional. I mean, that much was clear from yesterday. He assumes a woman is ghosting him and his solution is to steal her. I don't even think that was his contingency plan. Can you say deep end?

"What, Corn? No! I'm upset because I'm basically married, I've gotten diagnosed as a sorceress, and I've been kidnapped all in one month. My last wax hasn't even grown out and my entire life has imploded. I am stressed."

"Oh, so you do like me?"

Remember what I said about men being men regardless of the species? Exhibit B, everyone.

"Cornelius! Focus!" I hiss. "Of course I like you! I just didn't plan for this, ok? It's Wednesday, and last week I thought I'd be getting off work, grabbing discount sushi, and prepping for Bingo Thursday. Instead I'm summoning shit from hell and finding out my vagina spits acid like some Alien Vs Predator subplot!"

Corn slowly raises his hand to stroke my back.

"I really need to get caught up on the last fifty years of TV because I don't understand any of your references. But they sound pretty good. Are they good?"

"Don't make me laugh," I snort. "I'm supposed to be stressed."

Corn's spade-shaped tail snakes out to wrap around my left thigh while he pulls me closer onto his lap, and then my entire body goes slack. Magic is a fucking trip. There's no amount of meditation and Xanax that could've ever gotten me this relaxed, but close contact with my giant soul bound demon does me in almost immediately. Goodbye anxiety.

"There's no point in stressing over what we can't control, Candri-ma."

"Says the man who kidnapped me," I shoot back.

"Well, yeah. But to be fair, I was literally losing my mind. You're the only being I can feed from now."

Wait, how is he eating? It's not like we've had sex in any capacity while he's been pouting and sleeping on the roof. I haven't had one of *those* dreams in days.

"You think of me when you masturbate," he says lowly while nuzzling my neck. "Perverted little witch."

My face heats from embarrassment. I wrongly assumed that was my private time and my nasty little fantasies would never see the light of day. Yet here Corn is, confirming that he knows about them.

Again, magic is a trip.

Especially because I can feel his erection growing against my ass, and it's making me want to buss it wide open on the waiting room floor of his brother's medical practice. This has to be the bond, right? Magic must be encouraging me to fuck this demon's brains out.

"Corn," I start.

"We should go," he finishes.

I nod silently, thanking whoever that I don't always have to say it. Then Corn stands and puts me on his back before summoning another iridescent portal.

"Wait! Not again!" I shriek, realizing we're going back the way we came.

"Sorry, little witch," he sighs. "This is the quickest route."

Corn immediately tosses his shirt once we land back in the cabin. I feel bad because the evergreen Henley looked nice on him, but now it's decorated in my electric yellow puke.

"Sorry," I mumble.

"It's ok," Corn says gently. "I know it's rough. Come on, sit down and I'll make you a tea for your stomach."

I waste no time collapsing onto the cushy sofa. My body is weak and I'm hot and dizzy. As far as modes of transportation go, the ether is F tier. Having a demon carry you off over a city of skyscrapers like a bird of prey has moved up to a solid C.

Rain begins to fall from the sky and softly pitter against the windows. I'm tempted to open the door and let the fresh air cleanse the house, but I settle for watching it instead. I sit up to get a better view of a few drops clinging to a wide blade of grass before they assimilate into a waiting puddle underneath it. The ground around us slowly transitions from the light brown of dry loam to a rich, dense, wet mud and I sigh in contentment. Nature really does have it all figured out.

"What are you looking at?" Corn asks.

I watch as he attempts to mirror my angle to try and see what I find so interesting, but his expression quickly morphs from that of curious to hopelessly confused.

"I'm watching the rain," I chuckle.

He tilts his head onto his shoulder while studying my sincerity. Finally seeing that I am, his brows marry.

"Why?"

It's strange, I've never had someone ask me why. Most people just accept that it's something I do with no further explanation. But not Corn.

Never Corn.

"It's refreshing. The whole area gets so hot and dusty within a week that the air gets heavy, then the rain will come and wash it away. It feels like a reset for life," I explain.

"Hm," he hums in response.

I expect him to return to his kettle and try to beat the whistle like he usually does, but instead he sits besides me. His eyes find the same blade of grass I was focused on moments earlier, then the faintest smirk stretched across his lips. Soon his tail is curled around my waist, and my head rests against his big shoulder. We're not talking but my heart is syncing with his, and that's all I need for reassurance. A wave of peace unlike any other washes over me in that moment, and I begin to picture the rest of my life accented by times like this. Until our quiet is pierced by the sharp whistle of the tea kettle.

Disregarding my silent protest, Corn moves to remove the water from the fire and prepare our tea.

"Honey or agave?" he calls.

"Honey please."

I'm still getting used to telepathic communication, but I have to admit it has its perks. It's like texting, only it doesn't burn my corneas out or overstimulate me. Plus there's no paper trail. I can say whatever I want and only Corn will know. No one's pulling up receipts from the time I said I wanted my partner to fill all my holes and make my pussy cream like whipped butter.

"Candrima," Corn growls while offering me a warm saucer. "Be a lady."

Oh right. I keep forgetting that internal thoughts aren't always just internal thoughts. Sometimes they're us thoughts.

Shit.

I'm now an us.

"Sorry," I say sheepishly, accepting the tea. "I'm working on it."

"I got something you can work on." he says with raised brows.

"Excuse me? What was that?"

Corn blushes when he realizes his comment was shared with the group, and he covers his mouth like a little kid caught cussing. What an adorable goofball. I guess we both have some adjusting to do. We can start by adjusting his pants. They look tight.

Particularly in the crotch.

The heat I've been carrying all afternoon starts to spread to my belly before it settles in between my legs. I realize that what I'm feeling is arousal. I thought it was just the tea but it's him. Then the longer I look at him, the worse it becomes. Who decided that demons needed to be carved out of moonstone? Who decided that this one in partic-ular needed to be strong, sensitive, and nasty on top of being cruelly handsome?

It's too much for one woman to handle.

"Corn," I say softly before abandoning my tea.

The saucer clinks against the oak table as I rise from my seat. He holds my gaze and I watch as his eyes fill with lust, inverting to a sinister black. I take a few brave steps forward, and when I reach him, I wrap my arms around his neck. We fit like a lock and key. One of his hands meets the small of my back immediately and we stare at each other intently, knowing there's only one way for this to end.

And that's with me, folded into a croissant and stuffed with cream.

Our chests brush and his firm against my soft ignites the spark between us further. My need is plenty evident. Ever the gentleman, Cornelius tries his hardest not to look at my budding nipples, but cu-riosity eventually over takes him and he does anyway, sharply inhaling at the sight. He stares far too long to pretend he's not interested, but when he finally does look away, he doesn't notice that my face is closer and our lips graze. The tender sweep is too much for him and the white finally leaves his eyes.

"Candrima," he says, tilting my chin upward.

I hold my breath, hoping he'll be the one to resuscitate me should I pass out, and bend forward to meet his lips. Only to hear,

"I should go."

"Wa-"

He's transformed into a fit of inky shadows before I can get my protest out, and suddenly, I stand in the middle of a too hot cabin alone and frustrated.

Mine

Corn

"Is this how you tell me you're mated? Popping in here looking like sex, with no shirt on like this is an early 2000's romcom?" My mama asks. "Ok, Love Jones."

Damnit! I was in such a hurry to leave that I forgot to grab a shirt. Still don't understand the reference. Man, I really gotta catch up on TV.

"Hi, Mama. Hi Baba. I just need to hang out here for a minute," I say, trying to catch my fleeting breath.

"Hello, Cornelius," my father waves cheerfully.

My father has always been the a/c to my mother's heatwave. Even a thousand years later. It's sweet seeing them in their normal, and it almost gives me hope for my situation.

Until my mother replaces the lid on her stew, grabs a book from the endless stack on the dining room table, and joins my father in the living room. He shoots me a look that quietly says, "save yourself." But I'm too slow to listen before she starts.

"Mhm. Cyrus said she was very pretty. Unfortunate set of powers though. Is that why you're trying to avoid her? You're afraid of the EUM?"

"I don't appreciate you calling me out," I grumble.

"I don't appreciate finding out my son has been soul bound from someone other than him," she scoffs.

And checkmate.

How was this better than letting a gorgeous, curvy, witch milk me dry? I don't know, but it is less scary.

"Cornelius, you are a literal demon. Fall in love. Eat dessert first. Break a few rules. Live a little," she scolds.

Not by much though. Not by much.

"I just... I don't want to make it harder when I have to let her go. She's going to want to return to her life, Mama. We're looking for a way to sever the bond as we speak."

My mother cackles, sounding every bit as accurate as her title, First Priestess of Hell.

"You're never going to sever that bond. You might as well go home and let her have her way with you. You'll feel better afterwards," she chuckles.

Yeah, I wasn't so sure about that. I knew my mama was probably right about the bond. I paid enough attention during sexual education to know that a monogamy bind was serious business. But part of me still held out hope that we could one day go our separate ways and say, "this was fun."

Why? I wasn't sure, but I think deep down I didn't trust myself. I liked following the rules. I liked staying out of trouble. I enjoyed order. But then I went and blew all that up by wetting my dick in a sorceress, and the worst part is, I enjoyed the chaos Candy brought me even more. I had gotten so used to just existing that I forgot there was more to do out there. In just a month I had learned why calm precedes a storm, why grass grows green, and why the EUM is adamant about preventing species mixing, but I also didn't care anymore. I was starting to not mind a little lawlessness. A little chaos. A little love. So maybe I was afraid that if it came down to it, I wouldn't be able to make the right choice.

I'm allowed two hours of hiding before my mom scoops me two portions of stew and sends me back on my way to, "handle my re-sponsibilities." Apparently she could smell Candy's heat on me, and she was sure to let me know how cruel it was to abandon my partner during her time of need. What she didn't know was I was in my own rut, and I was sure if I acted on earlier impulse, my little witch would be somewhere comatose.

My little witch. What a strange thought. It felt right, but after living alone for the better part of nearly two hundred years, it was also strange. Just like the state of the living room when I walked in. Candrima had been busy. Various spell books and texts sat annotated and bookmarked, arranged in an oddly efficient reading circle. From what I could see, she had three main books she was working out of while the five in the rear were used as references. Part of me wished I had met Candrima during college, because I know she graduated top of her class with study habits like this.

"Candy?" I call.

There is no response but I can feel her presence in the house so I shrug it off as simple disinterest. She wasn't necessarily wrong to be disinterested in dealing with me right then anyway. I ran off to a whole nother realm just because I was afraid to kiss her. As far as I'm concerned, we're even.

I place our stew in the fridge and arrange the flowers I bought before I notice a pitcher of what looks like fresh squeezed OJ.

Jackpot.

I love orange juice, so my immediate instinct is to rinse a cup and pour myself a healthy glass. Part of me knows I probably shouldn't be drinking strange juice, but I'm 80% sure Candrima summoned it since she couldn't leave. There's also strawberries, bacon, and ice cream included in her haul. Plus little cheese puff snacks. Something feels ominous about encroaching on her drink, but I shake it off because I'm sure she won't miss a little juice.

I tip the spout towards the rim of my glass, filling it three quarters way full, and now this is the unfortunate part, I knock it straight back. The drink retaliates, and I find out that it was in fact **not** orange juice. I slide to the floor as the liquid sloshes down my throat into my stomach, leaving a scorching sensation in its wake.

"Why is it spicy?" I hiss.

The glass clatters against the floor with me, the shards scatter with a loud jingle, causing Candy to come running in. "Corn! What happened?" she shrieks.

I point to the deceptive container of liquid on the counter.

"What kind of juice is that?" I choke.

Candrima's eyes blow wide and guilt settles onto her pretty face.

"That's not juice, Corn! It's a sleeping potion!"

She says it like a sleeping potion is a perfectly reasonable thing to expect in your fridge. It was even in a beverage dispenser! The good one with the flip spout at that.

"Why was it in the fridge!?"

"You know I don't like room temperature drinks," she sighs. "I was just letting it get a chill."

"Goddess, you're going to be the damn death of me! Why do you even need a sleeping potion, Candy?" I wheeze.

This sleeping potion sucks anyway. I wasn't tired at all. In fact I was actually feeling very energetic. A little too energetic...

"I just do, ok? It's been like three days since I got some decent sleep. I'm hot, dizzy, and restless all the time. I don't have an appetite, I just want-"

"You're in heat, Candrima," I groan.

I've known for days. That's why I was finally able to find her. She went into heat in the middle of the day on Monday and her sweet honeyed scent reeled me in instantly. It was like the real life version of that cat and mouse cartoon where the smell of a freshly baked pie carried them to glory.

"What? Humans do not go into heat. I might be ovulating, sure. But I'm n-"

"Candrima, you are not human!" I say, pulling myself from the floor. "You are a sorceress and you have heats. Plus you're wrong. Human women do have heats, you all just prefer to put lipstick on a pig instead of calling it what it is! It's a heat. A natural need."

Speaking of natural needs, I notice that I am in desperate need of some relief. My corduroys are growing tighter with each passing breath, my eyes are inverting, and my humanoid form is becoming unstable. First with my second tail making an appearance, then with my wings, and finally, my horns.

"Candrima, where did you find that sleeping potion?" I ask lowly. "Hold on, I have it bookmarked."

She scurries off and returns a short while later, handing me not a spell book, no, but an aphrodisiac recipe booklet instead. "Why did you think this was a sleeping potion?" I query calmly.

"It says guaranteed to put you to bed," she replies, pointing to the faded Latin script.

At this point I can't stop the laughter that escapes me. It's warranted anyway. I tried so hard to control myself only to be brought down by a tasteless gag gift from Nilla and a sweet, anxious witch.

"Sweetheart, this says guaranteed to get you to bed. Bed, meaning sex. This is not a sleeping potion. It's a lust punch."

A few moments of loaded silence pass between us and a guilty Candy avoids my eyes while I finally succumb to the effects of the potion. My tails move to unfasten my pants and free my throbbing dick with haste, and when I see myself swollen and slick with desire, my eyes fall on the breathtaking witch standing in front of me. Ripe and sweet. Perfect for eating.

"Candrima," I growl. "Come here."

I can see the mischief in her eyes. She's going to make me work for it. We both know I'm not above chasing, but today isn't the day to test my control with games. I know she knows that.

Still, she takes a step backward.

"Don't," I warn, flexing my wings outward like the predator I am.

A smirk briefly plays on her lips before she folds herself into a flash of light.

Then just like that, the hunt is on.

Locating her is a bit more difficult than I originally thought. She's become quite proficient at teleporting in the two hours I've been out, but that sweet scent of hers is always on my side. It calls out to me like a beacon.

"Candyyyy," I call. "Come out, come out wherever you are."

"No thank you," she goads.

My ears turn, searching for any discernible sound that might allude to her location, but she's gotten better at this. I guess getting kidnapped will do that to you.

"Why not, little witch?" I laugh. "You don't wanna play with me?"

"Is that what you're calling it?"

She's one to talk. I've heard her version of *playtime.* Loud and clear.

Still I'm not in the mood to call her out on her hypocritical tendencies. We have bigger fish to fry.

"I'll call it whatever you want as long as it ends with you creaming on my dick, sweetheart. I know that's what you want, I can smell it on you. Why make it harder on yourself?" I say, hoping she'll adhere to reason.

"Why make it easier for you?"

Note to self: Heats make Candy a difficult little thing.

"Because when I finally do find you, no God you pray to in your time of need will have the courage to listen," I growl.

A few seconds of silence pass before I hear a telling chuckle in the recesses of my mind.

"Tempting, but no thanks." she replies.

I smile because I love a challenge. That much is clear from the amount of peace lilies I have in my home. I enjoy dramatics and stubbornness. Mental stimulation is an aphrodisiac like no other. So if she wants to play hide and seek, I'll seek. I'll seek her to the ends of the Earth. I just hope she can keep up.

It takes me fifteen minutes to narrow down her location. She's somewhere in the washroom.

I shadow in to avoid tipping her off, blending in with the darkness that the candle light cannot reach. Flames of varying hues dance amongst each other, creating a mosaic reflection on the pool of steaming water below me, one that shimmers and ripples unexpectedly.

She was so confident that she took a bath. I love misplaced confidence.

I creep from the ceiling, keeping my form liquid, and focus on blending with the steam. When I'm close enough to sense her body heat, I notice that she's floating on her back in the center of the pool, completely invisible to the naked eye. Candrima is continuously impressive. In just two hours she mastered teleportation, summons, and invisibility. Plus drove me into a maddening state that makes me want to dissolve into her.

"Little witch," I chuckle. *"You can't hide forever."*

Unaware of my new position, she smiles silently, assuming she's triumphant.

"Aw, baby. You sound upset."

Baby.

I had every intention of drawing her out slowly, but hearing her call me something other than my name turns my resolve into goo. I fall into the water with a loud splash and pull her toward me with my tail, chuckling darkly when her shocked little expression is once again visible.

"Corn, I-" she starts.

"I'm your baby?" I interrupt.

She smiles, drawing me closer to her pretty little mouth. "I'm your baby?" I ask again, this time against her lips.

"You are," she confirms with a nod. "My big, handsome, bratty baby."

I know this is bad. I know it's going to be difficult and painful to sever our bond. I know I shouldn't enjoy this, or touch her, or indulge in her heat. But how long am I supposed to follow the rules only to be rewarded with more rules? How long am I supposed to pretend that she isn't everything I could ever wish for? How long am I supposed to fight?

My mama is right. I am a demon, and it's high time I start acting like it. Starting with working the *kinks* out of our relationship.

"Possession is a sacrificial act, little witch," I say, kissing her pretty feet. "Are you sacrificing yourself to me?"

Without taking a breath, she lowers her eyes into a submissive gaze and answers,

"Yes."

My heart skips for a moment, but I work fast once I regain control. I pull her hips flush to mine and raise her torso upward. Immediately after, her lips meet mine in a passionate kiss, one that makes my wings unfurl. Our bodies glide against one another as we find our rhythm, and we sync quickly, but I know it's the friction that Candrima craves. Her hips rock against mine aggressively, seeking pleasure from contact, and being the good demon I am, I indulge her.

Dipping a finger in between her delicate folds, I find her soaking wet and burning up. Her clitoris is firm and ready, throbbing in anticipation of touch. Not wanting to deny her for any longer than I already have, I lightly press the pad of my thumb against her bud and rub vertically. I keep my movements nice and slow, gathering more slick from her entrance when I need to, increasing pressure when I see fit. Then, when she's all worked up and ready to come undone, I remove my touch completely.

"Corn!" she hisses. "What the fuck?"

I smile at her irritated scowl. She's gorgeous even when she's angry.

"Well I thought you didn't wanna play with me," I tease. "Have you changed your mind, Candrima?"

There's still fight in her eyes so I gently graze her clitoris with my free tail, encouraging her to squirm against my steeled length. Her soft against my hard feels wickedly right and it's taking every ounce of restraint I have not to make a home inside of her.

But if she were to say yes...

I just need her to say yes.

"Yeah, Corn. I changed my mind."

Her response comes out like a whisper, but it has the same effect as a roar. Candrima's yes resounds in my mind repeatedly, becoming my personal theme song, guiding me, demanding me, soothing me.

Most thoughts leave me, but a handful stay. The ones that remain consist of all the ways I'm going to wear her out and what we're going to do after. The latter can easily become a recipe for overthinking though, so I leave that one alone and focus on the former. I relax my body to lean backwards into the pool, and when I begin to float I use my wings to make lazy laps, circling around my little witch like a curious shark.

"Come here," I demand.

Candrima slowly turns her head, dipping her tight curls further into the water. I know she's trying to figure out how she can possibly come any closer, but she's thinking about it too much.

"Candrima."

"How?" she asks.

The smile that crawls on my face is insidious but I can't help it. I'm going to have fun corrupting this little witch. There's so much I can show and do to her that her human lovers can't, starting with this pool. I hope after tonight, she won't be able to come near this room without shuddering from reliving the memories of what we've done in here.

"Let me show you," I smile.

"Ok."

She nods her confirmation before pressing her pillowy lips to mine, and while she's in the middle of sucking my tongue, I pick her up and flip her around so she can suck something else.

"Wait, Corn. Is this safe?"

I become irritated at her question because I know her skepticism is a result of her weight. Someone somewhere has convinced her that a measly 257 pounds is unreasonably large, but I'm a demon of means and muscle. So all I want her to do is,

"Sit on my fucking face, Candy."

Goddess bless heats because all of those hormones have Candrima eager to comply. She's ass up head down in seconds, looking every bit as delectable as she smells. I grip her hips with two hands, greedily palming her plush bottom to satisfy my need to dominate. Then my tongue snakes out, probing her slick lips and swollen pearl hungrily. She tastes like bottled sin and she sounds like it too. The more I eat, the louder she moans. The sound is breathy and pregnant with pleasure, putting pornography moans to shame. Especially when she calls out my name in desperation while her first orgasm descends.

She's loud.

She's passionate.

She's mine.

Mine.

That sounds dangerous coming from me. Any other time I might be concerned about my inability to control my thoughts, but I'm too busy eating a buffet poolside to care. Candy is living up to her name.

Sweet, memorable, and addicting. Then the way she's swallowing my dick?

I'll never complain about my rut again if this is the result. Pleasure builds in my belly as her tongue tickles my length. Her mouth is so soft and warm and it would be the perfect place to unload if not for her perfect pussy. That's the goal, even if I have to think of dead puppies every ten seconds to make it there.

Luckily though, I don't have to wait long. Candrima's second orgasm comes on hard and fast, just as victoriously as the first. It's messier though and it's how I find out she can squirt.

Goddess.

I'm going to have fun fucking this woman.

She will be my demise, and I will follow her to the abyss happily.

Candy comes down and I pluck her trembling body from mine then hold her above my head so I can open my wings. I'm temporarily mesmerized by the beads of water trailing the length of her marbled body, coming together into a stream that eventually flows from the curve of her supple ass. I know that she's rewired my brain because I'd usually be disgusted by the idea of drinking bathwater and rightfully so. But now I can't bear the thought of something so perfect going to waste, and I open my mouth to catch a few sweet drops on my tongue.

It's official.

I'm obsessed.

I shoot out of the bath and join her in the air. My grip on her never loosens, but she jumps like it has.

"I got you," I say softly.

Candrima looks at the water below us that's still swaying from our recent evacuation, and then her eyes find the ceiling, which is so close

I could press my fingertips to it.

"I'm afraid of heights," she confesses with a whisper.

Her grip on my forearm tightens as if mentioning her phobia will doom her, but I'd never let her fall. I'd never let anything happen to her.

"Do you trust me?" I ask.

Candy's eyes rise from the pool and meet mine. I can see the moment her breath catches, and the moment she remembers to breathe. She's nervous, but she still gives me an eager nod. One I won't take for granted.

"Show me you trust me, baby," I say, leaning into her for a kiss.

I expect hesitation, but her lips meet mine immediately. The kiss is rough and demanding, making any blood I'm not utilizing to hold us in the air rush to my dick. I can barely think let alone breathe. Candrima's hungry and salacious, but also so vulnerable. I know she's giving me a lot and I have no intentions of forsaking that.

"I got you," I say again.

I then secure her against my torso with one tail before dipping her just low enough to squeeze my aching dick inside of her, and when our hips finally meet, I growl in relief.

"Oh, fuck," I moan, as Candy settles on my length.

She's wetter and warmer than I remember, and so much tighter. That makes me break into a nervous sweat. One over-confident pump would be all it takes to send me spiraling.

"You ok?" she asks sweetly.

The kindness reflecting in her stunning brown eyes is doing absolutely nothing to help the situation. She's ruined me in a month and being back inside her is like getting a sip of water after working under the August summer sun.

"I'm trying my best not to cum," I groan.

Candrima quickly mumbles the contraceptive incantation after I say that, remembering what I've easily forgotten. I'm thankful though because a baby is the last thing we need.

"Sorry," I moan.

"It's alright," she whispers, kissing me. "Heat of the moment."

She's exactly right, because once I adjust to her grip and wetness, I start pounding away without a care in the world. I'm definitely acting on all of my impulses, and so is she.

She meets me measure for measure, tightening around me when I enter, and rolling her hips when I retreat. We're synchronized in a way that transcends individual existence. We're one, and it makes me never want to be apart again. "Candy. Why do you feel so fucking good?" I groan. "Baby, why do you feel so good?"

Intimacy has never been this enjoyable for me. I adore every second of this. Candrima's curves, her warmth, her nails in my skin, and her sweet scent are all working hard to turn me into a madman. And I don't need any help with that. I've already Candy-napped her.

"Co-corn, what are you doing to me?" she cries.

At first I'm confused. But then Candrima's tight asshole contracts from pressure of a looming orgasm and I finally notice that my other tail has made a home in her previously unoccupied hole. My lower left thumb is resting against her wet tongue, my other hand is ravelled in her damp curls, and I'm fucking her so hard that the thrusts are ricocheting against my open wings. I know exactly what I'm doing.

"I'm claiming her."

This is not good.

I'm going to reinforce these bonds and she'll never be able to get rid of me. She'll never have peace. *I'll never leave her.*

I should stop.

I should unsheath myself from this beautiful brown-eyed creature and act like I have a little bit of sense. I should let go before it's too late.

But I can't.

Nor do I want to.

I purr in delight, my mind under siege of all her yielding softness. Then I become distrustful of my mind's ability to catalog every ripple and peak of her softness, so my hands roam over her curves in a selfish attempt to imprint a physical reminder there. My speed increases as my skin glides and grips hers and she continues to meet me measure for measure.

Beat for beat and pound for pound. Until I can't take it anymore.

The pressure building in my belly shoots down my spine, into my sack, and rips from me in a deafening roar. The speed of my flapping wings combines with Candrima's inhuman heat, creating instability in the air, and we produce a cyclone as we peak together. The summation of our pleasure quite literally rains down around us, leaden and thunderous. In contrast, the blinding platinum light Candrima produces is just barely contained in the dark mass of our destructive storm, and as she sings my name, I know this woman will be everything. My beginning, my end, and my damnation alike.

Candy

Oh, God.

Everything hurts. Including my elbows.

I guess fucking for eight hours straight in any and every available space will do that to you, but I can't say I regret it. That shit was fun, plus I feel much better. According to one of the many books Corn supplied me with on the subject, magic ejaculant has a chemical compound called esfraxin that is absorbed into the bloodstream from the vagina. It skips the liver so it can get to work soothing all the rampant heat hormones, and I'm extra lucky because my lust demon husband naturally produces nearly double the esfraxin than the rest of the magical population. Plus he needed to relieve his rut...

I'm sore as shit, but completely satisfied.

So satisfied that I keep ignoring my screaming bladder and slipping back into sleep. It doesn't help that Corn makes it easy to doze. He's warm and safe while his contented purring keeps my body in a catatonic state. Who would've thought that demons purred? Definitely not me.

I would've let him hold me until the next sun rose, but then I dreamed of a toilet. As soon as I sat my booty on that fake seat and started to go I knew it was time. There was just one problem...

I move to get out of bed and Corn's tails tighten around my hips and waist like a sensitive seatbelt. It's obviously bad timing, but I can't say I blame him. Fool him once...

"Corn, I gotta pee," I groan.

He cracks one eye open to look at me then he has the audacity to huff. But at least he lets me go, because I'm ten seconds away from finding out if he appreciates a golden shower.

I make it to the toilet in a nick of time to avoid pissing myself, and as the seemingly endless stream pours out of me, Corn joins me in the bathroom.

"Are you sore?" he asks gently.

He looks so guilty and I'm tempted to lie to assuage that, but then I remember he can likely feel the acute pain through our bond. Lying will do me no good here. Especially not if I want to rebuild our trust. "A little," I nod.

"I'm sorry," he sighs, prepping a compress. "This should help."

The bidet sprays a jet of cool water against my battered cooch, and once Corn is confident I'm clean, he presses the warm cloth to my sex.

It should be awkward having an eight foot tall man service my pussy in a tiny water closet like we're at a five minute oil change joint, but it's decidedly not once I stop thinking so hard, and I melt into the sensation. It's tingly, refreshing, and doing wonders for my stretched muscles. It's exactly what I need.

"I'm going to make us some breakfast," Corn says after a while. "Is there anything in particular that you're craving with the bacon?"

I raise my gaze from the navy and white tile I've been fixating on from the past four minutes and meet Corn's eyes. He's genuinely curious but I can see some sadness lingering behind his eyes.

What's going on?

"No," I say with a shake of my head. "I just like it for BLT's."

"Ok," he replies, moving to stand.

I don't know why, but the gesture makes me anxious and it's a reflex to reach for him and pull him back to me. He immediately halts, placing his hand on top of mine, and moves closer. We don't speak, we just watch each other's eyes for a moment. His are filled with warmth, hope, and sincerity, and I can even see the curiosity in my own eyes reflecting back to me.

Looking at him like this now, I can see exactly why that dream scared me. He's brushing my knuckles tenderly as if my bones would shatter under further pressure. And while that's not the only way he's found to touch me, all of his touch is gentle and soothing, including the way he scratches my scalp. There's even tenderness in the way he watches me. Corn is a sweetheart. He's thoughtful, funny, protective, and kind when he isn't going crazy from rut hormones. That dream terrified me because I know it's inevitable.

Corn's the perfect being to fall in love with.

I remember all the gory details of that fucking dream, and I ruin our moment by jumping away. Whatever spell Corn was under breaks and he returns to standing while offering me a shy smile.

"I ran you a bath," Corn whispers. "Soak for a little bit while I prep breakfast."

I'm silently kicking myself for throwing us back into real life, but I nod and rise, hoping that the day leads us back to another moment like this. Another moment where I can get lost in his pensive eyes and melt into his gentle touch.

"Come on," Corn says, sweeping me into his arms.

"Eep!" I shriek. "Corn, I can walk!"

"Yeah, I know. But I'm headed that way anyway. You might as well preserve your energy and let me carry you."

I blush because it turns out chivalry isn't dead, it's just exclusive to Hell.

"Oh, ok. I guess you're right," I conceded.

"Of course I'm right, baby," he chuckles.

You ever see a candle burn timelapse? You know how the wax goes from perfectly formed and symmetrical to a liquid, shapeless, melted, puddle? Well that's exactly what happened to me in real time when Corn called me baby. I became putty in his hands, so much so that I had to grip the landing to remain upright when he slipped me into the tub.

The water was the perfect temperature, steamy and relaxing, but when it ripples I'm thrust back into a memory of last night and I shiver like there's a breeze.

"You cold?" Corn asks.

Not wanting to explain my flashback, I quickly shake my head.

"Uh, no. Just thinking," I say.

Knowing Corn's inquisitive nature, I expect him to push back with further questions, but he just smiles and exits the room, chuckling to himself over what I can only assume is an inside joke.

What if I wanted to laugh though?

Before long, I'm so calm that I nearly fall back asleep. The plants, the heat, and the creamy blue of the water is conducive to unproductivity, but then I reach up and make the mistake of attempting to lace my fingers through my now-matted curls.

"Eugh," I grimace, feeling the knots.

I start to climb out to find a comb, but Corn comes in with a small tray stacked high with tea and fruit.

"I made you a mint and turmeric tea to help with the swelling. Also, do you like onion jam? Wait, what's wrong?" he asks, seeing my sad attempt at rising from the water.

I'm way too unathletic to be dealing with a man who's preferred method of movement is flying. I know he doesn't cling to this bath ledge like a one-legged lemur.

"Uh," I start, easing back down. "I need a comb for my hair. It's hella tangled."

"Oh, I'm almost done. I can comb your hair for you," he offers.

Suddenly the temperature increases by ten degrees. I look around, attempting to locate the source of the sweltering heat, only for Corn to reclaim my attention.

"Candrima," he says firmly.

His voice is rough and authoritative, like he's chastising my unfocused mind, and while that would annoy me coming from anyone else, it's perfect coming from him.

"Yes?" I nearly whimper in response.

"Is that ok?"

"Yes."

Corn chuckles before stepping closer to place the tray on my side.

"Let me wrap up what I was doing and I'll be right back," he says softly.

"*Please.*" I say silently.

Whether I say it just to myself or communicate my desperation between us, I don't know. But Corn smiles at me knowingly either way.

"This tea is really good," I say.

"Thank you. I make a big batch about twice a year."

I look down at my neat tray. The tea is the perfect color, a hypnotic amber hue that matches the honey it's served alongside.

He remembered my preference from yesterday.

There's also a small wedge of creamy brie, grapes, cherries, and the strawberries I summoned last night. All prepared in a perfect portion to tide me over until breakfast.

"How often do you do this?" I ask.

Corn drops the section of hair he's working on and reaches for a clip. "Do what?"

"Take care of women after sex," I say boldly.

The demon is 188 years old, it's a given that it was someone before me, but I still can't help the tiny twinge of jealousy I feel knowing that they got to experience him too. I want this all to myself.

Corn chuckles,

"Not often. I'm demisexual. You are the sixth being I've been intimate with."

Good lord, my body count is three times that. And here I am with the audacity.

"Not that it matters. I tend to believe that each instance of intimacy is unique to the person, so counting is arbitrary."

"Oh," I say, feeling humbled by his answer.

"Mhm. But to answer your question, Candrima, I've never taken care of anyone else to this extent. This experience is unique to you."

He twists down the final section of hair and plants a kiss on my forehead before rising out of the bath.

"When you get finished, there's a new dress in the bedroom. I hope you like it," he says, leaving me with my thoughts.

Once my embarrassment dims, I amble from the washroom and locate the dress. It's a silky velour emerald green dress with bardot sleeves and a slit. Something that looks like it would be a Kita Castille special. I'm not surprised though. Corn seemingly memorizes everything I say, do, or wear to use at a later date, so the dress makes sense. Especially because of the black dress he found me in.

I clothe and follow the sultry scent of cooked meat and fresh bread into the kitchen.

"You look beautiful," Corn says immediately.

He's dressed in a pale yellow Henley and a pair of deep brown corduroys with a black apron around his waist, holding a fresh pan of what may be the world's fluffiest biscuits. There are even flowers on the table, and seeing sunflowers in the morning brings me an unexpected jolt of joy.

"So do you. I mean, you look handsome. Not beautiful. But you are pretty," I ramble.

I look to the floor hoping that by some miracle of life I can be rendered unconscious and develop amnesia specific to this moment.

God, why am I so awkward? Is it because I like him?

"Are you just saying that because I'm holding breakfast?" he jokes.

"Yes," I nod. "The biscuits are distracting."

"I put in all that work last night just to be bested by bread. Oh well. Sit down and I'll make you a plate."

I do as I'm told and Corn rewards me with another generous plate. I have what looks like a fancy eggs Benedict breakfast sandwich, potatoes, and some steamed veggies.

"Thank you, it looks great."

"You look great."

I look up from my plate to see him gazing at me with predator eyes again.

"Corn…" I say sternly.

"I'm not going to bother you. You need to eat. Especially since you used a fair bit of energy last night for our games. What's up with the invisibility by the way? That seems new."

It was new. After he ran out of here like a man being served child support papers yesterday, I busied myself with learning new skills for the sole purpose of exacting petty revenge.

"I learned it so I could hide from you and have you think I found a way to leave."

"Candrima!" Corn chides.

I understand the implications of my admission, but I still don't feel bad. So I offer him a lazy shrug before tucking into my breakfast.

"How is it?" he asks with raised brows.

"It's really go-"

"I'm sorry for leaving yesterday. I hoped the flowers would help," he blurts.

So he buttered me up with food and flowers and now he wants to talk about it? Hm.

I carefully replace my fork onto my napkin then fold my arms over my chest. It's hard not to immediately melt while looking at his handsome face, but him dipping on me was fucked up.

"Why did you leave?" I query.

Corn grimaces like he didn't expect to have to provide an explanation for his behavior. While normally I wouldn't care if a man left, this isn't a normal situation. I can't ghost a guy my soul is literally tied to. So I need that reason.

"Candy, I- I don't want to reinforce these bonds. The more time we spend together, the harder it's going to be to separate. Last night shouldn't have happened," he sighs balefully.

Reality hits me like a pillowcase full of bricks. He regrets it. This is one-sided.

He doesn't want me.

I've experienced rejection before, but at the moment his words feel like a thousand pound weight crushing my entire body. It hurts so bad that I burst into tears.

"Shit, Candrima!" Corn cusses. "Please don't cry."

He moves to catch my tears on a tissue, but that act of service just pisses me off more. He's being nice just to let me down easy. What kind of game is this?

"What the fuck am I supposed to do, Corn? We have a mind-melting sex marathon, you hold me all night, and then you give me the best aftercare of my short, pitiful life just to tell me you don't actually want me!?" I holler.

His face twists in agony. I can feel the anger and frustration wave through our bond before he speaks. He tries to hold it in but then his wings flex and knock over a book which makes a truly obnoxious thud against the floor, and after that it just comes out.

"I DO WANT YOU AND THAT'S THE FUCKING PROBLEM!" he roars.

Corn's eyes start to do something I've never seen before. His normal rust consumes the entire surface of his eye and deepens to a color that is reminiscent of fresh blood. Then the room starts to warp, with distorted walls cracking and oozing a black shadowy smoke.

"That's the problem, Candy," he laughs sinisterly. "A partnering between a succubus and a sorceress is illegal. We could be killed for this. I know that, and yet I still want you. I want to hold you, and kiss you, and fuck you, and age with you despite knowing the repercussions. It's only been a month since you walked into my life, and in that short time you have made consequences meaningless. What are you doing to me?" he gasps. "Do you even know?"

I shake my head no, admitting my ignorance, and Corn inches closer. We meet somewhere in the space between us. His gaze draws me in and I feel I'm a clueless moth dancing around a hypnotic flame, unaware of the potential danger.

Indifferent to it, actually.

"Here you are in front of me. Being both everything I shouldn't have, and everything I need. Why are you so complicated? Why is this so complicated?" he asks.

I've asked myself that exact question so many times in the last forty eight hours.

Why was this so complicated?

Some people spend years hoping to meet the right person. The person whose smile lights up your entire day. The person you can share a comfortable silence with. The person that makes it all click. Only for me to stumble right into that person's life by complete accident and leave us both in shambles. It's not what I would've chosen, given the chance, but I can't say I regret any of it. Because eating breakfast with Corn after a disastrously long week is a pleasure I cannot believe I went so long without.

"It doesn't have to be complicated," I whisper against his lips. Corn rears away when our mouths brush, and I ready my pride in case he decides to disintegrate like yesterday. But to my surprise, he charges forward and claims my lips between his.

What a fucking kiss.

I feel fireworks. Literally.

Currents race up my fingertips and shoot up my spine, gathering in what feels like the center of my brain. My body becomes molten as I yield to Corn's affection, warming more with each hungry kiss, satisfied moan, and subtle squeeze. Unfortunately I get too excited and climb in his lap. That's when everything starts to go downhill. As soon as his erection brushes against my center, the energy I was holding rushes out and charges through the house. All of the light fixtures buzz from the inundation of electricity and burn platinum, until they begin to shatter one by one. The flying shards of glass land against the floors and the walls, burning holes in every soft surface they touch.

"Shit, I'm sorry!" I yell. "I'll clean this up."

I'm still shaking from the discharge, but I hop up and grab a broom and dustpan. This is embarrassing. It's like premature ejaculation but with electricity. Then it happens every single time he touches me. Once would be understandable, but every time!? I can never make fun of minute men ever again.

"Candrima, stop," Corn bellows.

I was cleaning furiously but Corn's voice flipped some weird switch in my brain and my arms fell to my side immediately. The glass I was gathering falls back to the floor with a loud bang, but the unnecessary noise doesn't even bother me. It's like I've been entranced.

He comes to my side and takes my hands in his.

"It's ok. I got this," he says gently. "Saniti Aboda."

The house creaks under Corn's magic as his shadows spread and then everything is snapped back in place. The lights, the glass, the knits, everything. It all reverts to its original position. No sweat necessary.

"Thanks," I mutter, slightly embarrassed of my lack of skill and control.

Corn tuts, dismissing my unease. Then he takes my face in his hands and leans forward to press out foreheads together. That fresh citrus scent of his floods my senses and the sensation brings me an unprecedented sense of calm. A kind of calm I feared was only possible in death.

Luckily, Corn breaks the spell this time.

"Come on, Candy. You need to eat."

He picks me up from my position on the ground then puts me back at the table, and after another heated glance sends energy crackling down my spine, I eat breakfast.

"We need to find you a coven so you can learn to control your powers," Corn says, as I start to sweep our breakfast mess.

"Why, cause I clean manually?" I tut.

"No. Because you have a tendency to short circuit neighborhoods when you get overwhelmed."

Ah, that is a fine point. A mighty fine point.

"Alright, you got me there. But where do we even find a coven. Is it like a YMCA? Do you just look for one closest to you?"

Corn snorts, clearly amused by my ignorance.

"No, Candy. Covens are sorted by species. We have to find out what species of sorcerer you are and then we can apply for some covens."

"You have to apply?" I gasp.

I don't know why I assumed you could just pop in, zap something to prove you're a witch, maybe do a little blood swear, and then belong to a coven. Magic society is much more modern than I anticipated. There's an embassy, magic cops, computerized spell books, and magic medical equipment. Apparently there's even a spell to update a being's jargon and language skills that can be used every ten years or so.

That explains Kita Castille.

And here I was blaming Urban Dictionary.

"Yes, Candrima. You have to apply. But don't worry about it. We will find a place where you belong."

Cornelius is awfully confident and charismatic when he wants to be. I like that about him. I like a lot of things about him. His taste in books, his sense of humor, and the fact that he knits. I know it's dangerous for us to remain bonded, but I hope he will still want to be my friend when it's all said and done. I want him in my life.

"So what's the plan here? How long am I supposed to stay? I'm sure my family has filed a missing person's report by now."

"Don't worry about your family. I copied your voice and left a voice-mail on your mother's phone saying you needed time away and decided to take an impromptu vacation. But once we sever the soul bond, you're free to go. Obviously we'll still have to stay close though, seeing as my curse is..."

"Permanent?" I finish.

"Yes," Corn sighs. "Permanent."

I doubt Betty was satisfied by that explanation, but I'll tell her the truth eventually anyway. First though, we need to figure out this bond situation.

"It's ok. Accidents happen," I shrug. "So how do we sever the soul bond?"

Corn taps his chin in thought before the mental lightbulb illuminates. Then he summons a large, dusty book covered in cobwebs that looks like it could kill a man if thrown at the right angle, and plops it onto the kitchen table I just cleaned. "Damnit, Cornelius!" I scold.

"Sorry, sorry. Don't worry, I'll clean that up," he insists.

He fucking better.

"Anyway, bonds usually cement in 90 days so we kind of need to work fast. But depending on your species, we have a few options. Demonic acid baths, Sword Of Destiny, maybe even a first death."

I throw him a look, silently asking if he's joking, but when no smile appears on his lips I grimace.

"Ok. Mhm. Great options. But are there any that don't envoke what I can only assume is extreme pain on the participants?" I ask.

"Nope! Soul bonds are no joke. There is no easy way out."

"Then why make the way in so damn easy?" I pout.

The consequences of sex are as follows: STDs, pregnancy, yeast infections, and possible injuries. No where in there did it mention irreversible claim bonds and kidnappings. I just wanted a light back cracking. I did not sign up for this shit!

"Hey, I'm sorry. I know this is a lot, and despite my earlier accusations, I know this was an accident. But we'll get through this one step at a time. Together. I promise," Corn says, pulling me in for a hug.

I hate how easy it is to melt into him. I thought the clothing would help, but no. My body molds to his regardless of the barriers. So I give up and tuck my head under his chin, and with my silent permission, Corn begins to rock us steadily. At first it happens slowly. Our steps fall into a harmonic rhythm, then our breathing follows only for our hearts to be just one step behind. Corn is right. This is everything. Everything we need.

"What are you doing?" Corn asks.

It's been two hours since breakfast, but the house is in the middle of moving locations, so I've busied myself with another spell book. Although this time I made sure it wasn't some freaky ass recipe guide. Corn has been playing records, most of which are 80s and 90s R&B. He doesn't keep up with television but music is a different story. This demon loves him some Jodeci and Al Green.

"Studying, trying to get a hang of this power thing. Did you know witches and sorcerers were an integral part of medieval kingdom ministry?"

"So I've been told," Corn nods. "What else did you learn?"

"Well for starters, rocks and crystals are actually used as magic conduits."

"Yeah?"

"Yeah. I thought that was just a special interest some women used to mask undiagnosed autism, but rocks are actually useful for spells and focus. It's really cool."

"Well maybe we should get you a few rocks," Corn chuckles.

"I'm glad you agree. I prepared a list," I laugh.

True to my word, I do have a list. I do a quick double check and hand it over to Corn who's smiling the entire time. What's going on in that mind of his?

"Alright. This is something I can handle," he nods.

"Thank you, sir. Also, if I could get a stay or something for my dresses that would be nice."

"Ok. Do you like your dresses otherwise?"

"I do," I nod. "They kinda remind me of Renaissance faire dresses or something."

"Yeah, I could see that. My dress maker kinda enjoys dramatics. She loves RenCon influences."

"Maybe I should go to one after we work this out," I say. "It's always been on my bucket list."

"Wait, you've never been to a faire?" Corn exclaims.

"Nope. I've been working since it was legal. I'm kind of a busybody."

Suddenly Corn rips through the house, gathering snacks, canteens, maps, and a change of clothes. I'm starting to think I'm not the only busybody in this curselationship.

"Oh, no. We have to remedy this. Grab your shoes, we're taking a trip," he says, hopping into a very snug pair of tights.

I'm talking Toni Britts snug. So snug that mind is slowly losing its battle to my body on whether or not it's appropriate to stare so obviously at his now visible bulge.

Jesus Devonte Christ.

It's even big on soft.

"A trip where?" I gulp as he pulls off his shirt.

He could probably tell me we're headed to outer space and I wouldn't give a damn. As much as I enjoy Corn's mind, I have to admit that part of my attraction also lies in the fact that he's built like a 70's cartoon lumberjack. Tall, muscular, and just hairy enough. With that black minky hair of his trailing from his navel down to his...

"Medieval Moon," Corn chuckles.

Well I'll be damned. I was right.

This man is taking me to space and I couldn't care less.

I'm doomed.

Actually, we went to Hell. Hell is unlike anything my human-indoctrinated brain could imagine. The first plane is vast and picturesque with sloping mountains, green oceans, and intimidating botanicals, while the planet we're visiting is suspended in a horizon that feels like the prettiest auric sunset. According to Corn, Medieval Moon is a small tourist moon located in Hell's first plane that was purchased over five thousand years ago by a group of wealthy elves. They were fed up by modernization so they decided to basically go out and create an Endless Summer situation. An everlasting Ren Faire spanning a whole planet. Complete with a monarchy, landlords, and magical merchants. Permanent Residents got to experience Medieval Moon for free of course, but visitors were charged a small fee of...

"Ninety-two dollars!? We are not paying that."

Corn was kind enough to give me the gold to USD conversion but it backfires. Finding out we have to pay nearly $100 each to enter has sucked the adventure right out of my body. I know a tourist scam when I see one. I cross my arms over my chest to show that I mean business, but Corn and the Orc fellow at the gate are unmoved and they continue their conversation as if I never spoke.

"Can you change 5 grams of gold?" Corn asks.

"Yes sir, let me get your stamps," The Orc replies.

I watch as Corn's gold is weighed and melted before it's streamed into a rotating cauldron. I see why the sign says no refunds.

"Excuse me," I fuss. "I said no. Are you just going to pretend like I'm not talking to you?"

"Yes," Corn replies quickly. "Now hold out your arm."

I start to protest but the Orc's eyes travel behind me and rest on the gathering crowd. There's a being with Horns bigger than Cornelius' huffing and puffing about the unusually long wait. So I swallow the bitter taste of defeat and hold out my arm. I receive a stamp that's glowing with an iridescent purple ink, but when it seeps into my skin, its magic reacts with my own and I accidentally drain the energy from all the entrance lanterns. One by one, the flames snuff out and travel through the dried grass up my arms.

The Orc looks between us skeptically.

"What exactly did you say she was?" he asks.

Corn quickly sweeps in front of me, covering my comparably smaller body with his larger fully demonic form while bearing his sharp canines.

"I didn't," Corn snarls.

The Orc, seeing the sizable difference between himself and my demon protector, raises his hands and backs away. Clearly he's not one for picking a fight he can't win.

"Ok. Just so you know, it's a 500 gram fee for anyone you kill that you can't revive. Accident or not. Keep that in mind," he mumbles while stamping Corn. "NEXT!"

The interaction at the gate made me nervous to join the crowds, but Corn doesn't let me freeze. He scoots me along like a man on a mission, only stopping when we reach a modiste.

"What are we doing?" I ask.

"Getting your stays," he replies.

"Oh, yeah. I forgot about that."

I look down at the ground while I try to organize my thoughts. Orcs are real, elves are real, Hell is real, and I'm standing on one of Hell's moons. There's a Centaur playing a gilded lute nearby. A lizard lady just passed me and she was holding hands with an owl man.

What the fuck is happening?

"Everything alright, Candrima?" Corn cooes softly while raising my chin.

His eyes glow like the rust sun above us and I appreciate the gorgeous view, but unfortunately my mind is still racing.

"Is murder legal in Hell?" I blurt out.

"To an extent," Corn shrugs. "If it can be proved that an unforgivable wrong was committed against the murderer by the murduree. One that could only be rectified by their death, then yes. Otherwise, no. And if you do it on accident you gotta be able to bring em' back. But no one goes around murdering because of the fines and prison time. A life sentence when you're human is one thing, but a life sentence as an immortal or a millennial? Absolutely not."

"Oh, that makes sense," I nod.

"Mhm. Ready to go try on some lingerie?" he asks mischievously.

"I thought you said we were here for stays?" I say with raised brows.

"Tuh-mayto, Tuh-matto," Corn shrugs. "They both involve a beautiful woman being squeezed into a silky lace garment."

"What a gentleman," I say teasingly. "Lead the way."

Turns out I didn't want a stay, I wanted a jump. I've only seen stays in paintings and TV shows, and it never occurred to me that there was no molded cup for your tatas when it came to stays. It felt like my girls were being forced up by duct tape. Luckily though, the seamstress was kind enough to explain all the differences and suggest a few things. Including some sheer gowns that Corn insisted I might need. For any hot climates the house might move to.

He's not slick.

"I'm hungry," Corn announces while taking my bags. "Can you eat?"

We spent two hours in the modiste on top of the hour ride to hell. Breakfast was delicious and filling, but not that damn filling. I heard my stomach singing in the dressing rooms.

"Yeah, I can eat."

"Ok, I know just the place."

Corn takes my hand to guide me off the merchant path, into what feels like a residential area. Beautiful brick homes sit side by side on a long cobblestone street. While some yards offer a view of well kept vegetable and flower gardens. We walk for a mile before we come to an arrangement of shops. Among which includes a tea and herb shop, a leather shop, and a butcher shop, which must be our destination guessing by the savory scents of spiced meat and hot charcoal wafting out of the building.

"Come on, let's see if we can get a seat," he says.

Corn opens the door and scoots me into the tavern by the small of my back. The actual butcher and deli portion is located in the back of the building judging by the neat rows of hung cured meats and frosty display cases, while the front is a cozy restaurant with comfortable leather booths and intimate tables that's warmed by small lanterns and floating tea lights.

"It's nice here," I whisper.

"It is. It's one of my favorite places in Hell," Corn replies.

Suddenly a large minotaur comes charging out of the back. He's stocky but limber and quick, and he seems to let his horns lead the way as he comes to greet us.

"Cornelius! I haven't seen you in at least three rotations. Welcome back!" he exclaims excitedly.

His voice is loud and the restaurant is unexpectedly acoustic. The bass sound rattles off the walls and shakes the windows. That spooks me and I cling to Corn's side, prompting one of his tails to wrap around my waist. The minotaur's eyes bore into mine, searching for something to explain Corn's protectiveness, and when he finds what he's looking for, he relaxes his shoulders and smiles. His eyes are pinched high and the curve of his nose dips, allowing the ornate septum that's strung there to rest against his top lip.

"You've gotten partnered. Finally. That's why I haven't seen you," he laughs heartily. "I can't be mad. It's about damn time, Flower Demon."

"Candrima Castille, this is my best friend, Glee. Glee, this is my wife," Corn says proudly.

"Nice to meet you, Candrima," Glee says, shaking my hand. "I'm actually his only friend."

Corn waves him off, feigning irritation with a loud huff.

"Is my table available, Glee? I thought this was a proper restaurant, not a hen coop."

"Oh, poor thing. You must be starving," Glee teases. "Right this way, your querulousness."

We're seated at a corner booth near the rear, just around the corner from the butcher portion, but still in a great area to observe all the comings and goings and preserve the privacy of our conversation. Glee summons a large pitcher of water and two glasses, then hands just me a menu and walks away.

"Why'd he only give me a menu?" I ask.

Corn shrugs while pouring us both a little water.

"I've been coming here for the last ninety years or so. I've long memorized the menu. I know what I'm getting," he answers.

"Oh," I say.

I've thought about the differences in our ages from time to time, but hearing Corn say he's frequented this restaurant nearly three times longer than I've been alive really cements it for me. He's lived two lives in a half before me. Clearly he's made a name for himself.

"Tell me about your life," I say firmly.

Corn chuckles loudly and the rich timbre of his voice coats every individual brain cell of mine, distracting me from my original question.

"What do you wanna know?" he asks.

I take a deep breath and a nice swig of water to gather my thoughts before responding, but seeing the way he watches me swallow does not help. So my first question becomes,

"Have you always been a freak?"

Smooth, Candy girl.

"I see that heat is kicking your behind," he laughs."But to answer your question, Candrima. No, I have not always been a freak. My appreciation for reciprocal sex is very recent, and I owe thanks for that gift to a five foot nine witch who orgasmed so hard that she accidentally cursed me."

I narrow my eyes in his direction, silently warning him to wipe that smile off his face. However Corn is amused by my sad attempt at intimidation and he offers me an even bigger smile instead.

So I move on to my next questions.

"You said reciprocal, so does that mean you were just getting folks off and going about your business?" I ask.

I don't know why I'm curious about this. It's private information, and in any other situation, I'd let it remain private. But my brain is eager to learn everything it can about the man I'm bound to. Temporary or not.

"Yes. Succubi need consensual lust to survive, utilize task magic, and hold appearance charms. Without it, we're reduced to hunting instinct or "feralness" as some call it," he explains.

"I see, that makes a lot of sense," I nod.

I read about feral succubi in the pamphlet that Cyrus gave me. Feral succubi are not tolerated by the EUM since there was an event a few hundred years ago called a "flocking". Where thousands of hungry, uncontrollable lust demons flooded the human plane and bred rapidly, tipping the scales of balance and creating many unstable offspring. Some of which, still roam the earth to this day, kicking up chaos.

"Tell me about your family," I say, redirecting the conversation. I can tell by the slight pang of annoyance through our bond that Corn doesn't enjoy discussing the treatment and unfair categorization of his species, and there's nothing I'm that curious to learn that I can't likely find out through all the books at home.

"Mhm, let's see," Corn starts. "I have three siblings. Cyrus who've you met. Nafisa, who you've heard of. Then finally, Nilla. Who you should avoid at all cost."

"Why?" I ask.

"Because she's a bounty hunter with an endless supply of crude jokes."

"She sounds fun," I giggle.

"You would think that wouldn't you? Miss lust punch."

"Cornnnn," I whine. "I already told you it was an accident."

"I know," he snickers. "Don't feel bad. When I was learning task magic as a youngling, I accidentally automated a stamp licker spell on the guest toilet instead of the writing desk. It violated Nafisa and she still brings it up to this day." "Oh, Corn. That's rough."

"I know," he says, shaking his head. "I got called a butt bandit for decades."

It doesn't take long for a hyper but beautiful faerie to come take our orders, and while we wait we fall into an easy conversation about our respective lives. I've learned that Corn's mother is a high priestess, his father is an accountant, and his siblings are doctors, lawyers, and a rogue bounty hunter. I've also learned that he and Glee are much like me and Betty. They went to primary school together some 175 years ago and they just remained friends. They even worked together at various points in their lives, including when they were firefighters, which I didn't expect from Corn. I know he now works a florist, but he's had a long list of careers before that. Some of which include firefighter, nurse, preschool teacher, and even a club bouncer for an exclusive night club located in the fourth realm of hell. Imagining a serious Corn all muscled up and ready to launch into action is not good for the integrity of my brain, so I'm elated when our food arrives.

"For the lady, we have our grilled trout with lemon bernaise, roasted winter vegetables, and white cheddar popovers," the faerie says, sitting down my reasonable plate. "And for the gentleman, we have two smoked rapscile legs with cranberry and orange chutney, roasted button mushrooms, mashed potatoes, roasted vegetables, and two king sized corn muffins."

Glee personally heaves Corn's massive plate onto the table, taking care not to spill the coffee mug's worth of gravy onto the freshly polished wood.

"Enjoy," they say, departing.

Out of the corner of my eye I can see the faerie pass Glee something that looks like a cigarette. I don't smoke, but I can't say I blame them. Corn's plate is absolutely massive. Apparently the legs took an hour alone even with acceleration magic.

Corn tears into the hot meat first, dipping it in the chutney as he eats.

"I need a little hot sauce," he says.

I summon it for him without second thought because I know Rapscille is a bit gamey based on what I read. Yesterday I found a hunting guide that was filled with pictures of creatures available for meat in Hell. One of which is a large bird-dinosaur being, dotted with sparse brown feathers, a bright orange beak, and razor sharp teeth. A Rapscile. Definitely not a fish.

"I thought you were pescatarian?" I say while nibbling my own dish.

I'm biased towards seafood, but this trout is divine. I could die happy eating this.

"I was pescatarian, but my new form requires a lot of protein. Way more protein than I could ethically source from fish. I don't want to be the reason trout, tuna, and salmon go extinct in the midwest," he says.

I think back to earlier at the gate. That Orc got a little too curious and Corn was quick to put a stop to that by pulling out the big guns. All four of them for that matter. Beckoning and rippling under that taut raspberry tunic...

"That's fair. I didn't think about that," I mumble, remembering last night.

I didn't think about the possibility of us fucking in midair either. But now that I've experienced it...

"Eat your food, Candrima," Corn growls as our gazes align.

His eyes are slowly fading to black the more we linger, and when I feel his spade tail slip up my leg to curl around my thigh, I know it's for the best to listen this time. I likely thought out loud, as I so often do when I'm thinking about him, which means he knows about my current preference to mount him like a throne. Let me not push my luck.

I couldn't even cut through half of my plate, yet I'm disgustingly full. I know I'm technically not human, but after witnessing many a being come in and clear a plate, I felt like the odd woman out. So I was too embarrassed to ask for a box, but Corn finished it off anyway, stating he was still a little hungry from the flight over.

God, I couldn't imagine us having a child. The fridge would be ransacked.

After Corn and Glee spend a little time catching up, we're made to swear we'll visit again soon. Like Cyrus, Glee also doesn't think we should separate. He's positive that I'm a good influence on the big guy although I struggle to see how. We're in an illegal partnership that we're hiding from the magical government by destination hoping. Plus we cursed each other.

That alone screams bad influence.

"Can you stand a little walking?" Corn asks as I trudge outside.

He gently takes the packages of sausage and shrimp I got from the shop from under my arm and places them amongst his other bags before sending everything off to the house. I'm unburdened and suddenly a walk does sound nice.

"Yeah, I can walk," I reply.

Corn leads me down the hill, into a grassy valley, and across a stone bridge. It's a little chilly out but I don't mind because we're hand in hand, and Corn's something of a space heater. Especially when he purrs.

"Can I ask you a question?"

"Don't you always?"

"Fair," I laugh. "But what causes you to purr?"

"Mhm. Lots of things. Mostly excitement or relaxation. But sometimes agitation or aggression."

That explains why he was purring the whole time Cyrus examined me. I thought he was excited to possibly sever our bond, but he was irritated.

"I was jealous," he confesses, correcting my estimate. "Unfortunately, I'm territorial. I try to keep it in check but it rears its ugly head occasionally. Sorry about threatening to eat your human friend by the way."

"It's ok, I know you were stressed," I reply.

I mean I did kind of abandon him and almost kill him. So that's fair.

"Who was he?" Corn says lowly.

I stop our movement and peer at him. He avoids my eyes but his mouth is tense and his jaw is set. So whatever he was hoping to hide is still visible plain as day.

"Corn, he was just some guy. We met at the party I went to before my accident and we chatted."

"Yes, but he was touching you here," Corn says, pulling me by my waist until I'm flush against him.

I see this demon enjoys his dramatics. That man had a respectful hand placed on my upper back. It was nowhere near as crass and explicit as this. Nowhere near as hard, warm, or excitable.

"Should we be doing this in public?" I ask as his erection grows against my thigh.

"Doing what?" Corn asks against my ear.

His breath is warm and minty, carrying the silent message of need across my skin with each exhale. I know he's up to no good, so I try not to moan when he kisses my collar only to fail. The heat that I tried so desperately to ignore yesterday begins to resurface, and it settles in my stomach, encouraging the space between my thighs to slicken and throb. I need to straighten my back before he bends me over this bridge and has his way with me. Because I know I'd let him do it.

"Should we be doing what I didn't do with that man here in public? What if someone reports us?" I gasp.

"Hell bows to no government but its own, little witch," Corn says. "Here, we're not illegal. We're just us, Candy and Corn. But I'll behave. We need to get going anyway so we can make it to the next shop before closing."

We separate and Corn regains his sense of urgency. I follow his brisk stride, finding my way by listening to the toe of his boot kick against the loose gravel, until we reach another section of shops. Then I look around, wondering what might be next. There's another modiste, a bookshop, and a shoe cobbler, but Corn guides me to a glowing hole located in the road.

"Come on, Candy," he says, scooting me forward.

"What the fuck? Come on, Candy, where?" I exclaim.

"Into the hole," he says matter of factly.

"Cornelius, I need you to be so fucking serious right now. You want me to crawl into a weird, illuminating hole?"

"Not crawl," he chuckles dismissively while scratching the back of his head. "Just jump."

"Go to Hell."

"Candrima," Corn chuckles, raising his brows at me expectantly.

Oh right. We're already in Hell. I guess I needed that reminder. But I'm still not jumping into a hole!

"Do you trust me, sweetheart?" he asks.

I soften in response to his tender nomenclature. Of course I trust him. He's been nothing but sweet and protective of me outside of the whole kidnapping thing. So I guess I'm jumping in this weird mystery hole.

"How do I do this?" I sigh.

"Legs straight, arms in. I'll be right behind you."

"I swear, Corn. You better not let me die," I fuss.

"Hush, little witch. This is perfectly safe. Stop being a brat and listen to your elders."

Oh wow? That's how he wants to play it?

Noted.

I take a deep breath and then jump in, as if the extra respiration is somehow going to help should I hurdle towards my end. But to my pleasant surprise, I find out that the hole is actually some kind of slide. My body twist and turns down the polished rock until the source of the glow becomes clear then I'm spat out onto a thick pile of unreasonably plush pillows. I don't sit there long though, knowing that Corn isn't too far behind me. And not even five seconds after I move, he's landing face down into the soft void, tail in the air, curled like an alfalfa.

"Did you just take me on a tunnel slide?" I ask.

"Yes. I love those things," he replies, joining my side. "Perfect entrance for this."

I'm spun around to greet a Dreamland. Large, ancient, hexagonal crystals sprout from the ground and emit an enchanting green glow, while smaller round ones outline the walls and the walking path.

"Corn, this is beautiful," I gasp.

"When you're right, you're right," he says softly.

I turn around to see nothing but want and adoration in his eyes, and I swear my heart starts to do backflips.

Fuck.

That dream was a premonition.

I try to be anxious about the progression of our relationship, but I'm too amazed by where we are. Vale's Crystals, Rocks, And Ropes is one of the only specialty stores of its kind. They mine 65% of their inventory straight from the ground and they have mostly every mineral available on the three planes. It's quite impressive, and of course Corn knows the owner. A ground troll who's just as ancient as the crystals they care for.

"How many can I get?" I call as they chat at the counter.

"As many as you want," Corn replies. "You haven't spent nearly enough money today."

I'm beyond grateful that I don't have a physically visible blush, because the way he leaves my heart fluttering and my lungs breathless is embarrassing.

Either way though, I'm grateful. I had a list but I also brought along a shrunk down version of Alexander Immortal's Crystal Guide

For Dummies. It's been instrumentally helpful in me understanding the breadth of my powers. Selenite will help with calm and focus so it's first on my list. Quartz helps with stability which I desperately need. Then Jade, which is a gemstone powerhouse, will help with my connection to the realms I cannot yet touch, harmony, and the kinship I'm cultivating with Cornelius. Jade also brings luck and fortune, and I'm hoping to quantify as much of those as possible with the looming threat of uncertainity that is my premonition.

I shop until I notice the floors getting swept. This must be why Corn was in such a hurry to get here. Because it's been two hours, but I'm nowhere near finished looking at all the selections. Crystals and gems are organized by color, size, ability and rarity, and each category contains hundreds upon hundreds of options.

"Ok, I think I'm ready," I say, heaving my basket onto the counter.

"Don't worry. We'll come back soon," Corn says, patting my back.

"Thank you."

"It's my pleasure, little witch."

Corn requests a few more stones that he thinks will be helpful, and after Vale finishes counting all 115 of them, they give us the total.

"Alright, your majesties. It's going to be 6 grams of gold."

My lips scrunch, knowing that Corn has spent nearly $400 on me at one shop.

"Does the sum offend you, your highness?" Vale asks.

I realize my reaction is noticeable and I relax my stank face.

"No, no. It's just, Corn isn't working right now and I'm slightly uncomfortable with the amount of money today has costs because who kn-"

I was going to say who knows when he'll be able to make it back, but both the demon and troll have interrupted me with truly obnoxious laughter.

"What's funny?" I ask.

"Forgive me, your highness. It is not my place," Vale cackles.

"Corn?" I frown, looking for an explanation.

He's nearly hanging over the side of the counter, laughing like we're at a King's Of Comedy show.

"I'm sorry, it's just... Bahaha. I've been alive for almost two hundred years, and you think six grams of gold is going to break me? Candrima, time is conducive to building wealth."

"Oh right," I say bashfully.

He has a point. If you've had two hundred years to stack your coin only for a day trip to break you, you need to reevaluate some things.

"I quite like her, your highness," Vale snickers. "A perfect princess for your lot."

"What do you mean by that?" I ask.

At first I thought Vale was saying that to get under Corn's skin. You know, good-natured ribbing. But they haven't faltered once in reference to the titles.

"Vale does that every time I visit," Corn says, shaking his head. "Ignore them. They're old and half blind."

"Not too blind to count though. Pay up, High Prince."

Corn laughs and drops the payment into the troll's weathered gray palm.

"Until next time, my friend," he says.

Corn flies us back up to the surface and while I've become used to being carried in that short time, I'm also eager to put my feet to the ground. I'm starting to feel dizzy. Hot and dizzy.

"I know someone in the fourth realm. A blacksmith who could fashion you a wrist brace with some of these to help guide your powers," Corn says.

He's telling me all about his blacksmith friend, but I can't really focus on anything he's saying. Hell suddenly feels far too hot for this many layers of clothes, and I feel far too unstable to stand on my own two feet.

I lean against him, pressing my entire body to his. Hugging Corn is always comforting, but right now, feeling his hard frame against my soft one is especially nice. God I love his tree trunk thighs, and his big shoulders, and his strong pecs. I could eat him for breakfast, lunch, and dinner.

"Candrima, you're molesting me," Corn says politely.

I look down at my hands which are firmly planted on his behind and chest. I hadn't even realized it.

"Am I? Sorry I can't help it. I feel weird."

Corn's brows furrow at the possibility of my discomfort then he bends slightly to sniff me, and when he returns upright his eyes are flooded with that signature black.

"Your heat is back," he says in the voice of his true form. "The esfraxin wore off."

He looks pained, but I'm not sure why. He can just take me back to the bridge and ravage me there.

"I cannot take you back to the bridge, little witch. It's likely already gone. The day is about to be done, the lands are changing to accommodate nightlife. Soon these shops won't even be here," he explains.

Shit, I do remember Corn telling me about Hell switching landscapes at night. It's done so they can have multiple businesses in the same spot. They've really mastered the whole tourism thing.

"What about that tree?" I ask breathily. "I just need a little relief."

Corn eyes the willow tree a few hundred feet away and sighs. I know he's considering it when he pulls us forward.

"Do you think you could turn us both invisible?" he asks.

"Probably," I nod.

I take Corn's giant hand in mine once I've located something for energy. Back at the cabin I usually borrow a little water or some heat from the fireplace, but that isn't an option here. Luckily, the newly illuminated street lantern that's shining above us seems like it's doing the trick. I focus my powers, directing my cells to use the borrowed energy to alter our reality, and just like that we're invisible.

"Ok, I know you're medically horny right now and you couldn't care less, but that is so cool," Corn commends.

"Thank you. Now will you please fuck me?" I ask.

"No, but I'll take care of you," he says.

Well why the hell not? What's a girl gotta do to get piped down in her time of need? Beg? I hate to say it, but I don't think I'm above begging.

"If I penetrate you now we'll be stuck in a mating frenzy here. Considering that we created a vortex last night, that probably isn't wise," Corn explains.

Fair enough. The last thing we need is that Orc testifying against us when I inevitably cause more property damage from the excitement of cumming.

Still I wonder what Corn's version of relief encompasses? We reach the tree and he turns me back towards the village and then sits on the ground behind me.

Weird.

I start to ask him what's going on, but then I feel my dress rise around my hips. My bloomers are split and they haphazardly fall around my ankles, which Corn throws on either side of his hips, and then I'm made to arch my back until my chest is resting against his thighs and my head is between his legs.

He's going to eat me.

My stellar detective skills are confirmed when Corn's thick tongue probes my outer lips. I'm a real Nancy Drew out here. The deft tip flickers against my hooded bud, teasing and exciting me. While his long, thick fingers thrust inside me gently.

"Corn." I moan silently.

Yes, we're invisible, but we're not mute. All it's going to take is one mistimed moan and we'll be discovered. I don't have time for that.

"That's my good little witch. Fuck my face, baby," he replies.

I want to comment on his sudden use of vulgar language, but I can't because I'm following directions. My hips roll to the rhythm of his thrashing tongue and thrusting fingers in an attempt to feel him everywhere. Luckily Corn meets my silent request, and splits his tongue like he did that first night. My nipples strain against the satin lining of my dress as I struggle to catch my breath from the sensation of his tongue licking my walls while simultaneously lapping my clit. My, the pleasure he causes.

Goodness, it's tremendous.

Not wanting to be branded as a selfish lover, I slide my hand into his leggings and take his length into my palm to stroke him according to the pace he's set for us. Slow, but firm.

It's wonderful torture.

He becomes rigid in my hands and begins to purr. Precum beads on the bulbous head of his dick, making his ridges warm and sticky, and I can almost feel them inside me. Oh, how I want Corn inside of me. Especially after hearing his lucid moans rattling from his chest while he's licking my plate clean. Especially as his tail slips into my mouth.

"Corn!"

This time my exaltation is audible as I ride out a familiar wave of pleasure. My stomach tightens with the force of my first release, especially when I realize Corn has lifted me onto his shoulders for better access.

His nose is firmly planted between my cheeks, and I'm terrified I'll accidentally smother my over-confident lover, but he doesn't seem to have any issue breathing. In fact, he's inhaling my scent like a paint huffer. Groaning and purring in delight with every breath. Monogamy bind or not, I don't think I could ever return to humans after this. After him. Besides the fact that he's licking my entire undercarriage like I'm a caramel sundae, there's also the purring, the cuddling, and the aftercare. He's officially ruined me.

I come down from my orgasm and Corn releases my trembling body with a dissatisfied grunt. I know that if not for the inconvenience of our location, he wouldn't have stopped. He would've probably stayed buried in me until a new day rose. I turn to gather my dignity in the form of my now shredded bloomers and I catch his stare. His face is wet and sticky, but it's his eyes that worry me. Corn's gaze is usually warm and kind, but not tonight. Tonight, eyes blacker than a moonless midnight bear into mine, demanding everything from me, including the air from out my lungs.

"Corn," I murmur.

He's purring again, but now I know enough about my bind to know it's not friendly.

He's on the hunt for flesh.

I take a step back, wondering how fast and far I could run in these flats, but Corn lunges forward to capture me before I can will the muscles in my legs to move.

"Mine," he growls, bearing his sharp fangs.

He's shedding his humanoid form fast. With his tails appearing first to tighten around me. One across my chest and one laced over my hips and thighs. Then his wings appear, and I'm certain I'm about to get carried off like feeble prey again, only this time my powers ignite instead. My eyes glow with that blinding white light as I snuff out three nearby street lanterns, and with a command that I did not initiate, we're teleported back across the realms at light speed.

Returning home.

Teleportation is not Corn's forte, so he's discombobulated when we land back in the messy living room. He's thrown against the couch with serious force, but our bond reassures me he's not hurt by it. He is confused, however, and I use that to my advantage. I could let him have his way with me, but why should I? I've never been the kind to go down easy, so if he wants to shred my guts like pulled pork, he'll need to work for it.

It's pouring down outside, but the house is stable and parked for the night, so I cross my fingers and swing the heavy wooden door open.

Lucky me.

The spell to keep me put has been removed. Thunderous skies greet me as lightning splits across the ominous black night, then I take off into the unknown.

<u>Ours</u>

"Return home, Candrima! Now!" he demands.

I've been running through this old forest for ten minutes, utilizing stealth and invisibility charms to stay hidden among the trees. Luckily I mastered a protection charm the night before, but that still won't save me from him.

He's angry.

I can feel it through our bond and I hear it when his wings slice through the chilled air. I shed my clothes a few hundred feet ago and transported them elsewhere to keep him from scenting me, but now I'm starting to regret it. My nipples pebble against the brisk autumn air and my skin pulls taut, erecting goosebumps over the length of my shivering body. I could pull energy from the rain to keep myself warm, but something tells me he's banking on that.

"If you want me, come get me." I taunt.

I know it's dangerous to tease a literal demon into hunting me, but it unearths some deeply buried desire I've had for a while. For a man to want me so bad that he'll track me down using any means necessary. I know that is screaming red flag for lots of people and rightfully so, but I've been that way for as long as I could remember. Since I started dreaming of him. Maybe that's why I could never make a relationship with a human man work. Some strange part of me knew that they didn't want me like they claimed to. But Corn, the picture of routine and order, is unraveling at the mere possibility of claiming my touch. If that's not powerful, I don't know what is.

I spend too much time thinking and not enough running, and soon, I hear his ragged breath grow closer.

"Do you know what I'll do to you when I find you?" he laughs. Branches snap under the weight of his full form some 600 feet away forcing me to resume my sprint.

"I'll tie you to the post and pleasure you until your vision fails and you black out, little witch. I'll dominate your body until the only thing you think of is me. I'll covet you forever. You won't be able to run next time. You will pay for this." □

The ire in his tone reflects his sinister intentions and I know he's serious, yet I can't help but egg him on.

"If. If you catch me, Cornelius. Good luck, on your coveting," I mock. I hear the wind catch beneath his wings as I run for the upcoming clearance.

Famous last words.

What little lead way I have is about to be decimated when he takes to the sky. So I reinforce my invisibility and press on. Luckily though, the clearance I saw turns out to be a graveyard, and not just any graveyard, but one with a church attached. I chuckle at the irony of it all. Here I am, hoping to find protection from my personal demons in the so-called house of God when I myself am something unholy: A sorceress bound to the infernal darkness.

I tumble over the rain-soaked headstones with precision, mentally willing my exhausted body to just make it a bit farther. The stone steps to the church lie just a hundred feet ahead, a silent savior in the stormy night. Lightning illuminates my ten yard dash while the corresponding thunder syncs with the sounds of my feet pounding against the sodden earth. I can still hear Corn's wings beating against the heavy rains, but I count down anyway, confident I'll make it before he can spot me.

Nine.

I lengthen my stride, utilizing as much of my legginess as possible.

Eight.

I dip low to avoid my curls tangling in the whipping branches of a nearby tree.

Seven.

I command my feet to grip the ground so I can maintain this pace.

Six.

I reach the first step.

Five.

I climb the second.

Four.

Lightning spreads across the leaden sky once more, illuminating the wings of my predator who is now directly above me.

Three.

His carefully extended claw reaches my flailing arm.

Two.

My feet are lifted from the wet ground as he captures my body.

One.

I'm pinned against the splintering wood and given the privilege of seeing I never had a chance in the first place. The church is abandoned, and the west facing windows are all without glass or a frame. He would've gotten to me regardless.

I know no one is coming to save me, but I still beat against the door until a strong hand restrains both my arms and secures them to my back. His touch, although malicious, sends heated shivers down my spine.

"Candrima," he whispers against my storm soaked skin. "I told you not to run."

Corn's sharp teeth drag against the skin of my shoulder blades, threatening to mark me at a moment's notice. Then his upper arms flank my sides to cage me in.

"Did you?" I query breathlessly.

His reply is a smooth chuckle laced with poison. He says everything he needs to say wordlessly. Daring me to continue my games.

"I'm not scared of you," I whisper.

Corn's chest vibrates with a facetious hum then his tails snake across my body, intertwining with one another across my chest and hips until I'm completely immobilized. I wiggle in an attempt to gauge how much room I have and his grip tightens.

"You should be," he growls.

I'm quickly lifted into the air, and my back is pressed flush against Corn's front. Then he transfers his hand that's restraining my arms to my legs, spreading me wide and allowing him to take advantage of my vulnerable position. Slowly, I'm lowered onto his pulsing length, and I nearly convulse from the stinging pleasure of my body stretching around his otherworldly girth.

A loud squelching sound emanates from the point of our connection as he works to fully bury himself inside of me, my body proving to him just how bad I wanted this.

"Cornelius," I cry, throwing my head back into his shoulders.

My damp curls are gently swept from my eyes with a tenderness that could only come from Corn, and he kisses my temples to calm me. Only to pound into me so hard that I shudder from the force. What a conflicting being.

"You ruined me, Candy," he moans, gripping my thighs tighter. "I wasn't supposed to be this way. This is all your fault, little witch. Look at what you did to me."

His hips piston into mine with machine-like power, matching the soul racking strength of the thunder narrating the stormy night, and leaving me breathless and unable to respond. Then he decides to press his spade tail to my throbbing clit.

"Corn..." I whimper.

"Is that all you have to say, you intoxicating vixen?" he asks while grazing the sides of my neck.

His upper hands find themselves busy with my breast and mouth respectively, while one of his lower ones takes over my clit so he can bury his arrow tail in my wanting ass.

"Oh, God!" I exclaim.

"God will not save you," Corn says, deep voice cracking with agitation.

"You are mine. Mine to touch. Mine to torture. Mine to protect. And mine to worship. Do not call out another being's name ever again."

Understood.

Corn's angry pounding halts to a slow, measured grind. One that starts to rock me right into an orgasm.

"Is this what you need?" Corn asks, ever so sincerely.

I nod, too delirious to action a coherent response.

"Tell me, Candrima. Tell me this is what you want," he urges against the shell of my ear.

He plants a supplicating kiss on my wet shoulder that coaxes the truth from my mouth.

"I need this," I gasp. "I need you."

The world allows us a half second of silence to get lost in each other's eyes before my confession sends Corn into overdrive. He purrs loudly while stroking me deep and slow, as if he's trying to become one with me and reunite our souls that were familiar long ago. I relax into his strength and let him take whatever he needs, and when what he needs turns out to be my overwhelmed release, I provide it happily.

I caught a cold. Turns out Corn wanted me to come home so I didn't get sick, but I was too hopped up on hormones to realize that. So now I'm slathered in the sexy scent of Vicks Vapor Rub. The plus side is I get extra attentive aftercare and a punch on my kink card. Primal play is definitely a yes.

"Candy," Corn whines. "I'm going to pass out."

Oh yeah. I also accidentally brought on the peak of Corn's rut and locked us into a mating frenzy, so we've been fucking for three days straight.

"I'm sorry," I say, reaching behind me to scratch his chin. "I'll leave you alone after this."

Corn holds me tighter in our spoon, continuing his lazy strokes while brushing my clit. Tremors of pleasure terrorize my body, warning me of what will happen if we continue.

"I don't think I'll be able to leave you alone though," he whimpers.

His ridges swell against my walls and the product of our sex begins to leak from my pussy onto my thighs. Sticky, warm, and white. Corn, who's living up to his lust demon legacy, collects it to smear it across my steeled nipples and then he takes his time licking it up.

Of course I cum.

How could I not?

"Fuck, Candrima. That's right, baby. Milk this dick with that pretty little pussy," Corn hisses.

He doesn't have to tell me twice. Feeling his fat, warm dick slither in and out of me is encouragement enough, but having him talk me through it?

Yahtzee.

My instincts take over and I rock against him furiously, making Corn drive his fang through his lip while emptying his sins inside me, and then our momentum peters out to a soft stop.

"That was nice," I say, relaxing into the mattress.

"I mean, I came so hard it made my stomach hurt, but sure," Corn sighs.

Rut has been hard on him. It's impacted both his daily routine and his body with sore joints, increased appetite, and fevers.

"Vara Nunca," I whisper.

Corn's eyes fly open as his body rights itself, the spell providing temporary relief from some of the rut's effects.

"Did you just heal me?" he asks.

I nod.

"Why?"

"You were uncomfortable."

"Candy, don't waste your energy on me. I would've healed with a nap."

I roll my eyes. We do this song and dance at least once a day now. I'll do something for Corn and he'll scold me for draining my energy. As if it's not already overflowing from my body at every minor inconvenience.

"Be quiet," I tut. "It wasn't a waste."

In fact, he was the only reason I learned the spell. Seeing him hobble around with his hormone-induced arthritis is hard on a girl.

I care about him.

It's kind of hard not to at this point. Every day I discover something new and wonderful about him. Such as his blanket project for his new nephew, his love of Beverly Jenkins Novels, and his appreciation for orange juice.

"Are you hungry? Do you need water or anything?" Corn whispers while rubbing my back.

Plus his insistence on taking care of me after sex.

Even if he's dead-ass tired.

His eyelids are heavy from the weight of an impending well-deserved slumber and his lips are pouty from unsuccessfully trying to fight it.

He just may fall asleep if he blinks too long.

"No, I'm ok. I just want to be held for a little while," I answer.

I'm repositioned onto the big guy's chest then rewarded with a deep, rumbly purr for my answer.

"I can do that," he yawns while wrapping his tails around me. "Easy peasy."

Several hours pass and I wake up alone in bed. A warm breeze carries the sweet scent of fresh spring lilies through the cabin, and the fire we lit earlier is slowly crackling out.

"Corn?" I call.

I can't feel him in the house, so I rise from the covers and search for a note.

Only there isn't one.

Though he may just be out reinforcing the barrier spell. He does it every time we move locations, and this funny flower field is definitely new. Last night we were in rainy, wooded autumn Oregon, but it's warm and green here. I dress in a skirt and shirred blouse, place a kettle on for our breakfast tea, and then head off to find my husband, only for that familiar feeling of dread to return.

This is the dream.

"I was wondering when you'd pop in here. Let me get you a robe," Granny says.

I woke up in a cold sweat after relieving what I now consider to be my worst nightmare, but Corn was still resting and I couldn't control my anxiety, which I'm learning is directly correlated to my powers, so I did the one thing I probably shouldn't have done.

I poofed back home.

"Candrima!" my daddy shouts. "What the hell do you have on?"

Teddy Castille is a quiet man who is perfectly content defaulting to his wife and letting her big personality shine, but not when it comes to me. I glance down at the pink sheer mesh sleep gown I'm dressed in and cringe.

"I am so sorry," I exclaim, trying to cover my bits and pieces with my hands.

Luckily, Granny is on top of things, and she quickly wraps me in a robe too thick to be anything but modest.

"Hush, Ted. She clearly didn't plan to come home like this. She was probably wearing it for her husband," Mama explains.

"What?" I gawk. "You know about that?"

Magic is genetic. That much I know. Almost every book I've read talks about how things such as curses, powers, and even fates can be passed through a bloodline. So the likelihood of my matriarchs being human while I was a sorceress were slim to none. But if that's the case, why didn't they tell me?

"Did you know about my powers this entire time? Why wouldn't you train me or at least tell me?" I press.

Mama powers off the TV and rises from her leather throne to meet me in the center of the living room. Where I stand both angry and scared.

"No, sweetheart. We didn't know about your powers. When you didn't get them at 25 like most water witches we thought it skipped you," she explains.

"I didn't," Granny interjects. "Especially after you kept having that dream."

"The dream," I mumble. "You knew it was magic and you let me think that I was crazy!?"

"No, no. It wasn't... Candy it's not that simple. Our bloodlines are so intermingled you could've been a number of things. A seer, a gollum, hell, even a sorceress or something," Mama laughs.

It's made clear to me by the mirth in her chuckle that she doesn't know, so I take her hands and give her the coming out talk for the second time in my life.

She sense my seriousness and immediately stops laughing.

"Candy, what's wrong?"

"Mama, I am a sorceress," I say softly.

The room falls silent, the weight of my confession weighing heavily on my entire family.

"Candrima, who told you that?" Granny asks finally.

"A doctor in the 4th realm named Cyrus. He ran some test."

Both my mother and grandmother begin to fidget from what feels like immense panic. Then they start to produce books I've never seen before from spots I've looked at my whole life.

"What's going on?" I ask as they clear the dining room table.

"I know Cyrus. He's an excellent doctor, so chances are he's not wrong," Granny says.

I have a thousand questions about everything from our family to our history, but I settle on one for now. One that may very well help prevent the 2.0 nightmare that's currently looping in my dreams.

"Do you know what kind I could be?" I ask.

My grandmother commands a large binder filled with names and it begins to turn pages rather violently, like a college kid cramming 30 minutes before their exam is in charge.

"No. We haven't had a sorceress in the bloodline in nearly three thousand years. She was my grandmother," Granny explains. "Amaka Kehinde. The summary of her powers was struck from the record."

I know sorceresses are rare, but I wonder why? Was the EUM even around back then to be all in people's shit? Or was there another reason? Something I should also fear?

They go through two more books together before my mother stops on a large page filled with Yoruba script. "Found it!" she exclaims. "A discovery spell. Ted, grab the candles. Make sure you trim the wicks."

My father moves urgently to complete the task assigned to him while my mother and grandmother began to wash the living room floor. Pinesol and Dawn bubbles together on the hardwood, taking the dirt and leaving behind the familiar scent of clean. Then they move onto repositioning the coffee table and rugs.

"Can I help?" I say, feeling very useless.

"No," they reply in unison.

"The spell won't work if we accept help from the being we're trying to discover," Mama explains.

That makes me feel worse, but my father takes over the heavy lifting, then my matriarchs scramble off to my grandmother's dress closet, and they return in long, cotton dresses with thick head wraps that are whiter than a Hollywood smile.

"Candy, get in the circle," Daddy says.

"What circle?" I ask.

As if that was the phrase to activate it, a glowing sphere consisting of spells and written offers appears in the center of the living room.

Who's fucking house is this? Because it can't be mine. Not once did I see this circle when I was making my Barbies kiss under a couch fort.

"Candy, we have limited time. Get to stepping," Granny says.

I try to swallow the knot in my throat, but it's decided to take up residence there. So with just the air in my lungs, I step into the circle. The emitted light changes from green to gold with my entrance, and then my matriarchs begin singing a song I swear I've heard once before.

Travel up the river and tell me what you see. Behold! A man who cannot withold arrives before me. A lion is just a lion until you tell me otherwise. Look beneath the waters, and tell me what lies. □

Sharp, piercing pain rips through the center of my spine and I collapse to my knees, unable to think or speak. The circle begins to rotate around my body, the color of the light transitions to my signature platinum, and my body heats as I try to soothe everything I'm feeling. Fear.

Anger.

Love.

Hatred.

Power.

So much power. I can feel the Chicago river waving below us, carrying ships and life within its waters. I can feel the Earth beneath us. Firm from winter, but warm from the molten core that sustains us. And I can feel the moon. Calling to me, lending me the strength from the sunlight she endures. So much strength that I could run right to her without ever stopping to catch my breath.

"Ted! Break the circle! She's unstable!" Mama cries.

I look up from my position on the floor and see my family clinging to whatever is heavy enough to keep them from meeting the same fate as the books on the shelves that are being thrown harshly against the walls. I'm in another power surge and I've created a windstorm, but this time I can't stop it. I don't know how and the being who usually talks me down from my fits is half a country away.

Luckily my father has the courage of steel. He marches towards me with a raised hand, singing a lullaby I remember from my childhood. I sway to the pretty melody, relishing a simpler time. A time when I wasn't an out of control supernova crammed into a 4 bedroom condo. The song distracts me enough for my father to safely breach the circle, and with his foot on the line, he pulls the flames from the candles and absorbs them into his body. "Fire gollum," he answers before I can ask. "Definitely made things interesting, falling in love with a water witch."

The spell breaks instantly and my powers relax, ending my giant temper tantrum.

"Now you have a disaster for a daughter," I chuckle awkwardly.

"Never a disaster," Daddy affirms, pulling me off the floor and covering me with a blanket. "Just a work in progress."

He smiles at me before ruffling my wild curls, and I understand more and more why I'm falling for Corn. Kind, aloof men are the bread and butter of my existence. Starting with my dad.

"Well that was informative," Mama says, rising from the floor.

She presses her thumb against her pointer fingers then swipes down the pads of her fingers, and the motion clothes my body. My grandmother is none too pleased to see one of her many florid designs hanging from my frame, and with a contented sigh, she rights the house as if that never happened.

"You're already dressed but go wipe the soot off your face, love bug. Dinner's almost ready."

"So what? I disappear out of here for a week, come back bound, almost blow the building up, and we just ignore that and eat dinner like a normal family?" I ask worriedly.

"Daddy made empress chicken," she adds.

I'll take that as a yes.

I get a rag hot and soapy to clean the last hour of chaos off my skin, and when the grayish-black suds rinse down the bathroom sink, I'm reminded of a very stupid decision I've made recently.

I left Corn.

Again.

Only this time, our bond is stronger. So who knows how long I have to go before he finds me again. I just hope I got a piece of lumpia before I had to leave. It wasn't on purpose this time though. I wanted to stay, be calm, and be reasonable about this, but everything about that dream felt as real as the concern I had for the being that slept beside me. As real as his anger, that was growing strangely close....

Suddenly inky black shadows spill out of every faucet, vent, and fixture until they stack to form a compelling vision of my cruelly handsome, irritable, demon husband.

"Wait, Corn. I can explain!" I yell.

Corn

I truly hate rutting. My body is trying its best to burden me with a child, I burn through an obscene amount of calories in the process, and if that isn't bad enough, it prompts mating frenzies which leave me as good as dead. I was so tired I didn't even feel Candrima leave. Not until she got caught in a summoning circle and got herself hurt. You best believe I felt that.

"No, Corn! No, no no!" she screams as I throw her over my shoulder.

She offered to explain, but I wasn't too keen on hearing any explanation on why she left.

Again.

We're going home, and this time I'll make sure to update the SIP spell to account for her newly acquired disappearing act. Fool me once...

However there's a knock at the door before I can utilize the tiny bathroom window for our escape.

"I'm coming in," the matronly voice announces.

Before either one of us could protest, the knob turns and in comes a disappointed glare topped with tight, graying curls.

"Cornelius," she says. "You could've used the stairs."

"Madam Kitara," I exclaim, bowing before her.

It's customary to bow before your elders in Hell regardless of their class or affiliation, and I do well to remember my manners.

"Wait, do you two know each other?" Candrima exclaims from over my shoulder.

Actually I mostly mind my manners. Besides the tiny instance of recurring kidnapping.

"Yes. Candrima, this is Madam Kitara. She's been our family seamstress for the last four centuries.

"Wow, that explains so much," Candy whispers.

"I'm also your new grandmother in law. So wash your hands and come join us for dinner," Madam Kitara says, voice final.

I look between Candy and her matriarch. The evidence is not only plentiful, it's also loud. The eyes and the enduring smile are the exact same, one is just expressed in a slightly more playful font.

"Dinner?" I ask, dumbfounded.

"Yes, dinner," she nods. "You bound my grandbaby, the least you can do is come meet her family. We'll be waiting."

I'm allowed not even a breath of protest before the door closes and we're saddled with her expectations.

"So what's for dinner?" I ask, as Candrima falls to my side.

"Who the fuck is that?" a voice announces as we exit the bathroom.

A fire gollum stands in the entrance to the dining room with his fist curled at his side. He's coming in hot, but based on his similar nose and curled brow, I can tell he's one of Candrima's guardians.

"Ted, that was rude," a woman replies.

"Mom, Dad," Candrima interjects. "This is my hus- Err, spouse, uh claim bond, Corn."

She stands in front of me as if she's going to protect me from any malice and I think it's sweet, but the fire gollum is disgusted.

"You didn't tell me he was a demon! You let our daughter marry a demon?" he shouts.

"We didn't know," her mother shrugs.

"Speak for yourself," Madam Kitara interjects.

"Well, all *I* knew was that she had a bind. It's not like she told me what happened."

"They fucked, that's what happened," Madam Kitara replies from the kitchen.

My insides begin to boil right along with the air in the room. There are hundreds of pictures of Candy on the wall and she's the only child in all of them. I put a monogamy bind on her father's only daughter. He's probably thinking of ways to poison me right now. Can't say I blame him.

"That's not what happened!" Candy argues. "And Corn is a succubus."

"Candrima, I was born at night. Not last night. Cornelius has a claiming bond engraved onto his ribs. You would've had to touch him there. Plus binds are an equal exchange. Y'all gave and received willingly," Madam Kitara says.

I thought Nafisa was bad, but this is a thousand times more awkward. The pressure of her father's gaze alone is enough to make me want to de-manifest.

"Ok, change of subject," her mother interjects kindly. "Corn-"

"How did you get in my house?" her father finishes.

Now I know this question is a set up. Any answer I give will be unsatisfactory, while the truth is ten times worse. He already dislikes the fact that I'm a demon. Telling him that I have shadow control is a bad move. Even I know that shadow demons are trouble.

"I uhm. I flew," I answer vaguely.

Suddenly, a slinky black cat chirps from his position on the windowsill, answering the question for me.

"Darkness." he says in simplified nocturnal Eldritch.

I growl at him, reminding him to mind his place as a lesser demon, but he seems rather amused. Especially given her parent's reaction.

"Goddess," her father says, bringing his palm to his face. "She married a shadow demon."

"It's a little more complicated than that, Ted," Kitara replies while fluffing the steaming hot rice. "Everybody put your powers away and we'll talk about it over dinner."

Candrima and I sit across from her parents, Theodore and Yvette as I've been introduced, while Madam Kitara occupies the head of the table. The food is excellent, but the interaction between everyone is awkward. Except for Madam Kitara. She seems most pleased that we're all here.

"So, Corn. What do you do for a living?" Yvette asks.

"I'm a florist and botanical planner," I reply proudly.

I love my occupation. It took me a long time to get here and lots of failed attempts at trying to be something I'm not, but it was well worth the journey. I'm starting to understand that a little hardship is worth enduring for a lot of happiness.

"A florist shadow demon?" Theodore scoffs.

Candrima straightens in her chair, scowling over her bite of rice before responding to her father.

"Dad, that's incredibly rude and unnecessary. Imagine some guy coming up to you and saying, *"Wow, a black engineer."*□

The strained look that sprouted up on his face told me he probably had at some point, and the loud sigh that followed said he didn't enjoy it either.

"I'm sorry. You're right. I guess I have my own biases, but I'm also a concerned father. You weren't even dating anyone then you came home soul bound. We didn't even get to know him first."

"I know it's jarring," I admit. "My family has had the same thing happen with my sister. We didn't even know she was dating, she just came home married one day."

"So you get it then?" Theodore asks.

I think back to the day Nilla returned home, hand in hand with some doting stranger. I was bothered about it for a week.

"I do," I nod.

"How did you two meet?" Yvette asks.

I'm ready to explain everything in very pg detail, but Candy replies first in a barely audible voice,

"The dream came true."

The air stills while her family exchanges looks of horror mixed with amazement. It seems they know exactly what she's talking about, but this is news to me.

"Candy, what dream?" I ask cautiously.

I feel her hesitation, but I try to calm her by holding her hand, and channeling calm through our bond.

Then she finally tells me,

"I've been dreaming of you since I was seventeen years old."

I'm told the anecdote of Candrima's dream and how she's lived with it foreshadowing her entire adult life. At first I find myself in disbelief, but I know premonitions are common in the magic world. She has piles of sleep journals describing our world in astonishing detail. Down to the stucco patch on the east window of the cabin. Even our reactions to each other.

Our coupling was no accident.

It seems that we're fated.

"This is Destiny's doing," Yvette murmurs.

"Destiny?" Candy replies irritably. "Destiny who?"

I gently recapture her hand before explaining.

"The entity Destiny, Candrima. Sometimes she meddles. Actually, that's all she does."

"So what is Destiny like a God?"

"No, no. Destiny is kind of like the universe. Vast, omnipotent, and formless. But conscience."

She searches my eyes for some sort of clue to make sense of all this, but truthfully, I know about as much as she does. All I can say for certain is that we were meant to come together. This was orchestrated by someone bigger than us.

"This is making my head hurt," she sighs.

I understand her frustration. I do. You live your life with routine and safety until an accident throws you left, and then a month later you find out your impromptu marriage was divinely arranged. Then your husband is a big idiot who can't explain shit properly because hormones are eating his brain. I'd be upset too. "We're soulmates," I say softly.

"What? What does this mean? Will we be able to dissolve our bond?" she asks.

Madam Kitara's eyes grow wide and cynical.

"You want to dissolve your binds?" she gawks.

Her father, who I'm sure would still be perfectly happy if I dropped dead this very moment, even looks concerned. Don't get me started on her poor mother. She looks like she could cry.

"Well, our partnership is illegal. The EUM forbades unions of any nature between sorcerers and cucubi."

"But it's an act of Destiny!" her mother argues.

"Yeah, but the damage is already done. I'm already wanted for questioning because I removed my location trackers and relocated our home. They could deny an appeal based on that alone."

"I'm not trying to be funny, but are you sure you're a succubus? I've never seen a lust demon with shadow control. The power is rare enough without the fact that it's almost exclusive to Hell royalty," her father says. "The EUM has no jurisdiction when it comes to citizens of Hell."

He's right. Shadow control is very rare. Even among higher rank demons. It's a form of ancient magic, kind of like Candrima's ability to manipulate air.

"I inherited it from my mother. She is The First Priestess Of Hell, but I am the fourth child. The EUM only considers two children for diplomatic immunity from the court. An heir and the spare," I explain.

Theodore leans back in his chair, contemplating what I've told him until a sincerely empathic lour arrives on his face.

"I'm sorry. I had no idea things had gotten that bad for demons with the EUM. They always did have it out for you all."

"Thank you," I say, appreciative of the acknowledgement.

The rest of dinner passes smoothly. Candrima's father and I surprisingly have a lot in common. He also appreciates orange juice, house plants, and textile work. He's a mosaic artist in his free time. That's his one true love outside of his family.

"So, now that we've all eaten, onto the subject of Candrima's powers," Madam Kitara says.

Candy's eyes drop to her lap that instant while her face twists with a strange guilt. She won't meet my eyes or anyone else's in the room. She must've lost control of her powers again.

"We're going to find her a coven as soon as the blood test comes back," I say, holding her hand tight. "She's been trying though. She taught herself teleportation and invisibility. She's studying an-"

"Cornelius, relax. Candrima is not on trial," Kitara says.

My tight shoulders suddenly ease down from my ears. I hadn't realized how fast I was talking. I was defending her like she was on trial, but that's my job. Every part of her is mine, including her heart. If I can't protect those parts I might as well be useless.

"I apologize," I say. "I just worry."

Candy's hand scratches under my chin with the same intense affection as earlier, and I purr from the soothing sensation of her sharp nails in my hair. It's so nice that I forget where we are for a moment, and I rub my head against hers to scent her sweet hibiscus smell.

"I'm going to be honest," Kitara says loudly with a clap of her hands. "I don't think you should try to sever your binds."

She's not the first to say that, and I know once the rest of my family meets Candy, she won't be the last. But I put Candrima's freedom at risk the longer she stays tethered to me. The reward is great, and so is the risk, but unfortunately it's one I can't take.

"I adore Candrima and I would do anything for her, but not this. She would be uprooted from her life, her friends, her family, you all. We would constantly be on the run. I don't want that life for her," I explain.

That is the truth. Candy has a long life to live, and seeing her spending a thousand years or more on the run from the embassy for the crime of partnering with me would break my heart.

She deserves better.

"Well, then we have two problems," Madam Kitara sighs. "Cornelius, your bind is permanent. It will only dissolve in the instance of true death. It can be sealed to some extent, but only if we take care of the first problem."

The air turns heavy and ominous, reminiscent of Kitara's glare.

"What's the first problem?" Candy asks.

"You," her grandmother replies. "You are a moonlight witch."

Despite the name, moonlight witches are in fact not witches. They are a very rare species of dark sorcerers who can pull energy directly from the moonlight as well as everything the moonlight touches, aka all other elements on earth. They are directly under the Goddess Of

Tides in rank, revered and highly sought after. Their powers, specifically their energy utilization and summons abilities, can change the landscape of entire realms and even bend the fabric of reality.

She is the epitome of dark magic, melted down and poured into the delicate shape of a woman.

"They will come for her eventually," I say, understanding the meaning of it all.

"They will," her grandmother nods.

"Our bind will be used as a bargaining chip for the control of her powers. We have to separate."

"It's not that simple, Cornelius," she warns. "Your entire immediate family and hers will have to help remove that bind. All living members. Plus you will need to acquire Destiny's Sword to initially weaken the tether."

"Ok, let's start there then," Candrima says. "Where is Destiny's Sword?"

Where is anything shiny and distracting enough that Heaven has deemed an important artifact of magic?

"The EUM history museum," I sigh.

Heaven is currently closed to tourists as they prepare for the season change, so we make a plan to visit during the pagan festival of Yule. We'll slip in with Madam Kitara as her guests and then grab the sword. So that gives us a little under a month to find Candy a coven and start training her to use her powers. As well as talk to my family about the plan, which I am not looking forward to. Luckily we have a couple of days to sleep on that though. We're both currently overdue for some rest.

"Well, Cornelius. It was nice meeting you, all things considered," Ted says, extending his hand. "I'm sorry for the way I started out."

"It's understandable, Sir," I reply. "It was nice meeting you as well. You have raised a remarkable woman. Thank you for trusting me with her care."

"You succubi sure are charming," he chuckles before moving onto Candy. "I love you, bug. We'll talk soon?"

"Of course, Daddy," she says, falling into his hug. "I'll start writing home every week since I won't have a phone."

"You better!" her matriarchs chide, joining the hug.

My heart pulls for Candy. Sure there were consequences for me too, but I didn't have to say goodbye to my family, and we're not nearly as tight knit as the Castilles. I almost wish they could come with us for her sake, but they have lives.

"Brrtt," Aster chirps as if he's reading my mind.

"Absolutely not," I reply.

He's asked me to take him with us, and outside the fact that I don't like other demons in my space, this one in particular is an asshole wrapped in a cheap fur throw.

"Are you talking to my cat?" Candrima exclaims.

"Yes, most cats speak Eldritch," I reply while glaring at the Hell beast. Candrima's curious brown eyes blink furiously as if she's trying to clear a hallucination from her vision, but alas we remain.

"Corn, I need you to explain this to me like I'm real slow, ok? What does that mean?"

I thought even humans knew about the origin of cats. There are so many jokes about it. Still, I explain,

"Most cats are part demon. Shapeshifter demon, to be exact. Some were lazy and got the bright idea to shift into cats so the humans would care for them and they just never shifted back. They lived as domestic felines in all aspects. So cats are tiny low-rank demons that can't shift anymore, but still speak the language."

"Are you telling me that Sir Aster Sweet Beans Castille is a demon?"

she asks.

"That's exactly what I'm saying!" I exclaim, pointing to the grooming beast. "You never wondered why cats and demons both purr? We're distantly related."

"So are you just a big, cranky, winged cat then?" she laughs.

"Absolutely," I nod. "I enjoy a fish dinner and a good scratch behind the ears as much as the next house cat."

"Mrrrh," Aster replies.

Why not?

"Well, because I simply don't like you," I answer plainly.

"What are y'all talking about?" she asks.

"He's trying to convince Cornelius to let him tag along," Madam Kitara says.

"Wait, is Aster not coming with us?" she asks.

"No?"

"Why not?"

"I just told him why. I don't like him. He's sneaky an-"

"He blew up your spot?" Ted finishes.

Yes, but I'll never admit that out loud. A demon has his pride.

"We're bringing him, Corn," Candy says firmly. "Aster's been with me since I was 19."

Jealousy flares in my belly. It makes no sense, but I'm upset that this fleabag has had more of Candy's time than me. And it's looking like it will remain that way since we're moving forward with separation.

"Fine, but I will not feed him," I sigh, conceding to her soft eyes.

"Prrbrtt."

I will hunt.

"You better," I scoff.

Candy

I find it hilarious that Corn has such strong feelings about Aster. An elder cat that weighs at most eight pounds on a good day. We stayed a little longer after dinner to hammer out plans and gather some of my things, and he's spent the entire time glaring at my poor baby. Luckily Aster doesn't seem to be bothered by Corn's antics.

"Is there anything else?" Corn asks, returning from transferring Aster.

He's been transporting my belongings back and forth while I catch up with my family. I offered to help, but he assured me it was not necessary and hoped through the ether before I could stop him. If severing our bond was hard before, the next month or so is going to make it downright impossible.

"No nothing else," I say, rising from the couch.

I'm trying not to be sad because at least I'll still have Aster, but this is the longest I've been away from home.

"Don't worry, Candy," Corn cooes. "I've promised Miss Yvette and Madam Kitara that we will be back to visit before Yule."

"Ok," I nod. "Then I guess I'm ready."

I hug my family one more time before joining Corn's side, and right before we jump into the iridescent ether, I remember the one thing I'm forgetting.

"WAIT! There's one more thing I need to do!" I exclaim.

"It looks expensive here. Are you sure this is the right place? I'm afraid to let my feet touch the floor," Corn says.

He's right. We're in a hall with a couch that probably costs double what my car did, the walls are wrapped in glittering gold leaf wallpaper that looks like it feels like silk, and heavy gilded sconces illuminate every foot of the walking path.

"She likes them loaded," I reply.

"Well, you two have that in common," Corn shrugs.

While he's got a point, it's not like I sought a rich man on purpose. Destiny basically dropped me in his lap. I guess she figured I've suffered enough.

"Are you sure this is a good idea?" Corn whispers as we tiptoe through the hall.

Honestly? No.

But I tried calling first, from both my mom and dad's phone as well as Granny's. Calling from my own number wasn't an option, seeing as my phone fell out of my pocket two weeks ago as I was being carried over the Tribune Tower. Plus it's still possible for a cell signal to track us. Being on the run is awfully inconvenient.

"It's fine. They're probably just having dinner or something," I reply, praying that's the truth.

Unfortunately, my wise old husband doesn't buy into my pitch of false confidence.

"Why do I let you take me on these adventures?" Corn sighs. "I could be at home with a nice cup of chamomile."

Goodness, we're more alike than I thought. I know I've said that exact same sentence to Betty plenty of times before.

"Hush, and stop griping! It won't take long, I promise."

I was right, it doesn't take long. Because the second we step over the threshold connecting the hall to the living area, the door slides closed behind us and a flurry of daggers woosh pass. Corn doesn't waste a second shielding me from any would-be threats. He quickly switches forms and pulls me to his center before his wings unfurl to cover the rest of me, including my line of sight. I can feel his body lunge forward as if he's swinging at someone though.

"Corn, what's happening?" I exclaim, unable to see for myself.

"Candy?" Betty calls.

"Uh, hi," I chuckle awkwardly.

"Hi, lady."

Corn is still in defensive mode even though I have verbal confirmation that we're safe, so I have to pry myself free from his grip to greet my friend.

"I have so many questions," Betty says as I smile at her.

She looks to the brooding figure positioned firmly behind me with curiosity. Oh right. I broke into her house with the help of my demon soulmate after disappearing for a week. So I guess it's my turn to spill the tea.

"Well, let me answer one of them for you. This is Corn, and he's my husband."

Once we make introductions, I sit down and tell Betty all about my last four weeks. The accident, the binding, my powers, Hell, Heaven, and everything in between.

"I knew I shouldn't have left you alone that night," Betty mumbles after I finish. "You almost died because of me."

I sigh because I knew Betty would take it hard. She's always felt responsible for my problems even though she's definitely not. She's also not responsible for my accident or anything that happened after.

I certainly wasn't complaining when Corn tongued me down.

Twice.

"Unfortunately her accident appears to be a symptom of Destiny," Corn replies from his section of the parallel sofa.

The men, who almost came to mutual blows barely an hour earlier are getting along just fine. They're exchanging war stories, jokes, and pain points of advanced age in this modern time. Callum was also made wealthy by the gift of time. It turns out he's a vampire while Betty really is a seer.

Yeah, I'm convinced that sex is nasty.

Dollar cheeseburger no ketchup, nasty.

"What does that mean?" Betty asks.

"It means that these two are true soulmates," Callum answers, motioning his large hand between Corn and I. "It's very rare to see. Even in this day and age."

"Well if it's so rare and wonderful, why are y'all trying to bust it up?" Betty queries.

Corn groans, exhausted from uttering the same sentence for the fifth time this week. His tone is arguing that he's irritated from the repetition, but his eyes swell with unverbalized angst over our situation.

"Our union is illegal. Sorcerers cannot mate with Succubi. Not even casually."

"What the fuck do you mean illegal? How is love illegal? Is the magic world stuck in Jim Crow times or something?"

"Honestly, yes," Callum answers. "The Embassy Of United Magic has their picks, and demons, among others, are low on the favorite list. Most demons don't care because Hell never joined the Union anyway, but the EUM compensates by making life especially difficult for the demons living on this plane."

"Why don't they just move back to Hell then?" Betty asks.

I prop myself up on my hands, waiting for the answer. Because I, too, am curious. It seems like it would solve plenty of problems surrounding the EUM's unfair policies. Especially all the tracking and fees cucubi are subject to.

"Because lust demons need humans, and humans need lust demons. The relationship is mutually beneficial. Sexual liberation pushes a large part of human development and societal growth, and cucubi are responsible. But we also need lust to live. It's kind of like mosquitoes biting humans, but feeding birds, which in turn help pollinate gardens and disperse seeds. It's a cycle just as natural as any other," Corn answers.

We stay for a little longer and discuss all of magic's messy politics, as well as our respective couplings. I was correct in my initial assessment of Callum. He's horrendously down bad for Betty in every way imaginable. I mean crying in the rain while singing R&B down bad. But as Betty points out with a sly smile and a tip of her chin when the big guy chills my water for the third time that hour, so is Corn.

All of his doting and consideration has me both praising and cursing Destiny. If she was going to stick me with someone I couldn't have, couldn't she have at least picked someone a little less appealing? Someone who couldn't care less about making me tarts, twisting my hair, or kissing me as if it heals his soul? This is unnecessarily cruel, because every hour that passes is one that reinforces the theory of our inevitable separation will destroy me.

I don't know if I can do it.

I yawn twice within ten minutes, and Corn begins to gather our belongings in preparation of our exit. Further proving his care and consideration.

Ugh.

"Thank you for your hospitality despite us breaking into your home," he says. "But we need to get going. It's been a very long day and we're both overdue for a bath and some rest."

He extends a hand to me to support my ascension from the overly stuffed sofa, and I take it to join his side.

"Ok, but promise you'll write," Betty says, standing with Callum. "I never thought I'd say that. Whew, this no phone shit is ghetto."

"Honestly, it's kind of nice once you get used to it," I shrug.

"Tuh. Listen, I love me some you, but we both know you vibe with the whole cottage in the isolated woods thing better than most people. This suits you."

I hate to admit she's right, but honestly this is kind of a dream come true for me. Days filled with books, tea, fresh scones, and a warm embrace accentuated with the heady smell of citrus and leather.

"You don't have to tell me. I know I'm right," she says, pulling me in for a right hug. "I love you, Candy. Please be safe."

"I will, I promise," I mumble into her raspberry scented locs.

"And please let us know if we can do anything to help," Callum adds.

Corn snorts loudly, disturbing the art hanging from the walls. He's tired, but he also isn't one to ask for help from what I've seen.

"If you happen to come across a coven for sorceresses, please let us know."

Callum's eyebrows rise in thought,

"Actually, my sister operates a coven down in the 9th. It's not all sorceresses, but there are a few members with such gifts."

As much as I cursed Destiny during the duration of this evening, it seems she didn't take it personally. Here she was dropping a gift square in our laps.

"Are you serious?" Corn asks in disbelief.

"Yes. Her name is Kira. They have a new recruit meeting on the 28th of every month."

The 28th was only a few days away, and with Yule approaching fast, it was perfect timing. Maybe Destiny had her own way of working things out...

"I can write down the information if you'd like," Callum says, summoning a quill and paper pad.

"Yes, please," Corn says. "I owe you a great debt for this."

Callum begins writing just as a mischievous grin sprouts on his face.

"Careful, demon. I just may come to collect," he laughs.

"I'm not one to offer blindly," Corn says. "Consider my word valid and binding if you should ever find yourself in need of my assistance."

"It's like watching the Black version of Pride And Prejudice," Betty laughs as the men continue their conversation in front of a thoughtfully situated fireplace.

They speak with one another in poetic old English as if they're men of high society, and funny enough I find it easy to imagine Corn being a titled man in an expensive, trim waistcoat, visiting the city while secretly longing to return to the sweet solitude of his country home.

"I know. It's kind of hot," I reply, watching the shadow of the flames lick across Corn's citrus skin.

"Very," Betty nods, watching Callum just the same.

Back home I find a similar fire blazing against the stone hearth. Aster has had no problem settling in, and lays atop Corn's favorite recliner, curled tightly into himself. My shoulders release the tension I was unaware of as Corn places a kettle on the old iron stove, and then I guide us to the couch so I can melt into his side like warm butter. The room calms in the wake of his soft caresses against my skin. It reminds me of the safety of a blanket swaddle, and wanting to hold onto that feeling, I say a little spell I've learned to make us a blanket fort.
"This is impressive," Corn chuckles, touching the supporting wall of quilts. "You never cease to amaze me."
"Well thank you, kind sir."

We fall back into a pleasant quiet, but my racing heart eventually spikes my guilt-driven anxiety about today. I left him again and I can't even claim ignorance. This time I fully knew what would happen, I did it anyway, and here he is extending me even more grace.

"I'm sorry about today," I say after a while. "I didn't mean to."

Corn raises his hand to scratch my tangled curls although he remains quiet. His heartbeat is steady and strong, and eventually it commands the blood coursing through my veins just the same. I fall into a blurry state of relaxation that would scare me in any other scenario, my chest rising and falling synchronously with my lover's. Then he presses a chaste kiss to my temple.

"What happened?" he finally asks.

He sits me on his lap and pulls me forward to face him. His eyes draw mine in with all the fervor of the fire in front of us. Asking a hundred silent questions and making double as many promises. I find that my lips part without much more thought, and I tell him.

"I had a panic attack from a nightmare."

His hand falls from my chin to my arm to trace soft circles in the plant flesh he finds there.

"Tell me about it," he says.

In the short time I've known Corn, I've learned that he prioritizes honest communication. Although his voice is gentle I make no mistake. This isn't a request, it's a demand.

So I tell him about the dream, the injuries, the pain, and the death. I spend what feels like hours reliving my worst nightmare, and Corn listens patiently the entire time. I know it's not the easiest thing for him to do considering I'm a blubbering, snot-crusted monster by the second act of my explanation, but he still listens intently and holds me through everything. Then when I finally finish he says,

"I'm so sorry you've been going through this alone."

Wow, out of everything that I expected to happen, him apologizing to me was low on the list. I'm a crybaby though so that's all it takes for me to burst into another fit of tears, causing Corn to secure my wet face to his chest with a strained sigh.

"It's ok, Candy," he cooes softly while stroking my back. "It's going to be ok."

"How can you be so sure?" I gargle.

"Well, because I'm old," he chuckles. "But also because I'll be by your side no matter what. Sweetheart, **if** your dream were to ever come true, and I say if because premonitions are sometimes just giant what ifs, then we'll handle it together. Until then stop worrying yourself, ok?"

"Ok," I blubber.

"Also, no more teleporting out of here after sex. That's really starting to hurt my feelings."

I tip my chin to look into his soft gaze. It's a cocktail of reassurance and also hurt, and I recognize I was just as responsible for him as he was me.

"I'm sorry," I sigh. "I'll try my best to reel it in."

"Good," he says, pecking my temple. "Now how about some tea? I made a tart earlier."

I poofed out of here, made him suffer the awkwardest dinner in history, then almost got us ambushed, and now he's offering me a little treat? Yeah, Destiny did her big one here. I finally understand why people run around claiming they're blessed all the time. Despite what Corn thinks about our union in the eyes of the law, I know he's my biggest blessing to date.

And I'm going to try to keep it that way.

Destiny

Corn

Candy's heat ended three nights ago when I fucked her into the kitchen table and got chocolate stuck in her hair. I paid for my crimes by detangling all her pretty curls, then she rewarded me by holding me all night as our hormones bottomed out. I was grateful because her hormones had not only cost me my sanity, but my body also. My overworked muscles were still recovering.

Since then, she had been dedicated to studying as much as she could for the Coven open house. We didn't know what the application would consist of, but we focused on the three main skill sets to be safe. Task, summons, and energy utilization. I felt like I missed my calling as a librarian the way she had me finding and recommending books and translating passages for her, but I quickly realized that the work I was doing was a labor of love, and I'd likely hate doing it for anyone else. With her though, watching her discover and learn was a drug I'd yet to tire of. She's smart, calculated, and capable. She's perfect.

Except for one little transgression.

"Candrima, are you feeling well?" I ask.

I woke up from my nap hungry and dehydrated, and while Candy wasn't at my side where I last left her, I could hear her contently humming from the kitchen. I nearly floated in here, trying to get a proper listen at her song, only to find her munching on a large bowl of disgrace.

"Why wouldn't I be?" she replies before pecking me.

I frown because the taste of that travesty lingers on her otherwise perfect lips. Even the smell of it is upsetting. Sickly sweet and oddly mapley. It smells how I think a conspiracy theory would smell.

"Because you're eating torch wax."

She rolls her eyes at my accusation,

"Haha. Corn is so funny. Just let me enjoy my candy corn in peace."

"I'm not being funny. We literally use that abomination as torch wax in Hell. I thought it was used for the same thing here on Earth, but then I find you in here eating it like it's Pringles or something. Why?"

"You have your period cravings, and I have mine," she says, referring to my rut cravings.

So I like my little crunchy snacks. That is not a crime. But this is.

"At first I was sad about our separation, but now I see it's for the best," I tease. "A wax eater for a mate. Who would've thought?"

I move towards the fridge just in time to witness Candy's perfect mouth fall open to release a strangled gasp.

"You take that back right now!" she demands, stomping her bare little foot against the floor.

"The truth hurts, baby," I shrug while taking out my dough.

Usually I'm all but willing to appease the little tyrant but wax eating is basically treason. I offer her a playful smile instead which she shoots down with a scowl.

"Well how's this for the truth," she nips back. "Your ice cream farts smell like a corpse, your blankets are in serious need of fabric softener, and your biscuits are mediocre!"

Candy shouts that last part with all the confidence of a cut rate chariot salesman, but we both know better.

"So we're playing two truths and a lie?" I chuckle, reining her into me by her waist.

Her breath hitches in response to her repositioning, blessing me with an extra view of her perfect chest rising and falling in conjunction with mine. Her lips never part to speak, but she still chastises me for teasing her.

"Fine, I'll go next," I say. "You have the loudest snore I've ever heard. I thought you had gotten possessed by a freight train that first night."

She rolls her eyes, trying to pull away, but I tighten my grip on her and let her lush curves overflow from the divides of my fingers before continuing. Indulging myself in the luxury of her proximity.

"You also make the worst tea I've ever tasted, and despite your penchant for those disgusting lumps of sugary wax, I absolutely adore you."

Her cinnamon eyes offer me soft curiosity in response. She searches my face, silently expressing both confusion and confliction before parting those sumptuous lips of hers to speak.

"Wh- Which one was the lie?" she mumbles.

I slip my hand behind her head and carefully scratch the soft, sweat-damp curls gathered at the nape of her neck before, against my better judgment, bringing her mouth to mine.

"The tea," I whisper against her pouty bottom lip. "I'd never chance that kind of disappointment with you. It would only prove my theory that we were made for each other."

"How so?" she all but gasps.

We're falling into something different. Something dangerous, but also something wonderful. Candrima watches me in these moments like I've painted the skies blue and the grass green. Like I'm holding the key to the entrance of Nirvana. The logical part of my brain is screaming UGK lyrics at me, begging me to reconsider, but the view from where I'm standing is far too perfect for me to do anything besides offer my absolute admiration. So taking her hand in mine, I leap from my perch of apprehension and answer her question,

"Because every cup of tea is made better with a little bit of honey, and a little of your sweetness is exactly what my life needs."

Her perfect, hooded eyes offer me plenty of warning about what's coming next, but I'm still caught off guard when her mouth presses to mine. Suddenly the sugar wax isn't so bad.

Goddess, what a kiss.

Explorative, and breathy, and so very torrid. It doesn't help that the upbeat tempo of Love An Happiness is thumping through the walls at that moment. Excitement surges beneath her skin, threatening to detonate her powers but I use our bond to blanket her with a wave of calm. She then falls further into me, mewling in satisfaction as our lips continue to seek one another's. The sensation of Candrima floods my veins with the aggression of opium. Making me forget everything and everywhere outside of us in this room while we seek air from one another's lungs.

Until the alarm clock sounds. Noting the final hour before our upcoming appointment, logic makes its grand reentrance into our lives. Unsorted and deeply rooted feelings aside, Candrima needs a coven. I can't just blow up her chance at stability with my dick. I'm better than that.

At least I think I am.

"We have to go, little witch. Tonight's the night."

She nods before taking my hand while I open the portal to the Ninth Realm of Hell, and we silently agree to put a pin in this for now.

The meeting spot is located in a rental cave off the cliff of Zetrh. A large volcanic mountain that at its peak, connects the 9th and 8th realms. Citizens of Hell move freely from the skies while customs processes tourists. Luckily, we don't have to stop due to my lineage and Candrima's IMB. So we make it with fifteen minutes to spare.

"Nervous?" I ask softly, taking her flailing hands.

We're outside the entrance so Candy can collect herself, but she's going to pace a hole in the pathway if I let her spiral continue.

"Very," she confirms.

"Don't be," I say as I stroke her soft curls. "You are more than capable. They're going to love you."

Candy pulls away only to fall back into me, pulling me into a tight, soothing hug. I used to hate hugs before her and now here I am, coiling my tails around her and giving it my all.

"Thank you for being here with me," she murmurs softly into my shirt.

"Always," I reply. "I'll always be here for you."

I've decided that a long time ago. That even if she can't be mine, I'll always be hers. No amount of legislation or fines could ever change that.

Ever.

The meeting started off with a brief history of Midnight Call's history. Kira, the founder, is a born-earth-witch turned vampire. Callum was turned by a malicious deputy and she followed shortly after, not wanting her brother to have to suffer the inevitable loneliness he'd feel when his family died. It was a selfless act of unconditional love. A selfless act that unfortunately cost her coven. Most covens have strict power agreements barring abilities outside of the general population's from membership, and she fell victim to that clause. As a hybrid, she was unable to find another sisterhood, so she set out to build her own. Hence, Midnight Call Coven, a sisterhood for the odd and uncategorized.

My little odd ball is practically vibrating where she stands while we wait on next steps.

Wait no, she's actually vibrating.

Not wanting her to accidentally erupt a volcano, I quickly take her hand and rub my thumb across her tight knuckles. It takes a few minutes, but she winds down and releases her energy in a more productive way. By brightening all the lanterns and warming the chilly, damp cave.

Unfortunately that didn't go unnoticed though.

"Um, mistress, did you raise the temperature?" an elven creature asks Kira.

"No, of course not. That would take an obscene amount of energy," Kira replies.

Yes it does.

She seems ready to dismiss the statement, but then a single bead of sweat rolls down her clove-colored forehead.

Perfect timing.

"Who did that?" she demands, facing the tenured members.

They all shake their heads no, rightfully denying involvement, so she moves on to the recruits.

Candrima twitches beside me as Kira examines each and every new face. Looking for any admission of guilt.

"It's ok." I assure her silently. *"I got you."*

She nods while Kira's intimidating steps draw near. Every one of her strides carries an unspoken accusation, aimed at Candy. She stops six feet away from her and turns on her heels with an unreadable expression etched into her features.

"What's your name, young woman?" Kira asks.

"Candrima Castille," Candy replies firmly.

"And Miss Castille, how did you discover Midnight Call?"

"My best friend's boyfriend, Callum Perry, referred us."

"I see," Kira nods before sending a cautious glance my way.

Her gaze lingers and writhing jealousy begins to twist through our bond and sink my stomach. Candy's magic surges through my body and glows underneath my skin, threatening to surface if Kira were to come closer. But luckily, she seems knowledgeable about the ominous force hanging heavily in the air between us.

"And you are bound to a demon?"

"Yes," Candy says defensively.

She says it with enough surety to make even me bristle, and I hate how right it feels. Things between us were of course complicated further since our mating cycle, but even moments like this, when she stood in front of me, willing to protect me from anything, and the silent moments we shared in each other's company were starting to erode my confidence in our ability to separate. Our bond was strengthening despite our attempts not to give this situation our all.

"Your bind to this Hell Spawn is strong. Why are you seeking a coven?" she asks.

I consider correcting her, but quickly decide against it. If she believes I'm Hell Borne, it just might work in Candy's favor. Midnight Call has 10 potential recruits but only three available slots, and I'm willing to use any advantage necessary to get her in.

"Corn is my mate, and his company is fulfilling, but I need guidance and sisterhood. My powers are uncontrollable currently," Candy explains.

Kira once again casts a wayward glance over where I stand. She's searching for something and when she finds it she refocuses on Candrima,

"I disagree, but I am curious to know why you believe that."

Candy's eyes quickly meet the floor. I can feel her embarrassment, and I know it's festering because she's wondering what's the best way to to tell a Coven Mistress that intimacy makes her detonate.

"I um, when I get excited... I-I expel energy."

She handled that well. My explanation would've been much less tactful.

"What does that mean?" Kira asks, tipping her head onto her shoulder.

"She loses control and causes power surges when we get intimate," I whisper.

Candrima shoots me an irritated look that proves my original sentiment on the matter. My explanation was definitely lacking tact.

"You think a coven would help with that?" Kira asks, trying to keep the laughter out of her eyes.

"I think a coven could help balance me. Just provide me with the tools to make lasting change. Not fix me and all my problems, " Candy answers.

Candrima is young by most magic standards, especially within her specific species. Most sorcerers will live for two thousand years or better, but here she is at 34 years old, able to articulate and champion her needs.

It's commendable.

"I see," Kira says with a dip of her head.

Her pensive eyes are eerily similar to those of her brother. They look different enough, being siblings of the opposite gender, but when she throws a mischievous smile in Candrima's direction, I see it clearly. Down to the slight curl of their upper lip.

"I like you. You'll fit in just fine."

I visibly relax knowing the hard part is over. All we have to do now is complete the application tasks and hopefully, Candy will be joining a sisterhood.

"What did you say your species was?" Kira finishes.

Or maybe not.

We both bristle at the question. I know the information would have to come out eventually, but I hoped it would be in a less public setting. Some of these potentials would definitely not be making it and the last thing I wanted was for one of them to snitch on a demon-part-nered-sorceress for taking their place.

However, my determined little witch didn't let the question stunt her. She quietly whispered a cloaking spell meant to mask the true meaning of spoken words, and after she's certain it took affect, she whispers her answer to an impressed Kira,

"I'm a moonlight witch."

Kira's eyes grew impossibly wide. Her previously rigid posture relaxed into something a little less certain, something vulnerable.

"I understand why Callum sent you here now," she replies softly. "You are apart of the 19th prophecy."

"The what?" I balk.

I've heard of the prophecies before, but I thought it was mostly folklore among Hellions. No one had spoken of a prophecy in thousands of years, much less referred to one. Looking to her elven assistant, she seems to pass off some non verbal command for the creature to take over. Then she waves us to the back of the cave.

I'm not surprised to see a tunnel leading deeper into the mountain and I'm even less surprised to find that it connects to some more modern accommodations. The dwelling has every creature comfort most have come to expect in this century, including a bathroom, a kitchen, sleeping chambers, and their official hall of records. A massive library hall containing texts of every fashion, including scrolls, papyrus, and prophetic rocks.

"I thought these were just a myth," I whisper, completely in awe of the slab before me.

"There is no myth in magic, Shadow demon," Kira replies. "If someone's taken the time to talk about it, then not only is it likely real, but also important."

I silence my comments as I review the prophecy. Thanks to my mother's insistence on language mastery, I'm proficient in the Ældlich this was written in, and I recite it out loud so that Candy can read it too.

"In the year eighteen hundred and thirty six, a male child will be born to two of royal demon lineage. His tether to one of the Earth moon's eternal children will be congenital, although he will bare no mark until their first meeting. They will mate and become bonded…"

I hesitate, knowing that this text could essentially prove what our family has predicted all along. That we were doomed from the beginning.

"Corn, what does it say?" Candy asks.

"It says the bond will be imperishable," Kira finishes. "And that the love and blood of The Moonchild and the Shadow King will usher in a new era, one marking the birth of The Time God."

"What? What does this mean?" Candy gasps.

"It means that we're stuck together," I answer plainly. "But there is a possibility it's wrong."

"Prophecies are never wrong, Shadow Demon," Kira tuts. "That's why they're revered."

I stop myself from rolling my eyes. Callum is very mellow, but his sister is not. Kira reminds me of Nilla: Imposing, pushy, and dominant. I suspect they are even the same age.

"Yes, but this clearly says born of two royal demons. I am a mixed-species succubus. My father is an Egbere. Hardly a demon, and definitely not royal. So maybe this refers to someone else," I argue.

Kira brings her hand to her chin in thought while studying the text. I hate to admit that there are quite a few similarities to The Mother Of Time as described and my dear little witch, but the inaccuracies are blaring. For one, it claims that we met in the springtime, for two, The Mother Of Time is described as a demure counter-balance to her raging, wrathful husband, and for three, it details that the couple lives in Hell. The ground was wet with snow when we met, I dislike being angry because it is a monumental waste of energy, and knowing what I know now, I would never try to move Candrima to Hell. She needs moonlight to synthesize power. She's like a plant.

A gorgeous, flowering plant that hypnotizes unsuspecting admirers with an intoxicating perfume and cashmere petals.

Or idiot florists.

"Perhaps you're right, Shadow Demon," Kira concedes. "You are certainly no powerhouse, and this text presumes The Father Of Time to be capable of splitting a continent in two with his bare hands."

Gee thanks. I know I'm not the most brolic, but I can still hold my own.

And I have no need for ripping apart a continent...

"I suppose I've gotten ahead of myself and I apologize. It's just platinum sorceresses and shadow demons are so rare that I knew it had to be you."

She has a point. This prophecy is nothing if not coincidental. However, it's also terrifying. If these events were to somehow come true...

"It's understandable, but Corn and I are definitely not the florid rulers of Hell," Candy says. "We prefer peace and quiet. That whole prophecy thing sounds very much like the opposite."

That's my girl! My beautiful, smart, candy-corn loving girl. However nasty that shit is...

"Are you certain you want to join a coven then? There's hardly a moment of quiet here," Kira sighs cautiously.

Just as she said that, a loud bang rang through the receiving area. Several more bangs accompanied it before irritated voices began coordinating in hopes of fixing whatever had happened in the ten minutes we were away.

Meanwhile, Kira summons a mushroom tea.

"I don't have any expectations of quiet here," Candy affirms with a nod. "I'm fine with a little chaos because the big guy provides all the calm I need."

My head snaps towards Candy immediately and our eyes meet. She seems infuriatingly content with what she just said. Does she know that we're falling for each other? More importantly, does she care? Should I care? Or should I just let her take me along for this wild ride and enjoy the sun on my face?

"Well then," Kira says, interrupting my racing thoughts. "I think congratulations are in order, Sister Castille. Welcome to Midnight Call."

"What!?" Candy screeches. "Seriously!?"

Her excitement swells our bond, and I quickly dispel some of the energy into the plants lining the walls, causing the pots to overflow with new growth. Kira watches in awe before motioning between us, specifically at our joined hands.

"You are obviously very powerful, because that Dracaena was near-ly dead. But you are also responsible and wise. You could've used your powers for a gaudy display of showmanship out there, but instead you warmed the cave and brightened the lamps. That shows care and con-sideration for others around you. Midnight Call would be honored to have you, Candrima," Kira explains.

My wings unfurl in utter relief. We finally found Candy a coven. She'll be able to train her powers and grow under tenured guidance. She won't be alone anymore.

Especially not once we separate...

Yes I know I just said I would consider letting us be, but this weird little rock has reminded me of the risks that lie ahead, and most of them befall Candrima. I cannot take her to Hell, and I don't want her to spend her life running. She'd be in good hands with Madam Kitara and her coven though. She'd be safe and happy. That's all I really want for her.

I watch idly while she signs her name in golden ink onto the coven contract, smile wider than the spring sky. My heart constricts in my chest knowing that one day those smiles will be limited, so I drink this one in greedily, praying that she'll sate my addiction with another sometime soon.

Candy

Coven initiation is hard. We stayed in Hell for 72 hours while preparing for the joining ceremony. Well, I stayed in Hell and completed my mile-long chore list for the coven. Corn was running around doing my bidding, including caring for Aster, however begrudging he was in doing so.

"It feels so good to be home," I sigh, stripping off my burnt dress.

One of my initiation tasks was to light the sisterhood beacon that sat high above the cave. The task itself wasn't so bad, especially since I could pilfer Corn's shadow magic and use it to boost my teleportation, but the lamp got so hot that my dress caught on fire.

Note to self, silk does not make a good magic fabric.

"It's great to have you back. Your fleabag wouldn't stop asking me questions," Corn replies.

Aster chitters a reply while I watch Corn place the kettle on the stove and pack two teaballs with mint and turmeric tea. It's been nearly a month since I first had the unique blend, but now it's part of my weekly care routine. Just like the demon brewing it.

"It's good to be back. I missed you guys. I don't know how I'm going to balance all of this and a job when things go back to normal."

"You intend to return to work?" he asks, shock lacing his tone.

"Well, yeah," I nod. "If Callum will allow me back."

Corn shifts against the stone counter, looking every bit as uncomfortable as our bond lets me feel. I don't know why though. Maybe he's worried about Steph or other men?

"You ok?" I ask.

"Well, I'm confused," he replies. "I don't know why you would want to put so much on your plate. Wouldn't you rather take some time to explore your powers?"

"Of course, but exploring my powers doesn't necessarily pay the bills. Being alive is expensive. Outside costs like 100 grams of gold a day."

"Is that what you're worried about?" he snorts.

"Yeah, kinda!" I exclaim.

He dismisses my concerns with a lazy wave before returning to the stove to heat oil for popcorn. Meanwhile if my brows scrunch any closer, I'll be rocking a unibrow well into the next century.

"Calm yourself, little witch. It's customary for demons to provide their mates with an allowance that reflects their wealth and lifestyle. As we've discussed previously, mine is vast. So there is no need for you to fuss over employment."

"What? But we're separating!" I argue.

"Yes, and? Look, at the end of the day, you'll still need me for your heats and other urges. You can't be intimate with anyone else because of my imposed bind. So I believe it's more than fair to compensate you for the inconvenience," he explains.

"So like a prostitute?" I scoff.

I never thought I'd see a day when I made Corn blush, but his citrus skin deepens with an unmistakeable rush of embarrassment. It's kind of cute.

"No, not like a prostitute. Obviously," he sighs. "Like my mate. Who I very much enjoy and delight in outside of our mind-melting sexual relationship."

Now's my turn to blush. Luckily Corn doesn't see me because he's focused on not burning his popcorn, but the butterflies rush my belly all the same.

"So, what do you want to do today?" Corn asks, breaking my focus from his strong back.

Damn he has nice shoulders.

Once I realize that he's seriously expecting an answer from me, I try not to frown at his question but I can't help it. For a man who's spent the last hundred years or so existing in leisure, he sure does love a packed itinerary.

"Babe, don't take this the wrong way, but I don't want to do shit. I'm going to summon a TV with a DvD player and I'm gonna veg out. I'd like for you to consider joining me."

"Are you sure? There's a festival happening today on Medieval Moon, we could just pop in for a few hours," he suggests.

I don't reply, I just stare at him and he stares back, completely oblivious to my souring mood. Why would I want to travel and spend the day walking in the heat when I could be naked on the couch, snacking on fruit leather and popcorn? I don't know, and I'm not trying to find out either. So when I've had enough of our staring contest, I decide to put my powers to good use and win this battle. First I summon the TV, then I borrow a few selections from the library back home in Chicago, and finally, I draw Corn over to me. It takes a lot more energy than I initially predicted since his magic fights mine the entire way, but eventually, he's plopping down on the couch with a gruff sigh. His body leaden from my newly learned defense spell.

"You know I could break out of this if I wanted to," he scoffs while wiggling against the invisible binds.

Both Aster and I watch him fail to do exactly that for a few seconds before I climb into his lap in a fit of victorious laughter.

"Whatever you say, big guy. What do you wanna watch first?" I say, displaying our options in a floating carousel.

Corn quietly watches the DVDs twirl in midair. I know he says he's behind on TV and I plan on rectifying that. Starting with the black classics.

"You're becoming far too proficient at this," he finally says.

Originally I thought he was referring to my magic, but that impressed glimmer in his eyes says otherwise.

"At what?" I ask.

"At making me question everything about my life," he replies cooly.

Our gazes align and suddenly all of the late nights spent studying for the coven with Corn come rushing back. All of his gently explanations. His animated narration voices. All of our inside jokes. All of our shared laughter. Our meals, conversations, and borrowed kisses. All of the times he looked at me as if I were the answer to the age old question: What's the meaning of life?

I suddenly realize that I'm in love with my demon husband.

And I think he might even love me back.

"But I guess we can go in chronological order. Media tends to build upon itself with references," he shrugs, refocusing me.

It takes me a moment to realize what he's talking about. Right. We were supposed to be watching stuff. Not battling life-alternating emotions. Definitely not falling in love.

"Ok, let's start simple. Here's Harlem Nights," I say, opening the case. "The perfect movie for old men."

"Hush, little witch," Corn scoffs while pulling me close.

I settle onto his firm chest with a pathetic whimper, soaking up all his signature scent before his heart beat renders me otherwise speechless, and in that moment I know for sure that we will never be able to separate fully.

"Wait, there's no way he's playing all the main characters in this movie!"

"Yes, Corn. He does this all the time. You just saw him do it in the Nutty professor."

"Are you for real? I thought he just casted his actual family."

"No sir. He the grandma's baby."

Our black classics catch up session turned into Eddie Murphython. We were four movies in, and after watching Norbit, Corn had noticed a pattern.

"So everybody just lets him get away with shit like this?" he asks.

"Shit like what?" I chuckle.

"Portraying the ugliest woman I've ever seen in this millennium. This is a crime."

"Probably," I concede in a fit of laughter.

I sling my body over the side of the couch in an effort to catch my breath, only for it to start all over again when I see Corn rewinding the movie to study "Mr. Wong." Out of all the characters, I personally believe this one is the most egregious.

"How is this not a hate crime?" Corn gasps, finally spotting the Eddie.

"I don't have an answer for you," I giggle. "Everybody just went with it."

"Everybody belongs in jail," he huffs.

"Even me?" I exclaim, straightening my posture.

"Especially you," he says, pulling me onto his lap. "Some demure counterbalance you are."

I begin to part my lips in protest but Corn silences me, pressing his mouth to mine. His kiss is respectful at first, but it's been a week since we last did anything and I'm eager to de-stress. I pull his warm tongue into my mouth and suck, enjoying the sweet taste of orange tea and the savory popcorn salt.

It's a move that gets me flipped onto my ass. My back collides with the conditioned leather and then Corn settles between my open legs, never once breaking our heated kiss. He only briefly tears away when his elected form sheds so he can drop his lower arms at my side.

"Candrima," Corn moans.

Those sinfully large fingers of his traipse up my right thigh, kneading my pliant skin masterfully with every passing inch. They leave a scorching trail in their wake. One that burns as bright as the desire in his blood-orange eyes.

"Cornelius," I gasp, succumbing to his covetous touch.

Nose to nose and cheek to cheek, I finally understand why it's so dangerous to belong to a demon. His beautiful mouth curls into a truly insidious grin as I arch my back to meet his beckoning hand, grinding my hips to the hypnotic twirl of his hungry tongue against his plush lips. My thoughts become just husks of ideas as he commands me.

Body, mind, and soul.

His hand remains an unrelenting source of pleasure as his lust magic works to increase my stamina. Orgasm after orgasm is pulled from my shaky body, making platinum tears spill against my marbled skin.

"Little witch," he laughs hauntingly. "Tell me what's wrong."

Every single one of his razor sharp teeth is made fully visible by his sinister smile. His fingers spread me wider as I struggle to answer. Every time I regain some measure of control his nimble thumb strokes my thumping clit faster.

"Corn," I sob. "What are you doing to me?"

I've never seen him like this before. His coal black eyes shine with the delectation he's deriving from my torture. Every time I writhe underneath him, his smile grows. Every time my breath hitches, his purring intensifies.

"Corn..."

"Cry louder, Candy," he responds, his deep voice curdling my insides. "Maybe it'll convince me to grant you mercy."

I move to grimace, but the stern edge of my expression melts into another breathless release, becoming all but useless. Corn is punishing me for something, that much is obvious, but I don't know what I did.

"Why, baby? Why are you doing this?" I sob.

My thighs are warm and sticky, I've soaked the couch and he's wet up to his elbow, yet he shows no signs of stopping.

I watch his hand grip around his challenging length in a daze, only realizing my fixation when my mouth waters. His bulbous tip is dripping with viscous pre-cum that almost sparkles underneath the evening lanterns.

I want a taste.

Luckily Corn reads my mind before I'm forced to beg like a starving harlot.

"You want me just as bad as I want you. Don't you, pretty witch?"

I nod my yes to be rewarded with a soft smile and his subsequent retreat before I'm lowered to my knees.

You know that meme of Tinkerbell hugging a truly unethical sized dick? Yeah, well I never thought there'd be a day when I'd be recreating that, but here we are. Corn towers over me impressively, resting his angry summer sausage against my bottom lip. I have to admit I'm appreciative that he lets me set the pace, because there's no way I'm not putting this in my mouth without some kind of mental pep talk.

So I start slowly by cuffing my hands around his girth and stroking him. It takes no time at all for his head to roll back between his shoulders, knocked loose from the rush of pleasure. I'm sure he thinks this is for him, but it's really scratching my itch. I love sliding my hands over his heated, throbbing ridges. It fixes my brain.

Can you say sensory issues?

"Candrimaaaaa," he moans as I take him into my mouth. "Fuck, you genitive little temptress."

The walls of the house shake from his soprano grunts as I slide my tongue down his sensitive frenum, the bass in his voice disturbing everything within 100ft. I also hear his horns softly scraping against the ceiling and it reminds me to fix the accomodation spell after we get finished, but I table that thought for now and focus on enjoying pushing him to the edge.

Until he slides one of his tails inside of me.

Fun Fact about Succubi: They have twice as many erogenous zones as most of the magical population.

Tails and armpits are included in that count. Meaning he's getting just as much pleasure as I am from the way his tail is thrusting in and out of me.

"Jamanichei. So wet," he hisses, pinching his bottom lip between his fangs.

"So hard," I reply, bobbing my head against his length.

It's honestly a wonder I'm still breathing. His steeled length is quite a bit more than the mouthful I'm used to from human men. It's so much I have to brace both my hands against his thighs to keep rhythm. It's almost too much, especially with his salacious tail fucking me and the big clawed hand he has laced through my curls.

It feels so good that another treacherous wave of pleasure begins to overtake me, and I know Corn won't be far behind me based on his sweet moans and bad language. Apparently I'm a very good little whore, and I plan to show him just how good before the day's end. With that goal in mind, I prepare myself to swallow that octuple shot with no chaser as his balls tighten from impending release, but as soon as I come to expect my reward, he withdraws from my mouth and de-manifests into a shadowy mess.

"Corn, what's wrong?" I ask, freeing my hair from his tightening grip.

He doesn't answer, but his ears do turn slightly when he returns to solid, searching for a noise that I'm not making. I'm beyond frustrated to have my orgasm snatched from me like shake-n-go a wig in a club fight, but I know there must be a reason for Corn to deny me, so I remain quiet and still.

Until Dart lunges at a vase.

It shatters spectacularly, decorating the freshly polished hardwood in shards of blue ceramic and scaring the absolute shit out of both me and Aster. But before I can scold him about his random bout of destruction, a form separates from the hearth wall in a fit of coughing from the dislodged dust. Once the debris clears from her skin, I can see that she's rightly beautiful. With bright yellow eyes that round against her high cheekbones, sharp upper fangs, small twisted horns, a heart shaped mouth, and hot pink skin.

"Nilla," Corn growls.

"Fuck, Corn. Were you trying to kill a bitch?" she asks.

"Yes," he replies simply, tail still aimed toward her person.

"This is how you treat your favorite sister? Yikes."

Oh thank God. I thought she was one of his ex-lovers, but no, she's his sister. That does provide some relief to make up for the weird way she's looking at me; Like I'm a meal she'd like to partake in. She snickers before tapping the small clear plastic piece in her ear.

"I found him, but I might need to come back," she says, tilting her head to look at me. "Looks like he was in the middle of mating."

I immediately summon clothing for both of us. Unfortunately Corn won't shift back so I have to sacrifice one of my stretchy Walmart mumus to cover all his bulging muscles. The cotton candy color and animated unicorn doesn't make him look any less menacing. The way the sleeves cling to his biceps make it worse, if anything.

"Who are you talking to!?" he demands.

"Relax, it's just Cyrus. He had me come find you because he got your blood test results back. Apparently you're really good at this location hopping thing," she says, flicking her braids over her shoulder.

"He didn't tell me she was so cute though."

She casts me a mischievous smile before reaching into what I'm 90% sure is the skin of her upper thigh to produce a phone, but when she aims at me to take a picture, Corn loses his shit.

"NO PHONES!" he hisses.

His tail launches through the back of the device, shattering the glass and camera lens, and before Nilla can attempt to recover it, he uses my powers to send it two continents over and a realm down. Essentially, her phone is in purgatory.

I'm still grappling with the fact that he's able to piggyback off my powers, but I quickly move on seeing that Nilla is terrified from seeing her brother's second set of arms appear. His upper eyes blink open and flash with undeniable fury over her intrusion, while his voice shakes the house with a tone of violent agitation.

"How dare you violate my home?" he growls, pacing closer to her.

His enormous foot stomps against the floor so hard that I fear the wood might splinter. Each step makes every living thing wince, including his sister.

"Corn, I forgot. I didn't mean any harm by it. We both know I play too much. Let's calm down for a second," she says, scrambling into the nearby corner for safety.

Her words don't mean much to the giant, angry, menacing demon. I can tell that he feels threatened by her presence, and when a vision flashes across my eyes of Corn putting a hole in the wall 60 seconds from now, it confirms that I need to take control of this situation. Sure, she trespassed, interrupted an intimate moment, and possibly put our safety and freedom at risk, but she was his sister! Betty was the closest thing I had to a sibling, and yet that felt pretty on brand for that sort of relationship. After all, I'd done that to her too.

So I teleport in front of Nilla, spreading my arms and legs wide to shield her against Corn's unpredictable tails. He's still mad, but he does hesitate, and so I do the only thing I can think to do in the moment.

I start to sing.

Now I know someone at BET would have a field day hearing that, but it's true. For some reason unknown to me, I begin to sing. The song is foreign to my ears but familiar to my lips, and after a while Corn begins to sway to the melody, confirming it's familiar to him too.

Finally he calms down. His form reverts back to classic Corn. Still tall and menacing, but with a manageable amount of appendages.

Relieved, I turn to help Nilla up from the ground.

"He taught you the family language?" she asks.

"You all have a family language?"

"Yes, of course. All demons have family languages. The song you just sang was a lullaby created for us specifically."

"Oh, I didn't know that. Something just told me to sing it so I did."

Nilla's eyes widen before narrowing to display what I believe is skepticism. She glances between me and Corn a few times before shaking her head in defeat. Which very much creeps me out.

"You won't separate that bond," she says. "You're too interwoven as it is. What do you think will happen in a month, let alone two?"

Right. Because we had a month before Heaven opened to visitors. A month before the separation was even remotely possible, and that possibility was getting scarcer by the second. But Corn doesn't acknowledge that, he just lowers his head and softens his tone to apologize.

"I'm so sorry for almost attacking you. I don't know what happened, you just felt like a threat," he explains to Nilla.

She looks at me one more time, tipping her head to look at my neck.

"I felt like a threat to your mate. I get it," she nods. "This bind is still new, but it's strong."

He winces hearing that.

"You said Cyrus wants us?" he asks, not so subtly changing the subject.

"Yeah," she nods. "He wants to go over your blood work. He says it's urgent, but that's all I know."

"Ok. Let us dress and we'll be on our way," Corn sighs. "Come on, Candy."

Cyrus is waiting for us when we land. Unlike our first visit, there are no staff or patients around. The room is dark, the curtains are drawn.

"Finally, I've been trying to reach you for weeks," Cyrus exclaims.

"About our car's extended warranty?" I reply.

NIlla snorts but Cyrus face remains grave and unmovable. I've only met him once before but this seems highly uncharacteristic based off what I have witnessed. Is this about my species? Is he about to tell us he's changed his mind and we actually should separate?

"Come with me to the back," he says firmly to Corn and I. "Nilla, wait out here."

He allows no time for questions before he whisks off toward a secluded exam room in the back. Based on the look Corn gives me, he doesn't know what's happening either, so we just shrug it off and follow wordlessly. Once everyone is safely over the threshold, Cyrus erects a literal firewall to guard the door, his eyes glowing with blue and orange flames that match the defense.

"Is this about Candy?" Corn asks, pulling out my seat. "Because we already know that she's a Moonlight Witch. Kita told us."

Cyrus chuckles, and the dark, throaty sound sends an eerie shiver down my spine.

"Trust me, that is the least of our worries," he says, drawing up a folder of paperwork.

He hands both me and Corn our own printouts, but it does nothing to ease my confusion because the paper is blank.

"Fi Han!" he demands, and ink appears.

It's a blood test result, but it's not for me. The patient this is referring to is one Cornelius Esqin Bankole, who according to the DNA results, is 75% Hell Spawn. Imperial Shadow Demon to be exact.

"What? What does this mean?" Corn gasps, reading over the paper for a third time.

Cyrus, who was the epitome of calm that last time we visited, hunches over his desk with a deep grimace accompanied by a maddening chuckle.

"It means that you're not a succubus, Corn. You're the King Of Shadows. The missing Sixth Prince Of Hell."

Reality

Corn

"That's impossible," I reply.

There's so much more I want to say, but it my mind is moving too fast for me to speak anymore than two words. I have what feels like the worst headache in existence because my brother just told me that I'm supposed to be a Son Of Hell. Which, by all accounts, is impossible.

"Nothing is impossible, Corn. It should be impossible for Candy to even have a claim bond considering she's nearly Primordial. Yet here we are. Bonded and shit."

I consider his words, but there are so many things about this that doesn't make sense. Demon monarchies are awarded to the first child of the current King or Queen regardless of gender. My parents aren't royal and I'm not even the first son, let alone the first child. I'm four of four. The only thing I should be awarded is a *You Tried* consolation medal.

"I'm hardly the prince of anything. I'm very clearly not the first child. One of you would in line well before me. What about Nafisa? Then seventy-five percent? There isn't even egbere DNA listed on here. This doesn't make sense."

"You're right. There is no egbere lineage listed here," he confirms with a nod. "Because we don't have the same father."

"What?" I stammer.

Cyrus shakes his head in disbelief before showing me two more files.

"I ran my own DNA against yours when I first got your results back, because you're right, it doesn't make sense. Here you are 75% Hell Spawn with almost negligible cuccubus DNA while I'm split 60/40. While the girls are split 60/40. I even ran the test thrice because nothing about this lines up. Until I got to thinking, what if the solution is simple? What if my dad, our dad, isn't your biological father? That would explain why you're so big, why your task magic is so vast, and why you have impeccable shadow control. You can transcend realms via shadows. Mama can't do that and she's five times your age," he explains.

His logic hangs heavy in the air. I never considered there was a reason for my excessive growth beyond the luck of the draw when my siblings were so small. The all had smaller statures from our father, *their father,* when I was eight feet tall in my hybrid form. I never questioned my need for darkness and solitude. I never gave Vale's comments a second thought. But now...

"Why would Mama cheat on Baba? Why didn't they tell me when I got to age?" I shout.

Cyrus jumps from the distortion waving in my voice, but Candy remains calm, stroking my back and channeling reassurance through our bond. My head snaps to her in that moment, rushing with a thousand new problems this creates for her. How could she possibly be bound to a Hell Spawn? What did this mean for her and her life?

"What about our bond?" I gasp.

"That's the other thing," Cyrus says, defeat lingering in his voice. "Corn, you both are nearly immortal. This isn't just a regular old monogamy bind. It doens't make sense for the immortal to be able to drop mates on a whim and create a whole bunch of potentially omnipotent illegitimate children. When you bound her to yourself, you bound her to your people as well. You bound her to Hell."

His words twist in my chest like a jack knife. I've damned Candrima to Hell. A sorceress who needs the moonlight like she needs air. I've committed an egregious wrong and I have to fix it.

"We'll get The Sword Of Destiny. There's still time. It's only been six weeks," I argue.

Candy's grip on my hand tightens.

"Corn, baby. I don't think we can sever this," she says quietly while cupping my face. "I think we're in it for the long haul."

Her soft hands sweep the fallen tears off my cheeks and finally, all the emotions I've been withholding for the past month seep out, and I wail, realizing the extent of damage that I've caused.

"Candy, you'll die. You cannot live in Hell!"

"Hey, Mister. I won't die, we can figure something out," she nods. "Can't we Cyrus?"

"Uh, yes! From what I've fou-"

"No! No! Don't tell me about all the ways you can give her a half life!" I shout. "Tell me how we can separate!" I demand.

My brother winces, his expression confirming what he's already said.

"Corn, I don't think you can. Time and sword aside, this bond is unprecedented, and it's strong. The next month is only going to make it stronger. Candy will go into another heat, you two will share another meal, another smile. Nilla told me that you can piggyback off each other's powers. She's just as much a part of you as you are of her. It may already be too late. Any possible solution at this point will come with great risks. Too many risks," he explains.

I can't accept that. I won't be the reason Candy suffers in this life or the next.

"I'm going to see Mama. This has to be wrong," I announce.

I stand to travel before Cyrus can begin to protest, but I linger just long enough to hear, *"Corn, no!"* before I land in the third realm of Hell, Candrima by my side.

It's still day when we arrive. I thought about portaling directly to my parent's house, but I decided against it, wanting Candy to see all the lakes and rivers since we were already here, That and I was trying to convince myself that this was all a gigantic misunderstanding. That Nilla would fall out the sky any minute now and tell me it was a joke.

Unfortunately she never did.

"Corn, how long are we gonna fly in circles?" Candy asks against my chest.

She points to the winding river that we've passed twice already. The fisherman in the area have long docked for the day, and their boats float contently, bracing the idle black current.

I realize that this probably isn't the most comfortable position for her to be in long term, and my guilt deepens.

"I'm sorry. I just don't know what to say."

"Start small," she suggests. "Ask a question."

Her recommendation does sound feasible, but it comes with it's own set of challenges. What would I even ask? Why did you cheat on your husband? Why did you lie?

"What kind of question?"

"Whatever feels right. Maybe ask about your powers?"

That was neutral enough territory. My mother and I shared these powers. It was a benign question if asked correctly. A nice light segway into who actually sired me.

"Ok," I nod, descending from the skies.

"Thank goodness," Candy mutters. "I was afraid I was going to piss on one of these poor farmers."

We're standing in front of my family home in no time. The stone entrance has been polished recently judging by the heavy smell of silica lingering in the air, and the roses I planted three decades ago have been trimmed. I could stand out here for hours, picking apart all the things that were different from the last time I visited but none of those things make me feel better about what's really changed: Me.

"Corn, we have to go in eventually. We look creepy standing out here and I have to pee," Candy says.

She's right, I know she's right, but my feet feel glued to the ground. What if we go in and my Mama confirms everything? Where does that leave me? The odd demon out, or the family bastard? Maybe I'll be the worst kept secret.

"You're none of those things," Candy says firmly. "Regardless of what happens in there, you're still Corn. Nothing will change that."

Our shared mind reading ability spooked me at first, but I don't think I'd change it for all the world. Especially given what's going on right here and now.

"Thank you for doing this with me," I whisper.

"Of course, big guy. It's like you said, we'll get through it one step at a time. Together," she nods.

My chest tightens when she blesses me with an extra bright smile. It's not particularly big or flashy, but it's so warm and comforting that it gives me enough energy to handle what's next: Raising my hand and knocking on the door.

The doorman charm recognizes me as a resident and the door creaks open to reveal a smile similar to Candy's. One belonging to the first Priestess Of Hell.

"Oh, Cornelius. I didn't know you were stopping by. Who's this?" Mama asks.

It takes far too long for her question to register, but luckily Candy is on it.

"Hello, Misses Bankole. I'm Candrima, Corn's bound mate," she says cheerily.

I'm once again conflicted by how right that sounds. My mate. My Candy.

"You're just as beautiful as Cyrus said," Mama beams. "Please come in, you two."

"Nafisa! Corn is here!" she announces, ushering us down the great hall into the living room.

"Uncle PopCorn!" Charlie shrieks.

As soon as I step over the threshold, my niece barrels into me head-first, her little wings still flapping while she wraps her sticky fingers around my neck for a hug.

"Hi, Crawly," I laugh, blowing her wild curls out of my eyes. "I missed you."

"I missed you too! I have a fang now, and Mommy says I'll have a little brother soon!"

She turns to Candrima, eyes as big as the 5th realm's sun and smiler wider than an Orc. "Hi, I'm Charlie! What's your name?"

"Hi Charlie, your uncle has told me a lot about you. I'm Candrima."

"That a pretty name," Charlie cooes. "I like your skin. It's cool. I'm purple."

"Purple's my favorite color," Candy nods back.

"My favorite color is yellow because Uncle PopCorn knitted me a yellow blankie when I was born. Uncle PopCorn, are you knitting my new brother a blankie too?" she asks.

Nafisa whisks in belly first before I can answer, Sven's blue behind hot on her tail. I know by the twitch in her upper lip that this conversation will not be a casual one. Not that it ever is with Nafisa. She's been Mom 2.0 regarding me ever since I could remember.

"Charlie, sweetie. Go with daddy for a second so I can talk to your uncle," she says, extending no formalities.

Charlie looks at me like she's been stabbed and my heart breaks. It's been so long since we've seen each other and it's 100% my fault. I can't be Uncle Sitting as a wanted criminal.

"Can I go with Uncle PopCorn and Miss Candrima for dinner?" she pleads while walking towards her dad.

"Not tonight, sweetie," Nafisa sighs. "Maybe next time."

"Ok, Mama," she says, slumping her small shoulders. "See you later Uncle Popcorn."

The defeated little wave she gives me when she walks off is enough to make me grovel at my sister's feet for forgiveness, but Nafisa was never a fan of groveling.

"Corn," she hisses. "How could you go on the run? Now I have a fugitive for a brother!"

"It's complicated Fis," I groan, throwing my head back. "This isn't something I can just pay a fine for or appeal."

Finally she notices Candrima.

"Apologies, where are my manners? I'm Nafisa Hark. You must be the witch who cursed my brother," she snarks, throwing an aggressive handshake in Candrima's direction.

The action is beyond rude. Still, Candy accepts rather graciously before correcting her.

"Actually, I'm a sorceress. And technically we cursed each other."

Nafisa has been working at the EUM for the last two centuries so she's not surprised by much, but hearing Candrima say our curse is mutual nearly pops her eyes out of their sockets.

"What do you mean?" she gasps. "Corn cursed you how?"

"I accidentally put an IMB on her," I sigh.

"You put a permanent mating bond on a sorceress!? Corn, that's illegal!" Nafisa shrieks.

"I'm aware," I nod. "Hence my current fugitive status."

"Who's a fugitive?" Mama ask.

Nafisa hesitates, but suddenly a hot bright ball of blue fire lands in the fireplace, and Cyrus materializes and answers for her.

"Corn!" he screams.

Nilla pushes from behind him, forcing him onto the rug while she shakes off the loose embers, which I'm sure we'll all hear about later.

We exchange puzzled looks because this is the first time we've all been in a room together since Charlie was born.

"Well, well. The gangs all here," Nilla laughs. "What Cyrus meant to say was, Corn is on his way to confront you about your lies."

Mama's perfectly plucked eyebrows arch.

"Who's lies?" she asks.

I shake my head, begging her not to, but it seems Nilla has her own agenda.

"He had a DNA test, Ma," she says.

I expected my mother to shudder or freeze, but she remains steady in both words and expression. Neutral, unreadable.

"Corn, what does Nilla mean you had a DNA test?" Nafisa asks.

Her voice carries all the concern and fear I thought my Mama might have. It's odd. Besides Vale, there's only one other person who's ever referred to me as a Son Of Hell. My sister.

"Did you know?" I gasp.

She shrinks back, her posture losing some of it's notorious firmness.

"It's complicated, Cornelius," she whispers.

I realize that I may very well be the first affected but the last to find out based on the looks that my siblings exchange. Cyrus and Nilla look apologetic, Nafisa looks ashamed, but my mother... She looks like she could punch someone through the chest. Which is ironic, given I'm the one who must now bare the consequences.

"How long have you known?" I chuckle awkwardly. "Why didn't you tell me?"

"I've had my suspicions for a few years now," Nilla admits.

"Me too," adds Cyrus.

My older sister remains quiet and stares at the clay tile, unwilling to volunteer testimony.

"Fis, how long have you known?" I demand.

Her eyes meet mine, and I swear I can almost swim in the regret present.

"Corn, you have to understand. Your birth…"

"You've known since I was born, Nafisa!?" I shout.

Candy takes my hand, pushing calm through our bond, but all that does is make me cry. She didn't sign up for the latest episode of Family Secret Fun. She didn't sign up to be Hell's concubine.

"Why didn't you tell me the night you stopped by and my form changed?" I sputter.

"Corn, I couldn't," she exclaims. "It wasn't my secret to tell."

Finally my mother chips in.

"Your form changed?" she gasps.

Irritated, that this is the first thing she says regarding the situation, I disgracefully shed my hybrid form and let the harrowing scraping sound of my horns against the ceiling fill the air. My mother winces as if someone has raised a hand to her.

"This was definitely not at your last checkup," Cyrus mumbles.

"This is my worst nightmare," Mama whispers.

"Ma," Nafisa chides. "Stop."

Fat tears fall against my hot skin, unfocusing my eyes and sparing me the full pain of the disgust in my mother's eyes. It's new and heartbreaking and all I want to know is,

"Why? Why would you hide something this important from me? Does Baba know?" I sob.

"Corn, you have to believe me when I say I wanted to tell you," Nafisa argues.

"Then why didn't you?"

"Because I forbade her," Mama interjects.

Silence befalls the room like a heavy quilt, suffocating everything except the sound of muffled breathing.

"I did not want you!" she hisses. "When I found out what you were, I did not want you!"

Her words punch me in the heart. It's been so long since I was a youngling, but the memories of my mother's strange distance come rushing back. I always assumed it was because I was the last child and she was tired, never did I assume that she didn't want me. After all, I was still her son.

Wasn't I?

I choke at thought of my self-imposed question, and Candy rushes forward, shielding me from my mother's wrath.

"We should go," she says.

I nod, the possibility of fleeing tasting sweet on my tongue before my sister extends a hand to stop us.

"Corn," Nafisa says, trying to reconcile the situation. "You have to understand that Mama didn't have a choice."

"Yeah, well neither did I! I just woke up one day in a body that I couldn't control, and I was so clueless about what was happening that I blamed it on someone else. You let Candy take the blame for this and you knew, Fis! You knew!"

"I didn't mean to," she cries. "I promise I didn't mean to hurt you like this."

"It's not just me anymore, Fisa. I didn't know what I was and I bound Candy to Hell. She's a moonlight witch. She could die in Hell. She could die because of me!"

"That's not her fault," Mama hisses.

Nafisa steps forward, her own tears streaking her ruby skin.

"Corn, we can fix this. If Candy surrenders to the EUM we can..."

"NO!" I growl. "You know they'll use her like a generator. She'll be a glorified battery pack for the whims of Heaven."

I've read plenty about what they do to dark magic beings. They turn them into energy experiments, vision mills, and weapons of war. I will not subject Candrima to any part of that, not for any amount of ease. I turn my back and rush towards Candy, hoping we can still escape this mess. Hoping I can lick my wounds in peace, but Nafisa is determined.

"Corn, just hear me out," Nafisa says, following after me.

"I SAID NO!" I bark, eyes filling with blood.

The entire house rattles and shakes from the bass of my voice, sending Cyrus and Nilla stumbling back into the walls. Candrima and Nafisa stand firm however, unmoved by my outburst. I realize then that my temper is once again getting the best of me, but before I can apologize, a spear lands between the tiles in front of my feet. Shattering the fortified ceramic.

"Stay away from my daughter, you insidious bastard!" Mama yells, jumping in front of Nafisa.

"Mama, stop it!" Nafisa yells, while trying to push forward.

My mother remains in a defensive stance, ready to launch another spear my way at a moment's notice. I'd never hurt my sisters, but it's clear that she doesn't care. Her eyes swell with a hatred I've only read about in books, and it's directed at me. Finally it hits me. I was never her child, I was just something she was burdened with. Some secret that's been looming over her, festering, threatening to erupt. I walk backwards until Candrima's hand latches onto mine, then with one final sniffle, I let her take me wherever she wants to go.

Candy

Hell is undeniably beautiful.

When Corn first described the planes to me, it was a little difficult to visualize. How were the realms layered? What was going on with the mountains? What did he mean the rivers flowed backwards? I just couldn't create a picture for it in my mind but now having visited thrice across three different planes, I see exactly what he was trying to describe. The winding rivers with currents that push upwards instead of down. The interplaneal mountains. The spry flora. The curious fauna. It's all so beautiful.

Too bad we'll never go back.

Listen, I know my family isn't always perfect, but at the end of the day we love each other. That shit there though, nah.

Fuck nah.

I could never imagine treating anyone I birthed that way, no matter what happened. Let alone someone as wonderful as Corn. Yes, he had a temper, but he had just found out that the last 188 years of his life were a lie. Then on top of that, he was going through a huge life change with an accidental partnership that is still very volatile. The only reason he yelled at Nafisa and Nilla was because I felt scared. He was protecting me. She had to know that.

But even if she didn't, as a mother, you extend grace. I can't tell you how many times my mom has forgiven me for doing something stupidly selfish. I've heard my fair share of lectures and lessons, but never did my Mama make me feel like I wasn't wanted. She often told me that she wish she could have had three of me.

Speaking of my mama, I'm supposed to be writing her my weekly letter, but I accidentally parked the house in Hell after Nilla brought a phone over. Glee offered us his help and his back lot of we should ever need it, and I accepted since the EUM has no jurisdiction in Hell. I wasn't thinking clearly though because I forgot I would have to bring it back.

Luckily the Amalfi coast has plenty of moonlight to spare. Tilting my head to my celestial charge, I bathe in the platinum warmth she exudes. I've always loved the moon, and now I know why. I am a representative of her. An embodiment of her power. I stand still for no fewer than ten minutes, and when I've finally collected enough strength, I bring the house back. It lands 200 feet behind me with a bright flash and an obnoxiously loud bang. I'm sure something has gotten knocked off the walls during transport, but luckily I've mastered task magic in recent days. I'm officially sworn off manual cleaning. Except for the occasional crumb sweep.

Once I check that the house is situated and get the fireplace going, I wander off to find Corn. When we first got back, he silently asked for some alone time to process everything. I didn't mind because I had malice to discharge, plus I needed to summon the cabin, but now it was getting late. The location charm would go back to work in a couple of hours, and we'd be moving once again. He still needed to eat and wash the day off.

"Corn?" I call, spotting a fire blazing wildly through the thick and thorny brush.

I don't get a response, but I quickly figured out why. Corn is in the fire, balled up into fetal position, letting death take him.

"CORN, WHAT THE FUCK!?" I scream, trying to figure out how to extinguish him. "No, no, no! You will not die on me!"

I'm not able to summon water fast enough to put out the death circle encompassing him, so I relocate some of the Earth, hoping the packed dirt will extinguish the flames. To my relief it does work, but as soon as the smoke clears from the air, the fire re-ignites on its own, engulfing him once again.

I stand there with my mouth open like a catfish while the big guy rolls over to face me, his eyes the only thing clearly visible.

"Calm down, Candrima. Fire can't kill me," he sighs. "I'm a Hell Spawn."

I've never heard something that was supposed to be reassuring said so resentfully.

"Do you want the fire to kill you?"

"In an ideal world, yes. But then again if it was that easy my mother probably would've offed me a long time ago."

Yikes on several fucking bikes. I don't know what to say to that. Partially because I've never experienced such a dysfunctional family dynamic, and partially because I'd be lying if I said he was wrong. She launched a spear at him.

"Corn, sweetie. You can't let her get to you," I sigh. "Come out of the fire and eat some dinner. You'll feel better."

"No thank you. I'd rather burn," he says, rolling back over into the ash.

The defeat I feel in this moment is bone crushing, but I know I just can't leave him. Distance will help no one. So I straighten my back and head towards the cabin, determined to get my husband out of his pit of despair.

I slowly rotate my skewer, careful not to let my snack catch on fire. It doesn't take long for the pretty pink to bubble and sizzle, eventually turning a nice toasty brown. But before I can pull it back to me, a large hand plucks it from the end of my stick.

Good thing I had two on there.

"What is this?" Corn asks, chewing loudly.

"You're just putting things in your mouth without knowing what they are?"

"Isn't that the whole reason we're in this situation? Nothing has changed."

I try not to laugh, but the chuckle sneaks past my lips anyway, eager to fill the air and mingle with the sounds of crackling embers.

"It's a strawberry milkshake marshmallow. One of my favorites," I answer.

"It's very good," he sighs. "Much better than that disgusting candle wax you try to pass off as candy."

He's yet to pass on the opportunity to call me a wax eater.

"You know I don't have to share right?" I say, biting into the deliciously gooey fluff.

"But I'm sad."

"Mhm, here with yo begging ass," I say, loading three more onto the skewer.

We sit in a companionable silence for a while, filling up on marshmallows and the peaceful sway of the nearby ocean. I'll have to remember to bring the house here again because it's a gorgeous area, and it's even better at night. Eventually though I hit the bottom of the bag, and when I announce that we're all out of little treats, Corn exits the fire with a loud huff. Smoke rising from his coal-hot skin.

"I'll be back," he says. "Head to the house."

I don't argue although I'm still a bit concerned. Regardless of how bad today has been, I trust Corn to come back to me.

Aster Chitters in my direction as soon as I step through the door, asking why I smell smokey. I still can't speak Eldritch, but Corn put a translation charm on audible speech so I can understand my little sweet beans better. After claiming that he still doesn't care for him.

"I sat by the fire. Did you enjoy your time in Hell?"

"Mrrll. Prt."

I caught a sparrow. It was delicious.

I wince at the vision of Aster ripping the wings off some poor bird, but who am I to judge? I'll take a twelve piece order of ranch rub flats with mild sauce down so fast.

Before I can ask Aster anything else about his day, he drags a large envelope from behind his and Corn's favorite chair. For the size, I have to admit that it's neatly packed. There isn't a centimeter of paper out of place, and when I pick it up I know why. It's from Nafisa.

"What's that?" Corn asks, water dripping from his limbs.

He must've taken a dip in the ocean to cool off.

He looks much more relaxed and my first instinct is to lie about the package, but I know he'll feel it through our bond. So I hold out the package with two hands and offer it to him. He immediately rejects it when he sees the sender, but the longer I hold it, the more I feel he should open it.

"I'm just going to open it for you," I say, placing the kettle on the stove.

Corn gives me a disinterested grunt and goes back to chopping his onions while I tear into the neatly wrapped parcel like a feral racoon. Eventually he stops prepping the veggies to judge what I'm doing, but I feel little shame for this. Envelopes are meant to be torn.

"It's a record," I say. "Actually a few of them."

I hold up a parchment filled with Corn's family tree, amazed that it's actually alive. Names are being added and moved every few minutes or so, including mine. It's just barely visible but Candrima Castille is slowly appearing next to Cornelious Bankole-Olakanye, King Of Shadows.

"Is that you?" Corn says, pointing to the shadowy text.

"I think so," I nod.

Seeing that the documents are worth investigating, he washes his hands and takes over my spot at the table to read through them. Meanwhile I take over dinner, and ditch whatever salad plans he appears to have. We need some comfort food. Something heavy and starchy.

"You're quiet," I say once I get my beans on the stove. "What'd you find out?"

"Apparently I have three younger brothers," he sighs, pointing to the side of the paper. "Also, I think this may be my aunt or something, but her name moves a lot."

"Interesting," I say. "I wonder why one of them hasn't taken over the throne."

"They can't," he sighs. "Hell is extremely structured, contrary to popular belief. If you inherit a monarchy, you must rule that monarchy. Robust magic enforces the birth order decree, and the consequences for trying to usurp a rightful ruler are grave."

"Even if you don't want it?" I ask.

"Even if I don't want it," he sighs.

I sense guilt eating at Corn as he continues to review the documents. Apparently his realm has not fared well without a ruler. Some villages are in a famine. Compared to other realms they have less schools, less tourism, and less children being born. His people, *our people*, are dying.

"I think I need to go down here," he sighs. "At least to meet my brothers and this maybe auntie."

"Ok, let me know when," I say.

That earns me a strange look. One that I quickly return. We stare at each other, unblinking until Corn looks away, eyes burning with tears. Seems I'll remain undefeated there.

"Candy, you aren't coming with me."

I flick his nose and smile at him like the silly goose he is,

"And that's where you're wrong."

"Candrima, we've talked about this," he grouses, dragging his hand down his handsome face. "You cannot survive in Hell."

"Actually we didn't because you wouldn't let Cyrus talk, but either way, you're wrong. I've done some research and the general consensus is that Moonlight Witches need about twenty four hours of the good stuff a week. Three days, with eight hours of night a week solves that problem. I'll pack Aster up and we'll plan to be Out Of Office for three days with an extra day available just in case, and as soon as I'm done with Monday's coven meeting, we can dip and go to Alaska or some shit," I explain.

We both know he's lost this battle when he rises from the table with a huff and stomps off.

Candy, 2. Corn, 0.

"Corn, now that's just big,"

I watch while Corn drags his tongue across the plate, licking up residual beans like it's his last meal. Red beans and rice is one of my favorites, and based on the way Corn damn near nibbles on the actual plate, it might be one of his favorites too.

"I remember when you used to lick me like that," I mutter as he continues to violate the dinnerware.

Suddenly he stops, inky black eyes trained on mine. It's clear he's turned on, but I really don't know if it's due to the food or what I said.

"Is that a request?" he purrs.

Listen, I promise I have a sense of self-preservation, but the way his gaze swallows my body makes me poke my chest out a little more. I've learned first-hand that it's a bad idea to incite a demon countless times before and yet I can't help myself. Besides, what do we live for if not to get our souls sucked out of our clits?

Corn raises a brow in my direction,

"Is there more?" he asks with a sultry smile.

I have as much brain as a mosquito at that point because I immediately reach to open my collar, confident that he's requesting a show only to hear,

"I meant more food, but this is nice too."

"Oh shit, sorry," I mumble, scrambling from the table to refill his plate.

"Please don't stop on my account," he laughs.

I'm flustered and I don't know if there will ever be a point in our relationship when I'm not. Even if we were to somehow remove my bond. There's just something about this demon that makes my cheeks tingle. Maybe it's his generosity. Although it could be the consideration I'm shown when he offers to twist my hair. Or maybe it's his slightly dry sense of humor coupled with that mischievous twinkle in his animated eyes. And that smile that could only be born of magic.

Thinking about that smile made me completely miss the plate when I dipped the spoon down to heap an extra serving. Thinking about that smile made me so loopy that I don't even notice the owner of said smile coming up behind me until he takes the plate out of my hand and places it on the counter.

"Candrima, a spoon would have sufficed," he says, raising my bean covered hand to his mouth. "But I do like this better."

I melt from the heat of his tongue crashing against my fingertips when he takes them into his mouth. The warmth rushes across my entire body when my back is pulled flush to his front, and it intensifies in my belly when his hand slides into the bust of my dress to cup my breast. His touch is gentle but sure, easing me into need and desire gradually. When he finishes licking my hand clean, his mouth moves to the curve of my neck, scattering soft kisses and hungry bites across my goosebump-taut skin.

"I thought you were still hungry?" I squeak.

Everything about this feels so right, but Corn had an emotional day, and a part of me feels like I might be taking advantage of his vulnerability. Although it's hard to say for sure who's taking advantage of who with the way he's kissing me.

"Who says I'm not?" he whispers while unlacing my corset.

"For physical food," I correct.

"You human Borne and your incessant need for labeling," he groans. "Must everything be categorized? Why can't you just feed me?"

"That's such a man ass answer," I snort.

I'm spun around to face him and my knees wobble, seeing mischief flash in his captivating eyes. His hand rises to stroke my jaw, the sensation attacking all of my common sense and self control.

"Can I please have you, Candrima?" he says gently.

That deep voice steals my breath away, so all I can do is nod in response and send Corn a pleading telepathic,

"Yes."

In doing so, I'm swept off my feet and into my husband's arms where I can appreciate the majesty of his true form.

"Let's go to bed," he says.

Corn

My succubus nature had recently taken a back seat with all the heats and ruts we've had to work through, but I missed it. I missed being dominated, I missed submitting to the whim of others, I missed giving pleasure first and receiving it second. I missed feeling Candrima's weight on top of me, and I missed the way she would drive her little blunt nails into my skin as my reward for being a good boy.

But tonight I didn't have to miss it. Because when I entered her from behind only to flop backwards on the bed with her on top, she indulged my silent request and wiggled her hips against mine. Satisfying my need to lie underneath.

Candy keeps our pace slow, but deliberate. Which I appreciate because the week we've been apart has been torturous for my stamina. I'd probably orgasm if she whispered the right way. I also delight in the prolonged, and I'd like to prolong the tender way she's tracing my jaw and kissing me for as long as possible.

"So eager," she moans, coating my tongue with her words. "Do you like the way I fuck you?"

"I do," I rasp between kisses. "Please don't stop."

"Why not? Does it feel good to have me bounce on your pretty dick?"

Despite the revelation of today, I still consider myself a lust demon. So it shocks me when I blush from the vulgarity of my little witch's words. *She* made *me* blush. What was Destiny thinking, throwing us together?"

"Candy," I moan, slipping my thumb into her mouth
"Oh, fuck. Show me that you own it, baby," I hiss. "Remind me who I belong to."

She does just that and I lose control of my hybrid form again and the weight of my true form creaks against the bed as I unfurl my arms and tails. Spades automatically seeks Candrima's swollen clit while Dart presses longingly against her tight little asshole.

"Can I?" I ask.

My mind and body races with anticipation while I trace the puckered ridge of her ass. Every swish makes her squeeze me tighter, pushing me closer to the edge of no return, but I hold out, waiting for her ok.

"Yes," she concedes, voice dizzy with pleasure.

And so begins the daunting task of entering her without cumming. Luckily she's so wet that I don't have to go through the hassle of lube, but I'm met with resistance even while soaking wet.

"Relax, baby," I coo while stroking her arms.

I try again and she shudders as an orgasm takes her. So I lift Spades slightly to ease her overworked nerves and slide Dart in. This time I'm successful and I can hear the blood rushing from my head to my toes as my entire being drowns in the forgiving current of Candrima Castille. Death has never felt so euphoric.

"Corn, fuck," she curses, driving those little nails into my skin. "Look how wet you make me."

I will not do anything of the sort should I like to remain tethered to a physical plane.

"I can feel it just fine," I shudder.

Her thrusts grow more urgent and I slowly begin to lose my self-control, and subsequently, my mind. The rest of the world around us is irrelevant. All I can think about is filling Candy's tight little holes with my seed. Even though I told myself I'd pull out. But deep down I knew that was a lie I convinced myself of to feel better about my addiction to her.

My right eye blinks before my left eye gets the memo and my mouth curls into a distorted smile when her rhythm falters. We've graduated from slow and steady to hard and fast, and I'm in no headspace to remind her to pace herself. So I delight in the feel of her warm silky walls gliding over my painfully hard length and meet her measure for measure. Her pleasurable cries ring louder with each stroke while she eagerly arches her back to accept all of me. I try to hold on, I try to wrestle more pleasure from her. But her tight little pussy squeezes me until all the tension and pressure building in my back erupts forward, coating my existence in an all-consuming pleasure, and coating Candy's insides white.

She wiggles against me some more to ride out the waves of after-shock but I have to hold her still when our cum drips out of her pussy and slides down to her ass where Dart is still occupied. The last thing I want is to accidentally bring on my rut from excessive sex, and Candy's sure to do exactly that if I let her. I need these last few weeks of mental clarity, especially given my family situation and our upcoming trips to Hell and Heaven respectively.

"Come on," I say, finally scrounging up the courage to exit her warmth.

"Let's get cleaned up and I'll make us some tea and pie."

I blink and I'm teleported into the bathroom, where a hot fragrant bath is waiting for us.

"You really have become far too good at this," I mumble, watching Candy free her curls from the tie.

"Well I need to be at least somewhat competent at magic, being a King's wife and all," she chuckles.

Her statement stings considering our impending separation. But I've had enough hard conversations for a lifetime these past twelve hours so I stay quiet and enjoy the moment with my intelligent, talented wife. Who just so happens to run a mean bubble bath.

"You seem sleepy," Candy giggles.

My head is resting on her chest and I'd be lying if I said it wasn't comforting. Actually it was the most comfortable I'd been in years. But I wasn't sleepy yet. No, instead of getting a night of much needed rest, my brain decided that it was more productive to replay the disastrous events of today on a never-ending loop.

"Not really, I'm just thinking," I reply.

"About what?" she asks.

I honestly wished she would just invade my brain. Because how was I supposed to tell her that I was terrified at my big age of 188? Terrified of the responsibility. Terrified of the future, past, and doubly terrified of the present. Terrified of my feelings, and terrified that I'd soon have to let her go knowing that she was one of the best things in my life. How was I supposed to admit that I didn't have all the answers?

"A little bit of everything," I sigh, feeling defeat settle into my stomach.

"Yeah, that's fair," she says, running her hand along my back. "Today was a hell of a whole lot."

"That is probably the only accurate human expression I've heard from you," I chuckle.

"Hush," she chides, playfully pinching my arm.

A comfortable silence settles in between us after our laughter clears, making it easy to focus on the feel of my curls being twisted around her nimble fingers and the silky skin of her exposed belly. I always considered my cabin home, but now I know it's just a dwelling. This little witch is actually home, and I seriously begin to doubt whether I'm strong enough to give her up. After all, I'm hardly strong enough to stand up to my own mother.

"It's not your fault. You know that right?" Candrima says, cutting through the silence.

I guess she finally felt compelled to pick my brain.

"I know, it's just," I sigh. "I think it's strange that I still love her. Obviously I know how she truly feels about me, but..."

"She's always going to be your mom, Corn. That will never change. She's the first being you've ever met. Of course you still love her," Candy replies.

I try to swallow the tears forming in my eyes but they fall anyway, evaporating into a tiny cloud of shadows while the wise little witch strokes my back.

"But none of that means that you have to accept abuse. You can love someone from a distance. You don't owe her your suffering. You deserve all of the good things, Corn. Whether your mom thinks so or not," she continues.

The tears fall steadily, soaking the thin fabric of Candy's sleep garment and making it cling to my face. I can count all the times I've cried as an adult between two hands, and it was never this much of a production. But instead of being embarrassed, I'm grateful. Because this time it feels good, like I'm letting go of the burden of unwavering strength. And for once, I'm sending prayers of gratitude to Destiny for the gift of my little witch. However this all turns out.

Home

Candy

"Prtt," Aster chitters, asking to be let out of his carrier.

The damp air carries the unmistakable bite of winter as we land on the mountain side.

"This is not Earth and you are not winged. You will die and I will have to console your owner over the loss of your miserable life," Corn tuts.

We're in Hell.

Again.

But this time we're in a different realm. This time we're in Corn's realm. We stand on the halfway point of the highest peak in their world, overlooking what is affectionately called The Valley Of Tenebrosity. Or Tens Val as a kind local referred to it. His six horned face will probably give me nightmares until I die, but he was very sweet. He even offered Aster a travel sparrow, which he rated a 10/10 for crunch.

"What exactly are we looking for?" I ask.

Don't get me wrong, the view is beautiful, but I'm still afraid of heights and it's unexpectedly chilly up here.

"There's supposed to be an entrance around here, but I can't find it. Perhaps I should've brought a map," Corn explains.

Suddenly, I remember the one thing that always gets people in a tizzy when it comes to Corn.

"What if you have to shadow in?" I suggest.

Astonishment settles into Corn's features while he studies the imposing mountain. It does make sense. What better way to fortify a castle than to make sure only royalty can enter?

"What if I accidentally drop us into a pool of lava?" he grimaces.

"As soon as we see oozing, bubbling, or crackling, I'll teleport us out," I shrug. "We got this. Just aim high."

Of course he checks for a conventional entrance one more time before bowing his head in concession.

"I don't know why you put this much trust in me. Just be ready I guess," he sighs.

He comes behind me and pulls my body flush to his, then his shadows take over. While my magic is white hot, Corn's is arctic cold. Ice floods my veins and flesh, turning me into a vessel of darkness. Then we surge forward, cutting through the jagged rock like a legendary sword. Much to my relief, we enter a throne room. Somehow it is filled with windows that offer a glimpse of the valley below, but that's not the only detail that catches my eye. The floors appear to be made out of polished lapis while the walls are coated with a sparkly matte black substance. There are several candle chandeliers affixed to the ceiling that match the wall sconces, and the platforms on which the thrones rest are filled with live white roses. It's beautiful here.

We land triumphantly, Aster in hand, and Corn exhales a ragged breath, releasing the stress from the potential mishap. But before we can get our bearings, a being comes charging forward, prompting Corn to pull me behind him while he changes forms.

"Brother!" the being calls. "It's so good to finally meet you. My, you really do favor father."

His statement makes me wonder what Corn's dad looks like, because the demon in front of us is damn near a spitting image of my husband. He has the same thick curls, rapt eyes, and sharp teeth, but his skin is a pale yellow color. Kind of like spring carnations.

He leans in close to examine Corn's markings and Corn retaliates by swatting at him with Dart.

"Apologies, I forget you're mostly used to the human realm," he huffs. "So I guess we should do introductions first. I'm Tobias, second born of Esqin Olakanye, and The Duke Of The Abyss."

"What's The Abyss?" I whisper.

Tobias jumps, suddenly aware of my presence, and then leans around his protective mountain of a brother to get a good look at me.

"This must be your bind!" he exclaims, happily wagging his tail. "I saw her name appear on the records. Congratulations are in order!"

"Thank you," I say sheepishly.

"Of course! This is so exciting. The Sixth Realm hasn't seen a queen in over 600 years. Perhaps now our birth rate will increase," Tobias explains.

"What do you mean?"

"Well, without a female ruler, our reproductive laws and advancements have suffered greatly."

"You all don't make those decisions without a female ruler?" I balk.

"No, of course not! We have no business creating laws about an experience we can't relate to. That's incredibly incompetent in my opinion."

"Tell that to the human rulers," I chuckle.

Corn finally jumps in with an irritated sigh,

"Candrima will not remain in Hell. She does not belong here."

I notice that his tone is very final, but that doesn't stop me from shooting him a challenging grimace. I've already accepted that we're likely stuck together, now I just need him to get with the program.

"Why not?" Tobias interrupts, completely oblivious to our tension. "Is she not bound to us? Where else would The Queen Of Shadows belong?"

"Candrima Castille belongs on Earth with the rest of her kind! She will not be bound to me past this year," Corn growls.

"Corn, we talked about thi-"

"Wait, you intend to dissolve your binds? Jamanichei! I'll be right back," Tobias says before dissolving into shadowy blue smoke.

As soon as he leaves, Corn's eyes return to mine.

"Candrima, we've talked about this," he gruffs.

"I don't know what you mean," I shrug while freeing Aster.

Aster, who's usually extremely shy in new places, prances right out and heads straight for the seat of what I can only assume is the King's Throne. Finding the cushion to his liking, he curls up and closes his eyes. New Realm, same demon.

Both of them.

"Candy, you cannot stay in Hell. There are consequences for such a decision."

"Yes, Corn. I'm aware," I tut.

"Then why are you getting Tobias' hopes up? It's irresponsible and selfish."

Upon hearing the accusation of me being "selfish" I stomp right back over to where he's standing and pop him on the tail.

"Ouch!" he exclaims.

I sneer because this demon really does enjoy his dramatics. I was barely able to make contact with Dart because his reflexes are so quick. I know it's actually his pride that was wounded, but I won't rollover just to make him feel better. People are suffering here without leadership.

"I'm being selfish? How am I being selfish because I'm willing to do what's right?"

"I thought we were clear on the definition of selfish," he says, crossing his arms over his heaving chest. "It means you're only thinking of yourself."

I roll my eyes, hoping they roll back so far that they get stuck so I don't have to look at his sour ass face for the rest of the night.

"Don't roll your eyes at me, brazen little witch!"

"Then don't call me selfish!" I hiss back. "And for the record, I wasn't thinking about myself. I was thinking about you and how content you felt when we landed here! Asshole!"

And with that, I exit the throne room and march down the hall.

Aster joins me sometime later. According to what I understand, Hell amplifies what little demonic powers he does have, so he was able to slink through the shadows on his own merit. Not that Corn would've helped him in the first place. Eventually we follow a soft yellow glowing light and find a library that has to be at least 4 Libraries Of Congress. There are shelves stacked in horizontal strips against the walls, shelves in the opulent oversized furniture, and even shelves embedded in the floor. Books move on their own, influenced by some kind of Classification Spell, and ladders adjust by sliding with my every step, offering me access to things far beyond my feeble humanish reach.

Somehow I find the middle of this gigantic ass room and locate the directory. It's initially in a language I can't understand, but as soon as I place my hand on the podium, it automatically translates to English for me. The information is organized by categories and then alphabetically, and it's such a great system that it takes me no time at all to dig up all the information I need about The Royal Shadow Family. With some texts dating back more than 75,000 years.

For now though, I chose to focus on the last 10,000 years, particularly Corn's parents and grandparents. Three volumes later, and I'm finally getting to Nasha and Esqin's story. I thought my own love story was sad, but this is fifty times worse. Especially when I find out how Corn was conceived. My heart goes out to the priestess because no one should ever have to suffer at the hands of someone they once loved, but that understanding doesn't justify everything she's put Corn through. Throwing the burden of lived trauma onto someone else doesn't do shit but cause more trauma.

I silently debate on whether or not I'm going to tell Corn what I've found, but right before I can come to a decision, a voice interrupts me.

"Candrima Castille, it's wonderful to finally meet you."

I jump, startled by the strong but feminine voice, and when I look up I see her. Her skin is the same rust color as Corn's, her horns are twisted like an intricate crown around her head and wrapped in a patterned fabric, while long locs flow down her back. Her expression is mostly unreadable since her lips are pinched and her round eyes are indifferent, but her body language seems welcoming.

"I'm sorry. I was just reading," I explain, abandoning my passage and rising from the table.

I feel like a kid who's gotten caught red handed poking around in the cookie tin. I've gotten way too comfortable here in the few hours since I arrived.

"No need to apologize, your majesty. After all, this is your home," she says.

Her pinched lips spread into a wide smile. One I realize I've seen before. In a dream once.

"Who are you?" I ask.

She takes two steps forward, making no attempt to answer my questions before linking her arm in mine.

"Come, let's find your King."

I joined the demoness, thinking she'd take me straight to Corn but no. Instead, we walked around enjoying the majesty of the castle, arm in arm, discussing everything from my favorite book, to "That dreadful Earth traffic," and even what Corn and I do in our spare time. I was sure to leave out the part about us fucking until we couldn't walk when I answered, choosing instead to focus on our movie marathons, cooking contest, and fireplace cuddles.

"He's always loved the fire. Ever since he was a youngling," the demoness says wistfully in return to my last admission.

I stopped walking, turning to her so I could fully read her expression when I asked her my next question,

"You've known Corn since he was a youngling?"

Again, she gives me a smile instead of a reply. However before I can call her out on it, we gain an audience.

"Candrima," Corn calls. "Are you alright?"

He's concerned, but not necessarily defensive. I think it's because whoever this woman is truly means no harm to either of us even though she's a stranger.

"Uh, yeah. We were just walking around. She found me in the library," I explain.

The demoness walks me to Corn, and replaces her arm with his before taking a step back to examine her work. Satisfied, she continues walking down the hall until Tobias fizzes in.

"Ninny!" he shouts. "I've been looking everywhere for you."

"Is that her name?" I ask Corn in a whisper.

"No idea," Corn shrugs. "I thought you'd know. You've been walking around with her for hours."

"Clearly introductions happen later when it comes to demons. You combed my hair before I knew your name."

"Touche," he replies.

We watch as Ninny gracefully flies through the air, landing in front of a hysteric Tobias with a sharp sigh.

"What is it Tob?" she says gently, lifting his chin.

Tobias sucks an obnoxious amount of air in through his nose before turning to point accusingly at me and Corn.

"They're trying to dissolve their binds!" he shouts, disturbing the walls of the castle.

Ninny's eyes pass between us, her indifferent expression instantly shifting into something disappointed and irritated when she finds confirmation in Corn's avoidant gaze.

"Bruh, not cool!" I hiss.

"What does he mean? Cornelius, you intend to leave your Queen?" she asks.

"I don't see how that's any of your business," Corn bites back. "I don't even know you."

The air falls silent, as if even our hearts have stopped. Ninny takes five steps forward, pausing when she's an arm's length away from me. She stares at me until I make the mistake of blinking and then she firmly presses her thumb to my forehead.

It triggers a vision.

I see Corn, small and nervous at a festival, standing in front of a fire pit. Night is falling upon Hell. He twirls Spades between his fingers, humming along to the pounding drums. Nafisa and Nataki stand a few hundred feet away, bargaining with a merchant over fabric and then a cloak figure joins Corn's side.

"Evening, my little prince," a voice cooes.

Corn glances into the eyes of the hooded stranger, plucks a flame from the raging fire with his little hand, and fashions it into a flickering red rose. He then hands it to the person with a fangless smile. They accept his offering, placing one hand over their heart, and the other in the thick curls of his head to scratch his scalp. Like the Corn I've come to know and love, he purrs sweetly in response to the affection.

"You will do great things, little one," the figure says. "I must go now, but please remember, your grandmother always loves you."

She bends, placing a kiss on his forehead and her hood slips just slightly, revealing Ninny almost 200 years earlier.

"Until next time," she says, disappearing into the shadows of the merchant stalls.

I'm thrown back to the present finding myself hand in hand with Corn who is now tearful.

"You're my grandmother?"

Enitan Tiwa Olakanye is the dowager Queen of The Realm Of Shadows, and also Corn's grandmother. Affectionately nicknamed Ninny, she switched her focus to orphaned younglings once her son ascended to the throne. Which is why her name moves around so much in the family tree. She is a mother to many.

Once the tears cleared, Corn had plenty of questions. Namely, why didn't they come find him if they knew about him? The answer surprised no one. His mother, Nasha, had suppressed his royal energy markers along with his true form so Ninny could only find him in dreams where Nasha's magic was weak. They could only trace him recently, after my bind eroded Nasha's seal and released the concealment spell. Tobias was the first to find him, but Corn was already in rut so they decided it would be best to let him find out about them on his own. Which he did.

His brothers, Tobias, Tayo, and Akanni are all excited to meet him. So much so that he can barely get a bite in between their questions at dinner. Ninny had done a fantastic job learning her grandson from a distance, and knowing his affinity for fish, she had the chefs cook up a big ass Hell Tuna. That's not the correct name for it, but that's what I'm calling it.

"How'd you mate a sorceress?" Akanni asks.

Akanni is the youngest of the royal brothers at just twenty one, and also the most unfiltered. His first question to me was about Corn's rut and how long it lasts.

Because talking about my spouse's mating period is perfect small talk for practical strangers.

"It was an accident," Corn sighs regretfully. "I got too excited and I bit her."

As Cyrus explained in a letter, the nip placed on my throat was likely the culprit behind both my bind and his. My bond reinforced Corn's claim on me, locking us in. Cementing our accidental coupling.

"Oh, well that explains it," Tob chuckles. "I'm surprised she's not gestating."

Gestating? As in pregnant? With a child?

"What do you mean by that?" I chuckle nervously.

"Well it was a mating bite. Mating bites are usually very effective, regardless of any contraceptive charms. You all must've gotten lucky," he explains. "Maybe next time you'll do the right thing and make me an uncle."

Corn chokes on his wine, while I make a mental note to keep him from biting me during my next heat. A child is the last thing we need. A winged toddler throwing a temper tantrum? No thank you.

"Unfortunately I will not be making you an uncle any time soon," Corn coughs. "We're not even supposed to be mated."

Ninny stops chewing and scoffs at his confession.

"Says who?" she asks.

Sensing his grandmother's less than subtle displeasure with the statement, Corn nervously scratches a patch of curls before whispering his answer,

"The EUM."

"The EUM!?" she tuts. "Some fucking High Strung Heaven bum kissers? Policing my child?"

She spits curses out at a rapid pace in a language I can't quite grasp. The only word I can identify for sure is the Hellion word for *fuck*, and I only know that one because it's Corn's favorite during sex.

"Eni- Ninny. It's fine, really," Corn sighs.

"It is not fine! Here, you reject your soulmate because of an agency that has no authority in our world? ***Your*** kingdom? Kasfiat," she cusses, sucking her fangs. "And let me ask you another question, oh wise one. Is that what Candrima wants?"

Everyone turns to me expectantly, even Corn. Did I want to separate from the one being who's laugh made my heart flutter? Who reminded me that I was in fact alive? Who made me feel like I deserved everything?

"No."

Of fucking course not. I didn't care about the EUM and whatever power game they're playing. I want to be with Corn, to love Corn. To hold him close at night and listen to his calm purr. That's what I want.

Corn shakes his head with a huff that contains enough palpable frustration to kill a man. I know his stance on this. His mind is busy exploring a thousand what if's while mine is living in the moment and enjoying whatever comes. He's always going to do the responsible thing, even if it isn't the best thing for him. For us.

"Candy is only thinking ab-"

"I love you," I interject. "That's what I'm thinking about."

I pictured that admission a lot differently in my head. Like in front of the fireplace after sex, different. Sans familial audience, different.

The table falls quiet at my confession and even Ninny's irritation calms. She instead looks sad, or maybe even hopeful. I'm hopeful too because Corn stares straight into my eyes, silently reciprocating those three little words, but what comes out his mouth next however...

"Candy, it's not safe. You know you can't live here. We can't avoid the EUM forever. You will need moonlight," he argues.

And there it is. The rejection I was hoping to avoid. At least for tonight.

"I think I've lost my appetite," I say, letting my exit be my reply.

I push my chair back with an obnoxious scrape and head off to find some solitude. If Corn wants to be alone, he can be alone.

Corn

Now I've done it.

Candrima storms out of the dining hall and folds herself into a hot angry flash of light, teleporting off somewhere. The only reason I don't immediately follow after her is because I know she's still in the castle.

Plus I know I'm the one in the wrong.

"I held onto hope that you would be smarter than your father," Ninny chuckles. "Alas you are not. The same fool will continue to haunt me in every generation."

"Ninny, that's harsh," Tob interjects.

"It is not harsh enough!" Ninny roars, throwing her chalice against the ebony table.

Wine spills over the lip of the golden cup, splashing against the floor in a way that reminds me of fresh blood. Maybe that's what will become of my heart if I keep down this path. Discarded and trampled due to my own stubbornness.

"You will never sever that bind!" she says pointing a long claw at me. "Not even in death! You are stubborn, and you are causing her unnecessary pain!"

"WE ARE ILLEGAL!" I roar back.

Blood pounds against my ear drum, making me feel woozy and unstable. I've never raised my voice at my elders, not even my mother. But Ninny knows how to pick a scab.

"Legality is hardly ever indicative of righteousness! Tell me who benefits from a law dictating what feelings are acceptable between two beings? The oppressor or the oppressed? You have every opportunity to be a catalyst for change! You have every opportunity to fight! Why are you just accepting this?" she shrieks.

"I don't want to fight! I just want to protect her!"

"From what, Cornelius? From your anticipated failings as her life-long partner? Or the monster you fear you may become?"

I swallow my rebuttal, finally understanding Candrima's human expression, *read for filth*. Yes, I'm scared. But rightfully so. Candrima's my whole world and we all know the Earth is just a rock without its guiding star. I am no different from the celestial bodies surrounding us and I know that despite the lies I feed myself.

"Thank you for dinner," I say pushing away from the table. "I'd like some time alone."

"I figured I'd find you up here," Tob says.

It's been two hours since my blow up at dinner and I've discovered a new thinking spot in that time. High up on the mountain, overlooking the East side of the valley. The air is frigid and dry up here, but it's so peaceful.

"Yeah, you can see the three rivers," I reply.

The Sixth Realm has three major rivers that converge past the royal mountain. OkuKun carries life upstream, Efun down, and the Red River changes direction based on the wind and temperature. They all beckon me forward, the view offering me solace.

"Yeah that's why father enjoyed this spot too," Tob says solemnly.

Ninny said we had more in common than just looks and she's right. The more I learn about him, the more I learn about myself. I never met him, but I can attest that I'm my father's son.

In some of the worst ways too.

"You know, father never loved our mother," Tob says after a beat of silence.

I bristle against the proclamation before meeting his eyes and shaking my head in denial. That can't possibly be true. And if it is, why would he make it known? Especially to his children.

"It's alright," Tob shrugs. "We had Ninny to show us what love looks like, and now we have you. Which is nice."

The chilly wind picks up a few of Tob's loose curls and blows them out from his face, highlighting yet another one of our similarities. Tob's eyes are starry and blue, full of dreams and tangible hope. We both wear our hearts on our sleeves.

"Tob, I-"

"Listen, Cornelius," he says, interrupting me. "Shadow Demons live for tens of thousands of years if they mind themselves and stay out of trouble. Tens of thousands of years is far too much time to spend denying that you love someone. Someone who loves you back. So maybe just accept that you've been blessed to find her early in your life, and figure out everything else later, yeah?"

He stares at me with every expectation that sense will fall from the night sky and conk me on my head, and it's odd because after a while, it does.

In the form of cold rain.

I've become used to watching the rainfalls with Candy in the last six weeks.

It's only been a few hours but I miss her.

I nod, and Tob clasps his hand over my shoulder, using it to rise. And here I thought I was the older brother.

"I hope to see you in the morning, brother. I bid you a goodnight," he says, dissolving into his signature blue.

He leaves me and I stare out over the range one last time, watching the point where the rivers converge. Then as platinum lightning stretches across the open midnight sky and pierces the heavy, gray clouds, I realize where I'd rather be.

Home.

I find her in the library in another study circle. This time I can see that she was working out of six books while at least fifteen books sit along the perimeter of the table, annotated and tabbed. The quill is still in her hand, drawing itself in lazy circles to document the pattern of her hazy dreams. I rid her of that first and make note to wipe the ink off her skin before we lay down for the night, then I tuck her in my upper arms against my heart and take her notebook underneath my lower left. Candy instinctively snuggles closer against my chest, making my purr rip through the quiet night air. Oh, my sweet little witch.

"Let me show you to your room," Ninny calls from the upper floor.

Jamanichei, I don't ever think I'll get used to how stealthy she is. How do you creep a demon out? A demon king at that?

"Aren't there staff around for this sort of thing?" I ask.

"Of course," she says, offering no other explanation.

I could be difficult, but it's late and I'm too tired to journey back to Earth. So I immediately resign my argument and follow her quick strides down the hall.

We fly up a few stories before landing in a hall with a singular set of doors. The wood is ebony just like the dining table, and it's decorated with intricate carvings unique to the Olakanye family. Including Candy's bind script.

Wait.

Does this mean that she's been solidified onto our family tree? Is it already too late?

My rising panic is interrupted by my perceptive grandmother's reclaiming scoff.

"Your father preferred his room at the very top of the mountain, but something tells me you'll like this better," Ninny says, pushing open the doors.

They give way to a room with sky high ceilings decorated in fine crystal chandeliers and velvet draping. Impossibly large windows offer a generous view of the three rivers, and a visibly plush demon-sized bed draped in darkness sits in front of them.

Just like I like it.

Most notable though, is the library tucked against the far wall closest to the door, and an entrance big enough for Aster to slink through next to a small study area.

"Did you do this?" I ask.

I don't hear any response from my grandmother, so I turn to see if her reply is one of those silent ones she likes so much only for her to be gone.

I guess I have my answer.

I find the bathing room and wipe Candrima down with a warm cloth before finally carrying her to bed. Poor little thing passed out mid-sentence according to her notes. Right in the middle of writing an S. She's also dead to the world, so I don't expect much of a fight when I begin to unlace her corset, but as soon as my fingertips graze her bare skin her powers ignite and she fires a wayward bolt across our room. Luckily it's absorbed by a fireplace that I'm almost certain wasn't there before.

Ninny is good at this.

"Where am I?" she shrieks.

I don't supply her an immediate answer because I'm distracted by the now raging fire, but seeing her breasts sway while she tries to pull her dress over her head refocuses me.

"You're in bed," I sigh, looking at her cream speckled areolas.

Despite the fire, the room is still a bit nippy and her nipples pebble against the brisk current. My pants grow uncomfortably tight as I try to resist slipping the mismatched peaks into my mouth, but they are tempting.

So pretty and soft.

"Corn, you're drooling," she scoffs.

"Am I?" I say, wiping excess spit from my bottom lip.

Definitely was, but it wasn't my fault. It was her breasts. They were calling to me. Distracting me.

"What plane are we on?" Candy asks, standing to remove her bloomers.

"Still in Hell," I sigh, enjoying the sight of her round hips.

"What? What do you mean we're still in Hell?"

She stops stripping and that's when I finally notice the shock lacing her tone. Does she want to leave? Does she feel unsafe?

"Yes. It's late and you were obviously comfortable enough to sleep here. Is that a bad thing? Do you want to go back to Earth?"

Candrima's movements slow as she resumes her undressing, becoming an artful display of control as she unlaces her jump and climbs out of her skirt. Showing off little peekaboos of her decadent body. She's aware of my entrancement, teasing me by tracing her curves with delicate fingers and a soft smile. Her creamy marbled skin puckers with goosebumps that are just barely visible under the flickering light of the fireplace, while her curls shine with oil and perspiration from the rising temperature.

"No. I just can't believe you let me stay," she says, climbing back into bed.

Candy moves to straddle me and I invite her closer by leaning back into the pillows. Feeling her soft skin underneath my grip is all it takes for my hybrid form to deteriorate and I moan when Dart finds purchase on her left thigh opposite from Spades on her right.

"Possessive tonight, aren't we?" Candy chuckles while stroking the tip of Spades.

Her gentle touch once again prompts my purr, but this time I feel it warming my entire chest. How can this creature be so powerful, yet so forgiving, and so lovely? How could she possibly be mine?

I stroke her cheek softly just to make sure she's real, and although I know she probably is, it still takes me by surprise when she leans into my affections. I don't think I'll ever get enough of that. Not in any lifetime.

"Yes, because I love you," I confess, reeling from her increasing warmth.

Her mouth falls open in shock from my confession, revealing her tiny pink tongue which is practically glued to the roof of her mouth. I know I fucked up earlier by not saying it back, but I need her to know that she affects me. That I belong to her.

Willingly.

"Corn, what?" she gasps.

"I love you," I say again, hoping to dismiss her disbelief. "I'm terrified, anxious, and cynical. But those feelings haven't stopped me from falling in love with you. There isn't a future I've pictured in the last month that you're not in and I think I'm finally ready to admit that I prefer things that way. You have my heart, Candrima Castille. You've had it from the moment I found you in that field."

She makes a small whimpering sound while I swipe away the tears streaking her cheeks with my thumb. My emotional little witch. I eventually move to kiss her tears away, but she stops me with a gentle but firm hand to my chest.

"Does this mean that you'll stop trying to sever our bond?" she asks.

She tries to keep her expression neutral, but I can see anxiety simmering in her eyes. I stroke her back to comfort her. I've been insistent on separating from the beginning so her skepticism is expected. Honestly, I still don't know how things will turn out with the legality of our union. I'm not foolish enough to believe we can avoid the EUM forever, and I know we can't avoid returning to Earth. But here and now, I'm ok with that. I'm ok with whatever consequences there will be as long as we can face them together.

"I'm yours. Wholly, magically, yours. Bind and all," I nod.

Candy grows closer, letting her lips graze against mine in a way that is dangerous for my unraveling mind.

"Then I'm yours, Cornelius. Wholly and magically, yours," she smiles.

All four of my eyes blink to focus on the perfect vision of a woman in front of me, and when I capture her mouth in mine, I know that she speaks the truth.

We are undeniably in love.

I open my eyes with a groan in the morning. Our passion outlasted the blazing fire last night, and it was not without consequence. Judging by the heat swallowing our quarters, we've slept well into the day. I intended to go meet with all the farmers in this area this morning but instead I'm still wrapped around Candrima. Whatever productivity I had planned yesterday is now out the window because my rut has begun on top of that. I can't leave her alone even if I wanted to.

And I don't.

She's too busy imitating a bulldozer to notice, but my tails curl around her soft thighs like pumpkin vines. I know I should be getting up and handling the lands, however, it's difficult to resist indulging in the peace of gazing at her drool-crusted face. Soon enough I'm tempted to lie beside her once again and my hands find purchase on her plump, pliant tummy. I begin to purr, then I begin to knead. Squishing her belly between my greedy claws in repetitive waves. I've denied myself the pleasure of kneading her for this long because I knew it'd be indicative of strong love and now I'm addicted. It's so comforting to touch her like this. So comforting that I barely hear the mismatched purring syncing with my own.

Barely.

I snap my head towards the door, my midsection contorting oddly to avoid completely separating with Candrima. And standing exactly where I expected to find a threat, is Tob. Purring away with a dumb smile plastered on his face.

"What are you doing?" I ask after a while.

I only ask because he seems rather content not to volunteer an answer for his intrusion.

"Watching you," he answers plainly.

"Why?"

"It's very sweet. After seeing Father, I didn't think imperial demons were capable of this kind of bond. It gives me hope that I will find my own soulmate some day."

His answer makes me choke. Tob has been the stereotypical annoying little brother since I met him but I'm starting to understand that he looks up to me in some strange way. I'm no one's role model, but he doesn't seem to care.

"What do you want?" I ask in a defeated sigh.

I know that my time in bed with Candrima is coming to a draw, and Tob confirms it when he offers to accompany me on my trip to the farms after a modest lunch.

"Alright," I say, rising from the warmth of the bed.

Tob averts his eyes and I quickly realize why when a gust of wind pushes through the open doors. I'm naked and hard as a brick.

"It appears you started your rut?" Tob asks, facing away from me.

The air is awkward, undoubtedly. But he came in my room while I was lying with my wife. I didn't try to flash him my goods. Still I feel ashamed. No one wants to see their brother's morning wood.

"I did," I sigh, trying to cover my dick with my hands.

"Can I interest you in a loincloth?"

"No thank you. I can manage pants," I say.

"Right, ok," he says, sounding unconvinced. "Well, I'll let you get to it. And we'll meet in the great hall in thirty minutes?"

"Sounds good."

He leaves, closing the door behind him, and I uncover myself. As awkward as that was, I still haven't softened because I can smell the ever enticing musk of my sex on Candy. I honestly don't know if I can manage pants, and while I know loincloths are common wear for demons, I don't particularly enjoy the idea of my first introduction to my people being one where they can see my bare ass.

I guess the human realm has changed me.

I wash and dress, making sure to conceal my dick to the best of my ability. I tried to think about shit like rancid meat and my brother's face wrinkled with disgust, but it doesn't do much since Candy's still technically in the same room. I do like that the bath house is ensuite but still far enough away from the bed so as to not disturb my little witch. She's still sleeping when I'm finished, so I take it as a sign that her body needs the rest and leave her be. Besides, I wouldn't want her toiling under the heat of the Sixth Realms twin suns all day anyway.

Lunch is amenable. We're served a simple pear salad alongside a steak flatbread wrap. I was starving after a long night of mucking around in Candrima's guts, so I eat wordlessly, but that doesn't stop Tob from asking me endless questions. He's trying to make up for the last 80 years in two days and I have to remind him that demons still need to take the occasional breath.

"I'm sorry, there's still so much I have to learn about you," he says.

"Well, we have a few thousand years," I reply.

"You're right. Plus we can talk on the way there," he says, patting my knee.

I just barely swallow a groan. That's not what I meant. That's not what I meant at all.

"You know, some people prefer to travel in silence," I sigh, trying to maintain my tact.

"Well good for them," Tob says cheerfully.

As expected, my brother talks the entire four mile flight to the first farm. He talks so much that I'm surprised he hasn't caught a bug in his mouth.

As if I could be so lucky.

I answer his questions regarding my first few occupations and we land in a dry abandoned Siaki field with a big thud. Dead stalks snap underneath our weight, alerting the owner to our intrusion.

His stance is defensive until he spots Tob, who greets him with a kind wave.

"Afternoon, My Grace!" he shouts before bowing.

"Afternoon, Lucien! I have someone I'd like you to meet!"

The farmer, Lucien, quickly meets us where we stand. He's squat and strong, with long braided hair falling to his midback, vermillion colored skin, and deep creases around his silver eyes. When I notice that he's older than me, I bow forward, forgetting for a moment that I am technically his king.

"Hello, I'm Cornelius," I say, offering my hand.

"Afternoon, Cornelius," Lucien nods, taking my offer on a handshake. "What brings you to my model of The Haxiatchira desert?"

I try not to laugh at the self-deprecating joke but it is funny. The Haxiatchira desert is the driest place in Hell, with annual rainfall accumulating to less than a ¼ inch. Unfortunately this barren field has a striking resemblance.

"Cornelius is The King Of Shadows," Tob snorts.

Lucien abandons my hand like I'm poison before dropping to the ground and bowing at my feet.

"Forgive me, Your Majesty. I-I did not know," he stammers.

His reaction makes me wince. I don't know if it's my size of simply my station, but the smell of Lucien's fear scents the air. I look to Tob for answers, and all he gives me is a frown coupled with a slight head shake.

"He's not Father," Tob sighs, helping Lucien off the ground. "There's no need to worry."

I haven't heard much about my father so I don't know if that's a good thing or a bad thing, but based on the pride rising from my brother, it's probably the best case scenario. Curiosity makes me want to dig deeper into Tobias' explanation, but I know we don't have the time right now. So I put a pin in it and focus on the task at hand.

"I'm not here to impose or wield my title. I'm actually here to help," I say, motioning to the fields.

Lucien is hesitant in his acceptance, but he does eventually accept my offer.

"Forgive me, Your Majesty, but I'm not sure that this can be helped. The last hundred or so years have been unforgivably dry. Last night was the first time we saw a decent rain in eight months."

My eyes find the waning lilac moon high in the sky. If it keeps on it's path, I'm sure we'll witness an eclipse. I wonder if that has anything to do with Candrima. I really need to do some serious research on the breadth of her capabilities when I find the time.

"Well, I'd like to try anyway," I reply.

"Of course, Your Majesty. But it will take several days to clear the lands," Lucien says sheepishly.

A broken plow sits on the horizon, tinged with rust and overgrowth from weeds. I'm sure it would take days with that, but luckily I've mastered my powers.

"No need," I reply.

My lower arms separate from my sides, joining my primary set to command my shadows. A chilling darkness descends upon the land, reducing everything on the ground to a petrified, frozen mass. Then I stomp my foot against the terrain which makes all that my shadows have touched crumble into a fine powder.

The fields are cleared.

Lucien's eyes are a second away from popping out of his head when I'm finished.

"Your Majesty!" he exclaims. "This is incredible."

His compliment makes me swell with pride. After all, it is incredibly difficult to impress a demon. Especially old ones. The shit that they've seen...

However, I'm not one to linger for the sake of my ego, so once I ensure the field is ready by rubbing my toes through the soft soot, I redirect the conversation.

"Do you have seed?" I ask.

Lucien nods excitedly.

"Yes, Your Majesty! I have seed. I also have sons. One moment please!"

Lucien returns with his three sons and several hundred pounds of seeds. It takes us less than an hour to sow the fields with his sons in the air and me and Tob prepping the ground. Dart and Spades work quickly to perforate the soil, while Tob utilizes his shadows to clone himself and expedite his hand sowing. Then as soon as we finish, it begins to drizzle.

A column of platinum light erupts in the distance, piercing the clouds with a deafening boom.

"What is that?" Lucien exclaims as the aftershock pushes us back a few feet.

I watch as a horde of mothbirds, Xilathias, flock towards to luminance, black wings contrasting against the pure white energy.

"That would be my wife," I answer.

Candy

I stand before my newly erected school in awe. Stone pillars frame a large entryway. Two ramps flank the sides of the stairs, and a playful door hangs thoughtfully in front of them. Pride swells in my chest.

I made this.

This is not where I saw the day going when I woke up in bed alone this morning, but thanks to Ninny's meddling, we're here.

"Yo, this is insane," Akanni mutters.

He's standing next to me, holding my newly updated spell tablet with his mouth hanging wide open. I have to manually close it for him before one of those weird ass moths fly in there.

"Thanks," I smile. "Now all I need you and Tayo to do is hire a few teachers. I'll try to find a headmaster before we head back to Earth."

Akanni's youthful face creases with a sourpuss frown, reminding me of his brother.

"Remind me again why you have to leave?" he huffs.

I never had the opportunity to scruff my siblings hair like they do in all the 90's sitcoms, so I relish the opportunity to do it to Akanni now. It's only been a day and he's grown strangely attached to me.

"Because my powers are directly tied to the Earth moon," I laugh.

"Wack," he tuts.

When I woke up, ripping through the castle searching for Corn, Ninny brought me a nice hot tea and sat me down. She explained that Corn had went to examine a few nearby farms, and when I started asking questions, she assigned Akanni to me. Ninny isn't much of a talker, she's more of a doer.

At her leisure, of course.

Akanni is the youngest out of the Olakanye's so at first I was hesitant, but Akanni is actually quite knowledgeable. He also was willing to break Corn's no device rule and get me a tablet. That's when this relationship really blossomed. Me and trouble makers always end up locked in.

"I'll bring you back some Earth snacks," I offer, collecting my tablet from him.

I scroll through my scanned annotations in search of my next task. I'll need to build three more schools in this town. Another elementary, a middle school, and a high school. Plus I also need to start drafting an incentive to lure medical professionals to our realm. It's weird because when I was working back on Earth, a list this long would've sent me into a three day long panic attack, but somehow this feels right.

"Hide your shit! Your husband is coming!" Akanni exclaims in a hushed tone.

I throw my tablet into my portable void, a space I enchanted on my bangle to carry books, non-perishables, and now also secrets.

Big horn-tipped wings block out the sun, casting a wide stretch of darkness in the center of my light. My husband lands on the top of my school with a big thud, and I breathe a sigh of relief when the roof doesn't collapse.

"Candy, what is this?" he asks, sliding down the shingling.

Tob lands besides Akanni, and his jaw also goes slack with admiration.

"I erected a school," I answer sheepishly.

Corn's eyes grow wide while he examines the outside of the structure. He runs his hand over the brown stucco, marveling at its integrity.

"You made this?" he asks.

"Isn't that what she said?" Akanni scoffs.

Corn narrows his eyes at his youngest brother, silently cursing him while Dart flickers menacingly.

"Why are you even here?" he tuts.

Ever the antagonist, Akanni, keeping his touch respectful, places both his hands on my shoulders and pulls me closer.

"Because I'm spending time with *our* wife. Especially since you abandoned her without a word this morning."

He's just fucking with Corn, I'm certain. But the look on Corn's face could render a dozen human men as good as dead.

"I don't like you very much," he growls.

"And I don't care," Akanni laughs haughtily.

Corn's wings fly open like windblown shutters while all the hair on his body tenses. Akanni does the same, barely flinching when Corn hisses at him.

Shit.

I do not wanna be in the middle of a demon fight.

Luckily Tob has inherited the sense his brothers clearly passed on, and he snatches me out of the way before thumping both of them on the forehead.

"Act like you have some sensibilities!" he chides. "Candrima has built a school, an entire campus really, and you two idiots are ruining it!"

One look at me and they both adopt the same endearing look of shame.

"Sorry," Akanni whispers.

"I apologize," Corn adds.

"Alright," Tob huffs. "Candrima, would you like to give us a tour?"

"I'd love to," I nod.

I walk through the doors with the world's biggest grin. It's better than what I imagined. Large windows let in the warm sunlight while deep vents keep the space cool. Offices are available to the right for the administration staff, while classrooms are placed side by side, three to a hall. The boys enter a room right off the entrance in their full forms and it automatically adjusts, moving the ceiling high to make space for their horns.

"This is amazing. Everything adjusts," Tob whispers, while approaching the floating board.

It rises slightly to meet his height and lowers when he steps away. Repeating the motions again when Akanni steps forward.

"Our queen built this," Akanni chuckles. "For our people."

The word our hits me in the chest full force. Sure, these guys aren't my born brothers, but hearing their praise makes me teary eyed-all the same. I'm accepted here. This is my rightful place.

Corn approaches me slowly, eyes shimmering with something undisclosed. For a second I'm afraid he's going to tell me that I can't get attached because I belong on Earth, but he doesn't. He just wraps his arms around me and pulls me close. Drowning me in that heirloom leather smell of his.

"Yes, our queen is extraordinary," he says, pressing a kiss to my temple. "We're so lucky to have her."

He lifts my chin to meet his grateful gaze, and I swear my heart melts into my ass.

"As am I you," I say softly.

Corn

We get ready for an early dinner after calling Ninny and Tayo out to look at Candy's school. Hordes of demons flock to the area, enchanted by the first sighting of all the royals in nearly a hundred years, and the possibility of seeing The Sixth Realm's new queen. Word had spread quickly and towns had begun organizing festivals celebrating a first in 600 years, a reigning queen. I'll admit I was hesitant to involve Candy in my realm's affairs at first, but when I saw her look at her school with all the hope in the universe, my fears abated. This was her home as much as it was mine. After all, my bond made sure of that.

Tayo slides Candrima's tablet back across the table with some updated applications for our new headmaster. The tablet I specifically forbade her from having. I shoot Akanni another irritated scowl, but at just 22 years old, there's not much he takes seriously. Especially not the potential, and admittedly unlikely, threat of the EUM.

"I starred a few Candidates. Desitol has 200 years of education and even helped found some hcus on Earth."

"HBCUs," Candrima laughs, tapping against the screen. "It means historically black colleges and universities."

"Oh, yeah. I forgot about that whole race segregation thing you guys had going on up there," Tayo grimaces before turning to me. "Did the EUM ever address that?"

I scoff in response.

The EUM barely has a handle on their own shit. They couldn't care less about what foul human fuckery is afoot.

"Alright, moving on. I know you all have to go back for Candrima's sunlight eventually, but is it possible to schedule the initial handover meeting with the High Council first?" Tayo asks.

From what I've gathered in the last 24 hours, Tob is the visionary, the bleeding heart, Tayo is the diplomat, and Akanni... Akanni is entertaining at the very least. While Tob and Akanni had question about my personal life, and mostly Candy, Tayo was focused on my plans or lack thereof for the throne. Ninny assured me it wasn't personal. Tayo just specialized in policy.

"Have they reached out?" I sigh while spearing a few of Candy's veggies.

She gives me a frustrated look, but I ignore it and continue chewing. She hardly ever eats her full plate, she won't miss them.

"No, but it won't be long before they do," Tayo replies. "Word travels fast through the realms."

That it does. Several letters have already arrived, addressed to The Queen Of The Sixth. We probably have 48 hours at best. I carefully scratch under my little witch's chin, grateful for her presence and flexibility with all of this even if I don't yet know what I'm doing.

"Schedule it for the day after tomorrow. It'll give me time to check on the rest of the agriculture lands and come up with a plan."

"On it," Tayo nods.

We return to dinner, back to my brothers' endless questions. Tayo is shocked to hear I was a bouncer at one point, and pleased to learn Candrima was an accountant before all of this. I'm happy that the night is going well, but as the head chef returns with a new bottle of wine, a loud clang from the first floor cuts through the happy table chatter.

"It appears we have a visitor," Ninny sighs before head-shotting her wine.

All three of my brothers turn to me at once, mildly freaking me out. I guess I am the biggest, but shit, I'm scared too. What if it's a spider demon? I hate spiders.

"Should I go get that?" I ask quietly.

I know I'm king, but I'm hoping I can claim ignorance a bit longer before I have to deal with something substantial. Unfortunately, my brothers aren't going to allow that.

"Yes, kinda, and who the fuck else is going to get?" they reply simultaneously.

Candrima gives me a weak confirmation nod, so I rise from the table with a huff. Something about this still feels off though, and I figure out what as soon as I take two steps towards the door.

"No need to move, your majesty," a foreign voice mocks. "I wouldn't want to ruin your dinner."

Unsettling anxiety causes tension to ripple across my skin, and my hair stands straight on edge. The demon, who seems to be affected by a disease that must have driven him mad, has a dagger to Candrima's throat. The gleaming silver tip has made a small indent in her skin. One mark to many.

"Let her go," I say, my voice channeling a calm that I do not feel.

She's staying as still as she possibly can, but the panic waving through our bond is inciting my tendencies towards violent resolutions. My sweet darling witch, caught because I let my guard down. Tayo and Tob sneer at the half-skinned intruder, seemingly looking for the best way to separate him from our queen, but Akanni steps forward first, his darkness creating whirlpools in the floor.

"You come any closer and I'll cut her eye out!" the demon yells.

Candrima stiffens and a single tear rolls down her cheek, starry and white hot.

"She cries platinum. Her eyes will fetch a fine price, even without her being your Queen," he laughs haughty.

The walls begin to bleed along with my eyes. I'm already in my biggest form, but the anger pulsing through my veins makes me feel like there's something else waiting to break free. Something every bit insidious as foretold in those prophecies.

Tayo tries to diffuse,

"To what end are you seeking?"

I don't know why he asked, because it's clear to me that this demon is seeking a violent end. Bloody and haunting.

The demon moistens his lips with a rotting tongue stained black from festering gangrene. I think of tearing it from his mouth, but he still holds my wife.

"I have a simple request," he smiles. "I want what all demons want who have suffered under late King Esqin. A chance to prove his bloodline unfit to rule."

"So this is a challenge for the throne? By law, citizens of the shadow realm are not allowed to challenge a king with which they share no blood relation," Tayo explains.

"By law, we should all bow down and die while you imperial maypoles sit in your ebony tower, eating filets and caviar!" he shouts.

I become more and more irate as Tob gently raises his hands and offers an explanation that the creature doesn't deserve,

"You must understand, King Cornelius did not know of his station. He only just learned of his birth right and responsibilities."

"You're only proving my point further," the demon laughs before tightening his grip on Candrima's neck. "You are unfit to rule. Submit to my challenge or watch this pathetic excuse for a daughter of Hell die."

Anger boils my blood, but before anyone can think to react, the candles are snuffed out. Total darkness engulfs the castle while my shadows are called from me by Candrima. I smell the acrid stench of fear rising of our intruder right as my shadows flow into his respiratory system, choking off his air supply. My brothers purr in excitement over her display of power.

"I will not be some defenseless victim," Candrima hisses while stepping back from the stifled demon.

Seeing her safe amongst my brothers, I charge forward, letting my full form free. But then something strange happens. Right as my shadows are pulled from the intruder, my body mass triples, my maw unhinges, freeing a second row of teeth, and I get the overwhelming urge to consume any living threat. Including the peccant demon in front of me.

The desire to cause devastation for his slight against my queen is untameable, and I tear his head from his body with one fluid motion. His steel bones make a pleasant crunching sound in my mouth and the crimson blood that was once contained in his useless meat sack is now spilling at my feet. His body twitches once, then twice, and once I'm satisfied with the limpness, I toss him aside like soiled laundry. Exhilaration floods me and the sensation is frightening, but I don't get the chance to work through why before I'm called back into action.

"There are more coming," Tayo says, while checking his own tablet. "There must be a mob of two hundred and so."

He shows me the screen of demons armed with arrows, spears, and swords and I take to the sky before I can realize it. My monstrous arms work in tandem with my wings to get me to the highest point of our mountain, relishing the challenging burn emanating from my muscles. I feel more alive than I ever have before. The rush I feel is second only to the feeling I get when Candrima holds me. This is what I'm made for. This is what I'm destined to do.

Defend and protect.

It takes me only a few seconds to reach the top, but by that time my body is comparable in size to the mountain I'm hanging off of.

My inky shadows billow around my body, casting an ominous hallow around The Valley Of Tenebrosity. My enemies began to reek of fear upon the sight of me, some utilizing the sense they were born with and abandoning the fight before it even begins, lest they want to die a senseless death tonight. Our lilac moon beats it's light against my onyx horns and I smile, knowing this is how I claim my birth right. This moment, will undoubtedly be one for the records.

Arrows begin to arch down from the skies, tipped with fire and laced with toxins. Some land on my palm, but they do not affect me. I throw them back from where they came and enjoy the harrowing screams that follow. Slowly, my shadows descend upon my land like a dense fog, creeping over peaks and settling into valleys. A few warriors succumb to my personal poison instantly while the rest move to higher ground. Even still, I know this won't take long. I've already slashed their numbers by half in just five minutes.

And then Candrima appears.

A flash of light erupts near my cheek before the sorceress settles onto shoulder. She says nothing as she grips the side of my neck, but when the second round of arrows descend from the clouds, she raises her free hand and absorbs them into a sigil. Seconds later, squelching fills the air as the weapons pierce their original wielders, followed by the sharp coppery scent of blood. I use my shadows to reduce our fallen enemies to ash while Candrima continues to redirect their blades. It takes less time than a bathroom break, and when the fields are clear, I make my declaration.

"I am Cornelius, King Of The Shadows. This is my Queen. Submit to her mercy or perish under my austerity. No challenges shall be honored under the duress of my queen!" I growl.

Pride swells in my chest when the few remaining challengers bow before me followed by the people of the valley.

I am king, and I will protect my people and my family.

Heaven

Candy

I don't consider myself much of an authority, but I have to admit seeing assholes bow down to my husband after trying to kill me was very hot. Not hot, however, was the dead demon in the dining room.

"Jamanichei, someone has to clean this up," Corn murmurs.

He's back to normal, but he's absolutely drenched in blood. It's matted in his skin and hair and I would be concerned if not for his imperial immunity. I'm more worried that he's butt ass naked. His clothing shredded since I didn't think he could get much bigger than his second demon form, so I reluctantly sacrifice yet another nightgown to clothe him, making note to fix my accommodation spell. I really need to get more nightgowns. Is there a Walmart in Hell? It feels like there'd be a Walmart in Hell.

"We have staff for that. Although unfortunately his body does appear to be diseased. They'll need to dig their suits out. They don't have royal immunity," Ninny explains, interrupting my mental checklist.

I silently examine the body. His head rests in a corner fifteen feet away from the other parts of his mangled corpse. Corn definitely killed him dead. However, I think I could revive him. Now I know what you're thinking; Why would she revive a creature who threatened to stab her eye out? I won't deny it's a strange course of action, but I have my reasons.

Magic is an equal exchange as is everything else in life. You cannot give without taking, for that is the law of balance. So I stretch out my hands, palms facing the dismembered. Light flickers in my irises as my powers swell, borrowing life from the eggshell roses planted around the room's perimeter. The blood spilled against the blue tiles slowly begins to return to the body, drawing into the flesh, and then the demon's head snaps back on with a satisfying popping sound.

Of course, Corn looks displeased. I can't exactly blame him seeing how my life was threatened, but he waits patiently for my explanation as the demon becomes re-acclimated to the world of the living. The once-dead intruder draws in a sharp breath,

"What happened?" he screams.

His once disintegrated skin is beginning to grow back in patches, which he only realizes when he touches his clawed hand to his previously severed throat.

"Well, to make a long story short, my husband ate your head," I answer.

He glances at an irritable Corn, but quickly tears his gaze away when Corn bears his fangs. I can only imagine the horrific memories that comes with being revived from a gruesome death.

"What is your name?" I ask cautiously.

He reacts to the sound of his beating heart like an animal being exposed to a vacuum cleaner. It's clear that he's in shock, and the last thing I want is for his reaction to the fear he's feeling to set Corn off. I can't keep killing roses. It's unethical...

"My name is Kirin, Your Majesty," the demon says, bowing his head.

"Kirin," I nod in acknowledgment. "You're free to go."

Everyone's heads snap towards me like finger-fired rubber bands almost immediately, even Ninny. I'm sure they've think I've lost my fucking mind, but they hold their tongues, waiting on the other shoe to drop.

Only there isn't one.

Kirin also shares their disbelief.

"Free to go? Your Majesty, I am beyond grateful, but was I not killed for treason against the crown?" he asks.

"Yes, that's correct," I confirm.

"And you're letting me go?"

Corn's brows quirk up as they so often do when he's observing a situation, silently begging the earlier question of why. I'd like to be all dark and mysterious like Mr. Three Forms, King Of Shadows over here, but it's just not my nature. So I smile somberly and provide my answer.

"Your life was spared only as a courtesy to anyone else who would think of attempting something like this. You are free to go, but every second you spend breathing will remind you of what happens when you unfairly contest the throne of our king. You will live long, cursed by the memory of death. A fitting punishment in my opinion."

Minor displays of admiration creep onto most every one of the royal brother's faces in the form of smiles. Every one except for Corn. Instead he stares at me like I've grown a second head, and it's so intense I start wondering if I have. His pulsing rust eyes will not leave mine no matter how many times I look away. Not wanting to face whatever that is, I turn to Ninny and ask for Kirin to be escorted home, *without* being murdered *again.* The brothers are quick to volunteer and I'm quick to shoot them down, not trusting the sinister smiles upon their handsome faces. Even Tayo looks like he's calculating Kirin's final demise. Once I make sure he's off, I leave the dining room and scurry off to Corn and I's shared bath hall. Something is screaming at me to run and I've learned my lesson about not listening to my instincts. I was carried over Willis Tower last time I didn't listen.

Corn was still in the company of his grandmother and brothers when I left the great hall and they seemed to be wrapped in an important conversation about royal demon stuff. So I'm mortified to see him waiting for me in the middle of a hot bath.

"Hello, Candrima," he cooes.

His voice is so deep it's hypnotic. I start to fall into a thoughtless trance and approach him, forgetting that I witnessed him bite off a demon's head minutes earlier.

"What are you doing here?" I gasp. "I thought you were talking to Ninny."

"I was," he drawls. "But then you left."

The urge to run is back and stronger than ever, but inky shadows ripple over calm blue water until they spill over the edge I'm closest to. I make the mistake of blinking and he captures me in his darkness and guides me into the pool. I can see the water wetting my dress due to the only source of light coming from the east windows.

"You are a formidable queen, Candrima Castille," he rumbles, tipping my chin upward with his extended claw. "I was a fool to ever question that."

His eyes are pure black, completely devoid of any luminence, while his fangs are extended. His honeyed breath tickles my ear as he breathes the scent of my skin before striking, just like any other apex predator.

"Are you going to bite me?" I ask, hyper aware of his desire through our bond.

I know what he wants. He wants to sink into my flesh and claim me. He wants to mark me. He wants there to be no doubt that I am his queen.

"I'd be lying if I said it isn't tempting," he replies before licking the curve of my neck.

I shiver as his warm, thick, tongue glides across my skin like cold butter against hot seared steak. The urge to submit to his whims grows unbearable and evident. With my thighs becoming slick from anticipation. But if I let this demon bite me, he could very well get me pregnant.

Sorry Time, but you will have to wait.

I form a plan and try my hardest to keep it to myself despite our bond.

"Can we at least wash our battle asses first?" I plead.

A familiar smile settles onto his lips. One that reminds me of when we first met. If Corn knows something, he doesn't show it. He just lowers me onto one of the bath shelves, strips my soggy dress, and begins washing my back. He cleans me with care, making sure to scrub my scalp all the way down to the soles of my feet before turning his attention to his own body. It doesn't take long before I'm putty in his hands, and I don't realize that his purring is liquefying my brain until his soft lips sweep over my collar.

"Don't bite me," I whisper in a small voice.

Corn hesitates, but he doesn't withdraw. Our bond is pulled taut, with the energy that binds our souls tugging me closer to him. Giving in is hard to resist. I'm starting to need it just as much as he does.

"Please, Candy," he pouts. "Just a little one."

It's an odd thing, seeing a demon king beg, but endearing nonetheless. I won't lie, feeling the jolt of electricity surge through my body when he bites is addictive. Still, I have no desire to be bred any time soon. I must remain strong. I must remain firm.

Then the Chicagoan in me resurfaces.

I must get the fuck out of dodge.

I'm living in another dream. Running through the halls of The Shadow Castle, running from the resident darkness, running from my fate. My husband. His voice sends chills across my perspiring skin,

"Little witch, you will never outrun me," he taunts.

"I can and I will," I sneer in reply.

The air between us falls quiet before Cornelius laughs.

The sound ricochets through the cavernous hall, settling deep into my bones. Then the memory of the dream begins rushing back. My adrenaline surges. I pick up my dress and take off, staying just a few feet ahead of the all-consuming darkness.

One by one, the flickering orange flames of the candles lighting my path are extinguished. The rolling cloud of darkness containing the sinister intentions of Cornelius follows me wherever I turn, but just like in the dream, I come across a path to salvation.

The library.

It beckons me forward with its moonlit shelves and gilded ladders, plus the door to the balcony is open. I know this was the way I met my end in the previous dream, but I can't help but foolishly believe that this time could be different. This time, I think I might win.

I command the heavy doors close before barricading them with some nearby furniture; A large chaise and a corresponding sofa. I'm not stupid. I don't think it's going to stop Corn, but I do think the inconvenience of maneuvering it will slow him down.

Dream Candrima never thought of that!

Once I'm satisfied with my blockade, I sprint to the balcony, and let the cool violet light of Hell's Sixth moon bathe my skin. She doesn't have as strong an effect as Earth's moon, but she calls to me still. Feeding my powers, strengthening my body, and distracting me from the insidious darkness that now has a grip on me.

My Mama was right, procrastination finally bit me in the ass.

Just like in my dream, I'm pulled through the grandiose doors and down the expansive hall. My feet dig into the plush rugs that line the floor, unsuccessfully delaying what I know is inevitable. My hands grasp at the shadows and hallucinations my husband conjured up to placate me. He laughs and I know it's useless fighting it, but I still try.

Until I land in his arms.

Not quite a man, but not quite a monster, he is firm but gentle. He holds me like he never wants to let go and subconsciously I know he never will. This game that we play only proves that where I go, he will follow. His soul will seek mine until the end of time. We are two piece of the same puzzle.

"Little witch, it appears you were incorrect," he says.

We both knew it would end this way, but his haughty chuckle encourages me to deny it.

"No, I-"

My heels spin against the ground until I face those gorgeous eyes of his. Observant, bright, and mischievous. I would recognize them in any shade or shape, across any lifetime.

"Corn," I gasp.

A smile stretches his lips wide as he gently scratches the base of my curly head, letting the spirals form around his fingertips.

"Candrima," he purrs, placing my right hand over his racing heart.

I feel his power and vulnerability underneath the skin of palm and I lean into it. He catches my fall from grace with surety, pressing his mouth against mine. Greedy kisses send us spinning into a world of our own creation, far away from the realities of our current life, and we find a beautiful rhythm with each other.

We descend breathlessly into chaotic shadows, only re-materializing when we land on the soft down of our mattress. Corn's larger body cradles my smaller one while his deft fingers work to rid me of my nightdress and hair ties. It doesn't take long before my skin is completely bare as is his, and when I feel the uninhibited glide of his palms against my back I melt.

"You are mine," he says, seeking my mouth.

"I am yours," I moan, reciprocating.

"I belong to only you. My heart was born beating for yours and I will be yours even after this world has passed ten times over," he whispers against the shell of my ear. "I love you, Candrima Castille."

"And I love you, Cornelius. Until the end of the universe as we know it. Until we are nothing more than a memory trapped in a drop of rain."

He flips me onto my back, his body dominating mine. I feel the energy pulling taut between us again when we lock eyes. Corn's gaze a mixture of raw desire, love, and excitement while my own reflects vulnerability and need. My breath hitches when his lips part to put his sharp white teeth on display and I raise my chin to offer my neck. But instead of a bite, I feel his tongue on my sex.

It's really easy to forget Corn is a demon most days. He arranges table bouquets for me based on my mood, plus we play board games and eat campfire marshmallows. We have a wash day routine, a shopping schedule, and also a chore list for the cottage. Our relationship at it's core is normal.

But this isn't.

He keeps his eyes trained on me while the tip of his fleshy pink tongue swirls against my tender hooded bud. The sensation is overwhelming because I can feel the crown of his steeled length pressing against my entrance, but I can't move. I'm pinned under the weight of his upper arms while his tails tighten against my core and hips, pushing my breasts upward so he can work the sensitive peaks between his fingers.

"What are you doing?" I cry as my head falls backwards into the pillows.

The only response I get is depraved laughter, then I feel the slight sting of his girth stretching me out.

I dig my nails into his triceps when his stroking begins. He eases in painfully slow only to roll his hips into mine with the speed of a light rail, forcing me to take all of him at once. I wish it hurt, but having Cornelius take me this way feels righter than chilly March rain against fresh blooms. I cry out his name and it sounds like a hymn upon my lips. The taste of his moniker is addicting. I writhe from the relentless pleasure and beg for mercy, experiencing insanity and euphoria simultaneously.

All while he watches me with a sadistic grin plastered on his hauntingly handsome face.

"A pretty little witch got lost in the woods and sacrificed herself to a demon. Look at what's become of you," he laughs.

He's right. I've become a live reenactment of a biblical painting where a young, naive maiden is eaten by a demon. All the details are there, even the sumptuous velvet chaise that could only belong to a creature with more wealth than a large kingdom. However, those women looked pained to be in such situations. I'm having the time of my life.

Until there's a knock at the door.

I know we're married adults, but I still find the space to feel guilty for getting ravaged in a family castle. We could've at least waited until everyone went to bed. It's impolite to have my in-laws listening to my hedonistic cries.

"Don't," Corn warns when I begin to fidget.

His rhythm hasn't faltered once even with the impatient knocking, and even though my manners are screaming at me to stop what I'm doing and answer, his paced strokes and gentle licks are starting to push me over the edge.

"Corn," I wail. "Wait, please. I'm gonna cum."

I search his eyes for semblance of understanding but he offers none.

"Good," he purrs.

The knocking continues while the simmering pleasure in my spine boils over and evolves into a rushing hot spring. All the pressure, fullness, and finesse consumes me until breathing is the only function my brain can afford. Everything else is irrelevant.

The doors swing open with a loud bang, revealing both Ninny and Granny, as well as a grubby little man with some floating camera device. I don't know if it's surprise or disgust on their faces but I know I'll try my best not to find out until the following morning.

"I'm sorry," I mumble, as we make what has to be the world's awkwardest eye contact.

Unfortunately I'm square in the middle of my orgasm so I can't really stop, and it's not like Corn would let me anyway. With an irate snarl, he casts them out into the hall and binds the doors shut with a borrowed bit of my magic. The bed quakes while he realigns us both, making sure that he's the only thing in my line of vision.

Outside, I can hear Ninny arguing with the strange demon about using a different reference while Granny laughs. Inside, I'm blushing with embarrassment.

"Candrima," Corn says, refocusing me with a gentle head nudge. "It's just us."

Like a spell, his words nullify all other sounds and I realize that it really is just us. I melt into the warmth of his rust eyes, drowning in their beckoning depths, while my mind focuses on our union. It doesn't take me long to sync to our new rhythm, with my hips raising rhythmically to glide against his. Seconds turn into minutes of us staring at each other like this until any notion of separation becomes impossible, and Corn reclaims my mouth with his. Making us whole. The thoughtful shape of our room dissolves into a mess of us. With my light cutting through Corn's eclipsing shadows. Our powers mimic the movement of our physical forms, darkness dominating light, light subduing dark, until we reach the precipice of our pleasurable ascension.

"Candrima," Corn moans, my name sounding sweeter than honey on his tongue.

"Cornelius," I plead, taking his face between my palms.

Our passionate ebullition does not come quietly. Curses flow from Corn with an exasperated whimper, while I cry out to the heavens for salvation that I know will never reach me. And in the midst of it all, my mouth aches for a taste of my bind. So I reach up and bite his soft exposed neck, and he grunts even though my blunt teeth barely mark him. We stay that way for a while after our movement stops, only breaking when I feel a laugh sneak up Corn's throat.

"What's funny?" I ask.

"You bit me."

"So?"

"So now I'm pregnant. Congratulations, you made one of your little Mpreg novels a reality," he snickers.

I know it's impossible, but an image of a round and cranky Corn populates in my mind instantly, causing heat to flood my face. The best sex of my life ends with a joke. Goodness gracious.

"I thought I told you to stay out of my books," I fuss.

"I thought we both knew I had no plans to listen," he chuckles.

Before I can fire back, I'm repositioned onto his chest so his large leathery wings can cage us. Then dart throws a flat sheet across the apexing horns.

"I made us a little fort so I can tell you a secret," he whispers.

This is only our second covert fort, but I smile because I know this will become a staple in our relationship. A girl could get used to 10,000 plus years of this.

"What's the secret?" I reply in my smallest voice.

Corn places a soothing kiss to my right temple before his smile takes the lead on the conversation. Somehow I think I know what the secret is.

"You, Candrima Castille, are the best wife a demon could ask for. Leagues better than what a beast like me deserves," he whispers while stroking my damp curls.

Ok, so I was wrong. Because I didn't expect him to say that.

I almost think he's joking until I see the angst simmering in his eyes. Angst indicative of his skepticism. I'll never truly know why he doesn't believe he's deserving of a love like this, but I'll always reassure him that he does.

"Cornelius, I love every part of you. The florist bits, the snarky bits, and the murdery demon king bits. My kind, handsome, and patient baby. You are a perfect husband."

I kiss his exposed fang and it earns me a head bump, one that once again reminds me of his relation to cats. He purrs his response, his arms tightening around me to keep me safe.

"I love you too, my darling little witch. More than what can ever be transcribed."

Corn

I wake up when a familiar sharp coppery scent hits my nose.

Blood.

Immediately I reach for Candrima and when I move her from her spot on the mattress, I see her crimson blood spilled against the sand colored sheets. My mind flashes back to the first night we met, when she was truthfully too injured to live and panic swells in my chest. Did I do this or did someone else? Did she accidentally hurt herself? How could I let something happen to my wife?

"Candy, you're bleeding!" I exclaim, scooping her into my arms to examine her. "Can you tell me what happened?"

I'm moving too fast to think, but when I get to the third button on her night dress her very uncoordinated hand flops against my nose and mouth to stop me.

"Corn, it's just my period. I'm fine."

Disturbed laughter fills our chambers.

I forgot that women had menstrual cycles.

Or maybe I was just expecting that she wouldn't get one. That line of thinking is dangerous, I know. But I still can't stop from smiling at a vision of her caressing a high, round belly while she waddles around and makes demands. That could be inaccurate since I don't know much about pregnancy. My only experience witnessing it so far has been with Nafisa. But even still I know I would spoil Candrima rotten. She'd want for nothing.

"I'm sorry, sweetheart," I coo, placing a hand against her bloated belly. "I'll start you a shower and we'll spend the day in bed together then, alright?"

"Oh no you don't!" Ninny says, swinging open the doors. "You have guests."

I can tell based on the formality of her attire. She's dressed to the nines in Hell's finest cave silks and hides. The family gemstone hangs heavy against her neck while her commanding staff occupies her hands. I scowl as staff enter our room with fresh linens, towels, and breakfast, ready and willing to launch into action. Madam Kitara stands beside my grandmother with an amused smirk, clearly delighting in my irritation.

"Well, tell them to leave. I'm tending to my queen," I say gruffly.

I'm shocked by my abrasiveness. I've never once been so inconsiderate before and yet I don't regret it. Candrima is my top priority and everything else falls second. Royal ass kissing included.

Ninny raises one sharp brow in my direction, issuing a challenge. My grandmother is a formidable opponent but I'm still unmoved. She will have to pry my witch from my cold, dead hands.

"Listen, Cornelius. The High Council Of Hell is here because of last night's coup attempt. They actually arrived last night, but they were kind enough to wait for an audience once they heard your *celebration.*"

I notice some of the staff look towards their polished toes while some stare straight ahead, their eyes filled with suppressed laughter.

So everyone heard me claim my wife?

Good.

"Ninny, can I just have a little time?" I plead. "At least to get Candrima comfortable?"

Ninny scowls at my proposal.

I see where I get my sense of compromise from.

"I will take care of Candy, Cornelius," Madam Kitara offers with a chuckle. "She'll be good as new in no time. Go be the king your people deserve."

Damn, Madam Kitara is good at this. My people do deserve a capable ruler, so with that, I reluctantly place Candrima against the warm mattress and peck her forehead. She smiles at me, eyes still half-lidded, before waving me off towards the bath chamber.

I guess it's time to be a king.

I'm on high alert when I enter the war room. One, because I've never been in my third form this long, and two because I feel out of my element. I'm meeting with the other Sons Of Hell for the first time and I'm dressed in traditional royal garb. With my agbada flowing around me like a second set of wings, my hair braided with the pattern of our family, and my markings out for all to see. This is in sharp contrast to some of the demons of the upper realms who wear full suits and capes, and the demons of three realms below me, who opt for longer loinclothes made of leather and encrusted with their family gemstones.

Wanting to end this quickly, I speak first.

"Good morning, thank you for your patience," I say.

I get collective nods in response before a pale, silver eyed demon raises a question.

"So you're the infamous missing Sixth Son Of Hell?"

Like Ninny, his expression issues a challenge, but if I can handle a grandmother who is essentially an ancient Riddler, I can handle a frost demon.

"I am," I confirm, voice steady.

The visiting kings briefly exchange looks before turning to me and offering full smiles.

"Welcome, brother!" they exclaim almost in unison.

The Frost King, Simon, commends my battle against the coup. While The King Of Flames, Haco, who is still single, asks whether or not Candrima has any available siblings. He's saddened to learn that she does not, and the closest thing she has to a sister is partnered with a vampire already. While our initial conversation is light and friendly, even our descent into deeper topics such as Candy's school and the drought problem are approached with respect and understanding. Especially when it comes to my queen.

"So she is a moonchild? Does this mean that her time here will have to be limited?" Pashir, The King Of Luxury asks.

"Unfortunately so," I say. "She will need to return to earth every four days for moonlight. Her stability is dependent on it."

"Do you think she'd ever choose Earth over Hell?" Simon questions. "It is her born home after all."

His question catches me off guard, but luckily I'm saved by Candrima's graceful entrance. She's dressed in a lapa that coordinates my agbada, her hair is braided in cornrows with a pattern indicating her status as queen, and *my* gemstone hangs from her neck in a string of hammered gold.

"No," I answer before joining her side.

I take her hand in mine without thinking and she rewards me with a megawatt smile. Quickly, I forget that we're not the only ones occupying the room. Until the visiting Kings bow to her in greeting. Candrima freezes, looking unsure of what to do. At first she gives a little wave but once she sees Akanni's meddlesome smirk, she begins to courtesy. Which I put a stop to immediately.

"Women do not bow to men in Hell. Our society is matriarchal," I remind her gently, while raising her chin.

She straightens her back and responds with a strong, but kind, nod instead. While showing off that same dazzling smile that has successfully captured my heart.

"Welcome, your majesties. It's an honor to meet you," she sings.

She does a quick spell to make a flashing welcome sign in Eldritch and our guests smile at the thoughtful gesture.

"The Daughters Of Hell will be pleased with our newest addition," Simon says.

"So I'm a daughter of Hell?" she asks sheepishly.

"You are indeed, Queen Candrima," I smile.

The following weeks pass by in a blur. Our time is split between Hell and Earth nearly 50/50, with almost everyone of Candrima's free moments going to the coven and her school initiative. She's erected three more schools and hired two more headmasters while also coordinating volunteer work for Midnight Call. It's commendable how hard she works to ensure she's handling her responsibilities, but I still make her take breaks every once in a while. We have thousands of years of this routine, but she will only be in her 30's for a short period of time and I want her to enjoy them.

So on the days when we journey back to Earth, I curate a date based on her bucket list. Last time it was exploring the night markets of Turkey and I'm not sure if that was the best idea since I still can't think of anything to top it. But having her squeeze my hand as we wove in and out of the ornate vendor stalls and beckoning food stands filled with spiced meat, cold beverages, and honey-sweet desserts was beyond worth it. She even made friends with a lunar moth.

Maybe we'll visit Atlantis next...

"Are y'all ready to go to Heaven?" Madam Kitara asks.

"Excuse me?" I gawk.

It's a quarter past nine and here I am, reviewing the salaries for our newest teachers while thinking about sniffing in between my wife's legs when our elder asks a question like this. I'm an imperial demon. Imperial demons in Heaven is a big ole no. I don't want any issues with the EUM. I just want to harbor my little illegal super nova and mind my business.

"Well Yule is in three days. You two are my plus ones," she explains.

"Yes, but I thought you picked someone else after we told you we were no longer separating. Plus I'm imperial."

"You were imperial two months ago too and you entered just fine, Cornelius," Madam Kitara reminds me. "Plus I really want Candy to experience Heaven at least once. Yule is the perfect time to visit and she will likely be barred from a tourism visa once the EUM gets wind of her coronation as The Queen Of The Sixth."

Damn it all, the elder witch has a point. Heaven is beautiful, and I know Candrima would love all the niche shops and luxurious gardens, but that trip will be out the window once she swears her allegiance to the people of Hell next month. Journalists, no matter the species, are loyal to nothing but a good story.

"Can we Corn, please?" she begs, shaking my arm.

I'm stupid because I look at her cute little face the moment she touches me and completely abandon all my resolve. It doesn't matter how many times she gives me that sweet yet bratty pout, it'll bring me to knees every time.

"Fine, but there are rules. You cannot use your powers for any reason whatsoever, and you will need a disguise," I explain.

She swings her feet excitedly, practically vibrating with anticipation. Somehow I don't think she heard my disclaimer. Either that or she doesn't care.

"Candrima," I chide.

"Yes, yes. I heard you Mr. Grumpy Pants. No powers, mandatory disguises. I'm going to the library so I can make a list. Come get me when you're ready for bed," she says, folding herself into a flash of light.

"She's going to be spoiled rotten in no time at all," Madam Kitara chuckles. "You've created a monster."

I dismiss her comment with a wave and go back to my reports, but her excitement surges through our bond, making me smile.

Madam Kitara is right once again.

Yule is nipping at our heels in a blink of an eye, and Candy is gagging from the viscous texture of a Hellion deception potion.

"What is this made of?" she shrieks as her skin begins to transform. "Liquidized ass?"

I don't tell her how close her estimate is because despite the questionable ingredients and the admittedly foul taste, this is the best deception charm in all the realms. Not even Heaven can strip this. She looks just like a water imp.

"I know it's unpleasant, but look, it was worth it," I say, directing her towards a mirror.

Her marbled skin is now swirled with translucent green and deep, majestic blue. Her hair waves with every movement, her usually tight curls flowing free, while a set of gills protrude from the curve of her neck.

"Holy shit, I'm blue!" she exclaims while touching her hands to her face.

"Yes," I chuckle while lacing my fingertips through the ends of her hair. "You are blue."

"And you're the Geico gecko," she says, tracing my temporary scales.

"I really need to catch up on TV," I groan.

"How's everything coming?" Granny Kita asks.

Yes, I said Granny. I've recently graduated from formal names with Candrima's family since our decision to move forward with our bond. Her mother is now my mother, my Ninny is now her Ninny, and Ted... Well I'm just glad he stopped trying to incinerate me over dinner.

Aster chirps in reply, letting Granny know Candy just needs to put on her gown. I've grown mildly attached to the freeloader since we've arrived in Hell. Aster is quite helpful when it comes to keeping tabs on Candrima, plus I can tell he cares for her deeply. I still don't like that he tries to claim my seats, but that's something a spray bottle can correct.

"Ok, shimmy in that thang and come on!" Granny shouts. "We need to get going if we're going to make the parade."

"There's a parade?" Candrima squeaks.

"It's Heaven, my love. There's always some ostentatious display."

"I thought you were kidding," Candy whispers as we make our way through the crowd.

The "ass juice" worked well and neither one of us triggered the charm sensors, which means we made it just in time for the parade.

"Unfortunately not," I reply. "This is what all those cuccubi fees go to."

A float of solid gold slowly rolls by. Its ruby-lined chariot transports a pool of shimmering ether fluid, which acrobatic angles use to teleport in and out of different floats. The crowd cheers before being blanketed with delicate petals of black baccara roses, hundreds if not thousands of these beautiful flowers will lie trampled in the streets. Their beauty appreciated for a fraction of the time they deserve.

"I've seen enough," Candy says firmly. "Come on."

She pulls me along towards the museums where we meet Granny Kitara.

"Alright, I got some business to wrap up and I know Candrima has a list. So let's go do our separate things and meet back here at the artifact section in three hours. Sounds good?" Granny asks.

Candy produces her list, gives it a quick glance, and nods in agreement.

"Yep, if you need us before then, we'll be checking out the gardens."

"Mm. Ok. Check out the Earth exhibit," she says, before disappearing into a cloud of mist.

"What's in the Earth exhibit?" Candrima asks with a confused blink.

I scoff at Granny Kitara's obvious set-up and guide Candy back towards the garden path.

Ah, water witches.

"Corn, look at all the forget-me-nots!" Candrima exclaims.

I gaze upon the familiar field of periwinkle and violet flowers with pride. I'd only just recently learned that they were one of Candy's favorite flowers. The irony of it isn't lost on me. It seems everything in my life for the last fifty years has been aligning for her arrival.

"I planted these," I say softly.

She turns to me with all the admiration in the world simmering in her beautiful brown eyes. A disbelieving smile graces her plump lips.

"You planted all of these?" she asks, glancing out at the rolling field.

"Yes," I nod. "Sometimes the EUM will make a skill trade in exchange for reduced fees. Saves them money and time on vetting since they already keep tabs on how well cuccubi perform their chosen profession."

"That's honestly disgusting, but these are so beautiful, Cornelius. Hopefully when everything gets settled at home, we can build you a new garden."

It dawns on me then that she is referring to Hell as home. I think back to Simon's question and I realize how fortunate I really am. Our initial relationship was only complicated because I made it that way. Being with Candrima is easy.

Too easy.

"This is a terrible time for you to go into heat," I whisper against her waving curls.

"I know, I'm sorry," she sighs.

It's not her fault but it is inconvenient. Unfortunately, not even the best deception charm can block my physical response to my wife's hormones. My entire being craves to breed. My eyes darken against the pale Heaven moon while Dart sneaks out of my pants for a taste of that delectable honeysuckle trap. Sensing my intentions, Candy widens her stance to allow my tail to flicker against her sex, which is already slick with desire. I snake my tail around her thigh and sink into her, sending her melodious moan off through the night air. It's addicting and I instantly forget where we are and what we're *supposed* to be doing.

If she doesn't stop me I'm going to take her right here in this field.

Candy's soft hands glide up my chest and hook around my shoulders to guide me into her orbit. One kiss turns into a dozen, and a dozen turns into three. All of which blacksmith my length into hot, hard steel. My resolve transforms with it, my mind abandoning all gentlemanly inclinations for a chance to sink inside her once I feel her pert nipples against my chest.

"Candrima," I start.

"Please," she finishes.

Her little pleading voice is unfortunately agreeable in my ear. It's chilly out, the area is busy with tourist, and we're here illegally. There are so many reasons for me to tell her no, but instead I answer,

"Ok, sweetheart. Quietly though."

I memorized the layout of this land when I worked it and it hasn't changed in the twenty years since. So I lead us to the bottom of a steep hill where lush wildflowers grow free and high. Perfect for ambush sex.

"Candy, are you sure?" I ask carefully after laying her in the grass.

I have to admit she's a vision lying here with flowers gathered all around her crown and molding to the apexes of her curves. I do wish I could have her like this in her actual form, but I'll take Candrima however I can get her. As long as she says,

"Yes. Now stop being so polite and take your fucking dick out."

Her demand comes out rough and salacious. Likely driven by all her rampaging hormones. It's not her normal sweet, almost shy approach, but the sub in me is ecstatic about that. Especially when she rewards me for following directions by scraping her teeth against my bottom lip.

"What do you want?" I purr when she pulls me against her.

The silky fabric of her dress is pooled into my free hand so I can marvel at her expansive thighs and soft belly. Rubbing a finger along the inside of her left thigh, I find my answer.

"You," Candy says seductively, spreading her legs wide and pushing me forward by the arch of my back.

I bite back a moan when we meet. I don't enter her, but she's so wet and warm that it doesn't matter. I know I need to build some endurance though if I'm going to satisfy her until we get back to Hell. So I slowly drag my dick against her fat sex, inciting her by directing my movements towards her swollen clitoris. She looks like a painting laying here wide open underneath all these stars. Highly prized and valued.

"Corn," she whimpers.

"Quiet," I say.

I know it'll be nearly impossible for such a vocal creature to remain quiet while in heat, but there's a solution for that.

I feel her release approaching rapidly. Her body becomes an uncoordinated, twitching mess. Her heavy breasts rise and fall with each labored breath, and her skin begins to deepen.

"Corn, I can't," she cries.

"You can," I affirm before slipping Dart into her wet open mouth.

That's all it takes to send her over the edge and wet the grass with bliss. Being an opportunist by nature, I don't waste the chance for what I consider a grand entry, and I push into her at the top of her orgasm, throwing her right into the next.

The way she wrings me reminds me to recite the contraceptive incantation and keep my teeth to myself. Truthfully, I would love to see her fat and round with my child, but I know the timing isn't right. Our coronation is in 30 days, and her schools will begin to open just a few months after that. I want her to enjoy her pregnancy completely and not hobble around with a mile-long to-do list.

Speaking of to-dos...

"Look at you being so quiet for me," I laugh. "Good job, sweetheart. Such a good listener."

Candy's eyes well with tears from everything unvocalized while her hips buck against mine with determination. Any other time that might get me to punch my ticket, but she's not the one in charge tonight.

I am.

I pin the weight of my arm against her hips and force her to move at my tempo. Languid and chasmic, leaving nothing untouched. Greedy almost. Truthfully, I should be adapting to her speed since we're mating in public, but the feral beast in me is desperate to savor the first day of her heat. There's nothing in all the worlds quite like it.

Candy's slickness grips around my pulsing length like a hungry snake while her nails dig into my flexing back. The pleasure is towing the thin line of pain as I try to hold out just a bit longer. My fangs ache to sink into her pliable flesh with every indulgent stroke and her fertile honeyed scent is encouraging me to do just that.

Then she cums again.

Her body fits to mine like a missing puzzle piece, reunited at last. She ejects Dart from her mouth and captures my lips between hers in a bruising, breathless kiss. One that makes my already fragile state of existence dizzy. While she can't physically speak, that doesn't stop her from using telepathy to hurl me further into nirvana.

"Cornelius, you are all I ever wanted," she confesses.

I know she's not just saying that because I can feel it in our bond.

And here I am thinking imperial demons were cast out of Heaven.

Pleasure overtakes me in euphoric waves as it does Candrima, but even as she bears her neck to me in submission, I do not give myself permission to mark her in that way. Instead I bury my claws into the ground and force my urges onto the soil below us. It spares Candrima from being bred firstly, but I don't expect the secondary consequences. The earth beneath us surges us, new growth from the surrounding gardens bursting forward until the fresh, tender blooms cover us completely. Some shaken petals fall above us, cascading against our unionized bodies like freshly fallen snow and settling into Candy's gorgeous curls like crown jewels. After spending a second admiring it, I retract my claws and sit up to pull Candrima into my arms.

"Sorry for scaring you," I say, noticing her shiver.

She pulls away gently to collect my set jaw in her tiny hands and peer into my eyes.

"You didn't scare me," she says before looking at wild calendula, milkweed, and bees balm around us. "This is amazing."

She touches her fingers to the soft petals of a nearby black-eyed-susan and it waves under her power, opening even more from the light she emits.

"You're right. It's so amazing," I say.

She notices that I'm not talking about the plants, and we almost close the space between our bodies with a sweet kiss, but rustling grass interrupts us before we can.

Someone else is out there.

"Sassprhats," I curse. "We need to go."

Shadowing would be faster and more discreet, but it risks tripping the magic usage alarms and getting us discovered, and Candy's powers are incapable of being inconspicuous as she looks like an exploding super nova every time she teleports. So our next best option is to crawl through the grass until we make it to the main road.

Aster would howl if he could see us.

Unfortunately, we're not as sneaky as we need to be.

"I knew it!" A familiar voice shrieks.

In instinctively shield Candy, ready for wherever the night takes us, but standing in front of us with a walkie and a stolen pastry puff is Nilla. Grinning like I just told the world's biggest joke.

"What are you doing here?" I scoff.

"My job," she snickers. "Patrolling the gardens for Wayward Wanderers. Question is, what are you two doing here?"

"I can explain!" Candy interjects with a small finger.

"Oh, honey. The way you two smell explains plenty," Nilla laughs while raising a brow at her disheveled dress. "No need to be embarrassed. Heats are hard."

Candy bristles at the mention of her heat and crosses her legs as if that's the only source of her freshly fucked smell.

And I won't dare mention that it's not.

"Come on, let's go find y'all a recovery snack," Nilla says, redirecting the conversation. "Heaven's bread is fantastic."

We settle into a small cafe with a low crowd and order a 18 cheese grilled cheese. It's rich, salty, and buttery. So buttery that Candy moans when she takes in the first bite. I think the sandwich is good, but that isn't the reason I plan on having the cooks add it to our lunch rotation.

That moan hit different. That moan is the reason I keep rosemary on hand for her eggs.

"So did you do a skill trade?" I ask my sister who's busy talking to Candy about Heaven's frivolous fashions.

The wing stickers they have up here to mimic true angels are unsightly at best. Don't get me started on the togas.

"Yeah, I needed to save a little coin this time around," Nilla confesses with a nod. "Me and Phillipa are gonna start trying for a baby."

I open my mouth at my sister's confession, and then immediately close it again. I truly don't know what to say. This is one of the few times she's rendered me speechless.

Nilla lours before shoving me in the shoulder.

"Are you just going to stare at me like I'm growing an ass out of the side of my neck or are you gonna say something?" she shouts.

"I'm sorry!" I exclaim, while fixing my face. "I don't know what to say. I recall you being firmly anti-reproduction for the last 100 or so years. What changed?"

"Oh, Corn. That was so long ago," she tuts, eyes rolling in every direction but forward until she eventually settles on my face. "But I don't know. It's just, spending all this time with Charlie and watching her grow and learn and look just life Fisa... I want that too."

Seeing my troublesome sister so vulnerable and nervous squeezes my heart tight, and I reach across the table to hug her, completely ignoring the fact that she stiffens in my arms.

"You're going to be a great mom," I say.

"When the fuck did you start initiating hugs?" she whispers, dismissing my compliment. "Candy, girl. What are you doing to my brother? That pussy must be all kinds of magical."

"Ok, moment over," I sigh.

I retract back to my side of the table and finish the last of Candy's meal as per our tradition.

"Are you satisfied?" she asks as I slurp down the rest of her lemonade.

"Very," I answer. "What's next on your little list?"

Almost two hours later and we're in our fourth store looking for a spell book and an unmeltable lemon ice cream cookie that's only available in Heaven's art district.

"I need a case of these," she says, finishing the last bites of her cookie.

"I can arrange that," I laugh.

"That's the least you can do," Nilla interjects. "She's a saint to deal with your attitude."

My face falls flat as Candrima's lips twitch into a slight smile. She doesn't laugh outright with Nilla, but I can tell she wants to.

"Whatever, I'll be over here when you're ready," I say, heading off to the record displays.

I can at least get some music out of the deal while I'm being paraded around.

Candy

Corn described Heaven perfectly a month ago. Pretentious, prim, and pretty. We'd been in and out of several shops in museums and not one single thing was out of place.

Well, except for us.

I have to admit that nasty ass drink did it's job. Corn looked like the perfect lizardman while my nymph getup was nymphing. I even had several actually nymphs stop me, claiming they recognized me. Someone even reminded me to RSVP to her wedding.

I can't attend for obvious reasons, but she was nice so I'll definitely send a gift.

It was nice running into Nilla since Granny ditched us. Despite all of Corn's warnings, she was actually my favorite so far out of his two sisters. She was funny and knowledgeable and she knew how to get under Corn's skin. And he needed that sometimes. It sucked though, because I knew we wouldn't be able to hang out anytime soon with everything going on. She was a realm hopping bounty hunter and we were about to be coronated as the rules of the Sixth Realm Of Hell. Our overlap would be slim unless we suddenly developed a crime problem.

Goodness, I hope we didn't develop a crime problem.

"How many hours you got left on the sewer juice?" Nilla asks as we scour the shelves for The Magic Misfit's Universal Building Guide.

I was going to start on a hospital soon, but that wasn't the type of thing I could just wing. I needed to have actual instructions to make it functional. Hence the guide.

"About two. We drank it around 11pm. It's what, 3 now?"

"Correct," Nilla replies. "Just keep an eye on Corn. It's weight based magic and he's a hefty fellow."

I completely forgot that the magic was weight based! Hearing Nilla's reminder prompts me to abandon my book search and go find Corn. I race through the tight packed shelves and reach him in the nick of time. Both his tails are swinging freely behind him, and a demon poacher has a sharp pair of shears aimed right for Dart.

Platinum energy builds between my palms, and I don't think twice before firing.

I kill the would-be attacker right in front of the shop owner.

Corn swings around to face me, looking both mortified and concerned, but before he can scold me, he notices the Bastet owner's hand on the panic button.

"No, wait. Please!" he begs. "We can revive him!"

Not even a second passes before she slams her open paw into the button and triggers an alarm, prompting dozens of angels to flood the tiny shop.

They see the dead gryphon and then me with my hands raised in his direction. Several hand signals are exchanged and then the leader demands me to step forward and go peacefully.

"Candy, don't move a muscle," Corn growls.

His potion is sloughing off, and it's made abundantly clear that he's a demon of high station. His four arms fall at his sides and his second set of eyes appear like two crimson slits on his forehead, rapidly cataloging every movement and breath.

"You're not in control here, demon!" the captain grits. "Your friend violated a non-violence decree."

"She's my wife," Corn hisses. "And he was a poacher."

"Even if that's true, it doesn't mean that she had the right to kill him. Hands up little lady, you're under arrest."

"No," Corn bites back."Corn, it's fine," I argue. "I did it. I can handle the consequences like a big girl. It's fine."

"Candrima," he begs. "Don't."

You know that feeling you get when you gotta take a massive shit in public? What would you call that? Impending doom? Whatever it is, that's exactly what I felt when I disobeyed Corn and raised my hands above my head. Turns out that was my gut telling me that Heaven doesn't exactly play fair, because seconds later my body goes heavy from a poisoned dart that's launched into my wrist. My system rejects the foreign magic instantly and I vomit, trying to force it out. It's suddenly too hot to breath. Sweat pours from every surface of me and my vision blurs, but even in my state of pure dysfunction, I can hear why they did it.

"She's an S tier sorceress. The suppressant probably won't last long. She's already starting to sweat it out," the captain says. "Get a move on."

I try to crawl towards Corn and away from the gloved hands reaching for me, but it's no use. Someone picks me up by my collar and restraints me. But as soon as the cuffs touch the skin of my ankles and wrist, hot, sticky blood ends up gushing against my back.

"YOU WILL NOT TOUCH THE QUEEN OF SHADOWS!" Corn roars with a mouthful of ligaments.

Angels scramble to avoid being the next victim of Corn's wrath while he picks me up and slings my dead weight over his shoulder like I'm a bag of flour. He's expanding rapidly, and when his horns cut through the dry-walled ceiling, I know that he's going to end up tearing this building down. Seconds later I'm proved right when the chilly night air greets my bare skin. The remaining angels take to the sky to try and subdue Corn, but when he rips the wings clean off the fourth, they realize it's no use.

Instead an aerial tank materializes, armed with big guns, big angels, and a big net. I'm not exactly sure what they plan to do with that, but I can tell you I don't plan on finding out. My body is still weak, but I've soaked up enough moonlight for my magic to be potent. With one shaking hand, I focus on the tank and teleport it a half a mile away into the Embassy headquarters, setting everything within 300 feet ablaze. Embers crackle as the hungry flames lick up the sides of the grandiose building while screams of roasting soldiers fill the air, and I hate that my first thought is how much it smells like barbeque. But Corn finds that funny.

Even when the world is burning down around us, at least we have each other.

"Citizens of Heaven," an alarm blares. "Be not afraid. Please return to the safety of your homes."

The message repeats while hover screens fill with images of Corn's massacre headlined, *The Sixth Son Of Hell wages war on Heaven.*

War? This is not war.

This is retaliation at the worse. Corn was almost made into freaky deeky magic soup and I was poisoned.

"This is self defense!" I scream at a nearby reporter.

Suddenly the headline updates.

"Hellion Concubine Falsely Claims Self Defense."

Concubine? Isn't that a fancy word for some royal hussy with no real title? Did Heaven just call me a whore? I'll show them a fucking whore!

"Candy, we don't have time. We need to leave," Corn says, voice deep and gravelly.

I know he's right. Heaven is a mirage of smoke and mirrors, but one thing about it, they adapt quickly. Eventually they're going to figure out who we came with and how to detain us. Plus they have aerial tanks. Who knows what else they have in store?

"My bad," I say, adjusting myself on his shoulder. "Let's find Granny and Nilla and dip."

Luckily Nilla is right on our heels, and Granny is exactly where she said she'd be when three hours passed.

"I thought you two were being discreet," she says, eyebrows raised high.

"Long story, but we need to get that sword and go," Corn says, setting me down.

"Sword? The Sword Of Destiny? Why would we need the sword?" I ask.

"Corn," Granny mumbles disapprovingly.

She understands something that I do not and her gray curls shake from side to side sprinkling disappointment with every toss.

"Granny, I'm asking you to help me. Will you please help me?" Corn pleads.

"This won't work, Cornelius," she sighs. "Your fate is already in motion."

"PLEASE!" Corn screams. "Help me, Kita! I'm asking you to help me!"

Rain begins to beat down around us, washing the blood and ash from Corn's silky skin. Nilla holds my hand, also understanding the gravity of Corn's request.

"Why are you doing this?" I ask.

"This is what's best for you," Corn replies with a dry voice.

"No it's not. What's best for me is to go back home with our bond intact."

"Kita," he presses again, choosing to ignore me.

Granny looks me in my eyes with all the regret in the world before sighing her agreement.

"Fine, Cornelius. But you will need to work together. I won't be here to help you through this next part."

That same sense of dread fills my soul as soon as those words leave her lips. I want to question it, but we simply don't have enough time.

"I can trickle in with the rain, but you two will need to use your light and shadows to avoid the sensors. The sword is located in the pit of the third floor under a dome of diamond and graphene. You will have 60 seconds to grab it once we enter. Got it?"

"Got it," Corn agrees and I nod.

"Alright now, let's go."

It's dark out, so Corn takes my hand and transforms us into a fit of shadows to get us in. We move completely in sync. Heart to heart and mind to mind, dancing with a magic and a love as old as time itself. I still don't know why he wants to end this though, and when that doubt creeps into my stomach, our coordinated dance falls apart.

"Candy, what are you doing?" Corn asks as we involuntary separate.

"I don't know why you're doing this. Did you change your mind?" I sob.

Finally, I get a real response. He gently sweeps a few curls behind my ears and kisses the space they left behind on my forehead.

"No Candy, quite the opposite actually. I love you more than anything in all the realms. I love you more than myself. And I would send Hell into a war that we might not be able to win to protect you."

Thunder cracks above us, punctuating the sharp light from nearby lightening and I see his mournful expression. Finally, I understand. He's letting me go to guarantee my safety. Part of me knew this was always a possibility even when I felt the impenetrable protection of his embrace. I would fight it, but he's right. The Sixth Realm is in no condition to fight a war. I wouldn't put the people through that devastation.

I'm not selfish enough.

I dry my tears on my battered gown before taking Corn's extended hand. We rejoin and this time we do not come apart as we move through the stone entrance and up to the third floor. There's a wide, sunken display spanning 400ft that greets us there, and smack in the middle is The Sword Of Destiny. Granny re-materializes from a puddle on the other side, standing just close enough so that we can hear her voice.

"Candy, put a lil energy in your pointer finger and raise it to the floor!" she instructs.

I do what I'm told, and immediately, the whole room ignites into a liquid grid of laser sensors. They change erratically, every seven, three, or six seconds, keeping any would-be intruders on their toes.

"I know it looks daunting, but you got this. You done studies numbers your whole life, baby! It's a number game," she says. "Use the light current to your advantage."

At my grandmother's suggestion I start to think of the lasers like rivers and streams, converging and connecting to get me to my goal. Confidence flows in me and I do to Corn as he has done to me, turning him into pure light to move us across the floor. It's a good thing too because the lasers aren't just alarm sensors, they're also weapons. Any other being would've been cooked up like a sunday roast trying to play like this, but because of my gifts, I'm able to glide right through them. The speed of light is a much faster travel method than flying or walking, because we're to The Sword before I would be able to form a sneeze. However, as soon as my hand reaches up to touch the cloache of the display, the angel from the bookstore seizes it.

His face is marred, bearing the evidence of his fight with Corn and his subsequent defeat, and his blue eyes are full of hatred. If we had any more time he would probably crush my wrist, but just like light can exist in darkness, darkness can also lurk through light. Corn's shadows emerge behind the unsuspecting angel and Spades pierces the shoulder connected to the hand accosting me, freeing me and granting us custody of the sword. Time slows down for a split second when we realizes he's been bested, and he raises his hand to try to correct it, but his reaction comes too late and we fire across the room to the other exit before he can blink. We made it, sword in hand. The hardest part is over.

Corn swoops Granny into our shadows and we descend back to Hell through the center of the Embassy, Nilla hot on our tail. The hole left in our devastation swallowing some of Hell's stolen valuables with us.

We land back in the Sixth with a whoop. Somehow we made it out of Heaven unscathed.

"Guys," Nilla says cautiously while holding Granny's weight.

Or so I thought.

"Granny! What happened?" I shout while rushing over to her.

She uncovers the wound and silvery blood splatters on the ground, staining the singed remnants of the bodice on the gown she's wearing.

Seems like the angel's timing was actually spot on.

"It's alright, baby," she says, withering in my arms. "I had a good 500 year run."

The Sword Of Destiny clatters against the cobblestone ground. The sound ricochets off the walls, masking my slightly withheld sobbing.

"No, no, no. Kita, please no!" Corn shouts, picking up my grandmother. "I'm sorry. Please, I'm sorry."

She extends a shaking hand to cup Corn's face and with a struggling breath, she gives him a gentle smile.

"Take care of my baby for me," she says, giving my hand one last gentle squeeze. "I'll wait for you both on the other side."

I wait and wait for her chest to rise with just one more breath, but it never does. Not after five minutes, not after fifteen, not after I destroy an entire tree and a swath of sikai crop. I pound my fist on the ground, begging and pleading to Destiny for just one more breath.

But she denies me.

My hysterical laughter rips through the air as my grandmother is wrapped in cave silk and prepared to be transported back to Earth. I don't hear a single thing even as Corn contacts my parents to let them know what happened. I don't feel a single thing even as he scoops me up and places me in his arms. And the debilitating numbness is even worse when he hands me over to my parents and says his goodbyes. I can't even speak, but luckily I don't have to and neither does he. After one lingering apologetic glances, he kisses my forehead and de-materializes.

Taking the last living part of my heart with him.

Hell

Corn

"Your sister called again."

I hear sharp claws tap against the solid ebony door when I roll off my desk, plucking yet another report off of my drool covered face. My breath stinks because I haven't brushed my teeth in at least two, maybe three days. I can't tell you the last time I showered or ate something other than those damn marshmallows she loved so much, and Let's Stay Together is the only song looping through my brain.

I think I'm depressed.

"Which one?" I sigh before stretching my stiff arms over my head and neck.

My joints crack like milled pepper, releasing all the tension from my neglected posture. I'm feeling every bit of my 188 years, even though I'm still comparatively young.

Definitely depressed.

"Nafisa of course," Ninny replies while rubbing her claws through my dry matted curls.

I retreat from her touch when I hear how crunchy my hair is. It's properly embarrassing to have your grandmother call you out for your lack of hygiene as an adult, but again...

Depression.

"Did she leave a message?" I ask, swiping my hand down my face.

"As a matter a fact, she did..." Ninny starts. "She was wondering if we can possibly postpone the separation until after Marcel is born. February 16th at the absolute latest."

Truly, Ninny wants me to postpone our separation forever. She is fairly confident that we could win a war against the big bad EUM, but everytime I look over the valley, my confidence in her confidence diminishes.

"No. Once coronation commences, she will be sworn in with me and officially bound to Hell. At that point war is unavoidable. She would be a princess. A daughter of Hell."

"Well, maybe we should stop trying to avoid it then," Ninny says pointedly.

She's made no effort to conceal her opinion on the matter, and honestly, she's lived long enough to earn that privilege. But that doesn't mean that I have to listen.

"We have 4 days," I say firmly.

Four days. Just four more days and everything I feel will be gone forever.

Even the happiness.

"What the fuck is this?" I hiss.

Nafisa asked me only once to postpone my separation from Candy, two days ago. Then she left it alone like a reasonable adult. Akanni, however.

"It's an intervention because you've obviously lost your mind," he snarls.

Tobias, Tayo, and even Cyrus stand before me in a little gang-up circle, ready to get their asses beat. I say that because that's the only likely outcome from them trying to back me into a corner.

"I have shit to do. Coronation is in three weeks and I still have four farms to visit in the East."

"You need your queen, brother," Tayo says solemnly. "Demons can't die from exhaustion, but you are trying to prove that wrong."

I make sure there's no chance of my lour being misconstrued as anything else. How I choose to cope is my business and my business alone. I can't have the other half of my heart, so I will pour all of that love into my kingdom and people. Perhaps it won't hurt half as bad in 200 years or so.

It won't burn as bad as it does now.

"I need you all to get out of my face," I hiss.

Cyrus steps forward, the bravest of them all. His usually jovial face is creased with angst. His voice comes out paced and filled with what some would consider wisdom.

"Corn, please be reasonable. A separation could not only cause serious physical injuries, but it could also fail. And you will still have to mate with her. Severing your bond won't make her absence hurt any less. What do you think this will feel like when you can't even talk to her like you do every night from the mountain top?"

My eyes find a spot on the floor in an effort to stabilize my racing thoughts. Every single night I call out to her and she answers. Even if we never hear each other's voice, knowing that she's there is all I need to continue on. It feels so selfish but I need it. Right now I need it more than air, water or food. But Cyrus is right, soon I won't even have this to sustain me.

"Get out!" I growl. "Either you help me or you get the fuck out of my face. I don't have time for this shit."

And with that, I retreat into my own dark cloud.

Only to find an unmistakable light at the center of it.

My hair is braided by Ninny the night before. Tight to my scalp and wet with black castor oil. The oil settles into my parts with a certainty that will probably outlive even I, a testament to all those before me who leaves the story of their legacy into their curls.

"Everything will be as it shall," Ninny says, tying a scarf over my forehead.

"Ninny please, no cryptic bullshit tonight. I can't take anymore ominous foreshadowing today, let alone in this lifetime."

I won't lie, I half expect her to pinch me for my outburst, but instead she places a gentle kiss to the top of my head.

"It's going to be ok, little prince," she says softly.

My eyes meet hers for reassurance and I find it stronger than ever.

"Get some rest. We have busy day tomorrow."

"Good night, Ninny," I nod. "I will see you tomorrow."

The halls are the coldest they've ever been the next morning. My nerves are pricked with each step against the icy stone floors. Winter is upon Hell. That alone should be enough to banish me back to the solace of my empty bed, but I press on, following the melody of my family's voices into the dining hall. I see everyone and no one as I meet my mother's eyes for the first time in a very long month.

"Corn," Nasha exclaims.

She looks apologetic and anxious. Nothing like the two thousand year old Priestess who commands the sons of men. But we all started somewhere.

"Why are you here?" I ask, breaking my morning silence.

She winces like her skin has been cut with a serrated blade and while I have first hand experience with how bad words can hurt, I can't be burdened to feel regret for my question.

She disowned me.

As far as I'm concerned, she's no mother of mine.

"I-I think we should talk," she says.

"No. Leave," I snarl. "You've said plenty."

She retreats into herself and for a moment, I do feel some kind of twisted victory, but then my elective selfishness prompts Nafisa to stand.

Her belly juts straight out, my nephew pressing forward, ready to meet the world and all it's wonders.

"Corn, please?" she sighs breathlessly. "I'm asking for me."

My sister shares our mother's anxiety filled eyes, but the rest of her face is soft and pleading.

And I've never been able to tell her no.

"Fine," I say. "But I will have you jailed the second you look like you might attack me, Nasha."

"That's fair," she nods before motioning down the hall. "Shall we?"

We walk quietly to the library. A place I've avoided since Candrima left. Another part of home I simply can't access at this time.

My mother asks me to sit at the study desks before she goes to the axis and summons a record book. *Her* record book.

Pages are already tabbed and bookmarked, organized by the curly handwriting of Candrima, and that's where I start.

By the end, I'm truly mortified.

I find out that I am a product of rape, violent and unforgivable. So unforgivable that the high council found no fault when she eventually killed him.

"Mommy, I'm so sorry. I didn't know," I say, my tails tucking between my legs.

She gives me a melancholy smile before slowly reaching upward to scratch behind my ear.

"I didn't want you to know, Corn. I wanted to be stronger than what was done to me. And for a while I had been successful, but that strength cost me everything."

"You did the best you could I say," reality settling into my stomach.

The reality is, my mother had a whole life I will never know about before my existence. And any peace she found in it was snatched from her.

"No, no I didn't, Corn," she says. "I did enough. I did enough to make sure you made it, but I didn't do my best. I couldn't. And I know that now."

"Yes, but this was also so heinous," I say motioning to the passage.

"It's complicated, Corn," she laughs with a head shake. "As is life."

"Complicated?* I scoff. "Mama, this is rape."

"Yes, but it's also love. I did love him once, and I think that love made me cling to you even if I knew I couldn't love you in all the ways you deserved."

"How could you love him after this?" I exclaim.

"Because I loved him before. And hate is an emotion that could only come from something as strong as love."

I lean backwards in my chair with a thud, the fibers of the siaki creaking under my weight.

"I don't know what to say," I admit.

"There's nothing to say, really," she says. "We were a symptom of fate, just like you and Candy."

"You were soulmates, and he did this?"

"Yes. And for a long time I was happy with that. We were read our prophecy as bedtime stories when we were children. We would lay in the valley and he'd make me roses out of honed flames, and the suns would beat against our young faces and I loved him. But unfortunately I couldn't love every part of him."

"How so?" I ask.

"Well," she chuckles, looking at my markings. "Your father's warform terrified me. I saw it on accident once when we were just twenty five. He'd eaten an entire horde of angels in a fit of rage and I was so disgusted I couldn't even look him in the eyes. So three days before our binding, I ran. I ran to Earth, disguised myself as a human and met Baba. But Esqin never stopped looking for me. His life has essentially stopped when I fled even though mine was finally beginning. Eventually though, he found me, and when he discovered that his misery was my happiness, his fury gave me you."

If the vivid detail in the record didn't make me feel bad, that definitely did.

"I don't tell you this to make you feel bad, Corn," Mama says, patting my hand. "I want you to understand, because I want my apology to mean something. Corn, I am so so sorry for everything I ever did and I'm double sorry for everything I didn't do. I should have been a better mom, and I hope it's not too late for me to try."

"Of course not," I laugh, tears spreading into my sinuses. "Never."

"Well good," she chuckles just as equally as awkwardly before going in for a hug.

Tears brim in her ruby eyes while she squeezes my palms, but then the relief transforms into something else.

"But as your mother, I have to say I think this separation a monumental mistake."

"Goddess, not you too!" I groan. "Can I please just catch a fucking break?"

I don't think anyone understands that our only two options are war or separation. The Sixth is just beginning to get back on its feet and war would devastate us. We would be alienated from feeling the benefits of tourism, farming, or education. We simply do not have the resources, and at the end of the day I could lose both my people and my bride.

I can't take that risk right now.

I don't know how.

"Corn, I know you're scared. But I'm telling you that Destiny makes no concessions. I've seen what you two can do, you are both strong yet harmonious. I have faith in you two, and so does Ninny, and so does Simon. So I guess my question is, why don't you?"

"Because I can't lose her," I admit, my voice cracking with trepidation. "Heaven would never give her back. At least this way I have the everlasting comfort of maybe someday. But to go to war and risk her being locked away under a cloche of glass forever? I'm not brave enough today."

Truthfully I expect more of a fight. After all, fighting seems to be the name of my family's game. Instead however, I get a smile reminding me of how bright my mother's love can burn.

"That's ok. I can be brave enough for both us today," she cooes, hugging me. "Let's get this show on the road."

Candy

Today's the day.

My unwedding.

I woke up this morning to watch the sun creep up the skyline, its fresh light diffusing the horizon against the blue waters of the pier. The waves washed back and forth, looking both tiny and yet larger than life. But regardless of the perspective, the affect is the same. It makes me realize that all the worlds are bigger than me and my problems.

"Good morning," I say. *"I guess I'll see you soon."*

I half-expect silence but a familiar satisfaction comes with his reply.

"See you soon, little witch.'

I have to look him in the eyes for thirty minutes today and I won't even be getting my back cracked or my mint tea afterwards.

How depressing.

"Got everything?" Mama asks.

"I think so. Angst, anxiety, and crippling depression? Check, check, check. I almost took a wet wipe bath this morning if not for the very specific instructions regarding personal cleanliness."

Mama grimaces, her full lips spreading into a painfully thin line.

Perhaps that was a little too honest.

"Candy, we will get this. Even if we have to crawl," she says, hugging me tight.

She smells so comforting, like lingering incense, honey cornbread, and good hair grease. The perfect elder scent.

"Might I just say, you are doing excellent as the new Castille matriarch," I cry laugh, slightly choking on my own tears.

"And you are doing excellent as our legacy," Mama says, stroking my braided hair. "Come on, let's get going. Ted! Let's roll."

I put a charm on my glasses as soon as we come under the Sixth's twin suns. Darkening them to a near midnight to protect my sensitive eyes.

I can't say they're not helpful for the sleep bags though.

I can smell the brimstone burning in the center of the mountain and it calls me home. All I want to do is snuggle into my bed and watch the rivers with a good book on standby. That feels more right than anything.

"Queen Candrima!" A little voice calls.

Shit, technically I am still queen. That's definitely not helping.

Still, I put on my best game face and steady my voice.

"Hi, hello, little ones!" I say with a wave.

A crowd of little elementary schoolers stand before me, their parents waving excitedly in the background. I beam at their faces rounded with innocence and smiles full of youth demoted by the presence of milk teeth. One little girl is even a pretty blood orange color, making my heart pull. I think my daughter would look a lot like her if I ever had one with Corn.

"Queen Candrima, we start school after this week!"

"Oh?" I say. "How exciting. You'll learn all kinds of great things. Perhaps our next royal assistant is among you. Someone smart and outspoken."

"Me!" the cute little girl shouts, ejecting her hand into the air.

We lock eyes and I smile at her, impressed by her determination.

"I don't doubt it for even one second," I nod with a genuine smile.

Then the suns position triggers the clock in the center square, sounding the start of the new hour.

My last hour as Candrima Bankole-Olakanye.

"Well, I gotta get going. But I wish you all a very happy and successful school year. Be good students for your teachers."

"We will, Your Majesty! Thank you so much for our school. Yes, thank you! Thank you," they chirp. "I'll see you soon," the little citrus one says. "Bye!"

I watch them leave with all my hopes in dreams in their pockets, knowing I won't get to witness their evolution.

That definitely didn't help.

Reluctantly, we're ushered into the echo chamber by seemingly unwilling staff. The echo chamber is something Esqin built in his final fits of madness, meant to be a physical diary of sorts with the walls keeping immeasurable secrets. But today, we're using it to absorb some of the potential aftershocks from our separation. I'm prepared by my mother, Betty, and Nilla, dressed in a white cotton smock and marked with ash collected from Corn and I's fireplace, physical proof of our passion and comfort. Then, a short while later, I stand in front of him.

His eyes find me first, rapt, round, and commanding. My safe place, my constant. They smile at me even though the rest of him does not.

Which, rude by the way.

"Hi," he says after a while.

"Hi," I say back.

His eyes rove over my cotton-clad form, settling once on my hips, once at on my lips, and finally arriving to my eyes.

"You look beautiful, for what it's worth," he says.

"So do you. H-handsome, I mean."

That earns me a chuckle, reminding us of the hundreds of times I've put my foot in my mouth when he give me that sly little smirk. But when the laughter fades between us, something grayer settles in.

"I'm sorry," Corn murmurs, sounding every bit as heartbroken as I feel.

Our bond pulls, the energy between us warming my chest, and I long to touch him. I almost step forward to do just that but then the room begins to fill. So I settle.

It won't be the first time or the last.

"I understand," I reply. "We're going to be ok."

"Yeah," he nods. "See you on the other side."

"See you," I whisper.

We stand in a waist-deep pool of salt water, Cyrus stands in front of us on an altar of stick and bone. A fox skull sits to my right, a feather sits to Corn's left. Symbolizing both resilience and luck.

And we'll need all the luck we can get.

Corn's darkness snuffs out all light present in the room except for mine and the candles I lit on the altar, then our families join hands, oldest to youngest, with Nasha and Yvette leading their respective charges. Slowly, the pool fills with divine gold. Simmering and warming until our skin begins to soften and our pores begin to weep. Cyrus strikes an incense against an ancient panel of ebony wood and then the song of partition begins, deep and sorrowful.

Then I feel it; A pain so sharp that it makes a fool of death. I cry out when it begins to split the skin of my back, running along my exposed vertebrae like a hammer. Corn's face twists in agony because he knows that he cannot comfort me. No matter what happens we must stay apart. Even if I say otherwise. Even if I beg.

Our respective souls are exposed, vining out of our backs like overgrown ivy and laced with aerosoled gold from the pool. Corns is pulled open by the voices of each of his six siblings, his mother, his father, and his grandmother. While my mother, father, and Betty direct mine. Each part seeking out the corresponding person responsible for developing those attributes in us, our humor, our communication, our joys and our fears. All pulled outside of our body for a few harrowing moments. Then, once our souls are pulled taught, our bind materializes. A thick, corded, band connecting two hearts and two minds. Writhing and shimmering under the force. Pain spreads up my ribs, almost crushing my physical heart, and our bond pulls Corn closer to me. Not caring one bit about his resistance.

"This is the hard part," Cyrus says, raising the sword to partition us. "Hang on."

He recites the hymn,

"Goddess of all existence, sun of all suns. We come before you in respect and admiration, offering this pain and blood as a sacrifice. We seek not to defy, but to rectify. Please accept the offering of life returned to you."

Dart slashes both of our palms and we slowly lower our hands into the pool, the salt burning the wound while our blood turns the water from gold to vivid red. Something akin to ten thousand perfect roses. Then the swords comes down against our bond.

"Fuck!" I scream.

The pain is unbearable, like a six ton anvil smashing against my entire body, and I collapse into the water. Corn falls with me, tears of red, hot, blood spilling down the contours of his face. His jaw is tense and it vibrates from the force of withheld sobs.

But I can still hear them.

All of our memories fill the room while his voice reverberates in my mind, clinging to mine, singing a song of regret. Our bond bucks against the sword, sending embers flying towards the ground. Some land in the pool with an obnoxious pop, far too hot for the water to handle. Cyrus falters for a moment but then he presses onward, using more force than before.

This time our bond frays.

I scream so loud that it destroys my eardrums. The sound bounces off the walls and causes stones to fall towards the ground. My powers rebel, casting my light into the shadows so we can reclaim what was once ours. But Corn will not let me in.

Another rope severs, and this time I choke. A strange mix of blood, snot, and spit staining the white of my dress.

"Corn, I can't do this. I can't!" I shout. "It's too much. It hurts too bad."

"We're almost there, Candy," Cyrus says. "I promise it won't be long."

I don't care about the outcome. I just want this to stop. Corn has tried to transfer some of my pain onto him through the splitting bond, but it makes it hurt worse. Especially when I hear his roar rip through the air.

Then another cord breaks.

The sword is a third of a way though our bond, and it's red hot and nearly molten. The smooth edge cuts into my heartstring with the same force as a butcher cleaving hindquarters for ham, and although I know I shouldn't, I reach for him.

"Cornelius, please," I beg, choking on my own discharge. "I would rather fight a thousand wars and lose every one of them than to do this. I can't lose you. It hurts too bad. Please."

Please.

One pleading look is all it takes, and the demon lunges for me. Our bond recoils against the sword which sends Cyrus tumbling back with both sides.

The separation failed.

"I'm sorry, I'm sorry," Corn says while licking my wounds. "I was so stupid. Please forgive me."

My cuts begin to close before I'm cradled in his arms, my head tucked against the safety of his beating heart.

"All is forgiven," I nod weakly.

I feel sick like I haven't eaten in days so I try to heal myself. It fails with a triumphant fizzle and only then do I realize I feel this way because my powers were drained. I'm running on fumes.

"What happened?" Nafisa asks.

"Well, the sword shattered," Cyrus answers while collecting the shards from Tayo. "I think it failed."

"It most certainly did," Ninny quips.

"Well, shit. Now what do we do?" Nafisa asks.

The lot of them begins discussing alternative options among themselves, but I can't hear much by that point because Corn has caged us in with his wings.

"Do you wanna go somewhere cool?" he asks.

"Is it outer space?" I murmur. "Because I fear I might say yes."

"You have nothing to worry about," he says while rubbing his nose against mine. "Let's go."

We re-materialize on the other side of Earth on a mountainside overlooking the misty sunset. Trees surround us completely. Sloped homes are interwoven into the countryside landscape, gable roofs providing a hint for our location. Corn sets up a little camp from the bangle I enchanted before lighting a fire. I admire his handywork for just a moment too long and just as I start to compliment him, he disappears.

"Corn!?" I shout, my voice echoing against the rocky mountainside. "CORNELIUS!"

Dread settles into my stomach too soon, but my husband is smart. He poofs back in five minutes later holding a bento box full of sushi.

"It's Wednesday so I figured we'd get discount sushi and unwind," he says warmly.

Our bond tugs, warmth dulling the pain from our failed separation attempt, and we meet somewhere in the space between us,

"I'd love that," I say.

"Good," he nods. "Because now I have the next ten thousand or so years to think up even better ways to love you. So I gotta start small."

"I'm ok with that," I say, pecking his lips.

"Yeah?"

"Yeah."

Highwater

Fifteen years later, The Sixth Realm Of Hell

Corn

We had a long, harsh winter, filled with problems. I watched the outside world from our window every day waiting for the slightest sliver of sunlight, and finally, I can say we made it. Spring is my favorite season and I'm outside enjoying the gentler temperatures of the year when I'm interrupted with a warning.

"Your majesty, there is mutiny brewing in your court."

The delivery is grave but it makes me the opposite of worried.

"Is that so?" I chuckle while sitting my seed bag against the mud-died ground.

"This is no laughing matter, Your Highness! You must act urgently to prevent discord."

I throw my gloves at my irate messenger's feet, abandoning my task in favor of lunch and a nice view.

"Is this because I fell asleep during our movie marathon last night?" I say, pulling Candrima close.

"No," she giggles as I trace her collarbone with my fingertip.

"No?" I question, one eyebrow raised.

My hand drops to the swell of her hip with finesse that almost makes me shiver. This dress is doing terrible things for my sanity with her exposed midriff and just a hint of ankle. All it takes is one gentle squeeze and my eyes fill with an unmistakable darkness.

"Is it something else that you need then?" I say, my voice warping.

Her breath hitches as my fingers pioneer a path from her hip to her exposed navel, dipping into the cavernous indent and taking delight in the sensitive exposed flesh they find there.

"No, no. Nothing else," she rasps.

"Is that right?"

"Mhhm."

"Mhm," I purr. "You know what I think?"

I hold her chin in my hand and I delight in the sweet honey hibiscus scent rising from her skin. She moans her reply, just barely an audible what once my lips press against the curve of her neck.

"I think you want to lay with me in this field and desicrate these beautiful flowers. Tell me, Candrima. Am I correct?"

I hear her groan in my mind first and it sounds just as sweet passing from her lips a second later. So sweet than I can forgive her irritating response.

"Not at all," she says breathlessly.

I snake Spades up her back to tug on the lace of her corset as I test, and she fails it immediately, leaning into my salacious touch.

"Liar," I snarl, bearing my fangs. "Dishonest little witches get punished in Hell."

I take to the sky with a woman in my arms, flying with little to no purpose. Honestly I just want her to feel the rush she craves during this time of the month.

"Corn!" she screams. "You're going to drop me!"

"I have never dropped you once in the last decade and a half. I think I have more than proved I'm capable of lifting you up not only in prayer and praise."

"This is crazy!" she shouts as we climb higher through the magenta clouds.

"Its not any crazier than lying about what you want," I challenge with a laugh.

"Fine, fine!" she says, pounding against my chest. "I want you to ravish me! I want you to fuck me into the daisies!" she laughs. "I want you."

We nosedive into a soft landing and I let her feet touch the bare grass before I pull her back into me.

"That's all you had to say," I whisper against her lips. "Let me take care of you."

"Please," she moans.

We fall into the grass gracelessly, a mess of limbs and curls. I brace her fall and stretch against the ground as she moves to straddle me.

"Did you just crack a rock?" Candrima asks as rubble spills from under me.

"It's fine," I say, pulling her back into our vortex. "You're about to crack one too."

"You terrible demon," she laughs before melting into my kisses. "What am I going to do with you?"

"Whatever you want," I offer in return. "You can do whatever you want to me."

Our mouths meet in that moment, hungrier than ever. I devour her lips breathlessly and I'm somehow surprised when she begins to mount me. But I'm quite pleased when my iron is teased against her decadent silk folds.

Then she pushes down.

The moon eclipses the sun the moment we join, creating an artificial night. Crickets hum all around us, excited by the rapidly cooling ground. My lower hands find purchase on her hips while my uppers seek to cradle her perfect face, keeping her eyes aligned with mine even as she pistons against me.

"You are so impossibly wonderful, Candrima," I say. "I am so lucky you chose me."

I've come to that realization in recent years. That what she did that day was a choice. I was scared senseless but she was brave for the both of us.

And I am better for it.

Her small hand holds my wrist for support while she leans into my touch, her hungry kisses increasing with her speed. Spades curls against her engorged bud, tapping at her pace, while Dart resides in my favorite tunnel of darkness, feeling cozy and relaxed as her muscles massage him with every determined rock.

"Corn," she cries. "I-I…"

"Just do it already, Candy," I grunt. "Give me everything. I can handle it."

Famous last words.

She does cum and it's wonderful as always, except this time it's a little too wonderful. Reality warps around us and the flowers burst forth from our married powers spilling haplessly onto the lands. I blink and suddenly the moon is only a thousand feet away. Then I blink again and we're thrown into the ether. A kaleidoscope of colors both new and familiar assault my senses, driving me further into Candrima's orbit. Every breath becomes hers. Every heartbeat becomes mine.

"I love you," she says against my lips.

"I love you more," I moan.

Then I feel the beginning of the end. It's a wonderful conclusion, but it's so much pressure that my brain can't function. And when the feeling of release inevitably overpowers me, I lose control and sink my teeth into Candy's offered collar. The sweet taste of her blood fills my mouth and I drink before I realize what I'm doing, making Candrima collapse against me from dizzy, lightheaded pleasure. We stay that way until I feel my heart's no longer at risk of exploding and once I'm 75% sure it won't, I tuck her into my side.

The afternoon sun splashes against the field once again, bathing the fresh flowers in warmth while I draw lazy circles on Candy's spine. We lay that way for at least an hour until her fingers gently trace the new mark on her chest.

"You bit me," she says pointedly.

I trace the mark my teeth left, sealing it with a little more spit before scratching the scalp underneath her curls.

"Yeah, I did," I nod in response.

Candy, Four Weeks Later

"Go away," I say, swatting at Aster.

When I said I wanted my cat to live forever, I was ill informed. It turns out that they become even more annoying with age. Who would've thought?

"*Brrk.*"

"*It's midnight.*"

"Seriously?" I groan. "Fuck, I need to eat."

My entire body creaks as I exit bed. The hormones are already working on my joints. Don't even get me started about my sleep schedule. I would think I was a vampire if I didn't despise the taste of rare meat. These days I survive off bread, mushrooms, and cheese. If I had to eat anything otherwise I would've perished. Which is why I'm grateful that Corn stocked the cottage with my favorite snacks before he went back home. The Sixth was in the middle of tourism bus con-tract renewals when I tapped out on moonlight, so I had to journey to Earth alone much to Corn and I's dismay. We're closer than ever, now having shared more than just memories, and any large amount of time apart causes us to fall into Shakespearean-level dramatics. Corn seems distressed about that new change so I thought about telling him before I returned, but I know if I did our economy would collapse shortly thereafter.

And I can't have that.

That shit took me eight years to build up.

"Maybe I'll make us some chicken and rice, hm?" I ask Aster. "That way you can keep me company since you won't have to hunt."

Aster's conceding purr dances through the quiet for a moment, but when I turn back around I notice his tail is bone straight and his back is arched like a parabola.

"What's wrong?" I ask, checking behind him for any clues.

I get silence in return and then Aster bolts outside, abandoning me and our dinner plans.

"He sensed something lurking in the darkness," The King Of Shadows says, materializing.

A big demon with four arms, four eyes, and two tails steps forward with a sinister smile. All while holding the most considerately arranged rose and baby's breath bouquet. Perfect for my sentimental mood.

"Welcome home, baby," I chuckle while he wraps his arms around me.

Corn's deep purr tickles the shell of my ear while I soak up his distinctive scent. Sweet citrus and earthy leather wraps around my senses, calming my nausea.

"I'm happy to be back. Especially since you're too soft on that freeloader," he says. "You need to make him hunt."

I turn to face him, rolling my eyes as I spin. Unfortunately for me though he's too handsome and I begin to stare. Being fine and immortal is a double whammy. He just turned 200 three years ago and he doesn't look a day over 35. His braided curls allow his wrapped horns to steal the show. They're clad in beautiful sunset colored wax cloth and adorned with gold pins to hold everything in place which coordinate with his royal dress. Everything compliments his rich eyes, which stay trained on me the entire time.

"15 years and you still haven't stopped antagonizing my cat," I tut. "Anyway, tell me how it went."

Corn scratches his scalp nervously and for a second my stomach drops. Don't get me wrong, we have other sources of revenue, but I already worked this deal with the tourism department into our budget with the Treasury. I had plans to use it for an education expansion. One that we need.

"Please tell me we closed our negotiations?" I murmur.

"Yes, it's just that we only got a mere..."

"A mere what!?" I shout, vibrating with anticipation. Anything less than 20% would be a slap in the face, and I'd fight them myself. Well, come January, I'd fight them myself.

"A measly 40% during peak season and 30% during off," Corn smiles.

He gives me a wicked little chuckle while I storm across the living room to him, louring the whole way.

"You tease," I growl while swatting at his chest. "What happened to 35% during peak seasons?"

"I decided to negotiate higher, sweetheart. The worst they could say was no, but then where would they take all of your adoring fans?" Corn says, peppering my face in kisses.

When people learned the King Of Shadows was a romantic who built an entire reading garden full of forget-me-nots for his wife, they flocked to our realm for a chance to see it. Soon after, gardens were popping up all over the Sixth, hoping to mimic Corn's artistry and care. Even if they were only able to achieve half of it.

"Our fans," I correct.

"Ha, no," he snorts. "I am mostly terrifying but you are adored, my gorgeous dear witch. Rightfully so. You tamed the insidious King Of Shadows."

He purrs that last part while pressing his lips to the small of my back and unfortunately my stomach hits a high note like Mariah. I know I need to eat, but dammit if that one little peck doesn't feel like nirvana.

He presses a hand to my rumbling belly.

"I almost brought you dinner, but the kitchen keeps shooting down my suggestions. That and Liliana insists on no red meat." Corn says against my ear. "It seems like they might know something I don't."

I stiffen in his arms like a pair of socks belonging to an incel. I've worked hard to conceal my shifting smell and symptoms only to be brought down by my overly-considerate staff and overachieving assistant. I knew she'd be trouble from the moment I saw her with those other kids 15 years ago. But she makes an amazing assistant. Still, a newfound meat aversion isn't how I planned on telling him after he waited patiently for so long. I at least wanted a little fanfare. What to do, what to do? Lie? Scheme? Run away? A secret fourth option?

"But I'll let you keep your secrets until morning," he says softly while nuzzling my neck. "Just as long as you let me hold you tonight."

His loud purr disrupts the midnight air, blending in seamlessly with the last few crackling embers from the fire and the hammering of my heart. It all makes it so easy to dissolve into him.

"I find myself most agreeable to your terms, Your Highness," I coo.

"Good, because otherwise I'd have to take you as prisoner. I have a reputation to uphold you know," he says while spinning me to face him.

"Shut up and kiss me," I chuckle.

I place my open hands against his chest and there I find his heart racing for me, calling out to me like a familiar beloved song.

"My pleasure, little witch," he says, encasing me in his darkness. "You never have to ask me twice."

Corn

The wind blows slightly softer like it's dragging something, and then a faint but unfamiliar scent wakes me. Something's different, and no, it's not my wife. I knew about Candy before she did, but I've been waiting for her to mention it first. That excites me, but the feeling I'm feeling now is harrowing. I should be happy to take my wife back home. I should be relishing these last few hours of quiet. I should be in bed holding her. But instead I find myself slipping into pants, lacing up boots, and heading into the yard.

It could be nothing.

But something tells me it's not.

Despite my anxiety, the fields surrounding the cabin look benign. A gentle breeze rolls over the tender tulip starts and pushes them east of the house. Just like it has for the last six springs. Six years ago I started getting smart and buying specific plots of land to park our second home so we didn't end up on the EUM's radar when Candrima had to recharge, and so far it's worked.

Until now.

It all happens too quickly. I feel the piercing tip of a dart between my shoulder blades then my body goes slack before I can draw my second form. It's not enough to render me unconscious, but it is enough to paralyze me. So I can't fight when angels swarm the area and bind me in ropes wet with corrosive holy water. For a moment, I forget myself and I cry out from the pain of my burned skin. But then I remember Candrima sleeping so peacefully under her horde of covers. They can have me as long as she's safe.

"We finally got you after 15 long years, demon," the captain says.

His face is still twisted and marred where I bit him. It seems not even the best glamour can cover my curse and that brings me immeasurable joy. Even though I regret not eating him.

"Fifteen years and you had to ambush and drug me to make it a fair fight," I chuckle. "The mighty sovereign certainly does know how to pick them. You'll make a delightful snack once this is all over."

"You talk a lot of shit for a creature in chains," he spits, sending his pungent saliva into the grass beside me. "Let's get moving, boys!"

I relax my body, accepting my fate for now. Heaven cannot kill a Son Of Hell, it's guaranteed war and demon kings do not respect the politics of such a conflict. They will cause devastation in Heaven. Plus it's physically impossible. Only my bind can end me. They'll likely try me, assess a fine, and put The Sixth back on the sanctions list. All fine by me. I can handle that.

"Captain, we have movement by the cabin. Two heat signatures."

But not this.

My heart pounds in my ears, sending my adrenaline galloping, but my body remains concrete and unmovable. Fuck the EUM and the chemist who created this shit. I'll burn Heaven to the ground myself if they touch my wife.

"Well, would you look at that," he smiles. "Seems like we got a two for one."

"I'LL KILL YOU!" I roar, digging my claws into the ground.

"Not with that attitude you won't," he goads, placing his dirty boot against my cheek. "This is the best magic suppressant in all the realms. Made exclusively for you, Your Highness. You won't be able to do anything but watch and ramble as your precious queen is shackled. Enjoy the show, demon," he says before giving his commands.

Our bond has grown stronger every day for the last fifteen years. And it's so strong that I can't even convince her to stay away by saying I'm fine. She knows something is wrong and she's seeking me out. Her finding me in this field is inevitable.

"Corn?" she calls from over the hill. "Baby, where are you?"

"Candy, go home!" I yell.

She walks closer, rustling the soft grass with her skirt and my voice transitions into a whimper. "Please."

It's too little too late, and she runs over as soon as she sees me laying on the ground bound, bloody, and beaten.

"Corn, what the fuck happened!?" she shouts, pulling at the ropes.

"Heaven is here," I whisper. "Candrima, my sweet witch. It's ok, baby. Just let them take me and call Betty. You'll be safe with her."

I try to push her back over the hill, but she digs her feet in, clinging to me with all her might.

No!" she screams. "I'm not leaving you. Corn, damnit! I'm not leaving you!"

Tenacious women plague me for all eternity, but this specific instance is awfully inconvenient. I can't track the soldiers but I know they're not far. Especially since she's glowing with anger.

"Candy, they will enslave you!" I holler. "Go! I will not allow your life to be traded for mine."

Candrima's gaze shoots up, finding the soldiers I couldn't track and her powers charge between her palms. She opens her mouth to argue with me further, but before she can get the words out, a rogue angel fires. The last thing I see is the tip of the arrow piercing her jaw, but before her blood can stain the Earth, I catch her in my arms. She's injured but still alive. A seal of maternal protection appears on her throat. It appears Granny Kita's death wasn't completely in vain. While this news is comforting, it does not charge my heart with compassion. My warform spreads across the tainted field, my claws sink into the rocky, dense plates of the Earth, and my tails split into fourths, filling the air around us.

This is war.

Sulfur and magma creep through the jagged cracks, and that is where some soldiers meet their demise. Others are killed by my brothers, who joined the fight the moment Candrima's blood was spilled as did the rest of Hell. Tobias' rapidly multiplying shadows easily work to remove weapons, wings, and other limbs. Tayo's invisible shadows creep up and cause catastrophe from the inside out, while Akanni has created a black hole to offset the soldiers pouring out of the auric hole in the sky. My brothers in Hell command their men, infiltrating the clouds, the sea, and the rest of the untouched Earth. While monsters from every realm join the war. A few pledge allegiance to Heaven, but most choose to side with the realm who has accepted and supported them the most. Even the human military is involved, although they are mostly useless since Heaven's numbers are dwindling quickly. Angel blood is spilling everywhere while the air is charged with celestial fear.

And I delight in the carnage.

"STOP!" A familiar voice yells.

I raise a hand and the battle around me temporarily ceases while Nafisa makes her way towards me with Arcangel following closely behind her. I almost roll my eyes when I see the stack of clipped and stapled papers she's carrying. 203 years and she's still never heard of a briefcase or messenger bag. Says it's too convenient even though she sure loves the convenience of a washing machine.

"Make it fast, Nafisa," I growl while plucking another soldier from the skies. "I'm in the middle of destroying the Earth."

"Yes, I can see that," she huffs, dragging closer. "But what if you didn't?"

The angel between my claws makes a feeble attempt at stabbing me with a dull blade better suited for slicing fruit while my still unconscious wife clings to my back. It's not really a convincing case for amnesty.

"Not interested," I reply.

The Arcangel looks like he could piss himself at any moment but he still manages to be an asshole with a superiority complex.

"Mrs. Hark, I know your kind has made considerable progress in the right direction, but these Hell borne savages are clearly unwilling to cooperate."

"I'm going to eat your boss," I say calmly.

"Hey, Gabriel? Please shut the fuck up. You're making my job unnecessarily difficult," she spits. "Back to what I was saying, Corn, we can work something out."

"No, I don't think so. They shot my wife."

"Yeah, that wasn't a shining moment, I'll admit. But it was an accident."

I blink slowly, hoping my frustration and annoyance comes across clearly.

"I don't care," I sigh.

"Ok, ok, fair!" she says, holding up a packet. "But what if we could fix this with a signature right now, no war necessary, and then you could take Candrima home. Heaven would never bother her again. Her crimes would be wiped from the record. Demons would be properly integrated into society. Your people will be safe."

Nafisa wiggles her eyebrow in response to my visible consideration. As good as revenge would feel, I have to admit the possibility of guaranteed peace sounds twenty times better.

It's been 15 years but almost nothing about what I want has changed. I want Candrima to be safe and happy. I want to love her, hold her, and age with her. Without fear of retaliation from Heaven.

"I'm willing to listen," I grumble. "But I'm eating that captain."

Gabriel freezes, but all it takes is Nafisa to wave at fifteen minutes worth of damage before he agrees with an enthusiastic nod.

"Phew, ok!" she exclaims. "Let's get to work."

Tobias and Ninny take Candrima back home, and I spend the following five hours in negotiations with the other Nine Sons Of Hell. Surprisingly, fiscal negotiations weren't the most difficult part. Heaven was generous with their concessions considering I was a hair away from ripping them straight out of the sky, but the hard part was coming to a mutually agreeable conclusion about the future of my people and their loved ones. Whatever they looked like. Me and Candy had been through so much unnecessary pain due to mating bans, pain I hoped to help others avoid. And by the end of the sixth hour I'd done just that. 1,987 pages, over 25 signatures, and 35 ink pens later, we were finished and holding the first and only treaty between Heaven and Hell. With an addendum outlawing mating bans, affectionately called The Candy Corn Curse Clause.

I return home late that evening, and I find Candrima in our room waiting for me inside of a grand pillow fort. She's enchanted a few cushions to glow with a warm soft light that highlights her deep smile. And luckily, I don't see any scars on her beautiful face. Thank you Kita.

"How'd everything go?" she asks gently.

"Really well, little witch," I reply, cupping her jaw in my hand.

"We're no longer illegal."

Silence pulses between us like it does most nights. Silence charged with appreciation and pure magic. Candy's mouth says nothing but her cinnamon eyes say everything. A thousand beautiful words hang in the quiet air between us while we stare at each other. And for once, I truly thank Destiny for such a precious gift.

Finally she speaks in a low, tearful whisper,

"I have a secret to tell you."

I already know what it is, but that doesn't stop the rush of surprise I feel finally hearing those three little words. I tangle all my limbs around her, trying to hold her close to my heart as soon as she's done. I'll never admit it out loud but Ninny was right. My love is and always will be worth fighting for, and it can conquer Heaven, Hell, and even the high water in between.

Epilogue

Candy, Nine Months Later, The OkuKun River

A gentle breeze blows over my exposed back from the blades of Ninny's fan, cooling my molten skin.

"You're doing so well," Corn says while rolling his hand over my shoulder blades.

"I feel like I'm about to shit myself," I laugh, my voice warping from labour-induced delirium.

"That's because she's crowning!" Mama says.

Oh yeah, did I mention that I'm giving birth in a river? Because I'm giving birth in a river. It's tradition for imperial demons to be born in the realm's largest river. I let a big, horny, demon king bite me and now I'm pushing out his big baby. Lots of bad decisions all around. Thank goddess for magic because I couldn't imagine passing a set of horns through my cooch without it.

"Holy shit, that's a lot of hair!" Betty screeches as she points between my legs. "It looks like your giving birth to a pack of cotton balls."

When I made my birth plan, I thought it'd be a good idea to have all the women in my life present for the delivery. Turns out that optimistic hoe was naive. But to be fair, she didn't feel like she was about to take the worst deuce of her life when she wrote everything up.

"Beatrice!" I hiss. "Not helping."

"I don't think anything could help that," she grimaces as I suffer the ring of fire.

Corn snarls at Betty, bearing his big fangs, and she finds a seat. He then tries to give me a supportive smile but I can tell that he feels guilty, and probably even a little scared.

"I'm ok, I promise," I assure him.

"Ok," he whispers, nuzzling me. "I'll never ask you for sex ever again."

"That's a lie and we both know it," I giggle.

"Yes, but it sounded so good in the moment, all things considered," he chuckles.

The laughter we share soothes a little of my contraction pains, and my hips start to relax more with each gentle stroke Corn gifts my lower back.

"She's almost out, Your Majesty!" the midwife, Salima calls. "One more push should do it."

"The hard part is over," Nilla says. "You really are doing amazing."

I smile at my sister, and I can feel how crazy I look as my splitting lips curl upward. But I'm truly happy because I know it's not in vain. I'm about to meet my daughter, a combination of all my love for Corn poured into a little being, and I've never been so happy in my entire life. I never thought I'd be having my first baby at fifty, but to be fair I also never imagined the father being a fresh 203 either. Like Ninny frequently says in her infinite wisdom, everything will be as it shall. It all worked out for us.

The clock in the center of the square strikes midnight, and I feel a big rush followed by immediate relief. Both of which prepare me for the shrill, hungry, cry of my first-born child. My daughter, The Goddess Of Time, born on the first minute of the first hour of the New Year. I'm too eager to hold her but luckily I don't have to fight her adoring fans since my husband knows the boss. He waits for her cord to stop pulsing and clips it with his claws before plucking her from the midwife, and then he carefully lays her against my rising chest. We have another premonition for the records because she looks just like I knew she would. Soft orange with pure white hair, pitch black horns, and raven wings. Same as the dream I had a year ago. Corn kneels besides me as she takes my nipple into her mouth, purring and singing the family lullaby. His head presses to mine as a gesture of submission, and the second we touch we're thrust through the space-time continuum, into a future where Amarantha is queen. I cling to my family a little more than before, because I know that the love Corn and I share has just given birth to a titillating new era.

A better one for all of us.

Appendex

Pronunciations and definitions.

- **Names**

Akanni

(Uh-Kon-Ee)

- **Candrima**

(Can-Dry-Mah)

- **Esqin**

(S-Kwa-N)

- **Etin**

(Ee-Ten)

Kitara

(Key-Ter-Uh)

- **Nafisa**

(Nah-Fee-Sah)

- **Nasha**

(Nah-Sh-Ah)

- **Nilla**

(Nee-La)

- **Tayo**

(T-Ay-O)

Phrases

- **Jamanichei**
(Ya-Man-Ich-ee)
Fuck

Kasfiat

(Ka-Ss-Fe-Aht)
Bullshit

- **Sassprhats**
(Sass-Pr-Hats)
Damn

- **Ehikuzimu**
(E-Hay-Koz-E-Mo)
Hell Cow

Thank You!

I originally wanted this to be a goofy little novella without much else going on, but as things in my personal life shifted, so did this story. I often think about the reasons I write about love, or why we even love at all, and with each varying conversation, I have come to the same conclusion:

We love because we need to. And it's better to have known love even for a short while than to have spent this harsh life suffering without it.

So from the bottom of my heart, thank you. Thank you for reading this book and others like it. Thank you for following my journey, thank you the support through recommendations, reviews, and kind words, and thank you for giving me the tools to fight another day in the sometimes cutthroat world of publishing. I love y'all with all my heart, and I can't wait to surprise both of us with what happens next.

Human Resources

Sneak Peek

I want her.

God, I want her.

I want to coil her well-maintained curls around my fingers. The ones she's careful to keep under her ever-changing rotation of wigs. I want to caress her impossibly soft umber skin. The same skin I watch glow under the Los Angeles sun every Monday. I want to kiss her perfect lips when they're wet with that peppermint mocha she loves so much, and peck her cute wide nose, and I want her to look at me with those low-lidded puma eyes while she's wrapped in my fresh sheets. I want her so bad that it hurts if I think about it too long.

Literally, because a lot of these slacks don't have enough stretch in the crotch and what a nigga lacks in height, he packs in girth.

But back to my main point. I've wanted her every day for the last seven years, and in a perfect world, she'd know that for as long as she lives. Anybody else would've made their move six years and four months ago and maybe by then the magic of Brittany Barnes would've long worn off. I probably would've made my move too except by now she'd be my wife and I'd be cleaning her car every Monday and serving her breakfast in bed every Sunday. But there's just one problem.

She's my boss.

Brittany Barnes is the CFO of marketing at Solei and I've worked in HR for the last seven or so years. She wasn't always the CFO, but she should have been. Luckily the company got acquired by a New York venture capitalist named Marvin Rosenbloom, and after he fired approximately half the staff between here and Rosencorp, he personally appointed Black women in the positions left behind. I've long-learned not to applaud white men for taking a step in the right direction with their power, but he seems like a good one. Because Brittany has been killing it ever since. Sales are doing fantastic, engagement has sky-rocketed, and while most of the economy feels like it's at a standstill, we've had unprecedented company growth. And it's all thanks to the 5'9 brown-skinned beauty who runs a tight ship.

Which only makes me want her more.

Now I know what you're thinking: "Dimitris, why don't you just leave that woman alone if she's doing so well?"

Believe me, I've tried.

Sometimes I stare at her so much I creep myself out, and I tell myself that I'm definitely going to get over her, that this will be the day.

But it never works.

As soon as I see her lick that airy whipped cream off her glossy full lips during our Monday catchups, I fold. It's a tragic cycle and it probably won't ever end, and that's why I'm going to do something about it in one week, five days, 4 hours, two minutes and 45 seconds.

During our company Holiday Party.

About the author

Aria is a die-hard romantic and her main goal is to always be drying her eyes from something sickly sweet. She has been dreaming up romance stories since she was seven years old, with the first one being a Toy Story fanfic. She's also a Neo-soul and R&B enthusiast who's forever got a song stuck in her head. You can find her looking for good food, (especially ramen), reading, writing, or enjoying time with her family in her free time. She lives happily in Saint Louis, Missouri with her middle school sweetheart-turned-husband and their adorably chaotic son. Her dream is to one day write inclusive stories that center BIPOC full-time, but for now, she labors in fraud as a working stay-at-home mom and a part-time social media comedian.